Mary Brock Jones lives in New Zealand but loves nothing more than to escape into the other worlds in her head, to write science fiction and historical romances. Sedate office worker by day; frantic scribbler by night.

Her parents introduced her to libraries and gave her a farm to play on, where trees became rocket ships and rocky outcrops were ancient fortresses. She grew up writing, filling pages of notebooks and filling her head with stories but took a number of detours on the pathway to her dream job. Four grown sons, more than one house renovated and various jobs later, her wish came true.

To keep up to date with her latest news and releases, sign up to her newsletter here:

subscribepage.io/mbj-landing-page

Or find Mary here:

http://www.marybrockjones.com/

https://www.facebook.com/MaryBrockJonesAuthor

Also By Mary Brock Jones:

A Heart Divided
Swift Runs the Heart

Hathe Series

Resistance: Hathe Book One
Pay the Piper: Hathe Book Two
Aftermath: Hathe Book Three

Arcadia Series

Torn
Taken
Exiled
Broken

TOIL AND STRIFE

Hathe Book One and Two

Mary Brock Jones

Mary Brock Jones

Auckland, New Zealand

CONTENTS

CHARACTER LIST AND GUIDE TO HATHE i
RESISTANCE 1
INTRODUCTION... 1
CHAPTER ONE 3
CHAPTER TWO 23
CHAPTER THREE... 37
CHAPTER FOUR 47
CHAPTER FIVE 65
CHAPTER SIX 83
CHAPTER SEVEN.. 101
CHAPTER EIGHT 117
CHAPTER NINE 131
CHAPTER TEN.. 143
CHAPTER ELEVEN 159
CHAPTER TWELVE 177
CHAPTER THIRTEEN.. 195
CHAPTER FOURTEEN 215
CHAPTER FIFTEEN 233
CHAPTER SIXTEEN 243
CHAPTER SEVENTEEN 259
CHAPTER EIGHTEEN 281
CHAPTER NINETEEN 291
CHAPTER TWENTY 305
PAY THE PIPER 317

CHAPTER TWENTY-ONE 319

CHAPTER TWENTY-TWO 337

CHAPTER TWENTY-THREE 353

CHAPTER TWENTY-FOUR 371

CHAPTER TWENTY-FIVE 385

CHAPTER TWENTY-SIX 399

CHAPTER TWENTY-SEVEN 421

CHAPTER TWENTY-EIGHT 441

CHAPTER TWENTY-NINE 463

CHAPTER THIRTY 475

CHAPTER THIRTY-ONE 481

CHAPTER THIRTY-TWO 505

CHAPTER THIRTY-THREE 529

CHAPTER THIRTY-FOUR 551

CHAPTER THIRTY-FIVE 575

CHARACTER LIST AND GUIDE TO HATHE

GUIDE TO HATHIAN NAMES

Hathian names use the format: [First name] [prefix] [Patrilineal family name].

Further to this, family genealogy and marital status are very important on Hathe. The name prefix shows the marital status for each Hathian: for example, see the difference in names of the asn Castre family:

Bendin asn Castre—known by the single form.

Sylvan an Castre—The twins' father. He is considered married although he is a widower at the time of this book.

GOVERNMENT

The Hathian system of government traditionally has three main branches:

Council: The supreme branch of the Hathian government, in hiding on Mathe during the occupation. The members are appointed by the individual family lines and the rules of appointment vary between lines. Every Hathian 'looks to' both a matrilineal and patrilineal councilor, as well as having connections to the councilors of other lines depending on their individual family connections. Democracy is based on a fluid and well understood system of personal contacts through family connections. For this reason, the accuracy and integrity of the family genealogical records are fiercely protected.

Senate: Each region has a Senator elected by all the inhabitants of that region, who deals solely with regional issues. The Senate is suspended during the occupation.

Local bodies: These vary in name and rules, but deal with all the day-to-day issues of each local community such as provision of community facilities, school buildings, water and sewage etc. The status of these is variable, many becoming part of the Resistance structure during the Terran occupation.

CHARACTER LIST

Major Hamon Radcliff of Earth, head of the Terran Security Service on Hathe.

Marthe asn Castre: Resistance agent and a trained physician. Called Mimi by her closest friends and family. Also known as Riarda.

Bendin asn Castre: Marthe's twin and close friend of Jacquel des Trurains. Pilot who died in the original battle to delay the Terran invasion of Hathe.

Jacquel des Trurain: Resistance leader and trained historian. Closest friend to Marthe and Bendin asn Castre, the three formed a tight-knit trio from childhood. Known as Jaca to his closest friends and family.

Hathian Council

Councilor Sylvan an Castre: father of Bendin and Marthe, and good friend to Jacquel. Senior councilor heavily involved with the Resistance during the occupation.

Councilor Gilda an Rathman: senior councilor and closely involved with the Resistance.

Councilor Trundain an Delsin - councilor and computer comptroller (in charge of genealogical records, births, deaths, and marriages).

Councilor an Baktish: The oldest member of Council. Third cousin by marriage to Marthe an Castre's grandmother.

Councilor an Jordan: Large, bluff, but perceptive councilor.

Councilor an Heurain: Quietly spoken but very influential councilor.

iv · MARY BROCK JONES

Hathian Resistance

Gof deln Crantz: commander of the Security Department and a senior member of the Resistance.

Griffith an Castre: Senior Resistance member and cousin to Marthe.

Yurin an Begum: lawyer.

Agnethe: Chief cook and supply officer in the Citadel. Responsible for maintaining the health and well-being of the Resistance members forced to work there for the Terrans.

Other Hathians

Laren an Castre: older sister of Marthe and Bendin asn Castre. Married with young children. Lives in the moon base on Mathe during the occupation.

Jorven an Dufon: husband to Laren an Castre. Also Mathe based, but periodically serves in the Resistance down on Hathe.

Ruth an Cracknell Nanny appointed to Marthe's family. Known fondly as 'Ruthie'.

Representative an Truro: leader of the Hathian delegation to Earth.

Prosecutor an Koth: Hathian prosecuting lawyer.

Terran Forces on Hathe

Colonel Johne: Head of the Terran occupation forces.

Captain Ferdo Braddock: Senior Communications technician and close friend to Hamon.

Helen Ravensbot: Stores division and friend to Marthe.

Jocelyn Harp: Acquaintance of Marthe and senior Ballistics technician.

Mathilde Chong: Acquaintance of Marthe.

Jones: Security services senior team.

Hawarth: Security services senior team.

Markham: Security services senior team.

Hector: Security services senior team.

Hanley: young anthropologist seconded to the Security services.

Terrans on Earth

Administrator Freya MacDiarmid: Hamon's mother and regulator of the Hathian priority lists. Literally gets to decide who lives and who dies on Earth.

Alliance Ambassador Garth Radcliff: Hamon's father. Senior figure in the Terran faction opposed to Hathe.

Caitlin Radcliff: Hamon's sister and the closest of his siblings to their father.

Jake: A street level Terran.

HATHIAN TERMS AND PLACE NAMES

Aerion: family of predatory flying animals now found only on the plateau.

Kryptark: thorny bush.

Gnur - ground dwelling herbivore. Favourite prey of aerions.

The City: Hathe's capital. Protected during the Terran occupation by an illusory radiation field.

Dromorne: the larger of Hathe's two moons.

Mathe: the small, less easily seen moon. Visible more often in the early morning when Dromorne begins to fade. Secret home to the Hathians evacuated at the time of the Terran invasion and now living in hidden bases there.

Pillars of Mathe: Legendary and ancient arc of stone pillars placed on Mathe by unknown species. The Zenith of the Pillars of Mathe occurs when Hathe sits directly over the central pillar and marks the alignment of the solar system that causes disruption to Terran designed technological devices.

RESISTANCE

INTRODUCTION

The stars beckoned and man went, spreading out to populate the new worlds with new ideas and new ways. Shining among those new worlds was Hathe. It had peace, stability and wealth, all in sufficient abundance to bring forth a world in which there was a blossoming of the arts, the sciences and sheer curiosity.

Particularly, it had wealth.

But that was before the Terran ships appeared in Hathian space. Before a raw and untried Hathian fleet flew out in futile battle against the invaders.

Before the Terrans stole the most precious jewel in the Hathian treasury:

Freedom..

CHAPTER ONE

Voices, coming closer. Too close. Marthe asn Castre tapped urgently on the small, clear patch on her wrist. After four years of occupation, the secret code of the Hathian resistance was as familiar to her as her own Harmish tongue.

"Terrans. Everyone out, now."

The reply came straight back, a sharp tattoo in her earpiece.

"You too. Move it."

Too late. The voices were nearly at her position, and footsteps sounded in the corridor outside. Marthe looked around the room. Banks of com instruments and control panels, a simple table and chairs at the center. There, in the far corner, a space between the wall and an equipment stack. She flattened herself back against the wall and eased into the gap. It was tight. For once being small was a blessing. She checked the shadows on the floor. Straight lines only— no telltale, dark fingers of a human shape.

"Ten point kitty, fives high."

The ugly sound of the Terran Standard words stopped just outside the door. She froze. A narrow gap between the equipment banks allowed her to see the doorway and part of the room. One man walked in, then two more. A scrape of chairs and the clatter of men settling at the table in the center of the room.

"Get ready to be fleeced, boys."

"Sure, Charlie. Like last time," came the sardonic reply.

A rattle, then the unmistakable jingle of chips hitting the tabletop.

Fiver players. Just her luck. Officially banned by the Terran administration, the gambling game was rife among the rank-and-file occupation troops—and a game could last for hours. She peered through the slit towards the far bank of controls. This room was the heart of the Terran communication system controlling this sector of Hathe, her home world. Sitting in the input slot was a thin sliver, her sliver, downloading all the essential data captured in this room. A minute more and she would have her treasure. If the Terrans didn't see it, and if they didn't notice her before their stupid game finished.

"Marthe, are you clear?" said the rapid fire of tapping in her ear. She barely had room to reach her wrist to send a reply.

"Go ahead without me. I'm stuck here. Three Terran soldiers playing Fivers."

The reply was crystal clear and emphatic—her oldest childhood friend Jaca, Jacquel des Trurain, suddenly remembering he was the appointed leader on this mission.

"Report," he ordered.

She told him all, using terse shortcut codes, and could imagine his face at the other end. Jaca would not be happy.

She looked out at the room. Her sliver was still safe, still unseen. So far.

"We're coming in to get you," threatened Jacquel.

"No."

He had to give her time.

Jacquel was as stubborn as she. "Don't expect me to leave you alone. Would Bendin?"

How could Jaca use her twin like that? *"Leave him out of this,"* she stabbed at her wrist. No, Bendin would not have left her here. Nor could he now do anything to help her. No longer. The code she sent back was not in any official manual, but Jaca fully understood it. The silence in her ear lasted a long time.

Hours later the Terrans still played. Marthe blamed the first man who had walked into the room. Did he not know when he was beaten? She kept herself amused by totting up the phenomenal sums he was losing and wished it was Hathians benefiting from his obstinacy rather than the hated Terran soldiers. Mind you, maybe the winners would reward their Hathian servants. If she remembered rightly, her second cousin Jessamie had been assigned to this post and was working as a general maid in the troop barracks. Imagining the look on the men's faces if they ever learned that Jessamie was actually a highly trained chemical engineer helped pass the hours. From there, she moved on to dreaming of the day the Hathians would take back their home and formulating ever more painful and embarrassing punishments for the Terran troops to avenge every single incident she and her fellow Hathians had endured since the Terrans seized their world.

It was a delicious pastime, but even such happy dreams couldn't take away the growing pain in her knees, bent tightly under her. She dare not move for fear of making a sound that might attract her enemy's attention. Despite the enveloping hooded cloak of the so-called Hathian peasantry she wore, she could not risk capture. There was no way to explain how a backward pleb could have bypassed the sophisticated alarms that protected these rooms. The Terrans must never learn the truth behind the mask of their Hathian serfs.

Finally. The loser flung down his chips, growled at his one-time mates, and stomped out. Marthe peered hopefully through the crack at the winners. They leaned back in their chairs, grinned and clapped each other on the back.

"Down to the bar?" said one. A heavy jingle as they collected up their chips. "Or winner take all?"

"You think I was born yesterday?" the other man said, laughing. "Just hand over half that credit balance and let's go."

The first man looked about to argue. Marthe held her breath. Go, go, she urged, trying fruitlessly to flex her numbed muscles without moving. The man stared belligerently at his mate, totting up the balance on their tablets, then moved his fingers as he split it into two. Then he relaxed, reached out a hand for his tab and stood up with a resigned chuckle. "McElroy's or the Crew Stop?"

The second man clapped him on the shoulder. "Crew Stop. No greasy Hathians there. And the first round's mine."

Finally, finally, they were both standing, both walking out the door. They rounded the corner, footsteps tromping down the corridor. They were gone. She could no longer hear their boots sounding against the hard floors.

Marthe carefully eased herself up, gritting her teeth against the agony of long-cramped muscles, throttling back the cries that rose in her throat.

"Marthe?"

"The troopers?" she queried.

"Cleared the building. You are safe to move. Now get out of there."

"*Yes, sir,*" she messaged weakly. Jaca would know exactly how much she meant that.

An hour later, he was still massaging her aching legs. They were in the back room of the Hathian quarters, under full surveillance protection. Jaca had thrown back his hood and leaned over her, his face still half angry, half desperately frightened. "Don't you ever put me through something like that again."

"Just 'cause you're bigger than me, doesn't mean you can boss me around." The old joke fell flat, as usual. He was tall, Jaca, almost as tall as Bendin, but his lean frame had never been a match for her brother's broad build; and she had never let Bendin order her around. Just because since babyhood they had both imagined their purpose in life was to protect her didn't mean she had to buy into it.

"If Bendin—"

"Well, he can't," she shot back. Which silenced Jaca immediately. "I'm all right now," she said gently to his bowed head after a time, and wriggled her feet to prove it.

He looked up, was about to open his mouth in apology.

"No, don't."

He shook his head, rubbing his hand through his hair. Then took a breath, stepped back and gave her the lopsided grin that spoke of unvoiced trouble.

She pulled the sliver from her inside pocket and passed it over to him. "This make it worthwhile?"

"No, but it's a start." He took the sliver, inserted it into the reader he carried under his cloak, and shook his head as if to clear it. "So where are you off to next?" he said.

She allowed him the change in subject. "Furlough. A month of long showers and soft beds, then back here for pick-up duty. You'll be pleased to know I'm to be stuck on a road gang, part of dear cousin Griffith's crew."

His grin returned to normal. "How … fitting."

It was the same hill.

Marthe's hand reached up and tugged her hood forward to hide her face. The guards were patrolling nearby. She looked carefully around the circle of Hathians huddling around the miserable fire then lifted her head as slowly as possible to look beyond them and up at the skyline behind. Then took the risk of lifting her head a fraction more to see clearly, following the angles and planes of rock standing up from the wide rolling lands all around her, the solid black outlined against the shifting light of the evening sky. Yes, there was the ridge leading to the top. There, the jagged block of stone standing alone on the flat platform of the summit. And there was that same pile of rocks she'd stumbled over that long-ago night, the night after graduation, banging her toes and setting off the ever-ready laughter in her twin's eyes as he'd reached out to haul her up to safety.

Her hand reached up now, but it was to pull her hood closer to hide the memory of a grin that touched her mouth. She'd always hated needing to be helped, the only throwback to her mother's genes in a family of fair-haired giants, and Bendin knew it. She'd scowled back at him that night, making it quite plain whose foot she wished had stumbled. Jaca had been with them and watched warily, caught too many times in the middle of an asn Castre twin flare up. But Bendin knew when she was really hurt, and this was nothing, said the laughing gleam in his eyes. There was nothing for it but to burst into matching laughter.

"Come on, Mimi," he'd said impatiently, using her childhood name. He kept his hold on her until she was over the last of the rocks and standing on the summit with the two young men.

Both moons were out that night. The larger Dromorne was already high in the sky, its solid bulk starting to wane. Far off at the edge of the horizon, the smaller sliver of Mathe was caught in its endless struggle to be seen, disappearing against the battling clouds and dying shards of sunlight.

The three of them had stood there in silent awe, for that brief moment at one with the vast wilderness of the high plateau lands.

They had been free, that night, as they stood on the flat top and saw their dreams reflected in the vast plateau lands spread out below them—wild, empty and filled with endless possibilities.

She hunched closer to the fire. That was then and this was now. The world had turned in the last four years and she no longer stood free. In this now, her twin's body lay deep in the soil of the world they all loved—forever young, forever asn Castre, never to change to the an Castre of a married Hathian, never a father, grandfather, grey-haired old curmudgeon. And far across the plains, Jaca played a truly dangerous game.

Nor had the road cut across the plains, scarring the land with its raw newness. On that lost night, there had been no road, no huts … and no Terrans. Yet the night was the same—dark clouds scudding across an unsettled sky and surging waves of movement spreading over the vast tussock plains. The land endured, and for this brief time it was hers. With the wind up, fewer guards patrolled the camp and her small huddle of Hathian workers would be left undisturbed for a while.

She edged closer to the warmth of the fire. She had the information she needed, stored in the thin sliver hidden in the ragged depths of her cloak and, for now, there was no more to be done.

Almost, she smiled. Not the wide, laughing smile of her youth, more an easing of the muscles of her face. For a rare moment, she could pretend she was free as she lingered outside with the other Hathian road workers. Soon, her group would be forced into the huts for the night. But not yet.

She stretched her back slowly, feeling the twinge of newly abused muscles. Three days of carrying stones had awakened muscles she'd forgotten she had. Didn't the Terrans have any modern construction equipment? Of course they do, came the unbidden retort, but why use machines when you can have the pleasure of watching Hathians toil.

No, don't think of them. Pretend instead that this is an evening on one of her childhood outings to the high plain. She'd always loved this wild and empty corner of Hathe.

Never had she imagined she would one day live here.

She made the mistake then of looking at her companions, saw engrained in their faces the harsh suffering that had not been there on those long gone evenings. One hand twitched at her outer robe, pulling it tightly around her as if to ward off old memories. It was no use. Memories such as hers were hard to deny. Faces from the past danced in the firelight: funereal faces, crying faces, faces bleak with shock and bewilderment. The face of her brother.

Let me be, she begged.

Not while Terrans rule our home.

A stray beam of moonlight brought her group to the guard's attention. The Terran strode across, his military bearing unmistakable, then halted and nudged the man beside her with the butt of his weapon. There was no argument, not from any of the Hathians. They rose and moved off towards the confinement of the huts. She stood to go with the rest. The guard watched them and then turned back, his heavy boot scuffing at the dirt to destroy the last, glowing warmth of the fire. Intent upon his actions, he failed to notice her slip away from the others. With a quick farewell sign, Marthe melded into the shadows then disappeared into the ever-moving tussocks and the vast lands beyond.

Griffith an Castre saw his cousin leave but gave no sign of it. To the guards he was only Griff, the big foreman of the work gang. They looked for no more, and he was not about to let them see more. He continued with the rest in their shuffle into the hut. Once inside, he closed the door against the night and their persecutors, glanced once round then gave a tired stretch, his arms reaching upwards as a yawn overcame him. On its way down, one hand grazed the rough wall, leaving behind a thin patch of translucence against the top stud.

He turned, the yawn suddenly stifled, and his weary stoop abandoned.

"We're safe now." He jerked his head up at the top corner from where his patch fed a fake Hathian vid through the Terran scanner, blocking the Terrans' surveillance. Then he threw back his hood. The rest copied him, throwing back their hoods with a newfound eagerness belying the tiredness that lined their faces.

"Did your cousin get safely away?" asked a youth.

Griffith nodded. "Yes, Hanith, and with all your hard-won information for HQ. Marthe tells me those troop movements you saw yesterday will be particularly useful."

The boy beamed his youthful pleasure.

"She also had some good news. The date for the final assault has been confirmed. All is set for the Zenith of the Pillars of Mathe."

He heard the ring in his voice echoed in muted cries of joy from all round him. In one corner, a woman sat with tears starting in her eyes. Griffith saw and moved over, his hands clasping hers in comfort. She looked up, hope almost afraid to enter her face.

"Six months only. Is it true?"

"Yes, Lena, it is true. Soon, it will be over." He stood up, a fierce exultation filling him as his gaze encompassed them all. "Six months only and then we will show these accursed Terrans the truth behind the peasants of Hathe. Come that day, we will wipe them from our world and send them back to their squalid Earth. And then … then, we can go home!"

He stood a moment longer, letting some of the powerful exhilaration that surged through him pass over and fill the rest. Then he signaled for silence, the patch was removed from the surveillance device, and all settled down to sleep, a sleep for once free of despair.

Outside the hut, the night was still plagued with unrest, and black shadows skittered over the ground. Marthe moved slowly, a splash of darkness passing from clump to clump. Suddenly she froze. The tramp of feet approached, a patrolman on his way around the camp perimeter. Closer he came, till he stopped by a large clump of grass to survey the scene then gave a shiver, huddled into his big, heavy coat and continued on. Behind the clump, she let out a silent sigh of relief. As soon as the tramp of feet had died away, she hurried onwards. The last obstacle was behind her.

Moving quickly, she made for the safety of a nearby hollow. Once in the tussocks on the far side, she would be hidden from even the sharpest of human eyes. Then began a long night of hard slogging, clinging to the sides of hills, slithering into the protective cover of the bushes in the sinuous gullies that carved their way into the land and winding her way about the rocks thrusting up through the plain. Always she kept the road near, following its twisting path onwards to the goal they both sought.

It was nearly morning when the grey light of the still hidden sun showed her the jumbled shapes of buildings ahead. In the middle, towering over the surrounding huddle of shacks and closely packed houses, was a huge, white edifice. The Citadel. Home to the Terrans, and her goal.

Not far from the wall enclosing the town, Marthe stopped and curled up in the shelter of a bush. There was time to rest. She pulled the heavy outer wrap closely round her and gave in to the weariness of the long night's hike. An unforgivably short time had passed before she was rudely woken by the prodding of a boot in her back. She looked up, straight into the face of a Terran soldier.

"What's this?" snarled a voice in Terran Standard.

Like all Hathians, Marthe had long ago learnt the hated tongue. Even after years on Hathe, few Terrans had bothered to acquire more than a smattering of the local Harmish tongue, rightly surmising that if the natives knew what was good for them, they would soon master their conquerors' language.

The soldier poked his boot in again, hard. "What are you up to out here, girl? Trying to avoid your assigned duty, unless I'm mistaken."

Marthe ducked her head, hiding the quick gleam in her eyes. "No, sir, never."

"Then what? Explain, and make it quick."

"I was in a foraging party sent out here yesterday, sir, and missed the last gong. The gates had shut before I knew it."

"Why? Sleeping instead of working, I suppose?" The soldier prodded her upright and looked down in contempt. He was of only average build himself and clearly relished his height advantage.

"Not sleeping, sir. I'd found a jerbel bush and was trying to pick as many berries as possible. The Commander likes them particularly, sir, and I hoped to exchange them for extra supplies for my family."

"And what happened to all those jerbels?"

"I ate them, sir. I was so hungry last night."

"So, greedy as well as lazy. We'll see what the Committee can do about that. Come on, get moving!"

The words were reinforced with a heavy blow to the side of the head. Used to such treatment, Marthe merely shook her head to clear the momentary fuzziness before starting to walk, her shoulders bowed as if in fear. Beneath her hood, her lips twitched in triumph.

Soon they reached the great metal gates of the town. So far, her information was accurate. The only guards she could see were a troop of soldiers lounging carelessly near the outer posts. Her captor hailed the one closest. "Hey, Carl. Take charge of my work group, will you?

I found this one skulking outside, too busy last night gorging on jerbels to hear the gong. It's the Citadel for her, I reckon. Maybe a spell in prison will remind her of her place." He gave a loud guffaw and shoved her forward.

They continued on, through busy streets crowded with natives and the occasional Terran soldier. Many were the frightened looks cast the pair and not a few shocked glances. At one point she stumbled, falling heavily against a fellow native. The soldier was too busy yelling at her to get up to notice the swift movement of hands as she passed the precious sliver over from the hidden pocket in her robe, or the quick nod of reply from the other Hathian.

Now they came to the last street. Ahead, the houses huddled even closer, seeming to draw back from the fearsome block of the Citadel. No other street led off this, and it was as if she were passing through a tunnel leading inexorably on to the black emptiness of the slowly opening gates beyond. It was the only breach visible in all the vast squareness of the fortress. Nothing else of the outer world was allowed to intrude into this, the center of Terran control on Hathe. Equally, she could not help feeling that, once taken into the Citadel, nothing and nobody would be released lightly from the heavy gates that now shut behind her.

She was in a closed passage, blocked at the far end by another pair of metal doors. The lights came on, and Marthe saw a smaller door opening to one side. She was taken through it, to find herself in an immense triangular courtyard, bereft of natural life but for soldiers and nervous, scurrying natives. In an office, a clerk took down her particulars then tapped his voicecom.

"Sir, we have a native girl on report. Data through to your screen now. What period of punishment and duty assignment? Looks reasonably young and strong, as far as you can ever tell under that shroud of theirs."

"One year. Major Radcliff mornings, prison kitchen the rest of the day," came the reply from the Committee.

"Right, sir." The clerk switched off, then looked up briefly. "Thank you, Sergeant. That will be all for now," he said, dismissing the guard. Again, he spoke into the voicecom. "Agnethe, to Admin immediately."

After which, he turned back to his own screen, taking no further notice of Marthe though she now stood unguarded within a hands breadth from him and could have easily killed him. The man had no idea of the skills she had been forced to acquire these last years. Instead, she kept her head down like any sensible native girl who found herself straying into the home of the conquerors.

If only she were free to do otherwise. Marthe had known so many *if only* moments.

Ten minutes later, a large, native woman bustled in, the hood of her robe slipping from her head to reveal a red-cheeked, smiling face and wisps of unruly, damp hair beginning to grey. "My apologies, sir. I was busy checking this evening's meal for the officers when you called, and it needed a few of my own touches. These ignorant peasants know nothing of a gentleman's palate, but I, who served in the kitchens of Councilor Bodmin, understand these things. Not that that degenerate would have noticed," she added hastily.

"Enough of your prattle, Agnethe. If the Commander was not so attached to your cooking, that tongue of yours would've had you banned to the mines years ago. You're to show this new girl her duties. She's to clean for Major Radcliff in the mornings and work in the prison kitchens the rest of the day." With which he turned back to his work and took no further notice of them.

"Come on, dear, this way," said the matronly woman, hurrying Marthe out the door. "What's your name, now, and how did you end up in this godforsaken place?" she asked as soon as they were out of the clerk's hearing.

"Riarda, please ma'am," she said in a timid voice. The woman may be one of her own, with an innate likeability, but Marthe's briefings had not included this woman's security clearance level, and she was not about to trust her with her real name. "I fell asleep and missed the shutting of the gates yesterday evening. I also ate a bag of jerbels that I'd gathered to sell to the Terrans."

"Is that all? I remember feasts of best bortch, with jerbels scattered everywhere. Now we get imprisoned for a few! But times are what they are. Come along, don't dawdle, and call me Agnethe. Everyone else does."

Marthe followed her obediently, attempting to make sense of the maze of intersecting corridors and halls. Soon they passed into a new area and through a security door that was bland enough in appearance, but harsh experience had left her with a wary sixth sense for such entrances. It hit her now, the hidden surveillance screens setting off a fine humming throughout her body.

Beyond it, the building changed. The corridors widened and the feeling of being in a prison was no longer present. This must be the Terrans' accommodation quarters.

"Major Radcliff's rooms are along here," said Agnethe, waving to a doorway. "A word of warning. The Terran may be only a major, but watch him. He's the head of Special Services and from a powerful Earth family, I am told. He is also, I might add, very particular over the state of his room and will bawl you out properly if your work is not up to standard. But please him and he's been known to be extraordinarily kind—especially to a young lady like you," added Agnethe with a chuckle. Then she became serious again. "One more thing. He speaks Harmish, though Mathe knows why he ever bothered with learning it. He's a strange one, he is—very keen on asking questions, so you be careful."

She threw open a door as she finished speaking, ushering Marthe into a service cupboard. Then the woman opened the door on the far side of the small room and Marthe entered a whole new world. They were in an apartment, but this was like no place she had seen in all the long and miserable years since the Terrans first landed. This place was beautiful, filled with light, air and comfort. She could only stand and gape, taking it all in. The resistance's bare plans of the Citadel gave no hint of this reality.

A profusion of plants graced the room in front of her, particularly on the small balcony at the far end and, beyond it, she could see the second of the Citadel's great courtyards. It was as unlike the barren oppression of the first yard as the character of the girl Riarda was to her own true nature. She walked forward as if in a daze, needing to see more of this miracle. The courtyard flourished with trees and flowers in kaleidoscopic abundance. The sound of water played from numerous fountains and shaded walks meandered through garden beds.

Agnethe's voice broke into the girl's bemused entrancement, following close behind her. "It may look lovely but remember we cannot appreciate it. We lack the quality of taste, so I'm told," she warned dryly. "Staff enter through the service door only."

She went on to explain Marthe's duties, leading her through the elegant rooms. Marthe was silent, a properly cowed and frightened detainee. At one point only did she interrupt. They were entering the bedroom, Agnethe instructing her in the precise ordering of the room, when Marthe happened to glance up. She gasped, eyes opening wide in recognition. Agnethe looked across sharply then saw what had startled her. Above the sleeper hung a painting of a house, a very beautiful house. It was not a Terran house. Agnethe had seen

Marthe's shocked recognition. The older woman's hand came down on her shoulder, to all intents guiding her fussily onwards. In reality, the fingers bit into her skin. Marthe acknowledged the warning with a humble down casting of eyes.

"A pretty enough picture," remarked Agnethe. "One of the filthy Lieger's City houses. The Major has an interest in such relics, though why he keeps this particular one here is beyond me."

She guided Marthe onwards, talking of duties again. Marthe listened with half an ear only, unable to stop from giving the picture a last, quick glance as she left the bedroom. She had recognized the house of a certainty, every single, wondrous line of it. Her warning hum was back and at full magnitude.

It was with a sense of relief that she followed Agnethe back to the native section of the Citadel, almost welcoming its grimness. Here, she was put to work preparing the prisoners' evening meal, leaving no time to spare for thoughts of the beautiful apartment with its disturbing painting.

Later that night, she managed to catch a free minute, sitting down in a quiet corner of the large dining room beside a fellow native. The breeches sticking out from under the customary cloak proclaimed him to be male, but his face was hidden by his hood. The man shuffled along to give her room, in the process separating them even more from the few native staff still clearing up, then dipped his head close to hers. Both kept their voices low.

"So you made it, little Mimi? And what huge crime did you commit to be sent here?" It was the voice of a young man, a hint of laughter breaking through despite the surroundings.

"Nothing really, and don't call me Mimi. No one has called me that since school, apart from Bendin when he was trying to be particularly annoying. I'm to be known here as Riarda, even by our own people, so just you remember it, Jaca." Beneath her hood, she could feel her mouth twitching and there was no longer even a hint of submission in her voice.

"Does no one dare to tease the mighty Madame Marthe asn Castre?" he retorted, chuckling shamelessly at her hasty warning hush then throwing up his hands in apology. "All right then, what's your news? This area is shielded so we're safe from their eavesdropping but stick to Harmish. No point in making things easy for the Terrans."

"No, it is not" she very pointedly agreed. "You got my last transmission?"

"Telling me you'd met with your cousin Griffith? Yes. I assume he had all the deployments you sought, in clearest detail, right down to the color of each Terran's eyes?"

"Not quite, but close to it. And with very strict instructions for their passage." She laughed herself, though still quietly. "I don't think cousin Griffith will ever approve of me."

"By the Pillars, may he not! Life wouldn't be half as much fun."

"Thank you, I think. Though even I have to admit that his reports are excellent. Full visuals of weapon types, training procedures and detailed specifications on numbers of soldiers and their armaments. I passed it on as I came through town. Better still, his was the last group of troops to be surveyed. We've now all we need."

"If that's so, why were we sent here? All I've been told is to familiarize myself with the Terran staff."

"It seems a few of their senior officers are still suspicious of us. We're to study them and report back to the Council. Here's the list," and she beat out a staccato of coded taps with her fingertips on the clear communications patch on his wrist, a match to the one she wore on her own. "All their leaders are based here. We need to find out if there are any senior officers who might take action against us. If so, the plan will have to be modified. Whatever happens, though, the

Council has confirmed that all is set for the coming Zenith. Or so Father told me a few days ago."

Jaca dropped his head suddenly, and then raised it to look directly at her for the first time. She caught the faint shine of wetness tipping his lashes and took his hand, squeezing it as she nodded in affirmation. He dropped his head again, but not before she saw a fierce relief seize him. She allowed him a moment then touched his hand again.

A shudder passed over him, as if at the throwing back of a blanket. "I thought you'd been off planet recently," he said with determined lightness. "You smell a little too sweet to have been long dirt side."

She took the hint. To speak too openly of the hope they had all clung to so long was more than most could bear. She gave him a minute to recover, then copied his nonchalance, wrinkled her nose and said teasingly: "Unlike certain other people I might mention who are certainly overdue for furlough."

A disgusted snort was his only reply. She ignored it and continued with her report. "I arrived here yesterday, fell asleep outside town and was found this morning by a Terran sergeant. He was ready to book me for anything, but just to be certain I told him I'd been eating jerbels."

"You're allergic to the things."

"I know that, but the sergeant didn't, did he? It got me in here anyway. I'm assigned to the prison kitchen, with mornings spent cleaning for a Major Radcliff. Our people really came through there. He was top of our list—Special Services head; and now I learn that he speaks Harmish. Definitely a man in need of study."

"Radcliff!"

Jaca's head had shot up and she saw, with surprise, his suddenly pale face and grim mouth. "What is it, Jaca?"

"I wish you'd been assigned to anyone but that man."

"But he's ideal for our purposes. I hadn't dared to hope we could get so close to such a priority target."

"Maybe. All I can say is that if he so much as harms one hair of your head, I'll have him. In the few days I've been here, I've heard more than enough about him. Where women are concerned, he's trouble."

Marthe stared. "What are you on about? I can look after myself. I've done so for these past four years and more, and rather successfully, I might add."

Her argument did not impress Jaca. "Radcliff is no good," he growled. "I'd back you in a physical fight any day, but that man won't use his fists against you. Sheer, galling charm is his favored weapon, and he uses it only too well. You keep that hood in place. And remember, he and his kind are responsible for the deaths of many of our people, your brother included."

"That had better not mean what it sounds like. You forget, I was there when they brought in Bendin's body."

"All I know is, Radcliff's dangerous. You've got your com patch safely hidden?"

She nodded silently, her anger gone as quickly as it had come. She could hear the worry in Jaca's voice. She huddled closer to him, seeking comfort. He relented at that and his arm came around her and pulled her in for a short, hard hug.

"Look after yourself, little Mimi," he said, softly squeezing her hand as he rose to leave. The gong sounded just then for the beginning of the night rest period. Agnethe had stressed that all natives must be inside the large dormitories before they were locked for the night. All about her, others bustled past, hurrying round her silent, withdrawn figure.

"Riarda, girl, move," Agnethe called as she passed. "You'll miss out on a bed if you don't hurry. There are never enough."

As it turned out, the warning proved true and Marthe spent the night huddled on a cold floor, prey to a thousand thoughts.

CHAPTER TWO

Hamon Radcliff scowled at the man coming down the corridor towards him. Colonel Johne! As if this night weren't bad enough already. There was no way to avoid a meeting, and right now he couldn't afford to alienate his commanding officer more than necessary. Why must the man be down here now? This late in the evening, it should be safe to leave the gym unseen.

"Evening, Major," said the commander, coming up to him and running a knowing eye over his junior officer.

"Colonel." He gave the required salute then moved off. Not quickly enough to miss the smirk on the older man's face. He knew its cause. The normal fitness regime compulsory for all members of the Terran forces occupying Hathe did not leave a man dripping with sweat and gaunt from exhaustion. Radcliff might resent the Colonel, but he didn't underestimate his intelligence. A long-term career soldier, Johne would know exactly why his head of Special Services sought escape in exercising to the point of near collapse.

There were only two things either of them had ever agreed upon: Hamon's forced conscription from his rule-free and independent civilian life to this posting on Hathe was a thoroughly undesirable change to the life of both men; and neither of them could do a thing about it. Radcliff was too well connected back home for Johne to touch, and Hamon was barred by an inconvenient sense of duty from organizing a release from his commission. What he did here was vital to the survival of Earth. The urgonium mined only on Hathe was their principal energy source, and Earth needed more of it very badly. Nor was there anyone else with his particular mix of skills and experience who could take his place. That was not a boast—rather, a cold-blooded assessment of fact that he wished with every particle of his being was not true.

But brooding could not distract him from the scream of abused muscles as he entered his quarters. He was so tired he must surely be able to sleep tonight. The briefest cycle of the cleanser was all he managed before throwing himself onto his sleeper … only to spend yet another night tossing restlessly, prey to a thousand thoughts.

Now another day had begun. A beam of sunlight splashed through the long windows of the apartment, shimmering off the water droplets still clinging to the plants on the small balcony then falling in lazy patterns on the large, cube chairs dominating the inner room.

Hamon stared morosely at the beautiful room, seeking some kind of ease in the familiar spaces. He had made of these rooms a refuge, the one place in this military fortress he must now inhabit that felt like home. With the dividing wall drawn back, he could look out from his secluded seat in the bedroom to the main room beyond, and past that to the freedom of the sky. It was why he had chosen these rooms for his own

Despite the air of comfort, there was a sparse feel to the apartment. An outdoorsman at heart, he'd insisted the services team minimized the constraints of walls, floor and ceiling to the barest noticeable. Simple shapes and a pale wash of near white, broken only by a profusion of plants. In the bedroom, the sole furniture was the chair he sat in and a sleeper of subtly shifting translucence. The room held a single embellishment—a painting. It hung above the sleeper and showed a house of flowing lines and soft colors. A spire climbed to the sky while at the base a tide of tropical plants clung to the walls, doors and balconies. A beautiful home, but Hamon could not pretend it belonged here. Despite the presence of Hathian plants, his apartment was undoubtedly Terran. The house in the painting was not.

This morning, as always, it drew his eyes. He stood, paced a couple of times around the room then once again slumped into the chair, to stare at the painting on the far wall. The building's clean lines only fed the fires within as memories crowded him mercilessly. He thumped down on the corner of his chair and leaped up to resume his pacing.

All the while, his gaze remained glued to the house as yet again he was thrust back in time to when he'd first seen it. Before Earth had invaded Hathe.

It had been a home then, filled with a constant procession of smiling faces. The visitors had included the most senior members of the planetary administration, coming to call on the good Dr Sylvan an Castre, a member of the Hathian Council and a scientist known throughout the Alliance for his work on interplanetary communication systems.

Others had come too. Younger faces, their voices calling merrily through the beams and spires. The doctor had a son, well-liked by all, he remembered sourly, and two daughters, each unique in her own way. Both women had followed their father into the world of science: the elder in his own sphere while the younger was said to be destined for an illustrious career in the world of medicine. They were also very beautiful. His mouth twisted to a skewed smile. Many of the young men who came to visit their lively brother, twin to the second of the sisters, had stayed to chat with the lovely young women of the an Castre family.

He could see them still. Images bright with the sharpness of carved crystal. The elder sister had been blessed with the sea grey eyes of an ocean in repose—slow to anger and with a rock-deep sense of enduring strength.

Then there was the younger.

Ah, yes, the younger of the asn Castre daughters. A mountain brook was how he always saw her. Small and slender, with brown eyes alive with the ever-changing currents of a stream breaking on rocks or slipping into silent mystery under root shrouded banks—a small enigma in a family of tall guardians.

He grimaced. He, too, had wanted to meet the sisters. Particularly the younger.

Very badly.

His hands clenched as memory played back. His wants had counted for nothing in that long-lost world. The brother made sure of that. The young man had already crossed paths with Hamon, and not to Bendin asn Castre's advantage. A small smile of satisfaction creased Hamon's mouth, but only for an instant. Too soon afterwards, he remembered, the Hathian had repaid Hamon fully and in kind.

Marthe asn Castre was like no woman Hamon had ever seen, before or since. She'd been busy arguing the first time he saw her. Eyes flashing, body almost bouncing with the energy filling it, her fingers jabbed the air with each point scored.

It was a typical diplomatic affair; all dry nothings and subtle courtesies with a hidden knife edge to every word. In the middle, stood this tiny woman, glowing with her passions and talking avidly.

She suddenly threw up her hands. Stopped as if struck and he surged forward. But no, she was laughing. Her whole face lit up with it. Still laughing, she swept her hands out as if flying, and bowed elaborately to the slimly built man in front of her. He could only see the man's back. He didn't matter. Not with her in the room.

Something gave a single beat inside him. Perfect, said a voice.

He had to meet her. But the crowd around her was too dense.

That night, he pulled the records of every guest there. Hamon was good at details and soon had her name. Marthe asn Castre, younger daughter of a Hathian councillor, Sylvan an Castre. In the days that followed, he haunted any gathering she was likely to attend.

Yet he made no move to meet her. Not after that inner voice and that word. *Perfect.* No one was perfect. People lived to disappoint you. If nothing else, life had taught him that. Collect the facts first. Marthe asn Castre was a complicated pattern, one he couldn't stop trying to decipher, but she would have flaws.

His father actually praised him one day for his attendance at so many dry affairs. Hamon had only been included in the mission to Hathe at his father's insistence and so far, had done little more than stand mute attendance on the discussions between the Hathian officials and the Terran contingent and indulge in the usual entertainments offered to any young man in a foreign port. Now, he made a point of listening to the locals. He was good at fact gathering and at dissembling. When he knew her better, when this overpowering need for her diminished, then he'd approach her.

When she was no more than simply another beautiful woman.

It didn't happen. He heard her debate, laugh, and once weep at a vid screening. He bolted out of his seat at the sound of it, then stopped when he realised what he'd done and quickly walked out instead.

That's when he knew he was in trouble. That this was more than simple attraction. The next night, he watched her from an upper balcony as she danced and chattered below, plotting exactly how he'd introduce himself.

Unfortunately, he met her twin brother first. He'd heard of the closeness of the asn Castre twins, but gave it little attention. He liked his own half-brother and sisters well enough, but they didn't meddle in each other's affairs. The twin brother would be the same.

He was wrong. That night, he discovered how disastrously wrong.

He was suddenly grabbed from behind. Hamon had been in enough bad situations to escape from an attacker but turning, found himself surrounded and badly outnumbered. He left them with bruises. They left him sprawling and battered in the cold street outside, cast to the ground like some criminal nobody. The tallest of his attackers glared down at him, and he groaned inside.

"Stay away from my sister, Terran," said Bendin asn Castre. "She's not for the likes of you."

The words were carved into his brain. The rest of that night was murky and the next day, his father eyed his bruises in disgust. That day, the Hathians gave them their final answer and the Terrans had to leave for Earth. A failed mission. His father blamed him for that too.

He'd never forgotten Marthe asn Castre, or the words of Bendin asn Castre and his father, but looking back on his deeds of the past few years, Hamon was forced to concede that the arrogant Hathian may just have been right. It made little difference. One day, he would make Bendin asn Castre and the rest pay for the humiliation of that trip.

What had become of them all? Was she still asn Castre? Or married and become an Castre? A sudden clench of denial at the thought of her with another, and he glared at the picture. The beautiful home, once so full of life, had been ugly with the decay of desertion when next he saw it immediately after the conquest. It was protected from the attentions of his troops by the same deadly radiation that cloaked all the buildings of the people who had once ruled this planet: the Liegers, as the natives named them or the Haut Liege as they had termed themselves—the ruling class that had now so inexplicably disappeared, taking with them the secret of extracting the precious urgonium.

Earth could mine it, but only in quantities laughably short of what they needed. Urgonium, the rarest and most valuable mineral in the universe. The most efficient source of energy known in all the Alliance and found only on Hathe. Earth needed it, couldn't survive without it, and Hathe refused to give them more. So they came to take it…and look what they found.

All that remained now of this world's once vibrant society were empty shells and dull wretches—the peasants of Hathe, claiming to be only too glad to see the back of the Liegers who had treated them little better than serfs. Life under the Terrans was lenient in comparison. Or so the natives claimed.

Hamon shook his head and thumped the chair again. It wasn't true. Over and over, the refrain jangled in his head. He may have only visited here once before the conquest, but he would have sworn it was not a society built on cruelty. Yes, he'd seen servants in the mansions of the ruling group. Proud and free people they had been, efficient organizers of the household routine, not frightened drudges like the native housemaid now scuttling in through his service door. Something was terribly wrong. All of a sudden, he felt as if he and his complacent fellow Terrans were sitting on a time bomb set to explode right in their faces.

He rose and stalked through to the lounge. Ignoring the heavily shrouded maid, he stared broodingly at his vidscreen. At the moment, it was set to the view of the native courtyard, crowded at this time of day with scurrying Hathians

Those damn peasants. Ignorant, foul smelling, subservient. But try to get some answers from them, and you could almost see the mask falling beneath the hood of that all concealing outer wrap of theirs. The blasted thing was more effective than any wall in creating an impenetrable barrier to these people.

And underneath… He remembered some of the women he'd used to assuage the awful loneliness and brutality of this place. He may not have liked himself afterwards, but that was a luxury he'd forfeited when he joined the occupation forces. Earth needed him here if it was to survive. That was all he could allow himself to consider, and those fleeting moments of pseudo intimacy kept him going for another hour, another day.

Not that any of them were beautiful by Terran standards but some may not have been too bad if he were less fastidious. Cleanliness was not a priority of the Hathian peasant. And the hair of the women! Custom dictated greasy, tightly woven coils, covered by a ragged cap which added nothing to the wearer's desirability. Thinking of those encounters, he grimaced in self-disgust. What was this world, this job making of him? A thing he could only despise? And whether he could live with himself afterwards was something he refused to consider.

His mouth twisted. At least he would live, unlike the millions of Terrans back on Earth if he failed in his duty.

And the women he used to help him survive here—*used* being the only word that fit what he did with them? For all his contrived charm, he learned nothing from them, regardless of the tears they wept as he rid himself of yet another failure in a long line of unproductive encumbrances. They swore of love and passion but refused to drop the mask drawn over life before the Terrans. All he had ever got were tired clichés. Those Liegers, they would sneer.

Stars! Maybe they really were the unfeeling clods his fellow Terrans believed them to be and he should give up this stupid quest for truth. What did he care? But he did, and knew he could not avoid it. If he was right and failed to prove it in time, all of Earth would pay in lost lives and misery. And he would stoop to anything to stop that.

So, he returned to it again. The dilemma that was driving him in ever maddening circles. He *must* try to find out what lay behind the hoods and the veiled eyes of Hathe. Starting with the subject in front of him—probably to as little use as usual, he admitted heavily, and eyed the maidservant dubiously.

She was new. Despite the concealing robes, he knew she was not the same maid that usually came. The frequency of changes to his cleaning staff was one of the things that made him most suspicious. He stalked back into the room, determined to break open that cursed façade of theirs.

Settling himself into one of the large chairs, one leg draped over the side, he gazed in apparent disinterest at the girl. He waited in silence, like a spectator at a play, noting each small twitch or jerk of his victim. He kept up the unmoving scrutiny for half an hour, deliberately creating an air of edgy expectancy in the room. The girl had become a challenge for him, a do or die last attempt. This time, he would not be beaten and watched as she meticulously cleaned each small speck from the spotless floor.

He noticed she avoided his one Earth plant. Its presence on Hathe contravened every biosecurity law in known space, but he had brought it regardless. He needed it. A piece of home to remind him why he was here. And he found the reaction of the Hathians to it very instructive. This girl appeared to be unaffected by it, ignoring it and carrying on regardless, but yet no part of her ever touched its shining green leaves.

"There's more dust over there, girl. Behind the far seat."

As intended, his sudden words after the tense silence reverberated through the room. Her hand froze, but then she deliberately steadied herself. Steady, then walked across to clean the pristine area. He increased the tension.

"While you're there, the plant leaves should be polished every day," he drawled in the most officious tone he could summon.

This time, the woman's whole body showed an infinitesimal stiffening, but still she bent to the assigned task. She left the Terran plant till last, hesitating fractionally as she approached it. As if she must force herself to obey him. Not as calm as she tried to appear, then, he guessed, and he allowed a nasty smile to spread over his face. This might be interesting.

He'd read his victim better than he could have guessed. So that is the way it is to be, thought Marthe angrily. Two can play that game, Terran.

She had been discreetly studying her target since he'd marched so cavalierly into the room. Why he chose to watch her working, she couldn't imagine, but she again checked the escape routes she'd identified on her first visit with Agnethe. Jaca may think she could best the Terran if it came to a struggle, but now she'd seen him, she wasn't so sure. The man was tall and lean, with a breadth of shoulder suggesting strength, and the easy balance in his gait was that of a trained fighter. It was possible she could take him, but only by using the kind of deadly tricks not usually known by a cowed and beaten Hathian maidservant. Her cover would be blown as soon as she tried any of them. No, the only hope she had lay in Jaca's words of warning. Charm was this man's weapon of choice. His guile against hers. So be it, Terran. She bent to rearrange the objects on a side table as per his latest, meaningless command, turning her head slightly as she did so in order to observe his face.

He scowled at her, eyes closely tracking her movements, and she was suddenly grateful for the concealing hood of her outer robe that hid her face from his scrutiny. In the feared Terran uniform and with his dark hair, deep earth-green eyes and sun-darkened skin, there was an air of real menace about the man. The downward twist of his mouth only added to it.

Yet a smile would have softened that hard face.

Her hand jerked, touching a small, translucent globe, a perfect circle of light caught in stone. It nearly toppled, saved only by a quick recovery of her hand that made the movement look deliberate, and she turned carefully to wait his next order, head bowed in submission and innards churning. Where had that thought come from?

He snapped the next command and she obeyed thankfully. She had herself in hand again but was ever more wary with each ridiculous command. Wary and rather angry at this game the Terran chose to inflict on her. She fought back in the only way possible, and each increasingly humiliating order was obeyed with an unchanging blandness of demeanor. I will outlast you, Terran.

Hamon watched her in stony calm, his bored voice pronouncing his demands. Inwardly, he was fuming. This one was either particularly thick-skinned or far cleverer than any native he had yet come across. He stood, and quietly walked to a spot just behind her. She was carefully wiping an imaginary speck from the wall. His hand rose to twitch away the enshrouding headgear. Too late. Like a startled deer, she had sensed his movement and whirled out of reach, ducking her head. Her hands clutched at her wrists, fingers tapping a nervous staccato on her pulse.

"You require something, sir?"

"Yes, blast you. I require that you take off that stupid hood," he snapped, angered at being caught out. "Come here and see how generous a Terran can be to a friendly young woman." He softened his voice, let it deepen seductively, but at the same time his hand reached out to grab her arm as she sidled away. He held her still, not hard enough to hurt, but firmly enough to let her know she was going nowhere. "Stand still. You've had your little game. Now we play by my rules."

She kept her face turned away as he drew back the hood from her head. Then paused. Something was not right. Here was the common cloth cap, dull grey this time and jammed down right over her ears. It was dirty enough, but his fingers felt drawn to touch all the same. She flinched back, but his hands were strong. He caught both her wrists in one hand, holding her tightly as the fingers of his other hand confirmed what his eyes suspected. He gripped the cap and tugged it back from her hair.

He stopped, shocked into stillness. What exactly he had suspected, he knew not. It wasn't this. Here was no greasy, odorous mess. His hand resumed its motion with a mesmerizing slowness, releasing a cascade of rich, nugget brown waves, shining with the lights of sun and earth. As the cap slid farther back, he reached out in wonder. A wordless gasp escaped him as his hand lightly caressed the tantalizing strands. Gently, oh so gently, he reached to tilt her chin round, eager to see the face beneath this unique halo.

There was a cough from behind him and the spell was broken. He turned to blast the intruder. It was a mistake. Swift as the Hathian loeth, the girl was fleeing out the nearby service way. He whirled to stop her. Too late. All he caught was the sliding of the door and a stray lock of hair peeping from beneath its imprisoning hood. Eyes blazing, he turned on the native responsible. It was a young man, desperately bowing in appeasement.

Hamon's temper snapped. "What is it? And do not ever again come in like that! Sneaking around like the currish lot you are." Head still down, no answer came. "Well, come on, you've done your damage. What was so important that you should interrupt me at such a moment?"

"My deepest apologies, sir. Please, I did not mean… I did not know. She's only a native girl, sir."

Goaded by disappointment into a rare need for violence, Hamon silenced the man with a crashing blow. Stumbling, the Hathian rose again, bowing low to soften any further blows. "The Colonel is an important man, sir, and he told me to bring you immediately. Please, sir?"

Temper ratcheted to a dangerous level by the edge of guilt at his action, Hamon felt a twinge of relief at the excuse to leave. Beating up Hathian peasants, no matter how irritating, was one thing he had till now resisted. What could his blasted commander want? He had no choice but to answer the summons and marched out, fully intending to continue his study of the strange native girl in the very near future. He could feel it, that twitch that said he was finally on the verge of learning something.

Jacquel des Trurain stood forgotten by his enemy, staring for a long moment after Radcliff's retreating figure. One day, Major, you will pay for today, he promised himself. Then, with a silently mouthed oath, he quietly turned to leave by the service door.

CHAPTER THREE

Marthe was overtaken by Jaca halfway down the next corridor. After checking for passing Terrans, he drew her into a nearby service room. Then he exploded.

"You really do have a talent for making trouble out of nothing. That precious hair of yours may have just been your downfall. How many times have I told you in the past—tied up and powdered? If you imagine that His Lordship of Radcliff," and he gestured rudely, "is not going to comb the entire native section to find you, then you're wrong! He's notorious for pursuing beautiful women, with a vigor that's matched only by his confounded success!" He slumped to the floor, cradling his head gingerly. "And damn me if I haven't gone and set my head ringing again. Your Major swings a mean cut."

Marthe crouched down beside him, guilt riding her. "I'm so sorry, Jaca. I had to call you. Anything else would have blown my cover." She reached out to examine the bruised tenderness, but his hand caught hers.

"It's all right, Marthe. I'm fine, really. But you see now why I warned you about that man. After this, you have to hide that hair of yours. We'll change the roster and get another maid sent in to cover your duties."

He put a hand on her face, tilting it to look her directly in the eye. "I know you want to find out more about Radcliff but leave it to others. There's only one way you're likely to learn anything from him, and that's out of the question. Your face was too well known to go long unrecognized once he starts parading you as his latest mistress. Don't say no," he added, touching a finger to lips already forming a denial. "You've seen the man. If you stay as his maid, he will get that hood off you. And once he sees what you really look like, how beautiful you are, do you really think you would have any choice but to stay and do whatever he wants? The kind of hunt that man could start if you disappeared would end up exposing us all. No. We'll have your duties changed."

Marthe was torn between angry denial and reluctant acceptance. Reality won.

"You're right, of course. Not about the beautiful bit," she had to add. It was an ancient argument between them.

He shook his head as if to say 'not now'.

She touched a hand to her hair. "It's just… it was my last stand, you see. We may have humbled ourselves and blighted our world, but while I kept my hair as it was before, it kept the real me alive."

"I do understand, Mimi," said Jaca gently. "We have fallen so, so far. But remember, we descended to these depths of our own free will, that we might one day ascend again. We have yet to be forced downwards. The free choice of a free people, even if it be degradation, is never shameful."

She had to smile at that, even if somewhat weakly. "Your politician's mind was always able to render a useful sentiment poetic." Then practicality returned, and she glanced up nervously. "We'd better not linger here. And if my hair must be bound so horribly, you should have the honor. I could do with a hand down to the bottom of the pit."

So, solemnly but with a smile in his eyes, Jacquel took the vibrant mass, divided it into four plaits, and twisted them into a knot at the nape of her neck. Then he took a green powder and lightly sprinkled it over the whole, changing the glowing, earthen sheen to a mousy lifelessness.

"You look disgusting," he teased. "Come wench, to your chores."

"And you, boy, to yours, for if I look disgusting, then you look downright filthy."

Side by side, she went with him back to the kitchen area, where levity was soon dispelled by the fussing Agnethe. She bustled up as soon as she saw them, scolded their lateness and set Marthe, whom she knew as Riarda, and Jaca, whom she had never bothered to name, to work at the massive cauldron of watery soup. It was the staple diet of the prisoners. The Terrans never tasted it themselves, said Marthe's briefings—so were not to know of certain powder concentrates secretly added by the cheery, harmless old head woman—and merely assumed that the peasants were a hardy breed, able to thrive despite the poor food and everlasting toil of their lives.

Agnethe was indefatigable, bustling everywhere in her huge kitchen, chiding here, praising there. For all its miserable grey walls and thin wisps of sunlight, Marthe found that an atmosphere of contentment pervaded the cavernous hall. Terrans seldom intruded, relying for control of the prisoners on the surveillance vids that constantly monitored the Hathians. Or so the Terrans thought.

At one end of the kitchen were the four enormous cooking pots: two for the morning gruel and two for the evening soup. Fortunately, the less than appetizing odors from these were vented to the outside and did not pervade the large work benches extending the length of the room. When she first arrived, these were crowded with workers, chopping, cutting and slicing the ingredients to be added to the large pots. Then later, after a thorough scrubbing, the same tables became dining tables for the hundreds of natives confined here in the fortress—so many that they had to run the meals in shifts.

For all the hustle, working in the kitchens was rather pleasant, mused Marthe later. Her surroundings may have lacked the elegance of the Major's apartment, but there were no Terran guards here, and she was ideally placed to hear the gossip so necessary to her mission. Hathians from throughout the fortress passed through in a constant stream, bringing news and many of the secrets of their deluded captors to her receptive ears. Everything had worked out rather well. She checked the temperature of the great pot, absentmindedly watching the one beam of sunlight that penetrated the gloomy hall and dreaming of good times to come.

Suddenly, two guards grabbed her by the shoulders. Without explanation, they pinned her arms behind her back and swung her round to march her out, forcing her to almost run to keep up with their brisk, military stride. She searched for a familiar face and was reassured to see a quick nod from a nearby, averted head.

Up the steps they shoved her, across the courtyard and through a heavily guarded doorway to a set of offices far more imposing than any she had yet seen. A wary foreboding filled her. She was brought to a rough halt in front of a stark, white door as her guards signaled their presence.

They waited a bit, then the door slid back to reveal a room dominated by a large desk. Behind it sat a small, middle-aged man wearing a bored expression on a face that presaged little sympathy.

The guards pushed her up to stand in front of the desk, held in place by a strong force field and unable to move any muscles. They then took up a position between her and the door.

"Your name, girl?" the man said without looking up.

She made her voice as small and obsequious as possible. "Riarda, sir."

"Riarda what?"

"Just Riarda, sir."

"Hmph." He turned to a second man, moving into her line of vision from the far side of the room. "Is this the girl you complained of, Radcliff?"

She tensed as the familiar head turned to look at her, his eyes hard green and filled with a speculative light.

"They all look alike in that cursed shroud."

"Guard, remove the cloak," the older man ordered, motioning to one of them. The soldier strode across and whipped off her outer wrap, unaffected by the strong field that gripped Marthe and held her head rigidly upright as she vainly sought to duck, to hide her face for every crucial second. But her secret was out, betrayed by one bright curl rebelliously escaping the cap and plaits that entrapped the rest, to slip tellingly down her temple and rest over her eye. She longed to blow it away, make it disappear. Too late. Radcliff had seen it.

"This is the one, Colonel." He moved around to where he could better see her, coming to a halt right beside the Colonel. Right in front of her, where she had no hope of hiding her face from him. He cannot know me. He can't, she told herself.

The Colonel ignored him and barely looked up at her as he studied the report. "Girl, it seems you have failed in your duties. For this, you will have your term of punishment increased from … ah, let's see…" and the older man bent to read her small entry in the list of prisoners.

"By the Seven Pillars of Mathe!" Radcliff stood with eyes wide open, gazing at her face in awe.

"What is the matter, Major?" queried the Colonel tetchily. "And what might be 'the seven pillars of mathe'? You're getting too damn close to these natives. It's affecting you."

The Terran Major, the man she was increasingly coming to think of as her most dangerous enemy, stood in silence, his face rigid. The

Colonel looked up with a frown. "Really, Radcliff. Even supposing she were pretty, you've no need to stand there like that." He punched his console and rapped out an order. "Scan in target zone. Confirm prisoner identity."

"You would find the old Hathian files to be more informative," said Radcliff in a voice thin with shock.

"Why? Do you know her?"

"Yes," he said, and in that one word, Marthe knew all her fears come true. How could he? How was it possible? Then Radcliff seemed to shake off the spell of stunned awe, and those green eyes took on a wicked glitter. No, not all green. They showed touches of warm brown now. It did nothing to reassure Marthe. His next words even less so.

"Colonel Johne, may I present Madame Marthe asn Castre, daughter of the Hathian Councilor and Alliance Representative, Dr Sylvan an Castre." The Terran commander sat up sharply. "Yes, you have in front of you a genuine Haut Liege, one of the despised Liegers whom we had thought to have fled and disappeared completely. And how is the good Doctor, your father, Madame. More importantly, where is he?"

Marthe read truth in his face. This man had seen her before. When and how, she couldn't imagine, and try as she might, she couldn't recall ever seeing him. Which was surprising, for having seen his face as it was at this moment, alight with excitement, she knew that never again would she forget it, though the faces of the others in this room who equally threatened her would undoubtedly fade with time.

She was caught and knew there was no escape, no point in trying to deny who she was. She gave in to her anger, clenching her fists and making no attempt to hide it from him. Or as much as she could under the frazzing controlling field. With a huge effort, she discreetly pressed the communications patch on her wrist against her leg before spitting out a reply.

"I cannot help you, Major. It has been over four years since I last saw my father. He was as well then as a man could be who has lost everything and is being forced to flee his home."

"Leaving behind his beloved younger daughter? Your family was renowned for their closeness, as I remember."

"We had an argument."

"He abandoned you?" he said with a curl of his lip and a tilt of his head to look down at her. So, he didn't believe her. But he still had to prove it to his boss.

"I'd gone off on my own and missed the embarkation call. They couldn't wait. It would put everyone at risk of being captured by your invasion fleet, and not even Father could change that. I have no idea where they are now. All I do know for certain is that Earth doesn't possess the technology to find them."

Radcliff laughed at her brave challenge. "Perhaps you would prefer to see just what Earth's technology can achieve?"

She refused to succumb to the threat in his voice, remaining defiant.

"You would do well to heed the Major, girl," said the Colonel. "He can make life very unpleasant for you."

"Maybe, but I still can't help you. I have no idea where my father might be at the moment." Which was strictly true, if not in the way she made it sound. "The final destination of the fleet was known to only a few, in case any were left behind and caught."

Radcliff stared back at her for a moment, then shrugged, letting the first part of her answer ride. "And were there any others? Where are your fellow Haut Liege hiding? You can't be the only one. What about your twin, that brother who was so protective of you in the past?"

"Dead, killed trying to keep you off planet long enough to let our people escape." She saw it in his face—his recognition of the pain that, despite their presence, she couldn't hide at the memory of Bendin's loss. Yet still she glared her defiance. "We thought you our inferior in technology and you were, in all except warfare. It's a science we never cared for, never having had sufficient dealings with your world to learn of its necessity."

She knew, even as she said the words, the stupidity of her pride-driven insolence and wasn't surprised to soon pay for it. The guard lashed out with a resounding blow to her head that made her sway even in the strong field.

It was too much for Hamon. Even in his triumph and bitter need for revenge, he felt the blow in his own gut. "That's enough, Corporal." He glared angrily until the guard stepped back from their prisoner. Then he bent to check on the girl, on Marthe asn Castre—the one woman in all the universe he'd thought to never see again. Had hoped so badly to find again, to meet unhindered at last by the interference of others. He put out a hand to check her for injury and tried to ignore the flinch as he touched her face.

Her skin was so soft, but her beautiful eyes were distant and closed to him. One of his fingers strayed, one only. It traced the line of her cheek, followed the curve of her neck. Then stopped as he remembered his role here, and they were not alone. He signed to the guard to adjust the force field and pulled a chair over.

"Sit down," he ordered, gesturing to the guard to ease off the field a fraction to let her move slowly, then waited till she obeyed. "Watch her," he said to the guard, "but don't touch her unless you have to." Then he deliberately turned his back on her as he addressed his commander. Which didn't mean that he didn't feel the fierce glare of her eyes or each angry breath, and he fought not to grieve for it.

"Colonel, there is more to this than one mislaid Lieger. Yesterday, just as I was about to expose Madame asn Castre's face, a native interrupted me with a bogus message from you. You may remember it?"

"Yes." The Colonel was listening but his face wore the expectant air of cynicism that Hamon had seen too often, the face of one about to hear an argument he'd heard and refuted many times before.

"I am convinced that the girl called the other Hathian by some means unknown to us. Her father was a leading communications scientist as well as a member of their government. I don't think her presence here is purely coincidental. Nor is she on her own."

"It's a possibility, though it doesn't seem feasible that this simple people could ever organize the kind of resistance movement that you repeatedly claim exists. However, I daresay we had better investigate. It appears to be a matter that comes within your jurisdiction, so I leave it up to you."

"Thank you, sir. I take it that I am free to conduct this enquiry as I see fit."

The Colonel looked up suspiciously. "Why?"

"I would like to try an experiment."

"Explain."

"As you know, our prison regime has so far proven ineffective in breaking these people. Further, we strongly suspect that most Hathian prisoners remain in contact with those outside, though we've found nothing to prove it. I therefore propose confining Madame asn Castre in my own quarters. It means I can keep her under close personal supervision at all times, and at the same time, get to know her well enough to learn more of the present Hathian society. My men have never succeeded in penetrating the facade these people throw up."

"That you claim they throw up. You know my views on that well enough. What about security?"

"My quarters would be fully protected by fields, coded only to me. She will be well guarded, I promise, yet apparently accessible. We may even manage to net some others of interest."

"If they exist! Personally, it seems an unnecessarily elaborate cover for keeping the girl for your own use. If you want her, you can have her. Though I have to say that your good taste appears to have deserted you this time." The Colonel peered dubiously at Marthe.

"Aah, but you haven't seen her scrubbed and gowned. Marthe asn Castre was known as one of the loveliest women on Hathe and it was a reputation not undeserved, as I once saw for myself."

He couldn't deny the rush of pleasure that filled him at the blush spreading over her cheeks, though she refused to give any other sign she'd heard him. The Colonel continued to look skeptical.

"Whatever you say," he said, "What you do in your own quarters is your affair, but I expect you to maintain a tight security. Your suspicions aside, she's the only Lieger we've ever captured. As such, she is a valuable hostage if we should one day find the rest of her thrice-accursed people. Go ahead with your plan, but guard her closely. I want her fully searched, too. The one thing I do know of her people is that they were cunning and untrustworthy. The stars know what she may be carrying on her."

"Certainly, sir. And thank you for your confidence. Guard, you heard the Colonel." Hamon allowed himself a small smile of triumph as he turned to follow the soldiers out of the room. They had a tight hold of their captive, hands locked behind her but still marching proudly along with her head high.

CHAPTER FOUR

Inwardly, it was a different matter. Marthe seethed with anger, her derision aimed squarely at herself. How could she have been so stupid? Her foolish, misplaced pride was about to jeopardize everything for which her people had worked so long and hard. They were too close to victory to let the Terrans ruin it. If, that is, they managed to break her—and that, she vowed, would not happen.

There was an alternative plan, she reminded herself, but she also knew that it came with a drastically lower margin of safety—a margin which would realize itself in the loss of many extra lives, lives for which she was now responsible by her silence.

She had one consolation—the small, flesh-molded communicator patch fixed to her wrist, which she had managed to activate. Base control must even now be listening to all that took place and should have alerted the Citadel natives of her plight, and of their own danger. With luck, any further captures would be prevented—if she could only convince the Terrans of the truth of her tale. It might sound far-fetched, but without any other evidence, what could they do? Even if Radcliff doubted her, the Colonel seemed easier to persuade, and he was the commander. Radcliff would have to follow his lead.

Or so she told herself as they half led, half dragged her through the Terran quarters to halt at last before the doors of the Major's apartment. Radcliff entered his code, letting them pass through the field already set up to bar the door.

"Enter, Madame," he beckoned in mock civility. She marched past, coldly daring him to maintain the arrogance of his stance. An amused tilt of his lips was her only answer. "You, too, Sergeant. A search is required, remember. A full search."

An expectant smirk on his face, the soldier walked in with what was undeniably a spring in his step.

Marthe watched as he approached, a wary unease taking hold of her. The Major had pulled out a portafield control from his suit and switched it onto her, holding her rigidly in place where she stood in the center of the room with her arms slightly raised from her sides. They had returned her wrap to her as they marched out of the Colonel's office, flinging it roughly about her shoulders. The guard dragged it off her now, leaving her in only her tunic, long shift and boots. She tensed in readiness, looking beyond the walls of the room to an imaginary horizon as she waited for the slithering of his examining hands. She loathed being searched and could endure it only by passing as far as possible into a protective trance, ignoring the humiliation of her bodily shell.

The customary mantra she used, a collection of her mother's gems of maternal wisdom, began to unreel in her head. But this time it was different. She had barely begun the third quote: 'nice little boys and girls do not leave prindars, especially live prindars, in the boots of their cousins'. It was the one Maman had always produced at least once during a visit by their cousin Ermentruda. Those words would return her instantly to the world of her youth, banishing the horror of the present.

Not this time. The hands did not trace their usual, overly familiar, slimy path over her shoulders and down her breasts. Instead, they reached out to grab her clothes, and the overtunic was roughly torn from her.

She brought her gaze sharply back to the present, her eyes questioning the Terran officer in stunned denial. It was no use. He lay back in his chair, his lips twisted up in a mockery of delight.

"Is this necessary?"

"Absolutely. The boots, Sergeant." Her feet were lifted and soon she stood barefooted, with only the protection of her shift. For the first time, Marthe considered begging.

"I am concealing nothing. Why resort to this?"

"My apologies, Madame, but my colonel did order a full search."

"And you are always so obedient."

"Certainly. Especially when it suits me so well, I have waited a very long time for this moment." His smile widened. "Continue, Sergeant."

Again, she felt the hateful fingers pulling at her, and the coarse material was torn apart and slithered to a puddle at her feet, to be kicked to one side by a heavy boot. Her gaze had switched back to the horizon, but her usual mantra was no use here. Never would she let Maman's memory be sullied by a moment such as this. Held tight by the grip of the portafield, she could not even bring her arms forward to cover herself. Nor could she avoid seeing the smirk of the guard, thoroughly enjoying the sight of her.

Hamon saw it too and shuffled restlessly, angry somehow at what he saw in the soldier's eyes. A nervous finger pulled momentarily at the fabric of the chair. He had so often dreamed of winning revenge for the humiliation of the past and the misery of his years here. Years when duty to Earth had driven him to actions for which he could never forgive himself. Marthe asn Castre was everything he had ever imagined, and to gaze at her as he had dreamed of for so long affected him far more powerfully than he had expected.

He should not have seen her first like this.

Remember her brother. Her twin brother, jeering as Hamon lay sprawled in the roadway outside their house. A Hathian he could wish stood in front of him now. He let the cold mask of his face settle in place again, then adjusted the field strength and ordered her to turn fully about.

She could feel the heat rush over her face as she obeyed, too conscious as she turned of the two pairs of eyes examining every inch of her. Radcliff refused to look her in the face. Gruffly, he stepped forward with a cloak, wrapping it around her naked body. She reached up to pull it close. Then suddenly felt her wrist grabbed. She looked up, to be held by the slate green eyes of the secret service Major.

"This patch, what is it?" He was staring intently at a slightly shiny patch on her inner wrist.

"I spilt some broth there. It's only a dressing to cover the burn."

"Oh?" His hand rubbed over the patch, felt a loose edge and quickly peeled back the soft film. "You heal remarkably well. Not even a scar. His eyes rose questioningly. "What exactly is this, and I want the truth."

"You think yourself such an expert on my people. Find out for yourself."

"I will, never fear."

He stared searchingly at her for some time, and she battened down hard on the dismay she felt at the loss of her communicator. After a short, intent challenge, he shrugged and passed the patch over to the guard. "To the analytical lab immediately, Sergeant. As for you, Madame, you will come with me. It's about time you were restored to something nearer your former self."

He pulled her towards the bedroom, removing the cloak and shoving her into the cleansing unit in one, undeniable motion.

She gasped, stunned into silence by the microjets of tingling hot water, and by the sudden, repeated disrobing. Yet it was glorious to feel the scrubbing spray of the jets. Too many days had passed since she last felt truly clean. In her pleasure at it, she almost succeeded in ignoring the Terran major, standing just outside the unit and watching her, his infernal enjoyment obvious, both at her predicament and at her nakedness.

There had been a moment when she had sensed a softening in him, but it was gone. Now, there was a smirk of thoroughly masculine satisfaction on his face. But she guessed it wasn't the sole reason for his vigil. He did not trust her and would not leave her unguarded. So she chose to deny his presence, turning up her face to the water and luxuriating in the unbraiding of the hated coils, to let her hair be flooded and drenched, the dulling powder scoured completely away. Afterwards, the strands sprang to life, restored to their native vibrancy as the warm gusts of drying air enveloped her.

It was bliss, and for an instant she let him see the woman she was, a barely acknowledged mirage from her past, but with the shutdown of the hot air currents she retreated back behind her mask. She caught a look at his face then, a fleeting shadow of disappointment, then bitter recognition of her knowledge of it. Maybe a touch of defensiveness in his harsh tugging open of the unit door. Whatever she saw, he hid it from her as he handed her a sleeveless shift. Simple in design, she quickly realized it was made to enhance rather than cover.

"This will suffice in these quarters," he said, as if daring her to deny it.

She took the garment and drew it on. The material was soft, of a comfort she had often longed for over the difficult years. Right now, though, she would have preferred the roughness of her own concealing robes.

"You have this stored here for your peasant drabs?"

"And any other woman I may come across in my line of work."

"Spying!"

"If that is what you wish to call it. You are entitled, I suppose, since you're doing the same thing yourself. Isn't that so?"

"No," she exclaimed. "I'm merely a Haut Liege trying to remain inconspicuous."

"Don't take me for a fool. As much as you try to hide what you think, you are not a totally blank screen." She began to protest but was stopped by an exasperated glare. "I don't know yet what you're up to, but I will find out. Who knows, you may even tell me yourself after a night of suitable persuasion."

The words brought a quixotic mood change and a wicked grin. One that some traitorous part of her found far too attractive. He stepped closer, taking her by both elbows and forcing her to look up at his face. She gave in to her urge to retreat but his grip was stronger than the caressing of his thumbs would suggest. He desired her and was making no attempt to conceal it, the challenge clear in the seductive mellowing of his eyes to a warm hazel brown. She was suddenly very afraid. The cold, hard-faced officer she could resist. But this man, she was not so sure.

"Major Radcliff, I am your prisoner, nothing else. I would thank you to let me go."

"I don't want to."

"You forget, you are responsible for me to your colonel. A valuable hostage, he said. If you ever find my people, they're not going to be as willing to negotiate if they find I have been abused."

He gave a short crack of laughter and pulled her even closer. "I wouldn't call what you and I could do for each other abuse."

With his big hands stroking her, she feared he was right. "Your colonel entrusted my safety to you."

"I was ordered to keep you secure, not safe, and the Colonel is well aware of what I intend for you. If you think Earth sent its philosophers and chivalrous officers on this mercenary little jaunt, you are mistaken. I am afraid we are all quite, quite rotten to the core."

She believed him and pulled hastily back, as afraid suddenly of her own needs as she was of him. Logic seemed to desert her, and she made a mad dash for safety. He clearly didn't expect it and the surprise gave her release. She raced through the lounge and to the outer door, so grateful to be free that she forgot all about the field guarding the exit. Slamming the opener with her hand, she made to burst through. She hit the powerful force bars there, throwing her roughly back and leaving small, painful burns on her arms, knees, stomach and breasts.

Gasping, she stumbled back onto the floor. She was dazed but a moment, then came to herself and half turned to her oppressor, standing watching her from the doorway. A maddening smile had spread across his face.

"Satisfied with the security measures we employ? Though I've seen less violent ways of testing them." He strode across and, surprisingly gently, picked her up and carried her to the bedroom. Reaching into a cupboard concealed in the wall, he brought out a pottle of thick, white cream. "Here, this will stop those burns marking that so beautiful skin of yours, though it will still be painful for a few days. I wouldn't advise such heroics too often."

Still dazed, she lay quiet, suddenly uncertain as she watched this unpredictable man spread the cream across her knees and arms. She put her hands out in protest as he pulled her shift higher to anoint the angry burns spreading over her abdomen and up to her breasts.

"Easy there," he gentled. "At present, my intentions are not dishonorable. Or at least, I hope they're not," and he carefully spread the cream over the stinging brands, pausing slightly to caress as well as soothe as he reached her breasts, then found a new shift for her and pulled it gently over her head and down, lifting it over the burnt patches.

She shivered at his touch, but whether from fear or delight, she could not have said. She looked up, a strained question in the look she bent on him. He didn't answer it, but turned away, returning a moment later with a mug of warmly steaming liquid.

"Here, take this."

She hesitated, but then saw something in his quiet waiting that unaccountably made her trust him. She drank, recognizing the taste of the sedative he'd included. She needed sleep after these hours of tension and she doubted he had included anything other than the sedative. All he offered was sleep, said the look in his face. She shouldn't believe him. There was no reason to. But she remembered that fleeting glimpse of vulnerability she had seen in him earlier. She accepted and gave in. Her eyes drooped closed.

Hamon stood watching her, curled up so carelessly on his sleeper, and was aware of a rarely felt moment of contentment. To give her such a respite was strictly against any sensible strategy, but to hell with it. She would have little chance to sleep in the coming days. Then, disgusted with himself, he argued instead that the sleep would leave her unsuspecting and vulnerable to his questioning.

Stars, he was growing soft. Who was this man who stood here wavering? He had a job to do and a world depending on him. He stalked angrily away to set in motion the search for the male who had interrupted him so suspiciously the previous day.

As he stormed down the corridor leading to the native hall, the soldiers warily sprang to attention. "Something's eating the Major today. Better watch out," he heard more than one mutter. Did they think he was deaf?

He rattled off a staccato string of orders as he swept through the Citadel, and within a very short time was pleased to see the resulting chaos and consternation spread throughout the fortress. He had the Hathians rounded up and brought to the hall, where the men were drafted off to one side. The women could only stand by and watch as, one by one, the men were forced to step forward and speak to him. For once Hamon could sense real fear in the air, instead of the usual contrived duplicity.

The afternoon hours passed, and twilight's end approached. Hamon grilled native after native, never quite hearing the voice he remembered. He had nearly conceded that his quarry had escaped, when he was alerted by a sound at the back. A burly guard was dragging forward a struggling pair, a woman and a man. He pushed the woman towards the rest and pulled the man to a halt in front of Radcliff.

"Found him skulking in the women's quarters, sir," the guard said, contemptuously throwing the bundle down at the Hamon's feet.

"Well? What have you to say for yourself? What business had you there and why did you evade the guard? Didn't you hear the order to report?"

A whining voice, faintly familiar, begged forgiveness. "The woman, sir. She wouldn't let me go. I wanted to come, honestly."

"That's the one," said Hamon, gesturing to the guard to pull the man to a stand. Hamon shoved back the concealing hood. For an instant he caught a spark of rebellious anger in the bright blue eyes before the man dropped his head and assumed a pose of abject servility. Hamon whirled, scanning the ranks of natives. There was not a hint of motion, yet he would have sworn the man had responded to an order. *Do not cause trouble.*

He turned back to examine his prisoner. The Hathian was young, only a few years less than himself but of a lighter build; he had a finely boned face, silvery blond hair and those brilliant blue eyes. The combination was decidedly striking, a fact that galled for some reason, and there was a nagging sense of familiarity about him. Hamon shrugged, unsettled and ill at ease, and flicked the hood back over the native's head.

"Take him away, clean him up, run him through central information and lock him up for the night. Then bring him to my quarters, tomorrow at the second hour. Check the old Hathian records too. You never know." He turned to go, then, as if remembering something, turned and grabbed the native's wrist, turning it over to reveal a telltale shiny patch. Seizing it, he ripped it off and handed it to a nearby guard. "Take this to the lab," he ordered, "and search all natives for similar patches. Any found wearing one is to be treated as this one, identified and locked away."

He sensed the growing consternation in the listening natives. Absolute terror would be his preference. They all huddled down into their over robes, arms hastily tucked into sleeves and trying to appear even less visible than usual. He was right on the verge, he knew it. Of what, he didn't know, but after the months of frustration, he was about to learn something.

He didn't stay to see the further results of his orders, too eager to see the effect of his latest discovery on Marthe asn Castre. Excitement rode him as he strode back through the Terran corridors. At long, long last, was the enigma of this planet starting to roll back?

Once in his own quarters, he looked into the bedroom. His captive was still sleeping, her bronze hair waving gently around the strongly drawn face. He stood watching a second, but the need to defeat these Hathians was riding him too hard to allow himself to be lulled by her beauty, and he reached out to roughly shake one small shoulder.

Marthe came to slowly, still in that hazy, just awake state when all still seems bathed in dreams. She gazed up at him, forgetting for a moment the reality of her detention.

She sighed, stretching languorously upwards, and then grimaced with pain as she pulled on the injured skin of her stomach. She was conscious yet of only some of what had passed before her sleep and saw in Hamon merely the kind and gentle man who had carried her here and soothed her pains.

"Ah Major, how long have I slept? It must have been some time for I'm decidedly hungry."

"I can imagine," came the unexpectedly harsh reply, "but, unfortunately for you, Terran supplies only run to those who earn them. However, I'm certain your company at my table would enliven my own dinner. If you would come this way?"

He reached down and, grabbing her arm firmly, and led her to his balcony where a table had been set for one, though two glasses and a water decanter had been added to the extremely appetizing offerings spread there.

"Won't you sit, my dear?"

He politely motioned her to the empty end of the table. She did as ordered and felt her feet gripped by another restraining field. Still strictly polite, he filled her glass before settling himself to his own chair and serving himself with every evidence of great enjoyment.

Marthe was definitely awake now and on full guard. She remembered Jaca's warning words and vowed that she would not again trust the dubious charm of her captor. Yet her stomach growled, and it was only sheer pride that prevented her reaching out and attempting to grasp whatever she could as he tantalizingly swept one plate after another in front of her.

"Your Agnethe is one of the real treasures of this world," said Radcliff, sniffing appreciatively and helping himself to an exquisitely tempting morsel from the selection on the table, before leaning back to savor his wine. "It has been a remarkably full and profitable day, and to relax in the company of one so beautiful seems a rare and fitting end to it. The water is to your taste, I hope?"

She slowly twirled the goblet in her fingers. "Quite, thank you."

"I regret you could not have shared in such a pleasant dinner, but standing orders are clear. The Colonel may overlook most of my activities, but I doubt he would countenance wasting precious supplies on an enemy spy who has shown no sign of cooperating with us. You have not, for example, explained that so called dressing you wore, despite having no injury." He leaned forward, abandoning the smooth urbanity as he awaited her reply. After a few moments of her determined silence, he shrugged. "No matter. I'm sure the friend who rescued you so gallantly that first day will be somewhat more helpful. We have him in custody and I am quite confident he will reveal some small matter before his death tomorrow."

At the careless announcement, Marthe's hard-held composure cracked. "No, you couldn't. He is innocent, believe me. Please, you cannot. Not J—" And she stopped herself just in time.

"Not who?" he snapped.

"No one in particular. You get to know most of the staff in such close quarters."

It was too late, her false nonchalance, and she knew it. What was there about this man that had her acting like the rawest of new recruits? Yet still she must try to appear disinterested. He could not do this to Jaca, not to someone so vibrant and alive. Jaca of so many escapades and narrowly successful tricks, Jaca of her earliest childhood, to be finally brought down by his protection of her. It wasn't fair, she thought, anger welling anew in her at the Terrans and the ease with which they so callously disposed of her people. Yet, the cooler part of her reminded, the death penalty was a rare action; her people were far too valuable as workers.

Radcliff growled angrily as he broke into her thoughts. "Don't take me for an idiot. You are upset, too much so for him to be no one in particular. He also wore a patch like yours and, strangely, in exactly the same place. After tonight, we will have extracted its true purpose. If not from him, then from one of the others caught wearing one. We are rounding them up now and they shall also be executed.

She blanched.

"Unless," he added.

"Unless what?"

"Unless you talk."

She shook her head mutely, wanting desperately to plead that he spare her this.

"You have till the morning to change your mind." Releasing her from the field, he walked her into the bedroom and laid her on the small couch now set up beside the bed. Another field imprisoned her, holding her rigidly still, "I'm afraid you will have rather an uncomfortable night, but then a few sleepless hours of contemplation may do you some good."

He left her then, and she could only lie there, alternately railing against her captor then remembering Jaca's face in fleeting glimpses of past moments. Silently, in every tongue she knew, she slowly and carefully cursed the tall, arrogant man cleansing just meters away. Mathe, what a mess she had made of it! And now, for the sake of the plan, she must allow Jaca to die.

She heard Radcliff returning and shut her eyes, feigning sleep. He leaned over her, apparently unaware of his nakedness, and adjusted a control. She felt her eyelids dragged inexorably open. She stared angrily at him, blushing at his state of undress.

"Am I not allowed the simple privacy of shutting my eyes?"

"No, for it also offers the privacy to plan and plot. This way, I can observe those machinations. Your eyes are very expressive."

"Then have the courtesy to put on a robe."

"Why? Am I ugly in your planet's terms?"

"You know full well you're not. But we value personal modesty more than it seems is customary on Earth."

"It has never bothered the other Hathian…ah, ladies I have entertained. Why should it you? It's not as if you are still the girl barely out of her teens I saw on my first visit here."

What was he talking about?

His hand touched her cheek. "I was at your formal Presentation and a rare pleasure it was, I might add."

"If I had known you were there, I can assure you the feeling would not have been reciprocated," she snapped back. With a final, supreme effort, she managed to half shut her eyes.

It didn't stop her hearing his sudden crack of laughter, or his brazen reply. "I think I'm going to enjoy changing your mind on that one."

He leaned over then, to kiss her as he had longed to do since that day he'd first seen her so many years ago, gently teasing at her stubbornly held lips. If it was not all he hoped, there was yet an instant when he felt the beginning of a response, before she again retreated within her controlled shell. He lifted his head, the mocking grin he deliberately sent her touched with real satisfaction.

"Go to the darks," she spat, trying valiantly to turn away and failing miserably. But he seemed content with his taunting and rose, checking the controls once more before retiring to his own sleeper.

Soon, to her even greater annoyance, she heard the sound of heavy, sleep-ridden breathing. How dare he, and whether it was his peaceful sleep or his kiss that angered her most, she could not say. She lay fuming but, eventually, weariness began to overcome her, her heavy eyelids dragging against the relentless force holding them open. She strained to close them and finally managed to achieve it—but only for a moment. As soon as sleep blessedly came, her eyelids relaxed and were dragged open again. After the fifth time this had happened, wretched tears started, tracing a path of misery. The best she could do was to relax her eyes to an unfocused blur, taking refuge in a trance-like state for the rest of the long, weary night, her thoughts dwelling desolately on the fate of Jaca.

It was a tired and dispirited Marthe who greeted the Terran the next morning. As if oblivious to her state, despite the sharp-eyed glance he sent her, he released her and led her through to the cleansing unit, passing her the cream to apply to her burns. She was at least allowed some privacy for this, and she supposed she ought to be thankful. Afterwards, she was again forced to sit with him as he made a hearty breakfast. He never mentioned Jaca, and she began to hope that her friend would be spared. To that end, she set herself to further distracting him, whiling away the meal in pleasant small talk and questions about Earth.

The Major appeared to miss it and yet be glad to be away from it—an intriguing attitude she suspected was not unusual among the Terrans on Hathe. She encouraged him to talk more about his home world, mindful of why she had been sent here originally. Oddly enough in the circumstance, she almost found herself relaxing as she listened, even smiling at some of his tales, one so outrageous she could do nothing but join him in laughter.

The door opened right then. Hauled roughly in between two guards and haggard after a night in the cells, Jaca caught her mid-laugh. She gasped, and was answered with an accusing glare. Stricken by shame and still glued to the spot by the force field holding her feet, she struggled up and reached out a hand, beseeching him to forget that damning chuckle. He ignored her plea. She wasn't surprised, given what he saw. Her body highlighted by the simple lines of her shift and her ease with the enemy. She couldn't blame him when he turned to gaze insolently forwards.

Beside her, Radcliff had watched their unspoken signals. Deliberately taunting both, he released the force restraining her and put his arm around her waist. Then he pulled her with him as he walked towards his other prisoner, forcing her close to his side. She could only guess what it looked like to Jaca.

"Identification of prisoner, Sergeant."

"Answers to Jaca, sir, but we checked the old Hathian records as you ordered. His full name is Jacquel des Trurain." The guard handed over the file. Radcliff scanned it then looked up, raising a querying eyebrow at Marthe.

"Another abandoned Lieger? Your step-cousin, it seems, my dear." She was unable to answer him, her throat too full. Suddenly, with a strength the Terran did not expect, she flung herself away from him and into the shoulder of her childhood friend.

"Jaca, forgive me. I can save you if I answer their questions, but I can't," she pleaded in their own tongue.

At first there was no lessening, no giving way in her oldest friend. Then he looked down into her face. What he saw, she couldn't say, but there was a tightening of his mouth and he met her eyes for the first time. "Hush, Mimi. It's all right, I understand. The Terran has been playing his games with you?" She nodded. "Don't worry, he's probably bluffing. The depths of Hathe keep you safe," he managed to add before they were pulled roughly apart.

The Major dragged Marthe towards him, pinioning her arms behind her as he harshly ordered that Jacquel be taken out.

"Very touching, Madame, but I do not bluff. Whatever your *friend* may say." He spoke in Harmish—just to show her his fluency, she didn't doubt. "And don't count on des Trurain's value as a prisoner. I am fully aware that he is potentially as useful as you, but I need information now. If one of you must be killed to make the other talk, then so be it. Sadly for des Trurain, he doesn't possess the advantage of your sex, and so will be the sacrifice. I need the information you hold and I will do anything to get it."

"You're mistaken. I know nothing of use to you."

"I don't think so. In half an hour, unless you start talking, des Trurain dies. You see the red light there?" She nodded. "When that goes out, so does he."

Marthe stared, transfixed. She did not move, not a muscle, not an eye, for the entire half hour allowed, staring intently at the light and willing it to stay red.

"Five seconds to go. Well?"

Slowly, as if in pain, she shook her head. The light went dead. It was over. She slumped to her feet, silent tears cascading down her cheeks.

A long while later, she looked up.

"I grew up with Jaca," she said as if in a dream. "I dare say that one day we would have married. Now I've killed him."

CHAPTER FIVE

Hamon said nothing, turning abruptly and walking from the room. It was many hours before he could bring himself to return. He knew he should have pressed the attack while she was vulnerable; every single thing he had ever learnt told him he must. He refused to listen. There was nothing under the stars that could have made him keep questioning her then, not with that sheer human misery in her eyes. Nor could he forget her words as the light signaled the death of Jacquel des Trurain.

"We would have married…"

Haunted by her face, he spent the day searching through the files for every piece of information he could find on the Hathian man. Maybe in knowledge of his enemy, he could find a justification for his actions. *Or relief from your guilt*, jibed the silent thought.

He was not to be so lucky. Despite his hopes, it was an intriguing picture that emerged. On the one hand, des Trurain seemed to be nothing more than an irresponsible sprig of his world's political elite, ready at any time to join in with the more daring of the juvenile pranks of his friends—among whom, he noted in particular, Bendin asn Castre and his twin sister, Marthe. So, she had been honest there. Even through the spare lines of the news reports, he caught an image of a close threesome. If one was mentioned, so were the other two. A triplet of bright young things, eager for whatever adventures their world could offer.

But that was too simplistic a picture of Marthe, and it seemed the same was true of des Trurain. The man had been active in student politics and was also a highly regarded scholar of history—his particular area of interest the early development of the modern Alliance, that loose confederation of the planets that had been settled long ago by people from Earth.

Hamon cringed as he read des Trurain's work, with its caustic analysis of the warmongering prevalent in pre-Alliance societies. He couldn't fail to recognize how the current actions of his own people repeated the time-worn cycle of greed and conquest.

It was a relentless and unforgiving academic self-flagellation, but he forced himself to persevere. He must understand des Trurain. Perhaps in understanding Marthe's friend—he refused to grant the man any closer name— he would find an explanation for his own turmoil. How had he come to be in sole and vicious charge of one proud and learned woman who deserved to be loved, not tormented, no matter the truth? He knew all the clichéd reasons, but his own, more personal ones … were they good enough?

Grimly, he brought up screen after screen of damning records. Was he seeking justification for his present actions or escape from the burden of his Terran birthright—a heritage that seemed to promise only pain and dishonor whichever path he chose? Whatever Marthe asn Castre might be to him, she was also the key to this planet. She alone could deliver the secret to securing the quantities of urgonium Earth needed so desperately. He had to continue his plan, must believe that success would soon be in his grasp … if he could but live with himself for long enough.

He returned to his apartment, heavy-hearted and angry. He'd undertaken a project in good faith, and whose fault was it but his own that he'd not foreseen the consequences? He passed through the doorway with a quick check of the security lock then looked through the lounge towards the balcony.

There was no sign of his prisoner.

He checked all the rooms, hurrying into the bedroom to see if she'd managed to bypass the controlling fields cloaking the apartment and fall asleep. No sign of her. Panic goading him, he activated his screen, ordering a heat sensor scan of every room.

There, in the service cupboard.

So, her grief was not too deep to stop her trying to escape. He moved swiftly, warily alert, slamming the door opener and erupting into the cupboard. Then came to an abrupt halt. Marthe was there, still sleep deprived but not trying to flee. Her elegant shift covered by an old tunic of his, she was occupied in nothing so extraordinary as that. Instead, she was mundanely emptying the contents of the rubbish bin into a recycling chute.

"What are you up to?"

"Cleaning the apartment, of course. Since you see fit to imprison me here, you've had to forgo the usual cleaning maid. And while you may fancy living in filth, I do not."

"My apologies. I didn't realize a Lieger would notice such things."

She ignored his deliberate use of the insulting Lieger, instead of the more proper Haut Liege. But he knew she had heard it.

"It is years since I had servants to attend to such matters. I learned very quickly after you Terrans arrived that if I wanted my surroundings to remain in an acceptable state, I would have to do it myself."

"Then you have my permission to continue, and my thanks, but I should point out that it won't get you back on the rations list. Though the stars know you look as though you need it."

She looked ready to claw his eyes out at the reminder of what must by now be serious hunger. She had free access to water, but that alone wouldn't stave off what must be a painfully empty stomach. Yet she refused to give him the satisfaction of a reply, glaring her resentment as she brushed past him to continue with her work. A pity. A fight was just what he needed. Anything to bury his guilt. He caught her by the wrists and held up her hands, scarred by fresh burn marks on her palms.

"So, you had come in here to check whether my security fields covered this entrance. Even on such short acquaintance, you should know me better. You'll be sore all over soon. How are your other burns?"

He reached out to feel her stomach but stopped when he saw her flinch. Ignoring her curt comment that she was rather better qualified than he in medical matters, he drew off the tunic and lifted the shift to inspect her skin. A pink flush only remained of the angry burn marks. "Good. I would hate to mar such a beautiful body."

Suddenly, unable to stop himself, he pulled her into his arms and for one crazy instant gave release to this misplaced passion of his, this mad aberration that he knew not whether to curse or welcome.

And for one moment only, his kiss caught her unawares and he felt her response. There was warmth and a haven here and, buried deep within him, a long-neglected core of need flared up and demanded satisfaction. He could swear it was echoed in the pressure of her lips on his, her body clinging for one joyous moment to his.

For one moment only. The defensive shell she hid behind was too strong, forged in fires he could only guess at. He felt her fight to restore her self-control and saw the struggle on her face as she sought to hide her desire for him, before pulling angrily away.

Hamon watched as she jerked the shift to rights again, attempting to cover the telltale signs of her response. Disappointment wavered with amusement inside him at her abrupt change of attitude, and a sad wish rose in him: If only they had met under other circumstances. As it was, he feared sleeplessness and hunger would overcome her before he could achieve any of his goals, personal or professional. It was not something he dared consider, and he too sought safety in retreat. Hamon was too vulnerable here. Only the Major was safe.

He let a practiced grin lift the planes of his face. "It seems, Madame, that this forced intimacy may be more enjoyable than either of us had expected."

"Enforced by you, Major; and you can spare me further exhibitions of your much-vaunted talent for seduction." Another angry tug at her shift. "You may think to flatter your ego by adding a true Hathian Lady to the list of unfortunate women who have been lured into your keeping, hoping to find a man behind the tricks. But I am awake to you and owe too much to the memory of what your race has done to mine. Leave me be!"

"But you would be quite one of the most desirable I have kept," he teased. "And who, may I ask, taught you to think of me in such unflattering terms? Your friend, des Trurain?"

"He always was a good judge of character."

"Then it's a blessing he is no more. You seem to have had far too good an opinion of the man." He put his hands on her hips to tug her close, his touch gentle despite his intentions. He managed to at least school his face into grim resolve. "I spent a considerable part of the day searching the records for his details. If you ask me, the universe is well rid of him. Which reminds me, Madame: fifty others detained wore those unusual patches. They must also be disposed of. One a day, until you start to talk, if you remember."

She pulled back, the blush on her face and deliciously peaked breasts giving the lie to her defiant glare. "You, sir, must be the most callous man it has ever been my misfortune to encounter. To kill innocent people because they use a common wound dressing is ridiculous. And all to extract non-existent information from one very much abandoned Haut Liege, not much better than a peasant herself. What a waste!"

"You're lying, just as you lie when you claim to be indifferent to me. Perhaps you hope I'm bluffing. Do not. All those so innocent people will die. One by one, a day at a time, for as long as you maintain this stubborn silence." He stared at her, trying by sheer will power to break through her shell. It didn't work. He lifted his hands from her hips in disgust and escorted her over to the table.

Marthe had no choice but to sit in the proffered chair. He was just too strong for her. Or rather, for the pampered Haut Liege Lady she must appear to be. Once again, she was forced to watch as he slowly worked his way through a tempting array of gourmet delights. Always the dishes were just out of reach, but close enough to set off her digestive juices. And, again, her night afforded little rest. At irregular periods she was jerked awake by the hated force field. Some time during those long, dark stretches of loneliness, a dismal hopelessness crashed down on her. She couldn't withstand such treatment forever. One day, soon, she would talk, and there was nothing she could do to stop it.

Next morning, she once more watched the inhuman red light, waiting for the off signal. Who was the unknown man she condemned? Did he have a family, waiting somewhere for his long spell of duty to end? Or did anyone really die? Truth to tell, she wasn't convinced. The extinguishing of a light seemed so far removed from the reality of a life gone.

As it was, she missed the crucial moment. Her eyes closed, and she sank into blessed sleep. The harsh voice of her captor jerked her back.

"That is two you now have on your conscience, and forty-nine still alive. How much longer can such indifference last?"

She didn't bother to turn her head in answer.

He waited until he saw it was useless. Her will was too strong still. He stood up. "I have to leave you for now, but I strongly urge you to reconsider. And don't think that means I'll let you sleep. After two days awake, the field cloaking this apartment is probably no longer strong enough to stop you falling off, but this headband will keep you alert." He strapped a metal band around her forehead, the purpose of which was only too soon revealed when she nodded off. A sharp pain jabbed her head, yanking her painfully awake. Desperately, she stayed silent, fighting back the tears she must hold in. *Remember what is at stake. Remember the lives you hold safe. Don't give in.*

Hamon watched her, but there was no breach in the wall of her resistance. Give in, please give in, he pleaded wordlessly. She only stared back at him, defiance still strong in every tautly held muscle of her beautiful body. He kept his own face rigid. She must break soon.

He left then. He had work to do, a duty to fulfill. The lives of millions of his people depended on him. He marched into the lab, hoping against hope that something had been made of the strange patches. Marthe asn Castre had stamina, but she was no Amazon. Without results, how long before Johne ordered him to pass her over to his own, delightful soldiery and their barbaric methods?

No, never that.

And you are so civilized? jeered an inner voice.

Sanity demanded he ignore the taunt. Perhaps the lab could give him the breakthrough he needed. Something had to, soon. He passed through to the room housing the technical staff, only to be greeted with a disappointing negative from the chief communications technician, Ferdo Braddock.

"Sorry, Hamon, this stuff has us beat. We don't even know the substance it's made of but can only postulate it to be synthetic. Nor can we open it up. It's resistant to everything we've tried."

"What about signal activity?"

"Not that we can detect. We've been through the whole range of known particle and energy types and can find no trace of a transmission. Either it's as harmless as the girl says or, more likely, it's something beyond our technology. This planet was rather advanced at one time, believe it or not."

"I know. I was here then." Hamon's fist crashed onto the bench, setting the monitors jumping and Ferdo staring.

"Hold on there. I mean, you wouldn't think so to look at them now."

"Sorry," said Hamon. "Things are piling up at the moment. They must be getting to me. Are we off record?"

"Just a minute." Ferdo sealed the doors, checking the screen as he did so. "Now, what's up. You look like you've been asked to execute your own mother."

"I feel like that," admitted Hamon ruefully, throwing himself into a disgruntled heap on a nearby seat and staring at his feet for a long moment before lifting his head to meet his friend's troubled gaze. "Do you never wonder why we're here?" he asked. "Before we came, this place was one of the most advanced Alliance planets, and now look at what's left of its people—a backward, peasant race—all so we can get unlimited quantities of one mineral, and that we can't even do without the technology this peasant planet once owned, four short years ago."

He looked down, seeing the staccato of restless tapping his fingers insisted on beating out, and clamped down hard to stop it.

"Where is that technology now?" Hamon demanded, glaring at his friend. "Vanished, in one stupid month. Stars! That simple first battle against the Hathians cost us this war. A trivial holding action, we thought. They didn't have the ships to take on even one of our starcruisers, let alone a whole fleet, but guess what? They did manage to stop us long enough to let their elite escape—the ones who had the knowledge we needed—and that won them the war." He thrust up, then threw himself back down again. "Well I say good on them. What right have we here anyway? We're barbaric!"

Hamon saw Ferdo's eyes rest on his drumming fingers. "Your problem," his friend said, "is that you think too much. You know as well as I what will happen if we don't get the quantities of urgonium we need, and damn soon at that. Have you seen the latest reports from Earth? Food production is down so badly that we soon won't have a people to go home to. In fact, I guess you *would* be killing your own mother if you don't become a barbarian, as you so nicely put it."

"What a logician you are."

Ferdo chuckled. "It helps in this place. You should try it."

Hamon smiled wryly. Then stopped. "You're not in my position," he said. "We've captured a Lieger. The daughter of one of their Councilors, no less. I have the honor," his teeth gritted on the last word, "to be her interrogator."

The technician whistled in appreciation. "A Lieger. By all the stars above! Why the glum face? According to report, they were a remarkably cruel bunch."

"This particular one has brown eyes you could lose yourself in forever, hair just asking to be touched and the most beautiful face you are likely to see on a woman anywhere. Worse still, she's as brave, staunch and fine as could be, damn her."

The technical officer stared, an amused grin lighting up his features as understanding came to him. "So, the impregnable Major has finally been caught in one of his own webs."

"Caught?" Hamon grunted. "I've been half in love with the woman since I first saw her more than five years ago, on the night of her Presentation—the Hathian coming of age ceremony," he added by way of explanation. "They had to give a speech, she and her twin brother, and you should have heard her. So bright and full of the future."

"She must've been surprised to meet you again in such changed circumstances."

Hamon shook his head. "She didn't know me. I never got a chance to meet her that first time. I couldn't get near her, thanks to that brother of hers. One night, he actually had me thrown out. Would you believe it? I was there on official business, the son of Earth's representative to the Alliance—but it was as little use to me then as it has ever been," he finished with a grimace.

"What's the problem then? The brother isn't around now. You have her all to yourself."

"She just might be the key to the whole mystery of this planet. So she must be questioned, by me at least rather than that band of thugs Johne employs. But I must still deny her sleep and food, and think up every ruse imaginable to make her talk, before it's too late and Johne forces me to hand her over anyway." Hamon looked down, watching his fingers pluck at his trousers. His face felt like a smudge of cold clay and his voice dropped to a whisper, barely able to admit his thoughts. "It's not pleasant to watch a woman fade, day by day. Oh, at first I was angry enough to think revenge would be sweet. But it's not. Stars, it's not. What in hell am I going to do?"

He slumped forward, burying his face in his fingers. Ferdo sat silent. There was nothing he could say that would help, and both of them knew it. They had been on Hathe long enough to know that the only choice on offer here was the degree of cruelty Hamon must employ.

It was Ferdo who broke the silence. "You want me to say it? You have to give her a session. Or let her escape, thereby signing your family's death warrant, along with every other Terran's."

Hamon's mouth opened in denial, but Ferdo jumped in before he could speak.

"If you don't give her one, Johne's gang will, or worse, and she may die at the end of it. Even if she lives, she would probably rather be dead. Their little refinements aren't too nice. I watched them in action once on some rebels on Earth." A harsh light entered his eyes as memory yanked him painfully back. Then Hamon saw him realize what he'd said. "Don't worry about her," Ferdo promised gently. "I'll take personal control, and I guarantee it will only be an illusion. But keep trying your methods for another day or two, if you like. Who knows, you may break her."

"Have you ever had a session? I did once, in my not so illustrious youth, and it's the most damnable experience." A shudder rippled through Hamon at the memory of it, even now, after so many years. "To have to subject another person to it, especially one for whom I have a fondness…"

Ferdo snorted in derision but refrained from further questioning. Just as well. He had told Ferdo more in these last minutes than he'd told anyone before. His private life was usually that—strictly private. It saved a great deal of trouble. For now, he was grateful that Ferdo was considerate enough to change the subject, asking instead why Hamon had been on Hathe before the takeover. He was certainly the only Terran among the occupying troops to have done so.

"I just happened to end up here once. I liked the place and stayed on for a couple of months. Father took advantage of my presence and arranged for me to be seconded to the team negotiating to buy more urgonium. Mostly to keep him informed fully on what was happening, I suspect, but at least it gave me entrée to the houses of the ruling classes, even if only as a type of poor cousin. As far as our delegates were concerned, I was a very junior member of the negotiating team and expected to act accordingly."

"Did you get any more?"

"Urgonium? No." He felt his mouth tighten at the memory. "They just stared and showed us the door. A more patronizing pack I've not met before or since. Yet … their civilization was amazing. I guess we were rather like the country cousins. They had so much: pure, clean air, beautiful homes, an abundance of food, and the time and leisure to indulge in an orgy of the arts. As for the discussions. They talked and argued constantly, with a gift of freedom you never find on Earth. *How* they talked!" He smiled at the memory then it was wiped abruptly away. "I never saw this part of the planet, though. Would never have guessed that such a bleak wilderness existed. Maybe they did only let us see their best. Maybe the peasants are right and their society was as they claim. Only it's strange that I saw no sign of it at the time."

"What about the girl? You never got to meet her."

"No. Not for want of trying, but she was always in the middle of a large group of friends, and I couldn't get near her. Her brother's attitude didn't help either." He saw Ferdo's attempt to hide his curiosity and relented. "I had beaten him to a certain, delightful lady in a local shop, and he took strong exception to what he called my poaching."

Ferdo hooted with laughter. "Trust you, Hamon. There's always one somewhere."

Hamon rightly ignored this. "It was before I saw Marthe. If I had known… But that's pointless. Anyway, he made sure I couldn't get near his sister." He grimaced, then remembered images chased it away. "You should have heard her speak," he said. "She loved a good argument, and usually came out the winner. That family was one in which intelligence was definitely inherited. Her elder sister was already looking to take up her father's work. You may have heard of him; he worked in your own field: Dr Sylvan an Castre?"

Ferdo sat up suddenly. "An Castre! I'll say I have. Even on Earth, we heard rumors of his studies. You don't mean to tell me this girl is his daughter? What a catch!"

"That is exactly what I'm telling you," snapped Hamon sourly. "And if you don't mind, she's not a hunting trophy."

"Oh, yes, she is. And if I remember rightly, that twin brother you tangled with was involved in energy research. We never learnt more than the barest outline of the work of his group. For some stupid reason, no one thought it relevant to Earth at the time, but I bet it was, and that sister would know all about it. Hamon, you have to break her. Now isn't the time for you to turn romantic over a pretty face. You have a duty to your own people first."

They were the worst words possible, echoing as they did his own inner turmoil. "I am fully aware of my duty," he snarled, rising to leave, "and am not about to forget it."

"Did I say any such thing?"

Hamon stopped, his back stiff. Then slowly, his shoulders came down and he turned back. "My apologies."

"Accepted," said Ferdo quickly. "Bring the girl down tomorrow. Even if she can last longer, your temper won't."

Hamon grunted, forced to concede the truth of the words and the good will that prompted them. Ferdo's next words were less palatable.

"If it doesn't work, we can give her a repeat session the next day. Though the threat alone should make her talk. Sorry, but I can't think of a kinder way, and with us she'll still be alive at the end of it."

What could he say to that? Hamon left, feeling little better than when he had entered. At least he'd given his friend something to think about. As well as affording him a great deal of amusement, he thought sourly. It didn't feel amusing to Hamon. Neither Earth's plight nor his own.

The day had been no less difficult for Marthe. She soon learnt that trying to ignore the shocks from the headband didn't work. All it did was make her headache worse and she still got no sleep. What she needed was something to take her mind off it. Cleaning the apartment yesterday had helped distract her, so she decided to try that again. There was nothing else for her to do since she'd already searched the place thoroughly, without finding anything of interest. If she was going to be immured here for some time, she may as well arrange things to please herself. Hopefully it would also thoroughly annoy that cursed Terran Major.

She started in the bedroom, straightening the sleeper and restoring the clothes to cleaning and storage. Finished, she stood back, nodding briskly with satisfaction. As she turned to walk into the other room, she looked up and was caught again by the painting of her home, so inexplicably set on the wall of this Terran apartment. A wave of homesickness hit her, remembering the happier days of her youth. There was the east tower where she and Bendin had made their secret headquarters. In reality a dusty old storeroom, all but forgotten by the rest of the family, but to the twins it was a magic kingdom. In it, they had planned such campaigns as the Expedition to the Deepest, Darkest Depths of the Albanok, commonly known to lesser mortals as the kitchen. There, they planned to find and bring back the famed

Elixir of Life cleverly disguised as a jar of sweets the cook dished out to any child who had helped her.

She chuckled. That particular expedition had been a disastrous failure. Cook had caught them with their hands in the jar, as guilty as sin, the pair of them, and they had been allowed only boringly healthy food for the whole of the following week.

No, don't think of food. Her stomach was already churning at the memory, and Bendin was dead now, killed with too many others of her childhood. He had signed up for the fleet straight after graduation. Anything to get into space, he'd told her, and it was meant to be only a secondary part of his life. The Hathian fleet was never more than a part-time force, staffed by volunteers, and his research work came first; but with less than six months' experience as a pilot, he was called up to help man Hathe's outer defenses, one of the brave few who must hurl their small spacecraft against the massive ships of the Terran invaders. Hathe's forces hung on against truly awful odds, fighting desperately at the edges of their solar system to give their world what it needed so badly. Time.

Time was something she was running out of. Somehow, she must escape or get a message out.

She had tried yesterday to alert a passing native through the service door. It was no use. He couldn't see her, though she could see and hear him as clearly as if she were walking beside him. Frustrated, she had screamed and yelled, beating her hands against the force field and ending only with the burns the Major had noticed. Damn him, she cursed. He thwarted her at every turn and she had nothing to fight him with. What did she even know of the man?

Nothing. Absolutely nothing. His apartment must have been carefully screened by the Terrans in the short time before she was brought here, for it told little of the personal side of its owner, and she had still been awaiting a report from Central when she was caught.

Even Jaca, who was so violently opposed to him, knew only rumors. Yet the man seemed to know a great deal about her.

What a fool she was. She had been sent here to gather information on officers such as him. Yet here she was, perfectly placed to do just that, and she was acting like a witless child trapped in a mythical nightmare. That was going to change, she vowed. It was time to get to work.

First, Jacquel. He was *not* dead. The Terran must be bluffing, or so she would believe until she saw a corpse. Not that she would ask to. For all she knew of him, he might just kill the captives to supply the proof of his words, and she had seen more than enough dead bodies.

She ignored her moment of weakness, the memory of that kiss, when something had flared between the Terran and her. What had Jaca said? The man used charm as a weapon. That's all it was—an experienced, charming rogue using his skills against her. Nothing more. She would be much better concentrating on how to make the best use of her situation. She needed to plan a campaign, not moon over an infantile crush.

Second the red light was a ruse. She must not believe otherwise. Next: find out about Major Radcliff—but not in the way he intended, she amended angrily. That he was so very attractive was but a nuisance, and one that must be ignored, she told herself sternly, disregarding the amused voice inside that asked did she seriously think she could do that so easily.

Yes, she declared back. He'd made it decidedly clear that he would enjoy taking her to his bed and giving that kind of pleasure to an accursed Terran was not among her plans.

She lay resting that afternoon, with a wicked grin cheering her thoughts of the coming evening. She had discovered a way of enduring her lack of sleep, by passing the time in an open-eyed doze. When that failed, she lay still, making and discarding plans. As it turned out, she had plenty of time to prepare. Radcliff was late in returning.

CHAPTER SIX

After leaving Ferdo, Hamon fled the Citadel and escaped to the solitary vastness of the plains. A timeless emptiness where the grasses, shrubs, and native creatures were intent only on their relentless and unforgiving battle for survival. Here alone he had the space he needed—space to think, to find a way out of his dilemma, to remember Earth as he had last seen it: overcrowded and short of all but the most basic of foods, and those only in quantities sufficient for those still on the list of citizens entitled to full rations. So many essential services disconnected to conserve what little urgonium the Terrans managed to extract from Hathe, the preservation of life being the only priority. Not even his own home was exempt, despite his personal wealth and the power of his family. Neither could buy what Earth no longer had.

He remembered, too, his once beautiful mother, charged with control of the scarce resources left to Earth. He had been shocked at the change in her, haggard and worn down by the constant need to order ever harsher restrictions and sick with worrying over how much longer Earth could survive. They had gambled everything on their attack and conquest of Hathe. Now, there was nowhere else for Earth's teeming millions to go. The other Alliance planets were too wary, too well armed and had made it brutally clear they would refuse entry to any Terran migrants. Their only option was Hathe, and without its vanished technology, it could support no more than a small fraction of those needing refuge.

He could prevent the impending catastrophe. All that stood against him was one small woman, as unattainable as she was desirable. How could he consider putting in jeopardy the survival of an entire planet, just for her? It was unthinkable!

Then he returned home and was met by her welcoming smile and her luscious curves. All his memories of Earth couldn't stop his response to the sight of her. He had to fight far too hard for his liking to kill his threatening smile and replace it with a frown of suspicion.

She misread it for weariness. Deliberately so, he had no doubt.

"Major, I thought you would never be back. Come, a cleansing and change from that uncomfortable uniform and you'll feel much better." Gently but firmly, she took his arm and led him through to the dressing room. She reached out to take his jacket, but that was too much. He stepped back in refusal. "What? Modesty? How unexpected. Never mind, I'll fetch you a drink instead and leave you to change in peace. Your robe is laid out on the sleeper." She gave him another innocently sweet smile and left him to bathe in private.

What's she up to? Hamon stared after Marthe as he slowly removed his uniform and stepped into the cleanser, to relax in the clouds of the fine jet spray tingling against his skin. Then had a sudden thought.

"No!" He burst into the room, ignoring the water dripping on the floor. But there was his uniform, exactly as he had left it. So she was not aiming to search that. To make sure, he sealed it in storage, along with a couple of telltale scraps in the pockets, before returning to the cleanser. Yet he could not banish his suspicions, and it was not long before he turned in irritation to the drying air currents and emerged. He flung on the long, dark green robe she'd left for him and stalked into the lounge. No one could be so cheerful after two days and nights of no food and no sleep. Could they?

But she was, coming forward with that damned welcoming smile on her face and beckoning him to a seat near her own.

"How was your day? Nothing too troublesome, I hope?"

"No, fine." He stretched out his legs, surveying her uneasily beneath lowered lids.

The woman wasn't to be put off so easily. "Mine was rather enjoyable—almost fun, in fact. This apartment was pleasant enough, but I think you might find my changes an improvement."

He looked round in surprise and, yes, he had to concede the success of her day's work. Not that he was about to capitulate fully. "Why did you move the melkin plant?"

"It wasn't getting enough light. They need bright sunlight to flower."

"So that's why it never did before." Unconsciously, his guard eased a fraction. "I put it down to the effects of irradiation. I found it near your house, you see."

"Maybe but see how it goes in the light." She was determined to ignore any provocation, it seemed. "As for the rest, they should be happy enough where they are, though I have to say they seem a much richer green than is normally the case for Hathian plants. What's your secret?"

"Loving care and attention ... and a room air mixture with a higher CO_2 content than is normal for Hathe. You may have noticed a slight odor when you were first brought in?"

A lift of her brow. "It wasn't the room I was noticing then. You have quite a reputation to live down to."

"And don't I?"

She laughed gently. His callousness of the past days appeared to have had little effect on her. Surprisingly, it didn't at this moment bother him. In fact, he was rapidly forgetting all his hard-won resolutions. Not that he went so far as to offer her dinner, but then she didn't ask for any, too busy discovering what she could of him. He would allow it for now. It was harmless enough, and he was curious about her reasons. Gradually, she drew him out to talk of himself and his family and, despite his innate caution, he found himself telling her who his parents were.

She tried to hide it, but he was starting to know her well enough to see the shock in her face.

"You may well be surprised. What is the son of Administrator Freya MacDiarmid and Ambassador Garth Radcliff doing as part of this miserable outfit? Well, for starters, I was one of the few Terrans who chose to or had the means to travel. I happened to be here at the start of the expedition and was the nearest thing available to an expert on Hathe, so the military asked me to come on board. My mother wasn't happy about it but knows me too well to argue. As for my father, it's years since we've been on speaking terms. I doubt he was too bothered over any possible danger to his misbegotten offspring." He grimaced. "My parents' marriage was politically advantageous to both but not convivial, I gather."

"I am sorry. How sad, to be estranged from your own father."

"Don't be. It's merely one of life's incompatibilities. We're too alike. But you should understand. Didn't you say you were at odds with your own father?" he countered, unable to resist catching her out.

"Only latterly," was her quick reply. She cast her eyes down as if in great sorrow. "We were very close once, especially after Mother's death when Bendin and I were twelve, and now Bendin's gone too." He saw the sadness in her eyes when she spoke of her brother, but it wasn't enough to stop the flash of gratification he felt. Nor did he bother to hide it, needing to see her reaction. Her retort was instant.

"He died trying to defend us from a certain pack of primitive savages, who yet managed to win, defying any belief in the existence of natural justice in the universe!"

Hamon immediately wiped his face clear. Not such a good move. The surprising rapport that had sprung up between them was far too fragile to be threatened by his bad memories.

Marthe, too, had regretted her rash words as soon as spoken, remembering her own goals of this night, and listened without comment to his apology.

"Sorry, I didn't mean to gloat. I had a humiliating encounter with your brother once. It still rankles."

"You met Bendin? But how? When?"

"It was during my visit here, just before the takeover." He told her of the delegations' mission. "Your Council just laughed," he added bitterly.

"More urgonium? But why?" she said, swiftly hiding her stunned amazement at his words. Earth had been their largest buyer, taking far in excess of its needs surely?

"To survive, of course. How else were we to keep the food processors operating, let alone the de-polluters, transporters, heat exchangers and all the other paraphernalia a very, very crowded planet needs to survive?"

"Is Earth very crowded?" She knew exactly Earth's population but needed time to recover.

"Very. I do not think even your peasants could have any comprehension of what a hell that once-so-glorious planet has become. It's why, Mathe help me, we had to indulge in this sordid occupation." His shoulders hunched. "And then we get here and find we can't get the damned stuff out in any but the most minimal quantities. All your technology had fled. Stars, what a joke. What a razzing, cursed joke!" He sat back, eyeing her bitterly, the one person who could solve his problems.

She couldn't meet that look, turning away to hide her amazement. Granted the recovery rate of urgonium was not as high as in the past, but the Terrans were still extracting enough to supply the entire Alliance! She carefully began to question him about life on Earth and found it harder and harder to believe what she heard. They had always known the Terrans were backward in energy technology, but if what he was saying was correct, Earth was at least a generation behind the rest of the Alliance, relying on one source, urgonium, for absolutely everything. And that in a grossly inefficient manner. Surely they had heard of modern developments! Not even Earth's pompous self-absorption could have led to such isolation, could it?

What a mess. All that her home had suffered these four years past, simply because Terrans were too ignorant to look after themselves properly.

Anger churned in her, igniting a deep resolution. She would fight this man with all the guile at her command, and right now she felt little of the fascination he had earlier evoked in her. She was as angry as she had ever been in her life, almost as much as the day she had seen her brother's body returned, bloodied and mutilated.

She must not let her anger take over. Not yet, despite the gut wrenching scream lodged in her throat, making talk impossible. Anger was too dangerous now. Time enough to let him feel the full depth of her fury when Hathians again owned Hathe. Struggling for control, she leaned back into the comfort of the chair fighting for breath. A fake smile, and air returned to her lungs; but she twisted the talk away to safer channels, frightened of what she might reveal.

Hamon went along with the change but was not fooled. He'd seen the shock of his words in the subtle tension of her face. She was very interested in what he had told of Earth. Why? He fell to studying her, trying to fathom what lay behind those shaded features. Not only had she been trying to milk him all evening, but she was also hiding something. He supposed knowing that eased his conscience, if nothing else; but the lady had better start talking soon.

She shifted uneasily under his stare and spoke quickly, filling the deadly silence that had fallen between them. "You said you had a run-in with Bendin once. What happened?"

His mouth twitched. It was so obvious that she was trying to distract him. He answered her anyway, repeating the story he'd told Ferdo. "We both fancied the same lady and he took exception to my greater success."

"Fancied? Bendin never merely *fancied* a woman. He had a disastrous habit of imagining himself involved in the romance of the century every time he met a new ladylove. There were ten such, if I remember rightly. I can just imagine how furious he would have been at your stealing his latest from under his eyes. But surely that's not why you dislike him? Not over such a trivial matter."

"Your brother didn't think it trivial. I was at a reception at your house not long after, and he had me thrown out. An accredited envoy, visiting the planet on official business, and he treated me like gutter trash. All because I was gazing over a balcony rail at you and your sister. You were quite a woman in your younger days."

"Thank you, I think. The last four years have been rather trying."

"Have they? I wonder. And I don't want to hear that hackneyed tale of yours again."

The abrupt attack deliberately slashed at her defenses. He watched her desperately scrabble for purchase in their deadly duel of wits as he compelled her to meet his eyes. This time he was the better at hiding how much he longed to forget duty for just one night and ask her about something entirely different. "Two Haut Liege turning up in the one place is too much of a coincidence for anyone. Especially two such good friends."

She jumped up, a dark red flush of anger in her cheeks. "You should have asked him before you had him put down," she retorted, rising and whirling round away from him, as if desperate to escape.

It was a mistake. Color deserted her face, a stark white as the blood left it and her eyes glazed over. She clutched at a nearby table, fighting back against the threatening faintness. The table crashed under her and she crumpled to the floor.

She came to, cradled in his arms as he forced liquid into her unyielding mouth. A look of confusion on her face, she pushed out at him, fighting off his help.

"Stop that. It's only water and glucose. Drink it down before you faint again."

Weakly, she did as she was told, then struggled to sit up. Another wave of dizziness hit as soon as she raised her head. Drops beaded on her forehead as her body flushed then paled, and her hand pushing at him was terrifyingly weak.

Hamon looked at the woman in his arms and knew defeat. Her face was stripped of life, the etched darkness beneath her eyes a mockery to his precious duty. Cursing softly, he picked her up and carried her gently into the bedroom to lay her on his sleeper.

"Lie there, don't move, and be sensible for a change. After this long without food or sleep, you should be conserving your energy, not trying to pick my brains."

There was no answer from Marthe. Exhausted and drained, she looked ready to dissolve into tears and barely seemed to notice as he lifted his hand to remove the band from her head to let her fall into desperately needed sleep.

It was a long time before Hamon found any rest. He stayed all night by her side. She was as tough as the land she took her strength from, but surely even she would not hold to her silence past the point of survival. Would she? Even the cruelty of a session was preferable to that!

In the earliest hours of sunrise, Marthe was crudely woken. The Terran had thrown the frigid splosh of a wet cloth on her face. Spluttering and with a head that felt as if half the city had been dumped on it, she struggled to rise, staring bleary-eyed at her tormentor. Gone was the gentle man who had held her last night.

"Go away, I've only just fallen asleep," she wailed miserably.

"Six hours ago, to be exact. Plenty of time for anyone. Right now, there are questions that need answering. You've stalled long enough, and I warn you, if you refuse to tell me what I want, I am prepared to use less civilized methods. You will talk then, believe me."

She was dragged from the comfort of the sleeper and forced out to the lounge. As if caught in the middle of a brokenly repeating vidtape, she found herself standing locked in place once again by a force field, as he paced angrily in front of her, snapping questions from all sides.

"What were you really doing in the Citadel. Why were you sent here?"

"Eating *jerbels*. It's not allowed for natives. And shirking duties," she said defiantly, refusing to understand his real question.

"What duties?"

"The road. Repairing the road by the gate."

"For how long?"

"Two months since. They co-opted my street."

"Which street, your address?"

"Twenty-two First Circle. A room by the wall."

"How convenient. Was there a door through the wall?"

"No, it's far too strong and what with. . ." She glared angrily, her head buzzing from the battery of questions.

"And your neighbors? Their names and occupations?"

She gave them. All had since shifted, but the Terran records still had them registered there. Then suddenly:

"The patch. What is it really?"

"A wound dressing. Very common."

"You lie," he yelled, banging a hand on a nearby table, making her jump as the blow scudded through her aching head. If only she could collapse back into lovely, lovely sleep.

"Once more, what is it? An identification badge, a secret symbol? Or some device, a communicator perhaps?"

"No. A mere dressing," she repeated wearily. "Believe me, that's all."

She felt him studying her, seeking a flaw, some crack in the wall of her intransigence. She refused to give him one. Weakened she might be, but she was not beaten yet. He came closer, grabbing her roughly by the arm.

"You've had your chance, Madame. Now it's time to be introduced to our technology. Not as advanced or as utopian as yours perhaps, but very effective. Come." He pulled her towards the door.

The threat in his voice was not lost on Marthe. She had heard tales of the victims of Terran refinements. It was present ever afterwards, they said, in the depths of their eyes. Fear seized her, struggling to smother what courage she could still muster as she was forced to march down the unwelcoming corridors, deeper and deeper into the military heart of the fortress.

Too soon, they stopped before a pair of doors, much like any other, and were passed in, to be greeted by an incongruously cheerful "Hello" from the room's sole occupant, a ruddy-faced, pleasantly smiling young man. All around him was bank upon bank of instrumentation, looking stupidly like the navigation room of the only interplanetary ship she had been aboard.

Two guards kept an attentive watch in the outer corridor, and Radcliff locked the doors from the inside before turning to the young man who had, meanwhile, been scrutinizing her in far too familiar a fashion, decided Marthe, even given her curiosity value. Her best, frigid Haut Liege glare answered that. Radcliff, unfortunately, was not looking at her at the time.

"All set, Ferdo?" he said, in a tone indicating friendship with the brash young Terran.

"Just about. The Colonel wasn't too keen on letting me use his precious gadgetry. As though I haven't used a more pleasant version the stars know how many times. Now, if the lady would care to take her seat, we can begin." Ferdo waved her to a chair, placed in front of a newly installed panel. "By the way, we're still as stumped as ever with this weird patch of yours, Hamon." He frowned at the harmless looking strip on a nearby bench.

Her captor was still looking at his friend and missed Marthe's quickly hidden excitement. Could she do it, could she get to it? "Hopefully you'll find something soon," Radcliff said. "But forget about that for now. Come, Madame, the chair."

Marthe didn't obey. She stared at the board, edging backwards in fearful horror. "No," she whispered.

"Since you refuse to speak, there is no other choice." Radcliff grabbed for her, but she swung away and sprang towards the far side of the room, flinging herself against the back bench in cornered dismay—the bench on which lay that small, clear patch.

The Terran Major pleaded with her softly. But Marthe saw that his friend's eye was on him, doubting his loyalty it seemed. His mouth set, Radcliff beckoned to the other man and both leapt at her. Marthe acted as if she was beyond fighting, overcome by fear and allowed herself to be dragged to the ominous chair. There was just time for her to clench down hard on her wrist, before the force field gripped her and movement became impossible. Unseen to her tormentors, she felt the blessed coolness of the patch, latching on as if to a lost limb as she had brushed against the bench. She was once more in contact with her own people, whatever was about to happen.

The next minute, a concealing mask came down, blocking her eyes, and the darkness took her. A fraction of a second's grace only, then footsteps approached. Lighter, too abrupt, not Hamon's footsteps. Around her, surrounding her, coming closer and closer.

Hamon would not hurt her, not unless pushed to extremity. Why she believed that, she didn't know, but she did. But Ferdo Braddock, the other Terran? The one who watched Hamon and waited for him to betray Earth.

Then she remembered. This was extremity, for Hamon, for her.

A moment only, and the nightmare began. A touch, the brush of heat against her legs. Not direct, not yet, but a faint crackling sound sent her heart into overdrive. More footsteps, around and around the chair, then that brush of heat, closer and closer. The smell of singed floor covering. As if scorched by a living flame.

Surely not, her mind screamed. No, barbaric. Witches and ancient history.

One sweep, the lightest scent of singed cloth, and she jerked on her restraints, desperate to smother the burning cloth.

A rush of cold water and she breathed a sigh of relief.

"We can stop now, if you will answer our questions. No flames, no pain. Or you can be charred and burned, that beautiful body twisted and blackened."

Hamon's voice, but mechanical, modulated through a speaker and hiding whatever he felt.

Now the footsteps again, and a tapping sound close by her ear, the sound of fingers on a control pad. Ferdo was in control of the torch, not Hamon, and her breathing fractured. A roar and the crackle of flames, then the heat was back. He was brushing that live flame near her feet, near her legs, higher and higher. Still those foreign footsteps walked around and around, and on each pass, the blast of heat came closer and closer. That smell again, charred fabric, the smoldering of cloth. The bottom of her tunic, starting to burn and the heat almost touching her bare legs.

"Your allies? Who are your allies?"

"The flame, the flame," she moaned in reply.

Then it was gone. Gone the flames, the heat, only the smell lingered. Through a mist of relief, she heard the harsh tones of her nightmare.

"We have taken away the torch and smothered your burning tunic. The torch will be returned if you refuse to cooperate. Who sent you and why?"

Still she held to her vow of silence. Only just, her heartbeat surely audible to both Terrans.

"You wish further treatment?"

There was a whoosh and the crackle of fire, then a brief bout of searing pain, leaving her trembling and crumbling in terror. *Just do it* she found herself wishing insanely, nerves stretched to breaking point with each deadly circle of those hated footsteps.

"Once again, who sent you and why? What organization do you work for? What really happened to the ruling group? Where is your base?"

She whimpered in fear, too scared to speak lest all resolution leave her and she blabber on and on and on.

A hideous pause followed. Two minutes, four, five.

"God damn you," came an agonized voice from the blackness, just before the blistering heat hit her, creeping higher and higher.

No! Why me? I'm too young.

The fire reached for her legs in a malevolent caress. Flames, crackling into life and beginning to lick at her now, the heat searing. The pain, the pain, starting, threatening, beating at the gateway to the rest of her body. *Ice cold water, soothing balms, talk, talk!*

"Father!" she screamed, suddenly unable to bear it. "Father, Daddy. Daddy, Bendin. Help me, help. Stop it, make them stop it!"

She screamed, again and again. The heat, the painful, burning heat. Then, gradually through the waves of terror she heard a blessedly familiar voice, soothing and calming. And the heat, the cackling of the wicked flames? Gone, all gone.

"Mimi, little Mimi. Shush, little one. I'm here. Father is here. We have contact again. You're all right. The flame, it's not real. It's only an illusion, a nerve simulation like in the theatres. It can't hurt you. You are whole, nothing has happened."

Slowly, hesitantly, the words began to penetrate the near hysterical fog enveloping her.

"It's not real?" she whispered.

"No, little one, it's not real. Come, remember your neurology. It's a simple illusion. They're playing on your nerves as if on an orchestra."

She listened avidly to the voice, the sound of calm and commonsense from her childhood. The warmly reassuring words had been there when her mother had died, and again, when the loss of Bendin had left her so alone. And now, they were here again in her time of need. Then the voice changed, became the Councilor's voice, the voice of authority giving her back courage and sanity.

"Don't speak. We're feeding panic reactions through to their instruments via your communicator. Unfortunately, we can't get you out of there yet. Too much is at stake to risk having Terrans poking around in search of you, but we will get you out soon, I promise, even if only for a short time. You will have to lose that patch again, but we will do all we can to get another to you. In your food perhaps?"

"No," in a soft hush.

"Why not? Do they search it? Tap for yes. Or, do you not get any? Her fingernail's gentle scratch confirmed her father's dread. "Ah, my poor Mimi. Your courage enhances the honor of this family more than I can say.

There was a period of silence, in which all her fears returned. Again, she whimpered.

"I'm still here," came the steady, paternal voice, only a slight quaver revealing his anguish. "We cannot hold this channel open any longer. Your sister and the twins send their love and their strength. Keep that chin up, remember you are asn Castre and that in a few months, we will all be back home again."

"Jaca?" she whispered, her one big fear.

"Still in prison. We dare not release him either, but at least we are in contact and can block the worst of their brutalities. The rest who were taken at the same time are also safe, all fifty, and now have replacement patches. But I must go. We shall put you into a faint, to make the brutes give up."

Dimly she tried to argue as the black waves advanced with the receding voice. "Not brutes," she mumbled then gave herself to the welcoming depths, remembering only to let the patch slip back onto the floor near the bench to be found later. She was vaguely aware of rough hands dragging her out of the force, slapping her face and clinging to her shoulders.

"Ferdo, help me. God help me if she dies!"

"Calm down, Hamon. It was only an illusion. She's merely fainted and is in shock." Ferdo shook his wrist, wincing at the twinges in it.

He'd had to fight to hold Hamon back from yanking the girl out of the field when she started screaming, but nothing could keep Radcliff from her when she fainted. Ferdo reckoned he'd bruised all the tendons in his arm trying to stop him. Then he looked at his friend again and sighed in resignation. "I'm calling the medics in here immediately, for both of you. You're as white as a ghost. Not that I blame you. Don't ever ask me to do such a horrifying thing again."

The face that turned towards him made Ferdo want to bite the words back; but his words of apology were as to a deaf man. These cursed natives! They broke every rule in the book. How were they to know she would fall into a hysterical trance?

"Thank the stars," Ferdo said at last, turning in relief as the medical team arrived.

"What happened?"

"A prisoner under neuroillusion has gone into shock. You'd better check the interrogating officer as well."

Briskly, the chief medic set to work, checking the most obviously affected first, the Major. He barely acknowledged them, retaining his tight grip on the unconscious body of the Hathian girl.

"Come, Major, she'll be all right. Let me read your vital signs." The woman held her recorder over his chest and groin then infused a sedative before he knew what she was doing, sending him into a gentle sleep. "To the wards and keep a close eye on him."

Turning now to the Hathian girl, she gave her a cursory examination then stood up.

"Well?" Ferdo asked, "aren't you going to do anything for her? She may be just a native, but she is also an important prisoner and the stars help you if anything happens to her."

"No need. She's only sleeping. Better get her back to her cell, then leave her alone; she'll be fine in the morning." With which terse assessment the woman made ready to leave, signaling the porters to lift the unconscious Radcliff and transfer him to the stretcher.

"But she can't be. Not after neuroillusion," gasped Ferdo.

"Oh, it's a common enough reaction. I don't know why the Colonel still insists on giving prisoners a session. These Hathians may be human, but something seems to have been lost from their nervous systems in the generations they've been here." She looked at the technician's pale face, told him he looked as if he needed a stiff drink, then was gone.

Not even the guard, entering soon after to remove the still shape of the girl from the floor, could disturb a stunned Ferdo. It was a long time he stayed there, not moving at all, staring with grim memories at the seat to which the Hathian woman had been fixed.

CHAPTER SEVEN

"Madame asn Castre, breakfast is served."

The delightful words, in her own tongue, seeped through the murky layers of Marthe's nightmare. Gradually she woke, barely noticing the grim walls surrounding her for the heavenly sight of Agnethe holding the biggest tray of food Marthe had ever seen.

"Food," she breathed, sitting up in a rush and grabbing at the dishes.

"Now, now, not so fast."

And as if to punish her, the dizzy waves reached up to seize hold again.

"There, there. Those brutes were none too gentle, were they? Sit back and let me help you. And don't bolt the food. Your poor stomach won't stand for such treatment."

Marthe was beyond caring. She reached out greedily and between mouthfuls managed to gasp: "Where? I haven't seen food like this since … oh, since before the fall. It's real!" And she started laughing, crying and choking on a full mouth, all in one.

"Old Agnethe still has her stores. I used to be housekeeper for your great-uncle Kastoff. Now there was a man who appreciated his food. None of this synthetic rubbish for him. And you can't possibly eat two whole brovins in one mouthful. The second one won't go away while you eat the first."

Marthe barely heard her, completing the impossible and reaching for more.

"No, that's quite enough for now. It's not wise to gorge on an empty stomach. Don't worry, I'll bring more soon, and here is a new com patch for you along with a set of proper Hathian robes. Not as elegant as that slip of a thing you're wearing, but it covers a sight more of you. Don't worry about the switch of clothes. We've doctored the surveillance vids to make the Terrans think a guard gave them to you."

Marthe took it all with a shaky smile. "Thank you, Agnethe, for everything. This cell looks … so good. To be able to speak Harmish freely again!"

She could hold back the tears no longer. Agnethe shushed her kindly, patting her hand. "Relax, you're safe now. That nasty Major is in hospital, and likely to remain so for a while. Suffering from shock, they say. In the meantime, no one is likely to worry about you. With any luck, we can sneak you out for a couple of day's furlough. Someone else can substitute for you; *they* will never know the difference." Her backwards nod to the door spoke volumes. "Now, I must leave before one of those pesky guards comes along and wonders how I managed to get past their precious monitors." With which she bustled out, taking with her the telltale tray and the despised elegance of Marthe's Terran clothing.

Left on her own, Marthe shrugged on the rest of the enveloping native robes, then lay back and sighed in contentment. How good to feel again the slick promise of a wrist patch and the comforting roughness of the peasant clothing, with its promise of safety in the concealing bulk. She was still in prison, granted, but the Terran systems were easily foiled in this part of the Citadel. Unlike that other part. She shuddered, remembering the isolation of the Major's beautiful apartment. Here, she could forget the confusion that had beset her there: the unwelcome pity she had felt for the Terrans and that unwanted spark that had flared between her and Hamon Radcliff. That she dared not remember. Best of all, she now knew that Jaca and the other captives were alive. The last of her burdens was gone.

She settled onto the hard bench, her stomach blessedly full. Free at last from the pernicious drag of the force field and able to close her eyes in peace, it was but an instant before the gift of sleep claimed her again.

Her next awakening was to the familiar clamor of Terrans shouting orders.

"Stand to for inspection."

Normal and wonderfully anonymous. Terrans bullying Hathians. That evening, she slept again—until the early hours of the morning, when a signal from her patch brought her rest to an abrupt end with a warning of an incoming message. She listened and did as ordered, opening the now unlocked cell door and moving down the passage to await her promised escort. She was on furlough already, it seemed.

A shadow, barely discernible from the other shadows of the night, tapped her shoulder and beckoned her to follow. They passed by the prison's banks of concealed surveillance monitors, with only a moment's work needed to ensure that nothing unusual registered on the Terrans' screens. Soon, very soon, they had walked out the gates of the fortress and were strolling down the curfewed streets. The protective shields surrounding them deflected all signs of their passing. Only human eyes could penetrate their shields, and so secure was Earth in its assumed supremacy that they were unlikely to meet any of those at night.

Her guide led her down a narrow street to a squat collection of houses, in a door, through a typically small, drab room, and down the lift concealed behind a rough chest of drawers. Emerging, Marthe breathed a happy sigh of relief. They had entered a great, underground hall, filled with 'her people' as she best thought of them. Technicians monitored rows of panels on every side of the room. All around her, Hathian voices discussed problems, transmitted orders, quipped with work mates with not a trace of the defeated subservience of the so-called peasants of Hathe so familiar to their Terran overlords.

She was in the control room of the plateau sector, the most crucial part of the underground's resistance campaign. On the far wall, she could see a group checking the mass of incoming and outgoing messages: where to, who to, who was not receiving. Elsewhere, others were locked into the multitude of Terran monitors that constantly watched over the Hathians, altering one here, one there, to prevent discovery of the illicit operations of the resistance. Marthe stopped to take it all in, a huge grin lifting the corners of her mouth. It was true, all true. In the dark stretches of the past nights, she had begun to doubt, to think that she really was alone, her people gone.

But here they were.

Suddenly a tall figure detached itself from the crowd and, with a cry of joy, hurried forward to clutch Marthe in a shuddering hug. Her sister?

"Marthe! I thought I'd never see you again."

The warm voice confirmed it. "Laren. What are you doing here? I thought you were still on maternity leave. Where are the twins, and Jorven?"

"The twins are fine. They're over a year old now, remember, and with three very doting grandparents, they are not likely to come to much harm. As for Jorven, turn around."

Marthe did so, to see her silent guide throw back his hood and the face of her brother-in-law laughing back at her.

"You never said anything!"

"And have you shout your surprise to the world," he teased. "Who else should have come? You're on family leave, not official duty."

"I hope someone tells Father that," snorted Laren, linking arms with Marthe and her husband. "Hurry up, you two, or we'll miss our shuttle."

They walked quickly to the far side of the hall, down a sloping corridor and into the upper level of an enormous chamber that lay directly below the first. Through the protective window Marthe could see two short-haul vessels, one with its blunt nose already beginning to tilt in readiness for flight.

"Five minutes to departure. Last embarkation call. All passengers please move forward immediately to docking procedure."

"Come on," cried Jorven. They broke into a run, hurrying to catch the departing chute, whisking them down to the flight deck, through the barricade, a halt to check their IDs, then along another corridor and a dash into the ship just as the harassed crewman was about to close the door.

"Names!"

"Asn Castre, an Castre, an Dufon."

"Take your seats then. First three on the left. We are almost ready to leave. In future I suggest you make better arrangements to be here on time." He sealed the door, before walking off, muttering about death and glory special agents and did they think they were the only ones who had it tough in this war.

"Welcome home, the returning heroine," laughed Laren, buckling in and settling back for the anti-grav phase.

"I know. Isn't it marvelous?" Marthe flung off her cloak and settled back with a grin.

A rumbling below warned the passengers. The ship began to lift, rising up to where, far above, a dark, gaping hole appeared as the cavern roof slid back to reveal the velvety blackness of the night sky.

Tonight, there was only one light to compete with the tiara of the stars: the pale glow of the lesser of Hathe's two moons—Mathe, the insignificant, the secret, so often overlooked by the unknowing and the unwise.

In a room in the Citadel, a Terran technician registered yet another minor shake hitting the township.

"Hope nothing's building," he said. "These ground tremors are hitting us every day now." He checked his screens, but there was no sign of damage. Everything in the town appeared normal.

"Marthe," called Laren, leaning over to chat. She was stopped by her husband's warning shush. Marthe was lost to sleep.

Gently, Laren eased off her sister's harness, curving Marthe onto her side and tucking back a stray wisp of hair, just like her own little daughter's—but not the black cavities beneath the eyes or the finely drawn bones standing out tautly from the face.

"It takes more than one night to recover from four days without food or sleep," Jorven cautioned. "Leave her be for now. She will probably have to face a grilling from our beloved statesmen when we get home, and she's had to endure more than enough grilling already."

"I didn't know," gasped Laren. This was her baby sister. "To think … the rumors that have been circulating, that she had fallen for a Terran! Just look at the marks on her hands," she added, noticing for the first time the healing welts on Marthe's palms.

Her husband's face reflected what she felt. "If I ever get my hands on that thug, Radcliff… Mathe knows what she's endured while we were out of contact. If only she didn't have to go back."

"Back? No! Surely once the Council sees her? Yes, I know there have been atrocities, but when your own sister's involved, it's different."

"I wouldn't get your hopes up, love. There is too much at stake. For all we know, it may not have been so bad."

"You think so?"

He looked down at the still, now peaceful body beside her. His face said it all. No, he did not think so.

Marthe remained blissfully oblivious to their anxiety. She basked in a dream world where hunger was banished and nothing could beset her. Nearing the end of the flight, she passed from deep sleep to a light doze and slowly became aware of her surroundings. Clean air, the softness of the cushioning beneath her and, best of all, the hum of genuine, relaxed Harmish voices. A touch of nausea warned of the changing flight path of their ship as they approached their destination. Shaking off the vestiges of sleep, she pulled herself up, fastening the landing harness and peering out the window at the rapidly nearing mass of Mathe, the lesser, often forgotten second moon of Hathe. The Terrans thought the name similarity merely a stupid inconvenience. The Hathians knew better.

"What a quick trip." She yawned and stretched. "I could have slept for hours. Do you think Father will have a meal ready when we get home? I'm famished," she declared and was surprised by the rush of pity in Laren's eyes. What had she said now? She subsided, sitting in pensive silence until the docking doors opened.

The moment of disquiet was lost in the chaos and bustle of arrival, caught in a pushing, ever hurrying mass of people eagerly seeking loved ones they had been parted from for too long.

"I'd forgotten how physical civilization is," she cried, fighting through the crowd with the other two and grabbing for a place in the ever-present queue. But there were occasional advantages to being the daughter of a Councilor, and she was glad to see one such manifest itself in the form of an official, bowing her small party to a side room.

There to greet them was the genial but lined face of Dr Sylvan an Castre.

"Father! I should have known you would be here. Thank you. The queues are longer than on Hathe."

"We couldn't leave our heroine to the mercies of the mob," he said, hugging her close then standing back gravely, "and my fellow Councilors are at the end of that line you were in." She couldn't hide her dismay, not from her father. "Don't worry, I've arranged a detour. They can wait a few hours longer. First, we have a special celebration feast waiting. Bortch with jerbels."

Marthe gave a hoot of laughter. "Father, I hate jerbels."

"Oh, well, never mind." The worry in his face belied the heartiness of his voice. "Here's the transporter."

They all stepped into the square, open-topped run-around and the doctor punched in the coordinates of the an Castre quarters. He reached out a hand to help Marthe into her seat.

"Careful, you must be tired out."

"Nonsense, I've done nothing but sleep for the last twenty-four hours," she retorted, "but I am famished. No jerbels, though, thank you very much." A chuckle of laughter threatened, then was quashed as she caught the glances among her family. It was as if there was a 'Care–Fragile' sticker plastered on her forehead. What she was to do about it was beyond her, and she could only nod in reply to her father's questions as they passed through the subterranean corridors.

It was with relief that she saw the doorway to the an Castre quarters, and scrambled out before they had fully stopped. She slammed the door open and stalked inside to savor the familiar spaces for one lone minute: above, the high-domed ceiling and in front the great window, looking out over the starkly silvered slopes of the dead moon. There were other lights shining back at her, oval sparks set amongst the crags and crevices telling of the windows of other homes.

A rocky warren of humanity, the entire mountain was riddled with the quarters of the main secret base on Mathe.

"It's good to be home again," she breathed, turning to her family as they entered.

"We are mighty glad to have you here," replied Laren. "But you must be eager to change out of those dreadful robes."

"Strangely, no." Marthe smiled, remembering the thin, beautiful shift of her imprisonment. Nonetheless, she followed Laren and was soon relaxing in the warm vapor jets of the cleanser, washing away the prison dirt of the last day. She emerged and began to leaf through the wardrobe she kept on hand here.

"Your stomach! What have they done to you?"

Marthe glanced down at the remaining scabs, thin lines running across her abdomen and breast. "I'd forgotten about those. My own fault, believe it or not. I tried to run through a force field and this was the result. I looked quite a mess when it first happened, but Major Radcliff had a pot of excellent salve. I must remember to ask him what it was when I get back."

"Don't say that. Don't even mention that man. Surely Father can stop it? You can't return!"

"Of course I must. I'm only on furlough."

"But Marthe. Oh, my poor darling."

It was too much. Marthe eyed her sister in growing wrath. For once, she refused to pander to her sister's need for harmony. "Stop this nonsense, Laren. It's just another assignment, no more terrible than many I've been on before. I should think you'd have enough sense by now not to carry on as if I were the only agent ever to be placed in danger."

"There's a difference between working among our own people and being caught alone among Terrans. Those days when you were out of touch!"

She tried to hide it, but Marthe was trained to read faces and couldn't miss that fleeting look on her sister's face. Like a bitter stab to her heart, and her mouth twisted. "When the stories started going around? A Hathian from an old, respected family, lost to all sense of duty and consorting in a disgraceful manner with a Terran? That's what you were supposed to think. How could you, of all people, fall for it. My big sister, one person I can count on to remain calm and sensible when all about me is falling into idiocy. Or maybe you too believed the stories?"

"No, never."

Laren looked so distressed, Marthe had to apologize despite herself. "I'm sorry. It's just… I didn't expect my family to be part of this stupid nonsense I've fallen into. I have survived fine so far and Major Radcliff isn't quite the monster you imagine. Have you never considered that there might be two sides to this whole bloody mess?"

Ignoring the shocked look that greeted this, she twitched her gown into place and swept out.

"Father, where's this feast you promised me? I intend to do my best to become the size of this room before I go back."

"And I will do my best to help you; but first, you must greet our guest—another returning hero."

Turning, Marthe found herself face to face with one who, deep down, she had never thought to see again.

"Jaca." Slow, silent tears touched her cheeks. "Jaca, I'm so sorry. I had to." She could say no more. He was alive, praise Mathe, this man she had condemned to death. Silently, she stared at him and the half-open, cautious smile on his face. But she soon had to glance away, seeing what he could not hide from her; the questions and the accusations.

"Are you on furlough as well, or did they release you?" she said, retreating to the safety of the polite query.

"Furlough." Now she could also read ridicule there. "Your Major's illness gave us both a reprieve. My substitute must have the privilege of the guards' kind attentions for a few days.

"I didn't know you were so closely watched."

"You're not the only Haut Liege under Radcliff's care. I even receive the occasional, personal visit. To discuss the weather, the arts, politics. Quite … gentlemanly."

"His father is the Alliance Representative!" It was out before she knew it. She stopped abruptly, lost for words to mend what she had said.

She could see her father's confusion but could do nothing about it. There was too much between Jaca and her, and both had learned in the same, hard school to keep their secrets. The awkward silence was finally broken by her father.

"Plenty of time to catch up on gossip later. Jacquel, if you would kindly take Marthe through, we will follow behind."

Politely nodding assent, Jaca rose, offering his arm to Marthe then walking with a marked limp towards the dining hall.

"Your leg? What happened?" she exclaimed.

"Your dear friend, the Major. We don't get on particularly," was the unpromising reply.

"Has it been treated? You must let me look at it after dinner."

"No," he said gruffly. "I've had excellent care since I arrived back, thank you." He would say no more, carefully handing her to her seat with punctilious courtesy. She was saved by her father from having to reply. He raised his glass.

"I believe a toast is in order. To us." He lifted his glass and gave that quiet smile of his that always spelled safety to Marthe and an end to dissent. "May the food be excellent and the wine purest ambrosia."

"What better toast could there be?" seconded Jorven, chuckling. "Knowing your table, I doubt not that it will be granted."

He was proved right. Course after fascinating course appeared: kafka from Aeros, ciukh from Delion and, best of all, genuine bortch rescued from Hathe – with jerbel berries!

Her stomach already stretched beyond its limit, Marthe could only gaze in wonder. "Real bortch," she breathed.

"Mmm, better than gruel, eh?" grinned Jaca, finally showing signs of relaxing.

"Gruel nothing! Do you realize this is only my second meal for days? Hamon Radcliff's so-called admiration did not extend to feeding prisoners."

"But I thought… You were at breakfast when I was brought in."

"Radcliff was at breakfast. I was kindly given a glass of water."

Behind his still closed face, she saw she had shocked him. "I think that you and I need to talk." he said. "But later. For now, bortch and jerbels."

"Mmm," she agreed holding out her plate for a huge helping.

"Marthe, you can't possibly eat all that," laughed Laren, "and don't touch the jerbels. Remember what happened the last time you ate them."

"As if I could forget. I was so ill I couldn't move for days."

"When was that?" said her father. "I never knew you were allergic to them."

"You were away at an Alliance meeting. I was fine by the time you got home. You were there, Jaca. The four of us had raided Dufon's orchard, and your father came out breathing fire and thunder, Jorven."

"That's right," recalled Jaca, laughing even. "It's no wonder you were ill. You ate masses of the things and half of them weren't even ripe."

"No more than we ate, though," said Laren with a chuckle. "As for Bendin, he must have eaten more than all of us put together. With, as usual, no effect at all. That boy led a charmed life."

"I don't wish to hear any more," exclaimed their father. "Like so many of your past escapades, it seems best left alone. Instead, tell me about the gossip planetside? I hear you rendezvoused with your cousin Griffith, though I daresay that young man refused to bother with such trivialities as family pleasantries."

"No," grimaced Marthe. "Only that cousin Addie had 'presented him with a young crusader'. Which I take to mean that Addie's finally had the baby."

"About two weeks late. Goodness, I thought she would never have it," Laren laughed. "Mind you, she didn't carry well, I hear."

"Oh, I know, do I ever know. Along with any other poor unfortunate who happened to come within shouting distance. Why Griffith let her stay planetside, I have no idea." said Marthe in disgust. "It wasn't as if there was anything really wrong with her. Just prolonged nausea and tiredness. Plenty of women suffer that."

"Behold the sympathetic physician," teased Jorven. "God protect us when you are let loose again on an unsuspecting world."

"As soon as I am, I promise you will be my first patient," she threatened back.

Her father chuckled. "That day is not too far off. Setting up refresher courses for professionals is one of the Council's first priorities, after we rid ourselves of these Terrans. I have already booked you a place. You'll be back in practice in no time."

"Not straight away, thank you Father. I'll need a holiday before I tackle something like that. You've no idea how much I've forgotten these last years, even with all the field work that's come my way." She grimaced, thinking of the tasks ahead, but then thrust them away, indulging instead in the pleasure of family gossip.

Later that night, she stood gazing out the library window in quiet contemplation of the lunar landscape, escaping for a few moments' peace. A noise made her spin round. It was Jacquel, poking his head through the doorway.

"Mind if I come in?"

She shook her head, motioning him forward to a pair of seats ideally placed to view the lunar scene below. The light from the window cast gaunt shadows across his face, sharpening the usually merry contours into harsh crags, and his voice when he spoke held no trace of easy banter. She sat in the other and waited. She could guess why he was here. He soon confirmed it.

"The Terrans have told me one story. I would like your version."

She nodded, her mouth dry. Her one-time friend was sitting in judgement before her. Only the truth would do, so she told him of her imprisonment, hiding nothing yet revealing little beyond the plain, unemotional facts. Grimly she told of Radcliff's ultimatum.

"Your death, or my confession. I ordered your death."

"Oh?"

"Plus two others."

She sat still, neither defending nor attacking herself.

Jacquel leaned back, resting his chin thoughtfully in his hands. Their enduring strength belied the usually reckless air of the man. "You had to do it, for the sake of the cause," he said with an icy logic.

"It was the only choice possible," she agreed. "Were you told?"

"Oh yes, he told me. In vivid detail." Bitterness scored deeply into the shadows surrounding him.

"Major Radcliff?"

"I received a visit from your amiable protector not long after."

Marthe was quelled by the hate edging his voice. "You don't seem to approve of our mutual captor. I take it that his methods were not overly gentle. I would like to know the truth; he did not kill you, remember."

"Of course he didn't. As an Haut Liege, I am for too valuable, even if I do not possess your beauty."

"Beauty nothing. There is more than one kind of torture; the subtlest can be the worst," she snapped, guilt churning her guts.

"Oh yes. No food, no sleep, but at least you were clean, lay in a proper bed at night. And how intensive was your interrogation— every waking hour of the day with those ghouls of hell they call soldiers?"

"I had one session."

"One?" he jeered, throwing himself up from the chair and pacing angrily back and forth. The very air seemed spattered with his rage, spewing forth into the shadows of the room as he strode in front of her. Suddenly he turned, paused in mid-step, his face of agony upon her.

"Why?"

The word hung there, splitting to shreds the defensive anger she had so gladly thrown up.

"I don't remember a time when you and Bendin weren't my closest friends," he went on. "When Bendin died, it hurt me almost as much as it hurt you. I've trusted you with my life more times than I care to remember these last years, and vice versa. Then you just say 'No' and I'm gone? That's it?"

"I had to," was all she could whisper.

"Had to? Of course you *had to*. All those men who would have died. But did you *have to* so easily? You didn't even ask for a day's grace to consider."

"There wasn't one on offer," she replied in a voice as still as his was turbulent. "Major Radcliff is driven by a desperation almost greater than our own. He thinks his world is dying."

"So now you favor his cause. Take care. You soon won't have to worry about killing your friends. It will all spill out so easily."

Marthe shot up at that. "Jaca, stop it. Don't do this. I doubt if you can believe me, but the moment I thought you dead was the worst of my life, whatever our mutual enemy may claim. Worse even than losing Bendin, because I didn't cause that. I won't ask your forgiveness for my decision. You would've been forced to do the same if you were me. But I tell you, it wasn't lightly made or easy to live with." She smiled jaggedly. "In less than a day's time we both return to captivity. Let's not bear this burden as well." She began to raise her hand in supplication, then recognized the effrontery and let it drop.

Jaca didn't move, standing as one trapped, his chest heaving and pain scoring his face. She waited, knowing if she failed here, it would be one loss too many. She didn't know if she could face the coming ordeal without his support.

For a long time, it looked like she would have to. Jaca stood silent, in judgment, his clear blue eyes studying her and his face closed and rigid. Then, slowly, ever so slowly, the stiff shoulders eased, and fell, and the ghost of a smile flitted across the twisted mouth. He had made his decision. "You're right, Mimi, as ever. My hand." and he cautiously stretched out one, pale palm.

The relief of it flooded her. "A pact on it," she agreed eagerly, grasping his hand with pleasure.

"Yes, a pact on it."

CHAPTER EIGHT

That brief smile was all he gave her of warmth. The barest hint, but there was yet a promise in it and, for a moment only, he made her a party to his pain, the trace of warmth disappearing and his face open and exposed. He let her see all the grief of the days to come and a pledge that he would stand by her as they stepped through them together.

Then he gave a small shake and the old Jaca, the bright image of her youth, settled as a mask over his inner torment. She had no choice but to go along with the masquerade. She was the betrayer here, and when he spoke again it was as if the last moments had never been. They had known each other so long that the familiar habits of friendship fell easily into place, but Marthe knew the private soul behind the bravura and that nothing was the same.

"We ought to discuss our strategy," he said brightly, once more the fellow conspirator. "Decide what tale we shall string the Terrans. Two such tried and true troupers as we are must be able to come up with something special." He paced before her again, his considerable dramatic talents to the fore as he illuminated his words with vivid movements of arm and body. "Shall we be the revolutionary philosophers of our tribe, preferring to share in the peasants' poverty to a luxurious exile? Or did we run away, or were cast out for our flagrant contempt of their outdated mores. I would rather like to go down in history as a rogue, a lecher of young, innocent daughters and not so young or innocent spouses. What say you, Mimi? Can you see me as the disgraced ravisher?" And he flung his hand high before flourishing low in a sweeping, courtly bow.

"You've had an interesting reputation since your teens, and well you know it," she said, laughing at this display but not fooled for a second. Still beneath the surface, she sensed the tautly held control of her apparently volatile friend. But she was also a skilled actor.

"As for me, my story is told," she said as blithely. "Father and I quarreled, I took myself off in a huff and missed the ships' departure. Needless to say, it wasn't believed."

"I should think not. Everyone knew how close your family was. Couldn't you think of anything better? Why not stolen by bandits for ransom? Or you were knocked on the head, developed amnesia and wandered off?"

"They are just as unbelievable, and you know it. Apart from which, my tale is told and it's too late to change it now.

"You're right, more's the pity. It really is the worst load of garbage I ever heard, but it will have to do. As for me, I do think I was cast off in disgrace, because, because...

"Your father was trying to get you to marry Emily delns Varst?"

"Ugh!" His face crinkled. "Not even Father would try that one."

"You had got the President's daughter pregnant?"

"Who says I hadn't?" he grinned back.

Her eyes opened wide. "There was a rumor going around. I remember Jessamie saying something.

"Rubbish she did," he retorted, rapidly backing down.

"Thought that would call your bluff. But you must have told them something, if only to put them off the track?"

"There was no point. By the time Radcliff caught me, he was so suspicious that anything I said would only have made matters worse. So I played dumb: the spoiled Haut Liege in a sulk."

"Which you can play to perfection."

"Thank you." He lifted an eyebrow in some surprise.

"Well you can, so you needn't look at me like that. Save it for the Terrans." A thought caught her. "Since we can't avoid imprisonment, why not use it to reinforce the set-up of a society of Haut Liege and peasants. After what they've done to us, the least the Terrans deserve is to have a pair of insufferably arrogant Haut Liege thrust upon them. We won't be able to fool Major Radcliff—the man knows too much about what Hathe was like before they came—but possibly we can minimize his credibility with the other Terrans."

"By exposing them to a full blast of those exalted personages, the Lady Marthe asn Castre and the Master Jacquel des Trurain?" For an instant the old, wicked delight lit his eyes.

"Exactly!"

"And Radcliff? How are you going to manage him?"

She looked away at that, out the window to the rocky shadows of the valley below. Then she retreated to the sanctuary of a chair and sat tensely poised on the front edge. The air strained heavily around them again. "That will be a more personal battle," was all she could say. Who she must battle wasn't clear, even to her. Too many conflicted feelings invaded her whenever she thought of the Terran. Hamon Radcliff was her enemy. So why couldn't she think of him as one?

Jaca went to stand by the window, looking out it as he asked the question she knew he couldn't avoid. "He'll want to make you his mistress?"

"If I can get him to trust me? Yes, probably."

He turned half back. "Will you agree?" All the light was stripped from him as he waited, and she saw the effect of her slow nod in reply.

"If necessary to keep my cover. Yes."

"Can you bear it?"

A jagged gasp of laughter escaped her. "After what we've have endured these last four and a half years? This is nothing."

"Maybe."

He lied, and they both knew it. More than anyone else alive, he knew the cost of those strife-torn years, years which should have seen her youth and young loves. Emotionally, she was a novice. Did she really understand what she proposed?

"He won't tolerate our charade otherwise," she added then.

"You seem sure he'll know it to be a charade."

"Oh, yes. Sometimes, it's as if he can see right into my—" and she broke off in confusion. She shook her head and continued in a voice devoid of emotion. "But without proof, he can do nothing. Who's going to believe him if he claims I'm a spy, when he's the one keeping me safe, and you can be sure he will be fully aware of that too." Bitter anguish feathered her whispered words.

Jacquel watched the emotions chase across her face. *Damn the Terran and his charm.* And he was going to have to watch her do this, watch the two of them together, watch his worst enemy with his best friend.

Marthe shook herself mentally. *Enough.* She plastered a bright smile on her face. "He has no choice but to go along with my act anyway, if he wants to find out what I'm up to. I only hope he's so busy trying to figure me out that he eases up on you. Otherwise you'll be far worse off than me. You seem to have become Major Radcliff's least favorite Hathian."

Jaca's smile looked forced. "It's only for a few months, and I'm tougher than I look." Which was nothing less than the truth, thought

Marthe. "Don't worry about me," he continued. "I'll be such an autocratic, overbearing, conceited and spoilt *brat* that they will just beg me to escape."

She had to laugh then. She hugged him closely, trying to hold on to his strength and familiarity till the last moment possible. She was going to need it.

"You say they are not extracting enough urgonium to meet Earth's domestic requirements?"

Marthe passed a weary hand across aching eyes, before replying for what must be the hundredth time. "That's correct. They seem to know little of the recent developments in energy generation that use urgonium more efficiently or are based on other sources.

"That's impossible, child. The kind of alternatives you refer to have been in common use throughout the Alliance for years, well before the Terrans invaded. This Major Radcliff? Is he in a position to fully know about Earth's current situation?"

"As I have already stated, Councilor an Baktish, Major Radcliff is the son of Representative Garth Radcliff of the Alliance Council and Administrator Freya MacDiarmid. He was also part of Earth's mission to Hathe immediately prior to the invasion. He knew exactly how badly the Terrans needed the urgonium then, and how much they still do."

"Yes, yes, girl. You said that. But what else does he know?"

"I was not able to ascertain the exact extent of his knowledge of Earth's affairs, Councilor," she replied, politely resigned. "That must wait until I return to Hathe's surface proper."

She'd been giving similar answers for hours. The whole bunch of them now ignored her, leaning over their notes and talking among themselves. Marthe was set on a solitary chair facing what she could only think of as her panel of inquisitors. Barely attending to their discussions, she gazed speculatively at the lineup. Grey-haired and tetchy Councilor an Baktish, the oldest member of Council—a fact which afforded him a kind of precarious pride she had never been able to understand. Beside him, the quietly distinguished and completely unfathomable Councilor an Heurain. Though he spoke the least, she had quickly become aware of how readily the other three deferred to his judgment.

The booming, staccato voice now addressing her belonged to Councilor an Jordan. A large, hale man resembling a giant megalith in action, she knew not to discount him for he was a man of subtle deliberations. Then her own dear father, torn at present between his duty to his people and to his family, a slight pucker wrinkling his brow as he watched her closely. She could feel his concern, caught the frown that warned her to attend, the frown that had always accompanied worry for his children. Right now, she guessed he would rather have been anywhere than in a senior Councilor's chair.

She replied absentmindedly to Councilor an Jordan's rather rambling question, yet another that she had already answered over and over. In the past two days, she would swear she could count on one hand the minutes she had spent out of this room. Over in the far corner, the same crack still reached cautiously up the otherwise flawless wall, struggling to impose lunar forces on this antiseptic bastion of the organic invaders. Even the potted shrubs in one corner were a synthesized replica of the sprawling gardens of Hathe, the atmosphere here too precious for other than necessary organic life. Living plants were strictly confined to the hydroponic unit, as part of the tightly controlled, environmental systems servicing the colony on Mathe.

Thinking of this, she wondered cynically which were of the least use: the ornamental shrubs or the even more ornamental wielders of power sitting in front of her. But that, she supposed, was unfair.

Everyone had their own peculiar talents, as her father was wont to say and, right now, she couldn't really claim that her talents had been of the slightest use to the cause. In all probability, she may have hindered her people's plans, which was more than the garrulous an Baktish had ever managed. She answered the next question. Would they never stop? She'd begun to wish she'd never left Hathe.

At last her relief force knocked on the door with a message that Agent asn Castre was required Hatheside immediately if their cover was not to be broken. Word had come that the Terran major was to be released from sick bay, and he would be sure to ask about his prisoners soon afterwards.

Thank the stars, she breathed, hiding a grin of unholy joy. Her father knew her too well and ticked her off soundly as they passed down the corridor to the space bay shortly afterwards.

"Marthe, Marthe, will I never instill in you a proper respect for our leaders. We are in a very serious situation and here you are, still treating a planetside mission as an exciting holiday trip."

"It is after that grilling, and well you know it, Father mine." She smiled, linking arms affectionately with her father and sister. "You have no idea how lacking in imagination are our esteemed leaders, Laren. I swear, if they asked a question once, they asked it a dozen times. The scant information I had could have been delivered in half an hour at most; but no, they had to pick over every nuance, every slight change in tone."

"You poor darling," chuckled Laren. "Though Father is right. The Councilors carry a heavy load of responsibility. Even if it is only to provide our government with the essential essence of senility in the case of your favorite, dear old an Baktish."

"Dear old an Baktish nothing. The man is a public menace. If his family hadn't bred so profusely, he would never be there. I swear he must be related to half the planet."

"A point you would do well to remember, if you do exaggerate somewhat," said her father. "Dotty old an Baktish he may be, but to many of us he symbolizes the family ties on which our society is built, and without which we would never have survived the invasion. The planet couldn't have been organized in that one, short month we had before the Terrans arrived without a quick call to a second cousin, a word from uncle to nephew, sisters having a chat, your grandmother speaking to old an Baktish—her third cousin by marriage, I might remind you. Formal deliberations at Council would take an age if we had to find out the people's opinion some other way."

"Not everyone has a relation on Council," she pointed out.

"No, but enough do to get a cross-section of public opinion, and the relationships are well enough known to be accessible."

"I still think it's a rather hit or miss form of government."

"Maybe, little one, but it works. At least we make some attempt to involve the populace in the decision-making process, aside from the quadrennial vote. They don't even bother with that on your major's precious Earth." A grim frown marred his usually gentle countenance. "Conquering us because they couldn't be bothered ruling their own planet properly! To such have fallen the remnants of our ancestors."

"Now, Father," soothed Laren, the eternal pacifier. "Our ancestors left Earth, therefore these current Terrans cannot be their descendants."

"A technicality. We share a common, if distant, ancestry, and one would expect a semblance of intelligence from the present inhabitants of Earth. Their communication systems can only be described as primitive, and these are the descendants of the first Terran species to acquire the gift of language. It's criminal! Do you not agree, des Trurain?"

Jaca had chosen that unfortunate moment to emerge from an adjacent corridor. "Certainly sir, most definitely," he replied, shooting an enquiring glance at Laren.

"Father is upset that Marthe must return and is relieving himself by denouncing our distant cousins of Earth. Just keep agreeing in that beautiful manner of yours. The most polished in all Hathe, as my third cousin Juanine once said."

"Not, I take it, in a complimentary way?" he grinned.

"Not exactly. However did you offend her, or dare I not ask?"

"You dare, but Juanine would not thank me for answering."

"Jaca, not another!" Marthe shook her finger in mock approbation and, in reply, he fell into a pose of melodramatic dolor.

"Ah, but my Lady don't you know it's all due to my very sad background. Never once was I allowed to know the sweet pangs of hunger, to endure the strengthening discipline of refusal, the constraint of somnolent colors in my dress. It was all most tragic. Nor did my parents soil their hands with honest labor, choosing instead to depend entirely on the fruits of their disgustingly formidable intellects. Quite beyond the pale, I fear." A sigh of great lament escaped his anguished countenance and a trembling hand was pressed sadly to his twinkling eyes.

Laren applauded slowly, a wry smile on her face. "A remarkable performance, Jacquel. You have missed your true calling."

"Oh no, he hasn't," countered Marthe. "Ah, me, what a degenerate, what a good-for-nothing, what a filthy *Lieger* you are, Jaca. If that doesn't convince the Terrans that the peasants and Haut Liege are genuine, nothing will." She threw herself into a pose equally as haughty as his. "I vow sir, your lack of serious sentiment quite dismays me. A lost case indeed."

"Just as long as you both remember you're playacting," warned her father. "Some of our people have been peasants so long, you may just convince them you're important. Heaven help the day either of you has a jot of power in Hathe."

All he got in answer was a laughing smile from Laren, and the disdainful silence of the wickedly affronted from Jaca. Marthe chose only to grin and hug her father, holding on to his strength as long as she could.

His arms closed hard around her, and the mood suddenly changed. "Be safe, my daughter. You are so brave, so like your mother. You and Bendin. We never knew what you would get up to next. So stubborn, so wild the pair of you. I can't lose you too." Then he released her, and almost pushed her away. "Go and do what you must, and know we will always be with you."

She could say nothing, could do no more than lift her hand in farewell and in thanks, but his face she printed into her heart before she turned and walked around the corner and down the corridor leading her back to the shuttle and duty, back to Hathe.

Seated on board the transporter shuttle a short while later, Jacquel thought over Sylvan an Castre's last words. The asn Castre twins. Always they had lived on the edge. Jacquel knew well the fire Marthe usually kept hidden, knew too the times when she could no longer contain it, how it would burst forth in a passionate storm of misplaced energy. How often would she be tested when they returned to captivity, tested to her limit? Bendin had been big and strong, a tall, bright flame of a man.

It hadn't saved him.

Then again, after four years of rigid discipline, Marthe held herself in check rather better than had her younger self. As for the young Bendin! Jacquel grinned suddenly, remembering the one stolen, off-planet visit they had made together. Their conduct would not, he recalled, have commended them to their elders.

"What's so funny?" said Marthe, suddenly breaking into his thoughts.

"You were asleep a moment ago."

"No, just dream gazing. How long do you think it will be till we sit in a modern transporter again?"

"Five months of course, more or less." Though he knew her thoughts were of a more philosophical nature, Jacquel deliberately chose to answer the literal question. It was safer. Fortunately, Marthe chose to follow his lead, chatting instead of family trivia. The serious discussions had already taken place and no more was really needed than a short briefing once they landed, to bring them up to date with events since their departure.

For Marthe, disembarking shortly afterwards and once more assuming her dull peasant robes, it was as if she had returned from a dream. What did those clean, white corridors, those soft clothes of that colony in the sky have to do with this, the real world. A world of dirt, rough fabrics, harsh voices and the heavy boots of the conquerors.

First on their schedule was a meeting with the sector commander, Gof deln Crantz. Marthe had heard much of the bravery and resourcefulness of this man but had never before met him, as she had always worked under direct orders from the Council. What a surprise, then, to find herself confronted by a small, balding, cheery little man, most decidedly running to fat—a man she had seen on previous assignments to the Citadel scurrying along with supplies from the townspeople for the Terrans.

"Old Raphe!"

"Yes, old Raphe, as I am known. Affectionately, I hope." It was a beautifully cultured voice, quite at odds with the body of its owner and totally unlike the hoarse, crackly tones of the little carrier that she was used to hearing.

"My apologies, sir. I did not mean any disrespect," she said in hasty confusion.

"That's quite all right, my dear. Only a few of the permanent planetary staff know of my disguise—a very useful one for moving about the settlement, as you can imagine, though not exactly one to lend me dignity," and he gave a short chortle at his own expense.

He fixed them with a stern look that brought Marthe to stiff attention. "To proceed. We haven't been able to ascertain the nature of the major's illness, but a girl was ordered to clean his apartments by tomorrow morning so we must conclude that he could be returning to active duty any time after that. Both of you, in the meantime, have had a session with the guards." He waved his hand at the vidscreen. "Neither was particularly civilized, if you wish to complain at a later date, but your covers are still intact. We also have a new type of communicator for you, hopefully undetectable this time. So far, they haven't identified any of the others who were caught with the wrist patches. The major was only particular in his identification of you, des Trurain. An interesting point. Could it be that our opponent is a man of his emotions? A rare attribute among the Terrans."

He broke off to ponder the idea, ignoring them for quite some minutes.

"Where was I?" he said suddenly. "Yes, your communicators. Here you are." He handed over two, thin slivers of translucent material. "Fit them behind the left ear, into the cleft. They surely won't look there. Now you are ready to go. Asn Castre will leave first, with des Trurain to follow. In case anything happens, we don't want any connection to be found between you. Off you go, my girl, and good luck."

"Thank you, sir. I shall do my best." She turned to squeeze Jaca's hand lightly, before passing out of the room into the hands of her guide. She nervously squelched a wish that Jaca could have walked out with her, together one last time, for who knew how long. It was for the cause. Remember that.

Jacquel was about to follow when he was detained by the touch of a hand on his sleeve.

"A word with you first, des Trurain."

"Sir?" A surprised Jacquel turned back to face the suddenly serious little man.

"Agent asn Castre. We haven't let it be known that she has been instructed to cooperate with the Terrans and, in consequence, she is likely to meet with a great deal of hostility from our people. Can she cope with it?"

"Of course she can. Sir," he added belatedly.

"Loyalty—a truly venerable virtue." murmured Deln Crantz, "It's fact I require, young man."

Jacquel stood silent. What could he say? He took time to consider … what? His little Mimi, the lifelong friend and more, and agent asn Castre, the resistance operative. He took a deep breath and hoped his voice sounded surer than he felt.

"She's strong enough, sir. Deep, though, and it will hurt her greatly. Still, she has as much chance of coping as any other, as long as you don't expect her to take it in silence. She's as likely to rip into any stupid enough to sneer as she is to bow down meekly." He paused, thinking hard. How could he make this man understand Mimi? He didn't understand her, not all the time. "I have never quite figured out how she works. I've seen her hold herself under the most rigid control despite gross provocation, yet at other times a mere slight will send her off. I think, sir, all we can hope is that her control will last as long as necessary. Remember, she has endured much from the Terrans these last years, yet hasn't once lost hold of her temper while on a mission." He looked at the man, challenging him to disagree.

"Thank you, des Trurain. You have been very helpful. You may go now." The senior man seemed to lose all interest in him and turned in his chair to confront the far wall.

Silently, Jaca let himself out. Had he just damned or praised Marthe? By the Pillars, let him have helped her. She was going to need it.

CHAPTER NINE

The black waves receded in great, gulping ebbs as Hamon gingerly opened one eye. A blur of antiseptic whiteness greeted him—sterile and unexpected. He panicked and scurried back to the nothingness within, then opened his eyes again in a confused rat-a-tat of blinks. Slowly, recognition of his surroundings filtered through. The medic wards. How in hell had he come to be here? There was something about Ferdo, but what else? He tried to rise, only to fall heavily back as the tides crashed in again and set him adrift on warm, gentle currents of forgetfulness. Come, sink into oblivion.

Can't, mustn't, the voice within nagged. Why not? *Because, because,* came the insensate reply. No, he raged. Much easier to lie back and submit to the blankness.

Persistently, valiantly, the niggling inner voice pushed forward again and again, clawing at the breaches of his retreat. *A girl. There was a girl somewhere.* Just over those grey walls which kept him safe from the world. Her hands clung, white knuckles clenching tight, as slowly, slowly, someone dragged her inexorably down into whatever dread mire lurked on the far side. Damn them all to oblivion, he knew he had to follow the girl, catch hold of her and keep her dangling above the mire—not safe, but not engulfed either.

Back, back, he cursed to the kind darkness. Piece by piece, consciousness returned. One eye stayed open. The second joined it as he fixed on a notch in the far wall, a break from the perfect smoothness that trapped him. One point, one focus on reality. Grimly, he stared at it, determined to use that tiny notch as his key to awareness and, the stars help him, to responsibility.

It began to return. The enemy woman, so proud, so distant. The room. The screams … and the awful void of her face at the end.

Marthe—his *daemon* and his redeemer. *This time, Hamon, you've really done it. Your world or hers,* came the jeering, laughing voice.

A new voice intruded, real and solid with humanity. He could only welcome it.

"Major Radcliff. You've finally woken. How are you feeling?"

He opened both eyes, aware of a niggling pain in the base of his head, and saw a crisp white uniform and a kind, competent face. "Nurse Trenwyth?" he said, remembering a friendly, reserved woman from the early weeks of planetary acclimatization.

"That's right. Pleased to see your memory's not affected. What about the rest of you?"

He thought for a bit, reviewing what he could feel of the lump that passed for his body. "I feel a bit woozy and my head hurts. Nothing too serious," he finally decided, then attempted a smile. "Do you know what happened to me? How long have I been here?"

"The second question is easy. About five days. As to the first, we can't say for sure. There's no sign of any physical damage in your neuroscans. The doctor's current best guess is that some overwhelming emotional stress caused your brain to … well … shut down. You've been in a comatose state ever since."

He scowled at her, thoroughly insulted. "Stress isn't exactly a stranger to any inhabitant of Earth."

"Maybe so, Major. Perhaps you've been under an extra strain lately. Something certainly sent you into overload. You look much better now, though, and we should have you out of here by tomorrow.

"Tomorrow! After five days, my desk must be spilling over. I can't afford more time off. Another couple of hours at most. I have work to do, nurse."

It seemed that long experience had taught Nurse Trenwyth the value of a soothing, white lie. "You may be right, Major. Why not get some sleep now, and I'll send you in a bite to eat shortly?"

Smiling in reassurance—as if at a recalcitrant child, he thought gruffly—she made a small adjustment to the couch temperature then turned and left, leaving Hamon alone with his decidedly ruffled pride.

Hamon Radcliff, First Union son of Representative Radcliff and Administrator MacDiarmid, succumbs to 'overwhelming emotional stress'? That fool woman, he fumed, conveniently forgetting his swirling thoughts on waking. Stars, let me out of this bed and I'll show her. There must be a hundred and one things waiting me. First up, that damn native girl needs sorting out.

He grimly forced all thoughts to the contrary to a deep, dark recess where they were no danger to him. Should he let it be said that Major Radcliff was losing his touch, could no longer cope—even, the stars forbid, be sent home?

Home, to his father's scorn. Or, more unbearable still, home to add one more sorrow to all those that so cruelly sapped the youth from his mother's face. She had an intolerable load already, inhuman decisions which must be made each and every day until she had become but a grey shell of the loving woman of his childhood. No, he would not be the one to increase her burden.

He felt himself drifting. Just imagine his mother in that splendid house of the an Castres, free of her responsibilities and able to enjoy the light, the air and the music. What would she have been? Her grace, the beauty of his childhood still there, still alive in her face rather than buried deep by the lines that dug in, deeper and deeper each time he saw her

Even that picture was a lie, though; the house, that whole amazing city of his memory, was false—a dream world built on a nightmare of slavery and bleak drudgery, if what the peasants said was true. Fact or fiction? Only Marthe asn Castre could tell him. Marthe, who had been suffering the Pillars knew what for five days—and again the crashing pain gripped his temples.

He had put her through a session. He was no better than Johne's men.

Yes, but you made sure she lived.

This time, instead of drifting back into oblivion, he fought against it, struggling to a sitting position as he cursed in the blackest words he knew in every Alliance tongue. It was one of the few useful skills he had learned in his years of gypsying, he reflected cynically. The only other skill he had acquired of any use to him had been an ability to disregard injury or weakness—a necessity in some of the places he had visited. He called on it now to lift his body from the bed, denying the racking pain that squeezed his head, his body, every part of him. It wasn't real. There was no physical damage. That's what the nurse had said.

It felt damned real. He had to hold onto the side of the bed until the room finally agreed to stop rolling around him. Ignoring every warning from his abused body and head, he walked slowly across the room and out. He had to leave. He forced himself to keep walking.

From the look on Ferdo's face, he must look as bad as he felt.

"Hamon, what in hell are you doing up? Have you looked at yourself lately?"

"I'm fine, Ferdo. Don't fuss." Yet he sank gratefully enough into the offered chair, quelling further solicitude with a black look. "Five days wasted. What have I missed and what's the talk."

"You've missed nothing and the only talk going around is that you needed a rest after the hours you've put in lately. By the look of you, it was pretty accurate. Either that or you've been on an almighty bender."

"Something like," Hamon conceded, forcing a grin through the waves of pain. "But enough of me. I need to know what happened to that native girl we questioned?"

"She was sent back to the cells. Reports are she's had a session with the guards, but nothing came of it. The medicos tell me that coma she fell into is normal for Hathians. Their eyes glaze over, and any further treatment is a complete waste of time." His brow creased and he shook his head. "Why Johne persists in using sessions on prisoners is beyond me—unless it's to give those thugs of his a bit of a thrill. Go ask the guard on duty if you want to know more; but not now," he added hastily, as Hamon began struggling to his feet.

"No time. I have to get to the bottom of that girl urgently, and I've already lost five days."

"You're not fit. Stay a bit longer."

He left Ferdo protesting to thin air.

Marthe was woken by the clash of the outer door then her own cell door shot across.

"Up, girl. Major Radcliff wants you," from the surly guard was her sole warning before the tall figure of the Terran officer briefly glanced in and snapped at the guard to bring her to his quarters. Then there was only the major's rigidly held back, striding a few paces in front of her.

He's in pain, was her second thought. He should still be in bed, she decided next, watching his stilted gait and the tautly held head as she was hurried on behind him by the guards. Her professional eye analyzed her memory of that brief glimpse of his face: the pallor, the harsh darkness of the hollowed eyes. What could have caused them? For an instant she recalled a distraught man clutching her at the end of that session, but dismissed the memory almost as quickly as she shoved away the strange sense of worry it brought her. She was still in a puzzle when they arrived at his rooms.

"That's all. You may leave the prisoner with me," the major growled in a tone even harsher than usual. The guard obeyed only too quickly, clearly recognizing this was no place to linger.

"Now, girl. You've had five days' reprieve while I've been otherwise occupied. No more stupid prevarication from you. Take off that hood and let me see if you are as much a liar as ever."

"Sit down before you fall down," came her equally sharp retort. "Even in prison the guards gossip, and you shouldn't be out of the medical wards yet.

He gasped in anger, pulling his shoulders up stiffly as if to deny her claim. "They gossip too much."

Hamon had spoken too loudly, far too loudly for the hammers banging in his head. He winced, and hated the sign of his weakness, even if it did get him what he wanted. The girl threw back her hood, revealing the hair he had once thought so beautiful but now could only dimly notice. She took his arm and led him to the nearest cube chair, forcing him gently down.

"Major, you're not well. I can help you, but for now you must sit still. When did you last eat?"

He shook his head carefully. "Not sure."

She disappeared, causing a momentary worry. Hamon had just begun to struggle to his feet when she returned, carrying a bowl of hot broth.

"Shh, lie back. I'd only gone to fetch a snack. You have my word I will not leave. Please, Hamon, lie down."

Some part of him marked her first use of his name and liked it. The rest of him was beyond caring. She soothed the hair back from his brow, slowly easing him down, before offering the broth spoonful by careful spoonful.

He eyed her suspiciously, too conscious of the closeness of her yielding body as she cradled him to her shoulder. For a few moments more, he held back. This was Marthe asn Castre, his enemy and the woman he had dreamed of for so long. But none of that mattered now. With a silent sigh, he relaxed, allowing his throbbing head to find solace in the peace of her cushioning arms.

"Your head's on fire isn't it?" she whispered softly, seeming to know what loud sounds did to his jangled nerve ends. "Do you remember much of the last few days?"

"Not much," he admitted. "I woke this morning for the first time."

"Yes, and left the wards rather sooner than you should have. Do you never admit mortality? No, don't answer, just drink up." She leaned over to place a kiss on his forehead.

It seemed that a reverse had occurred, and at the touch of her chaste lips a part of him wanted to reach up and grind her mouth under his to assert his ward ship over her. But later, he again shrugged, as he let himself slip into deep and dreamless sleep.

For a long time Marthe sat there, at peace in a way she had not dreamed possible as she sheltered in her arms this strong and arrogant man. In repose, the stern face was softened, a smile lurking about the thin mouth; but it was offset by the dark shadows under the eyes, the gauntness of the high cheekbones and the pale, shocked skin. The doctor in her could not be silenced. A stress coma, she would have said. If he'd been under her care, she wouldn't have brought him to consciousness so soon. But, then, what else could be expected from primitive Terran hacks.

After eons, his hazel eyes opened lazily and looked upwards. Entranced, she returned his searching gaze, all thought of purpose, duty, role, fleeing out the windows of space, and saw—something. A commitment. The linking of that part of each, unencumbered by loyalty or tribe, unique to them.

"Truce," she heard or felt. She nodded dazedly. Then drowned in the warm lips reaching up to enfold hers.

In the following weeks, Marthe barely recognized the person wearing her voice and body. The truce of that strange evening persisted, as if both had agreed to call 'time out' in their battle of wills, had sealed with that overwhelming kiss some mutual pledge. Hamon made no apology for what he had put her through—he couldn't, both of them knew that—but it was there in his care of her and in the secure isolation he created for her, free of other Terrans. The weeks became a time of exploring what little each of them was able to offer openly. Marthe was still Hamon's prisoner, as was Jacquel; and she guessed, from the secret transmissions she received from Jaca, that her friend's treatment remained very different from her own.

It troubled her less than it should. If she tried to change Jaca's conditions, she would put at risk her own cover, and by distracting Hamon, she stopped him inflicting worse damage on her friend. Dubious arguments that surfaced any time guilt struck. Instead, she filed the matter of Jacquel as *business pending* and gave herself to daydream days wrapped in the fragile bubble of a growing enchantment with her Terran captor. For now, it was only Hamon and Marthe. Anything else she refused entry.

Together, they explored this world of hers. She showed him all the gaunt wonder of the upland plateau's grasslands, etched in clashing beauty under a full moon. First, the bright iridescence of the primary, Dromorne. Then, on one memorable night, there was the rarely seen, translucent glow of the smaller Mathe. They sampled music, and the simple delight of sharing a meal, then afterwards, a kiss and, one night, almost, there was more.

But not yet. For all that this man made her sing in a way she had never known before, she was not yet ready to let him take her fully. If her masquerade were to succeed, it would be inevitable—or so she told herself, knowing it for a half truth. She had come to want this man, this Terran, as she had never wanted a man before. Yet for now, she held onto this one thing, the inner hold of self, this one part of herself that she still owned.

It didn't fool him. By now he knew her, waited for the first, upward tilt of the outer corner of her mouth before she suddenly relaxed into laughter, gloried in her acceptance of him, knowing that she could be one with his thoughts in a way he had never till now found. Certainly not in the entanglements of his family, or the grappling, mercenary place-seeking necessary among his friends as he grew up. It was the search for such understanding that had first driven him to leave Earth. He had roamed the galaxy, acquiring qualifications in various Alliance universities, or dipping into the less exalted schools of the docks, the factories and the ships that happened upon his erratic passage, ever searching but never finding.

Now the loneliness could be banished. In this woman of his enemy, he had found his other half, though had not yet made her his own ... maybe never could. Too much lay between them.

There was no time to change that. This was only an interlude, temporary as were all such. One inevitable day, reality shoved itself back into their life. Hamon was called to his colonel's office and in short, chilling sentences, his commanding officer destroyed any hopes that Hamon might hold to the contrary.

"Have you made any progress at all," the Colonel finished in an exasperated tone.

There was a worrying threat implicit in the words. Both men knew the mantle of Hamon's Earthside connections limited Johne's authority over his subordinate. The Colonel resented it with all the bitterness of the also-ran, and right now Hamon dared not forget it. Within that protective mantle, he could keep Marthe safe, but only if he could furnish a reason.

And then there was duty, never to be long forgotten. Who was he to put the only chance at joy he might ever find ahead of the lives of millions of his fellow Terrans?

He did not answer his commander immediately. For days he'd been arguing with himself. Now, he used all those arguments he'd been turning over in his head, all the for and againsts, trying to find what would work best. He began to talk.

He could yet disarm her, he said. Trick her into revealing what she knew, as he had first proposed. Since then, he'd learnt even more of the toughness and courage she tried to hide and was convinced no other method would work. He'd tried harsher methods on des Trurain, the other Hathian Lieger, to no effect, and he had no reason to believe that Marthe asn Castre would react any differently.

"What about the other men who were caught wearing patches?" the Colonel asked at the end, having heard him out in a discouraging silence.

"We've nothing on them. Des Trurain was the only one to appear in our pre-conquest records. The rest have been given routine interrogation and are being held pending further developments.

"Are they a security risk?"

Hamon had to shake his head.

"Is there any point in holding them for longer?"

"No."

"You can't keep them in custody if you want to gain the trust of the asn Castre woman. Especially if they are her confederates, as you claim," pointed out the Colonel. "Put it out that you can find no case to answer and release them back to the Citadel workforce. Under full surveillance, of course. As for des Trurain, bring the two Liegers together. If they're in collusion, something should happen."

Hamon nodded, giving no sign of his inner dismay, and knowing it had nothing to do with duty or his plans to break open the peasants' secrets. He did not want Jacquel des Trurain anywhere near Marthe. *We would have married.*' The words rang in his brain, a constant companion to all his encounters with the Hathian man.

There was a nasty smile on Johne's face at his junior's reticence. "You could always release des Trurain to house arrest in one of the guest quarters. See what happens if he has the freedom to mingle with the girl in company."

"Not a good idea, sir," was all Hamon could come up with.

The colonel eased back in his chair, one hand fingering the badge of his rank pinned to the hat placed on one side of the desk. He surveyed Hamon, standing to attention before him. "The girl—is she your mistress yet?"

Hamon felt his body go rigid. "That is none of your business, sir."

"That's where you're wrong, Major. I want this girl broken. You can continue with your scheme, but I expect you to give it your fullest attention—and that means the use of *all* your considerable talents."

Hamon could almost smell the stink of degradation. Not that he didn't want Marthe, and in exactly the way Johne implied. He needed very badly to explore her body as he had begun to explore her mind; but he had hoped to do it in their own time, needed her to come to him of her own free will.

Time had just run out.

Marthe welcomed him home that night with a friendly smile, and anything else she felt at the shadow she saw in his eyes locked tightly down. He was exceptionally tender with her as they lay together for hours, bringing her to delight with the treasures gleaned from his eclectic education and with the caresses of his hands and lips and body.

And almost she would have let him love her, if she had not recognized in his careful embraces the end of their idyll. His hands traced her body as if trying to imprint her shape on his mind, as if she were some fragile memory to be stored away in the protective tissue paper of his deepest heart. It was an ending. Tomorrow would see the start of the ugly game they must play. For this one, last evening, Marthe would remain herself.

CHAPTER TEN

Hamon felt the tension brimming from Marthe. They were locked together in the shielded cab of an all-terrain rover driving towards the irradiated and abandoned capital city of the Haut Liege and forced by the small space inside the vehicle to sit close together. He could feel the rigid tautness of her body and, with just a slight turning of his head, could see the tight set of her jaw. More was hidden by the shrouding of the outer mantle she wore today, a finer version of the peasant's concealing robe.

"Would you rather we hadn't come?"

"No, no." She spoke too quickly. "I haven't been back here since the day of the fall, that's all."

"If it's the radiation you're worried about, don't. We have full hazard level shielding in this thing, and I brought our best protective hazbubble with us. Or is something else bothering you? You're acting like a cat facing a large dog. Unsure whether to run or stand."

"Nonsense, I'm fine. It's only that I haven't been down this road since the day your people landed. When I walked out of town that day, I never expected to be able to return." Under the fall of her sleeves he saw her hands twisting into knots. A sudden tilt of chin as if she swallowed, yet her voice held firm as she added in explanation,

"The Council had given plenty of warnings they were going to put the field in place to make sure your people couldn't touch the City. The peasants all knew to get out if they wanted to survive." More twisting of hands. "What's a cat anyway?"

"A small Terran animal, once kept as a pet, and don't bite my head off." He leaned over to draw her close, only partly in reassurance.

He'd known The City might distress her, but he also knew her well enough now to be aware of the steel beneath her gentle exterior. So why this barely held, tightly coiling of nerves? So different from his entrancing companion of the last weeks. The memory of those weeks shunted his guilt burden up a notch and it was high enough already.

Those weeks had been a precious gift of time. Ephemeral, yes, but during them she had allowed him glimpses of the woman he remembered from that long ago visit to Hathe. The woman he had fallen in love with. Her courage and grace he knew; her delicious sense of fun had been a rare bonus.

All that was now banished, and it was back to work after the holiday. He had known to expect it as soon as Johne had issued his ultimatum, but that didn't make the change any easier to bear. At the same time, and despite hating himself for it, his professional side couldn't stop puzzling over her reaction to this place. The grief he had expected, but why the fear?

Sensing his curiosity, Marthe attempted to quell her growing sense of doom. She fixed her gaze on the passing scenery, taking care not to look ahead at the white spires, the dreadful emptiness of the once great city now filled only with a sprawling scramble of shrubs and trees marked with signs of the radiation protecting the capital city of the vanished Hathians from its enemies—or, rather, the machine readings of radiation the Terrans thought protected the City. What would happen if they discovered the deadly levels registering on their equipment were as false as everything else they thought they knew about Hathe's people—that the signals, the burnt traces of exposure on the plant life, the deadly readings from the small animals that still haunted the area were all a fabrication, a vast blanket of deceptive camouflage blasting out from the resistance's planet-wide network of transmitters? The Terrans had no idea of the level of technology available to the Hathians and had nothing in their own techno arsenal to detect it.

They would remain in ignorance only as long as she could keep her secrets from this man beside her, this man she feared she might be falling in love with. The man who brought her now to the one place that could break her resolution.

The City; home for her and all her family and friends. So secure and safe, we thought—teeming with the life of the metropolis and housing Hathe's government. It had been a place of bureaucracy and individuals—such individuals! But she must not remember them, for they had children: sons and daughters who had died in the last battle, children and grandchildren now hiding on Mathe, or eking out a perilous existence planetside, their very lives threatened if any hint of the startling truth should be leaked to the Terrans. The faces of people long gone crowded in on her.

No, don't think of them. Look to the side. See the beautiful Pathan tree, the long leaves still swooping in gentle cascade to the ground, so wonderful as shade for picnics.

"The Pathan trees, they used to be lovely at this time of year," she said too brightly, as she strove to break the echoing silence.

He looked over. "Those drooping ones? They still are, despite the burn scars. Particularly the one up on that small rise." He was startled to catch a glimpse of a tear, quickly flicked away as she moved back a strand of hair. "You know it well, I daresay." he said casually, hating himself.

She nodded. "It was a favorite spot for lovers."

She takes swift revenge, he thought savagely.

"Bendin and I used to spy on them as kids." A half sobbing laugh accompanied this, then silence.

"I wonder if your people, wherever they are, also remember it."

"My people?"

"The Haut Liege. I don't suppose you have any idea where they had planned to go?"

"No, no." She stumbled over the words. "Somewhere far away, waiting for the day you decide to leave, I presume. When the urgonium runs out."

"Oh, we don't plan to leave. Earth is so overcrowded that the empty spaces of this planet are as valuable as your mineral wealth."

He saw her shock despite her swift attempt to hide it. "You can't mean to stay forever?"

"Why not? The peasants wouldn't know the difference. Serfs to Terrans or Hathians, what does it matter?"

He watched her closely. The slight signs of her face betrayed to him the struggle within. Then the conflict was over, and she turned, her entrancing smile on her face.

"You are so right, they wouldn't. Although it's a shame that my people should have to live out their lives in exile, there's no doubt they are quite comfortable wherever they have fled. They certainly took enough with them to have no need to return." She laughed in brittle denial. "Now, what would you like me to show you first? For this is still my city, however angry I may have been at my father."

She snuggled in against his broad shoulder and Hamon knew a huge sense of loss. The holiday was truly over. The beautifully charming Marthe he would have but that was all, she had just declared. The real woman he had glimpsed these past days belonged to those unknown others who held her loyalty and, of a sudden a fierce, personal hate for his foes seized him, never fully to leave him again. I, too, have my duties, he reminded himself grimly, retreating into the refuge of cold professionalism.

"Your city for now, my little enchantress." He lowered his voice, using a tone he'd never thought to use with her, smooth and heavy with a slick seductiveness. It was the cynical voice of countless seedy bars in space station layovers. "What would I like to see first? Let me see. I have seen already your government buildings, your libraries, museums and the public rooms of your home. What could compare with those?" He planted a slight kiss on her brow, lingering to nibble at her ear. True to her role, she moved slightly in her seat to ease his attentions … but not too much, he noted.

So the reserved Marthe had not been totally buried.

"You're right, you have seen our best, but the remainder is still very impressive."

"No. Give me no poor imitations. Let's go instead for a contrast. The peasants' quarters, that's what I shall see," and his treacherous hand moved quietly around her shoulder to caress, oh so casually, one round breast.

He had surprised her. She gasped and made to pull away, but he had trapped her too well, and kept her firmly in place with his elbow as his hand wandered where it willed.

She glanced briefly at his face and, for an instant, he dared to hope his own Marthe had returned. But no. Her resolve held, and he watched as she abandoned herself to the purely physical pleasure roused by his attentions, turning slightly to accommodate his exploring fingers as they folded back her veiling wrap and lifting her head to display the long, sensual line of her neck. Stars, she's becoming more Terran than me, he thought in despair, before returning to his role in this inhuman game of theirs.

Switching the controls to automatic, he devoted himself fully to her, the piled-up experiences of years of dalliance coming to his rescue. Nuzzling one, delicate ear, he whispered softly, "After the peasant's quarters, where next? The kitchens, the garbage disposal plant?" His voice dropped a fraction lower. "Your bedroom?" His mouth engulfed hers and, to his disgust, a tantalizing softening answered his probing tongue.

Beneath her melting exterior, Marthe's mind was cold steel. Mathe be praised for the obviousness of his practiced technique, she thought, as she deliberately lost herself in the physical sensations he alone could rouse in her. It was so much easier to sink into pleasure than face the haunted streets of her home. He pulled up outside a house, one familiar to them both. It was the house of the picture in his apartment, the home of the an Castre family, her home. It was a huge effort, but still she held her cover, merely lifting an eyebrow at his choice of destination as he activated a hazbubble around them and helped her out of the cab. That look was all she could manage. She was beyond speaking. So many memories, tearing and clawing at her. Too many, bringing her too near the point where the final strands of her control would be torn away and she must be lost. She, and all the hopes of the people of Hathe.

It was recognition of Radcliff's deliberate attempts to manipulate her emotions that saved her. So obviously designed to either crack open her silence or seduce her into lowering her defenses, they instead fortified her protective shell. This was business, nothing more. Radcliff's cynical use of his ability to manipulate and pleasure a woman freed her to seek her own refuge, to hide in the waves of physical desire set off by the expert caresses of this man who wore the body of her Hamon. She could hide her face in his cheek and refuse to see the ghosts calling her: Bendin, staring reproachfully, as she had last seen him on his death slab—white as powdered chalk and old, oh so old.

No, don't look. Explore instead this delightfully sexy man, feel the tingles as his expert hand releases your body from its useless coverings. Close your eyes and sink into his kiss as he carries you up the stair, pass a flippant remark to hear the sound of his voice drowning out Maman as she tells you not to race into her drawing room.

Up the next flight. Within the hazbubble, her near naked body flushed as it pressed against his welcoming chest; but even the resulting cascade of sensation could not protect her as they entered her old room, her graduation sash still hanging in pride of place over her couch and a hologram of Bendin, Maman and Father on a nearby table.

Momentarily, she fumbled, reaching out with barely shaking hand to crash the hologram to the floor.

"This couch is far too small," she murmured, desperate to be out of this room. "The guest suite down the hall is so much better."

"We won't need much room," he countered, seeing the minuscule signs that told of the near shattering of her defenses. "Come here," and he pulled her down beside him. He checked the bubble, enlarging the protective field, and then, in slow enjoyment, removed her last layers. As she did for him, in far too expert a fashion for the woman he knew her to be or thought her to be. But no, that way lay insanity. He had to believe the Marthe he held in his arms was an act only—even if she seemed as expert as he at this, he thought, cursing silently but never letting slip his sultry mask.

"And now, my love, shall we see if we cannot make the stars sing?"

The words were hackneyed but Hamon felt anything but. He rolled on top of her and stroked a hand down her exquisite length. She was so beautiful. His palm shaped each breast and reached up to cradle her head as his lips sought hers. The Terran Major was fading and Hamon emerged, fighting for ascendancy. He had waited so long for this. He flexed his hips and strove not to notice her shy flinching. Slowly, slowly, he entered her.

Then he looked down and saw her face. Suddenly, the wrongness overwhelmed him. This was not who he was, not who they were. He pulled back hard.

"No, don't do this. Stop acting, Marthe, not here, not between us." She stared back at him, her eyes hooded. "Please, if in nothing else, give me your trust in this. Let me love you, the real you," he pleaded.

But she knew too well the danger of that gentle path. She teetered already on the brink of telling him all her secrets, of giving way to the temptation of his body, and of the man she was discovering him to be. No, she mustn't. Planting a brittle, come hither smile on her face, she looked straight up at him and forced a sultry smile onto her lips. "Hamon Radcliff! After such a masterly seduction, am I now to be left in need?"

It was a mistake. A red haze of fury and pain roared through Hamon and he trapped her in a vicious clench, bringing into play all the seasoned muscles of his street brawling days. "Just remember you chose this." Then he thrust into her with all the force of his pent-up need.

It was short, brutal, and he supposed there was some kind of satisfaction in it. At the end, he collapsed in a disgusted, angry heap upon her.

After that first, smothered shriek, that first panic at his assault, she fell silent, but he could feel her shock. After a time, he looked up and saw her face. It was blank, the owner long flown. Guilt seized him and the only refuge he could find was anger.

"Stop that!" he shouted, shaking her with unfriendly hands. "You come back from wherever it is you go. Don't you dare play the victim when you know damn well you've won here today." He caught her face, forcing her to look at him. "What else did you expect to happen when you decided to play gutter politics?"

God help those bastards who forced you into this if I ever get my hands on them. Deep in some previously unknown place of his heart, a veil of tears fell.

Marthe could not answer him, hidden so far within herself that she didn't know if she could return. Why, oh why could he not have continued with the game, spared her the vicious honesty of that final, degrading assault? He had taken everything from her, right down to that inner vestige of pride that had kept her going so long, and now he had the gall to tell her she had won. Hah! Won what?

Gingerly, she eased herself from under him and off to the far end of the couch, aware only that her one remaining hope of salvation lay in her duty. This man truly owned her. All she could do now was to exact some kind of price in exchange.

No. That was too easy a label for what had happened here. *Be honest with yourself at least.* What really smeared her soul, left her empty and lost, was the truth his words laid bare. She had chosen to use him, used the sheer physical pleasure he brought her to hide from the dangers of this place, all the while knowing what he felt for her and what they could have been to each other. All Hamon had done was give form to the ugliness of the game they must play. Now, she had to find a way to survive it.

Slowly, cautiously, she pulled her clothes on, ignoring the grating tenderness between her thighs.

"Where to next?"

She meant her voice to sound cool and controlled, but it came out high and shaky. "The peasants' quarters, was it not? They're down below, well away from our own rooms."

Hamon jerked up onto an elbow, ignoring his nakedness and her refusal to look directly at him. "So, you still refuse to give in. What do you owe these people, these peasants you claim to despise? By all the stars, they barely speak the same language as you!"

"I owe them no loyalty, as well you know; but I owe your people even less. The peasants merely turned on us after we had succored them for years. But you and your kind? You killed, conquered and drove my people away, and now you've finally turned me into a peasant too. Four years of loneliness, falsely smiling at scum and what for? Nothing. In a few minutes, you destroyed everything I had left. Any particle of self-worth I had left is gone."

Her words were bringing her back to life, the awakening of her anger echoing in her rising voice. Disgusted, she turned away, only to be hauled back by his rough hands on her shoulders.

"Don't feed me those razzing lies. Your own people forced you into this situation. It was they who raped you as surely as I, and yet still you protect them."

"My people left four years ago. I would have gone too, but for my damnable temper."

"Temper, yes, you little hellcat, but I don't believe the rest of it. Your people are close by, this peasant society of yours is a complete fabrication, and you are in league with some underground group. That's the truth of it. Isn't it? … Isn't it?" he slammed at her again.

The devastation of shock fled under the storm of rage that swamped her. She flung his hands off and lifted up her head, staring down her nose at him.

"Don't you dare touch me like that again."

"I'll touch you however I like, and don't you forget it." He grabbed her, one hand possessively surrounding her as the other pushed her chin farther up for his kiss. Tenderness had no part in it. She managed to rake his face with one long fingernail. He gasped, throwing her off to dab at the red beads springing to life on his cheek.

"If you have sated your appetite, shall we go?" she demanded angrily.

"There seems little point staying longer. Hysterical outbursts after sex hold little appeal for me. Especially when the woman knew exactly what she was doing beforehand," was his mocking reply as that cold mask of his again slipped into place, that rigidly non-expressive face he could assume far too readily. He rose to dress, pulling on his clothes in short, jerky moves as if desperate to leave this place, then grasped her arm and bowed her out of her once dear room.

The hateful mask remained in place all day, further feeding her rage. She gave herself to it, acting the Haut Liege to the hilt with flashing eyes and proudly held head—more than enough to convince an observer less astute than Hamon. Through the kitchens she led him, barely deigning to notice such mundane objects as cookers, food preservers and storeroom. Holding her nose carefully, she picked her way through the cellars and through a doorway to a small, dark room, pointing to rows of crude benches, a few, poor wooden shelves and a store cupboard.

"The peasants' quarters, kitchen staff only. Household and outdoor staff lived farther down the garden."

Thank God they had anticipated such a search, she thought, and had taken time to turn the decanting rooms of the wine cellars into these horrid barracks amidst the turmoil of those desperate weeks before the Terrans landed. "You cannot wish to see more. It's too reminiscent of your Citadel, a place even you must wish to escape."

Hamon was silent beside her. Her words were so callous, yet he knew her to be sensitive and compassionate. Or did he? Everything she said rang so false, yet today she'd given him proof enough.

He said little on the trip back, brooding on the day. All except a few, violent moments which he refused to revisit. That night, he undressed in wordless challenge before her then lay on the sleeper.

The cover on the other side was folded back and he looked at her, waiting her reply.

Marthe accepted. Standing tall and straight, she slowly peeled off her robe under his unchanging stare then climbed in beside him. Despite all her will, she was unable to stop a shuddering flinch as his hands first found her. He let her go abruptly, then lifted her chin with one gentle finger and turned to show her a face of solemn grief.

"I won't apologize or ask your forgiveness. I don't know if I ever can, but this I promise. Never again will I bring what divides us into our bed. Here, in this one place, there is only you and me. On this, I give you my word." Then he gathered her close and with no more than a short "Good night" curled into her to sleep.

It was some time before Marthe could relax enough to join him in slumber, and she woke in the morning to find him already gone. The only lingering trace of his presence, a faint scent on the headrest.

Hamon had left her early and driven to visit the prison wing, hoping against hope to find the clue to his dilemma in his other Haute Liege detainee, the inimitable Jacquel des Trurain. The man had been—no, still was—a close friend to Marthe and must be able to help him. If only Hamon could set aside the anger that always overcame him at the sight of that insolent, jeering face.

But today was to be no different from all the days before.

"Ah, Major. Good morning. To what do I owe this … pleasure? A spot of the old physical hijinks again. What joy!"

Hamon could already feel his resolve faltering and his face stiffening. "I merely came to find out what you could tell me about a certain, mutual acquaintance of ours."

"Oh, and who might that be? My estimable jailer? I can certainly claim a close acquaintance with him." Des Trurain winced, shifting uneasily on the crude bench. "You will forgive me for not rising, but my head will not seem to withstand such exertion. Obviously due to the lack of mineral water—always most efficacious for the maintenance of mental clarity."

Hamon could not suppress a taunting grin at his enemy's plight. Des Trurain so rarely showed any sign of the effects of his imprisonment.

"I was referring to my current mistress, Marthe asn Castre. You were once very close, I understand."

It was with even more satisfaction that he observed the icy stillness of his prisoner.

"The Lady asn Castre's twin brother was an old and dear friend, until slaughtered in a battle you no doubt remember," des Trurain said bitterly. Then his face changed, and he gazed brightly back at Hamon. "Now I have it. Always thought I'd seen your face somewhere. You're that Terran Bendin threw out one night, and damn me if that wasn't over a girl too. Remember it well now. The boys thought it a great laugh—the backward Terran mooning over a Hathian lady."

"The very one," agreed Hamon amicably.

"So now you have the boot on the other foot and can take your petty revenge," snarled des Trurain "but, God help me, did you have to take it out on her too?" He launched himself viciously at Hamon.

Taken by surprise, Hamon was knocked to the ground. For an instant, shock gave the Hathian the advantage. Then Hamon shook his head, ignored a pummeling of blows and brought into play a few of the more devious tricks needed by any Terran school boy—a childhood education for which his attacker had no parallel. In a satisfyingly short time, the younger man was locked back onto the bench by a strong force field, glaring in sullen rage at his captor.

"So your dishonorable tricks win again," he sneered.

"Dishonorable, maybe. It's a word that became too expensive on Earth many decades ago. Effective: now that is a word we can afford. If you've finished with these petty distractions, can we get back to the matter in hand? My current mistress. Even you must see what a delicate matter it is to introduce a native into Terran society, especially a Lieger. She told me once that you two might have married if things hadn't changed, so what better person to consult regarding her loyalty to her … benefactor, shall we say?"

"Are you sleeping with her?"

For once the insolence was gone, Radcliff noted with satisfaction. Never had he disliked anyone so much. "But of course. Though I must admit that her lack of … experience … came as a surprise. What happened, des Trurain? Your famous expertise with the ladies desert you?"

"The Lady asn Castre is a close family friend—far too close for the kind of casual dalliance you Terrans seem to revel in; and don't tell me she jumped easily into your bed. Not Mimi."

"Mimi, how apt. Though I somehow feel she has outgrown it," mused Hamon, fingering the scar on his cheek. He watched as the Hathian's eyes tracked his fingers, and his face suddenly froze into stark whiteness. "I admit to needing to use a little persuasion, but the girl is shaping up well now. I always feel a strong hand does wonders for a woman—lets her know where she stands right from the start. Don't you agree?"

"Oh, you bastard."

Radcliff stared at the slumped figure in front of him. His first triumph over the taunting Hathian and all he could feel was shame. He'd learnt, what? Nothing he hadn't known already. The luscious Marthe of yesterday was but a counterfeit of a more precious woman, held for the briefest of interludes. A woman driven by loyalties Hamon could only guess at, but which had led him to assault her in the most despicable way. He needed to leave this cell. Now. As soon as he got rid of the other reason for his visit. Curtly, he spat out the words forced on him.

"You are to be shifted today. My commander feels I exaggerate the threat you pose and has ordered that you be released to civilian quarters. Oh, don't worry. You're not done with me. My own men will guard you. Not perhaps as sadistic as the Colonel's, but far more efficient."

There was no change in the man on the bench. Hamon made himself finish the message.

"He's also ordered that you be allowed to meet with Marthe periodically. You will therefore be dining with us tomorrow night."

Hamon refused to stay to see des Trurain's reaction to that. He left quickly, ignoring the globule of spit landing on the wall as the door slid behind him.

CHAPTER ELEVEN

His temper hadn't improved by the following evening. It was a quarter of an hour past the time set and there was still no sign of des Trurain. That Marthe was in full Haut Liege mode didn't help. Especially as he suspected this was to be the Marthe he must live with from now on.

"My dear Hamon, Jaca has never been early for any but the most important of occasions in his whole life."

"Don't 'dear Hamon' me, you little…" A tap at the door luckily stopped him finishing, and was followed by the entrance of his disturbing guest—looking, thought Hamon in disgust, far too impressive in a cast-off suit that had never become Hamon's larger body. It was only by remembering the image of des Trurain slumped in defeat that he could maintain any semblance of polite courtesy.

"Major, my dear Marthe, so pleasant to see you both. Marthe, positively enticing. Imprisonment becomes you, it seems."

It was going to be a long evening. Hamon wished just once he could best this man verbally and left it to Marthe to answer.

"Thank you, Jaca, love. And you also have been restored to your elegant self since I last saw you." She linked her arm with his and drew him over to the bar. "I trust you will behave in a more civilized fashion tonight, though. You were positively barbaric the other day."

"My deepest apologies, little Madame. I, of all people, had no right to reproach you. Bye the bye, Major, I don't suppose you're bisexual?"

Marthe had seen Jacquel in one of his outrageous moods too often to consider attempting to curb him. There was no point. He now chose to gaze pensively at his shocked host. "No, I didn't think so. Such a pity. My new quarters are an improvement, for which I thank you, but not luxurious, no, and I do so like my comforts."

He didn't get the retaliation he was no doubt hoping for from Radcliff, but he did at least elicit a bubble of laughter from her. It almost vanquished the grief lurking inside her. "Jaca, you're the most impossible man I know. Don't you agree, Hamon, darling?"

"Quite," was all she got from their victim.

"Oh, dear, the poor boy is a bit put out," she murmured dolefully to her exquisite compatriot. "Hamon, my deepest, most sincere apologies. It's such an age since I was last with a friend of my own. But we mustn't be so cliquey, Jaca darling, or my sweet Hamon becomes horribly offended. I think he must be an only child," she added in a loud stage whisper as she waved Jacquel to a seat near her own.

"Not at all," said Hamon, stiffly. "I have three half-brothers and one half-sister, to my knowledge, though little contact with my father's second-union children, I do admit."

"Half brothers and sisters? I don't believe I've ever seen a half person. Which half, pray tell? The head and shoulders, two arms and one leg? Marthe, how curious these Terrans are."

"I think perhaps he means they have only one parent in common," explained Marthe delicately. "Family relationships appear not to be as important on Earth as they are to our people."

"Oh?" Jacquel sank into thought a moment, gazing into his glass. "How very sad, one might say. On the other hand, it occurs to me that if family hadn't been so important to Hathians, I wouldn't be stuck here."

"Whatever do you mean?"

She put enough awe into her voice to make any worthwhile listener believe she was hearing the story for the first time. Not that she thought for a minute she was fooling Hamon—only the other Terrans behind the vids she knew watched them always in the public rooms of the apartment.

"If you hadn't been so caught up in that ridiculous squabble with your father," said Jacquel, a hint of a pout appearing on his ever-mobile face, "you might have noticed that you were not the only *enfant terrible* around at the time.

"Jaca!" And then she gave a peal of laughter. "You don't mean... Jessamie did hint that you were involved, but I never thought you could be so stupid."

"Well, I was, but did you ever meet the girl?" He lifted his eyes in exasperation.

"Yes. She was a mite dull, shall we say, but very attractive."

"Maybe, but looks aren't everything, as my dear Mama was forever telling me. This time, she was right. How a brilliant man like an Starne could father someone like Emeline defies all laws of genetic probability. She actually insisted on wearing the brightest of puce one evening when she knew I would be in yellow. The clash. It's too awful to remember. And damn me if I could persuade her to change. After that, what hope was there of long-term felicity with such a woman?" he demanded.

Hamon scowled. It was long past time he ended this nonsense. "Are you perhaps referring to the ex-President's daughter, Emeline asn Starne," he asked, half wondering whether either Hathian remembered his presence, while the other half of him was bleakly aware he was watching a performance. One aimed at him.

"I'm sorry, how rude of us, Hamon," said Marthe. "It was the most delicious scandal. Emeline was made pregnant, by a man unknown, and there was no marriage. He left her high and dry. Not at all the way to treat the Lady Emeline asn Starne. A prude, and simple with it, she was. It was put about that the man responsible had used *ungentlemanly* means with her."

"Rubbish," put in des Trurain promptly. "The girl practically dragged me off. How was I to know her parents had forgotten a vital part of her education. Falling pregnant after a brief flirtation. Downright irresponsible, if you ask me."

"Jaca, you knew what a numbskull she was. You should've thought to check."

"Didn't get a chance," he replied plaintively. "To cap it all off, daddy dear made sure I was left here in penitential misery, while that hussy rocketed off with the rest to luxury." He sighed, slumping back in his seat. "I don't suppose you could spare me a small ship, Major. Just big enough to get me to a civilized planet." A disbelieving snort answered that one. "It was worth a try. I did manage to make it into the control room of one of your ships once."

Hamon was immediately alert. "How, may I ask?" he said in a voice that would leave his tormentors in no doubt it was an order.

"Nothing devious," replied des Trurain airily. "I knocked one of your boys on the head and borrowed his uniform and ID card. At the time, I'd been assigned to a crew of cleaners at the port, and that got me through the handprint check at the gate. It was all very neatly done, I thought."

"What happened?"

"I couldn't make head nor tail of your controls, that's what happened. Beaten at first base."

A delighted chuckle from Marthe broke the rising tension between him and his enemy. "Jaca, you never told me that story before. What did you do next?"

"Got out of there as quickly as I could, dressed the soldier again and left the base, fast. A more pathetic end to an adventure I've yet to hear."

"Are you still keen to leave the planet?" Hamon made sure des Trurain could read the underlying threat in his voice and watched carefully the subtle signs of tension in the other man.

"Of course. Nothing left here for me."

"So where were you planning to go? To rejoin your people?"

The man had recovered enough to greet that with a mirthful hoot. "Devil a bit, no. Even if I had the slightest notion where the pack of them went, I'm the last one they'd welcome. No, I rather thought Etelia would do nicely. Not quite as civilized as Hathe was, but damn close, and no family scruples there."

"How would you earn your keep?"

"What, work?" demanded the shocked dandy. "Lord, no. Not a pathetic refugee such as myself. There must be plenty of Etelians only too happy to work out their guilt feelings on my support.

"In return for services rendered, I presume."

"Naturally," was the unabashed reply. "It's what I'm known for, after all. Isn't that so, little Mimi," and he leaned over and passed a light hand over her neck.

"So you tell me," said Marthe softly, smiling far too freely at her *friend* for Hamon's liking.

"Dinner is ready," he snapped, and glared a warning to any who cared to notice.

Marthe chose to ignore it and to further rile Hamon by linking arms with Jaca as they passed out to the balcony. "Any news?" she murmured quietly.

"Later," Jacquel said, a nod warning her of Radcliff's angry scrutiny.

The dinner passed in mixed enjoyment. She and Jacquel seized the chance to exact a shadow of the revenge due them from the Terrans, indulging freely in a biting raillery that succeeded only in deepening the black frown on Hamon's face. Raw from the turmoil of emotion the past days had dealt her, Marthe couldn't resist ensuring that her disturbing captor should know some of the humiliation her people had had to endure so long. Or was it retribution for the uneasy questions he set her? She missed her place in the latest verbal exchange, lost suddenly in uncertainty, then angrily scolded herself. Her loyalty was to her own people, not this Terran. For a brief interlude, she would be purely Hathian. With Jaca leading in his most outrageous of guises, they were both insultingly free with their wit, seemingly entrenched in an arrogant assumption of superiority. The Haut Liege in truth.

At the end of the meal, Marthe leaned back.

"What bliss. Beautiful food, two handsome men for company and conversation of charm and wit as accompaniment. Now, if you will excuse me a moment, a lady claims the privilege of a chance to freshen up. Why don't you move through to the sitting area and I'll fetch the drinks? Just please behave yourselves for five minutes." She leaned over to kiss both, gently stroking Jacquel behind his ear and pressing on the inconspicuous patch hidden there.

"The Major and I are used to quiet, little tete-a-tetes," Jacquel assured her with a touch of malice as the two men rose.

As he'd expected, Jacquel was soon rewarded for his jibe. Marthe had barely left when Radcliff's control broke.

"The lady's mine, des Trurain," he said angrily, "and I do not suffer rivals lightly."

"Mmm," Jacquel replied, distracted by Marthe's incoming report.

"So you can keep your razzing paws off her."

"Uh-huh."

"There's to be a special check on the Delta refinery at ten a.m. Can you tell Central to advise the surveillance teams there to keep low for a couple of hours?" came Marthe's message in his ear.

"Hmm now," said Jacquel to Radcliff, scratching his ear and pressing an affirmative to Marthe. "That could be difficult. We've been close friends for so long."

"Not that close and don't try to claim otherwise."

"A number of the staff appear to be on edge. Radcliff is not the only one beginning to suspect us. The following is a list of those needing attention." She paused to let him code for record then gave the names.

"Did you hear me, des Trurain?"

"Yes. Sorry. You were telling me of your masterly rights. The archaic notions of Terrans never cease to amaze me. Marthe must be quite intrigued by the novelty of it all. But, then, she has no alternative. How fortunate you are to have such a hold on a beautiful woman."

"I take it you've never needed one?" Radcliff sat back, as if to stop himself from treating Jacquel as he yearned to, crushing his Hathian rival from existence.

Jacquel assumed an air of blithe ignorance. "I admit I haven't but, to be fair, my background is rather more advantageous than yours."

"Oh?" Now Radcliff did lean forward in threat.

"Advanced technology, refined civilization, and so forth," explained Jacquel, deliberately blind to the insolent nature of his remarks. It was perhaps fortunate that Marthe chose to return at that moment. *"At least there was no blood,"* he signed to her.

To Hamon, it seemed an interminable time must pass before he could bid good night to his unwanted guest. His relief was so deep that he barely noticed the few, quick words whispered by Marthe to the man. It was only later that night that the message registered: "Daily at cockcrow's height."

Suddenly he was startlingly awake. An assignation? Slowly he turned to look at the sleeping face beside him. Could this be his proof, he wondered? Cockcrow's height. A place? But no, des Trurain was too closely guarded. Cockcrow? A time of course. But height? Dawn was when cocks crowed, or used to on old Earth. But this was Hathe. No cocks crowed here, or ever had. A pre-arranged code?

It had to be for some time in the morning. But how? She wore no device that could possibly be a transmitter. That patch of hers, he'd thought that to be one, but she wore no such patch now. His memory played over those few, precious minutes that told him he was right. Then less pleasant scenes intruded and he drove himself back to the original problem.

Some sort of contact had been arranged and all he could do now was watch and wait. With a grim smile, he nestled in to Marthe, safe in the innocence of sleep. Her only response to his restless tossing: to lay one, bronzed arm across the security of his broad chest. It soothed him and, holding one hand over hers, he settled into his own, guilty rest. Even then, his barely submerged consciousness kept plotting, planning, working out strategies to keep this precious beauty of his under his treacherous eye.

Marthe soon felt the effect of his night of planning. He began to insist on staying with her, for most of every day. All but those rare times when his duties could not be avoided. She might almost have fooled herself that she was back in the early weeks of bliss. But it wasn't the same. This was the game, the ugly masquerade that she had known would come and in which she, too, had a part to play.

Sophisticated, witty and charming. The elegant mistress. She was all of these and more, and it was the most trying of all the missions she had undertaken. She could see in his eyes his hatred of her falseness but knew he dared not challenge her. Not when duty must keep her beside him, probing at her defenses, seeking always to discover who and what lay behind her facade.

Yet surprisingly, there was still a place for courtship on the knife-edge they walked. Slowly, tenderly, in their nights together he made reparation for that first, cruel taking. She learned to let him hold her, then a kiss. Then, one inevitable night she turned to him and could have laughed at the relief he could not hide, had she not been as hungry for completion as he. On this night, he made love to her with all his heart and body, bringing to it none of his duty but all of the gentleness he usually hid so well.

It was a start. A promise for the days and weeks to come that, together, their passion could release the joy that was within them. That there would be many more nights like this.

Something more she learned that night too. The reason behind what she had always known, why this gift between them was so necessary if they were to tolerate the sham of ugliness of the roles they must play. Denied words, it was only in the language of lips and hands and bodies that there could be any truth between them—just as there had been in the brutal honesty of that afternoon in her bedroom in the City. She loved this man, she was forced to recognize, and he loved her. Inconvenient, inexplicable, but true. Without those fleeting instants when there was only Hamon and Marthe, she could not have endured the hateful game that was so necessary to her people. Nor, she knew, could he. Did she love him enough to sacrifice the lives of so many of her own? No. That was no true love. Love did not ask that, could not survive such evil.

So the game continued. She could never forget why she was here, in the heart of the enemy's fortress, that she had no right to abandon her people to their misery.

She always kept to the agreed time for passing messages to Jacquel—cockcrow height, as the locals labeled the daily parade of the Terrans. Even Hamon was forced to join in the ritual gathering of the military, to hear the Commander deliver his report and pass on the orders of the day. During his absence, Marthe was confined to their quarters, but with recorders in every room, she knew Hamon had no qualms at leaving her. According to the playback he would view later, she merely used the time to indulge in an obscure and complicated beauty routine.

Such trust in the infallibility of Terran technology amused Marthe as she signaled Central one morning to intercept the surveillance of her quarters.

"*His suspicion of me is growing,*" she reported to her father and Jacquel.

"Has he not been so all along?"

"Yes, but something in particular happened about a month ago that's made him even more suspicious; and no, I don't know what it was. He barely leaves my side now, and last week my entire wardrobe was replaced with Terran-made clothing. About which all I can say is, if they are the latest Terran fashions, as Hamon claims, then Earth is sadly lacking in design skills.

I told Hamon what I thought of them, but he refused to return my own clothes and instead detailed a tech to change the styles to my liking. Even our food is untouched by Hathian hands. Terran standard rations only. He says he prefers them after so many years. It's all a decided nuisance. I should be able to keep broadcasting at this time, but if I have to change, Central will let you know," she added to Jacquel. "I'll do my best not to, though, as I know you are as closely watched as I am."

"Closely watched is an understatement," said Jacquel, frustration lacing his codes. "Radcliff's troops are as paranoid as their master.

Their interference is seriously limiting what I can do. We need something to keep them better occupied, some sort of diversion."

"Such as?" enquired the elder an Castre warily.

"It's time for the emergence of a certain, highly intriguing Hathian rogue into Terran society. I'm sure I could set enough tongues wagging to divert the attention of our captors," Jaca announced.

"I'm quite sure you could," coded Marthe dryly.

"The idea has merit," Dr an Castre conceded. "You may go ahead."

"What!" Marthe exploded. "Have two possible conspirators for the Terrans to wonder at? Why not just come right out and give them all the details of the resistance while you're at it?"

"Are you two such clumsy actors then? The Terrans will think nothing of the kind, except Radcliff who suspects you anyway. I take it that we can trust Jaca to treat the Terrans to some of the less restrained facets of his otherwise quite admirable personality?"

"Thank you, I think," replied that worthy.

"You said yourself, Marthe, that none can play the Haut Liege better than Jacquel." Marthe gritted her teeth at the chuckle from Jaca on hearing this. Did her father have to remember only her silliest comments? *"May I leave the introduction in your capable hands?"* added that venerable man, knowing the answer all the time.

"There is a reception next week for the outgoing comptroller. He will be invited," she promised.

Marthe began her campaign the next day. She had become friendly with a few of the Terran woman, using her inclusion in their gatherings as a chance to gather valuable information, but this day it was she who let slip an interesting morsel, the merest hint of Jacquel's name and exploits.

"How fascinating. Do tell us more." Jocelyn Harp from Ballistics was bored with Hathe and, in particular, the men in the Terran forces stationed there. Her large, sultry green eyes gazed avidly at Marthe and her over-ripe mouth gaped ever so slightly.

"Well, I can't say precisely. But from what I heard, via friends of friends…"

"Marthe! You cannot leave us in suspense. He sounds quite delicious," protested Helen Ravensbot, a dark-haired and lively woman from Stores.

"Memorable, was one term I heard bandied about," Marthe said, spinning out the word to its most intriguing fullness. "He's certainly fun to be with, but I never had the chance to find out more than that. My brother and he were very close and, on occasion, even Jacquel remembers he has scruples—though I must have been only the only woman he ever singled out for such an honor."

"I have to meet this paragon," exclaimed Mathilde Chong, slowly licking her lips and conveniently forgetting a hard-working partner in senior administration.

"Not much chance of that, I'm afraid. Our families expected Jacquel and I to marry one day—before your people arrived, that is. I was silly enough to let Hamon know and now he keeps Jacquel closely guarded, claiming he is a dangerous saboteur. He loathes Jacquel, I do know that, but if you ask me, it's nothing more than simple jealousy."

"That's infamous!"

"I agree, but what can I do. Hamon would completely misconstrue any attempt on my part to have Jacquel released. A pity. He could bring such cheer into our lives."

"It is rather bleak at present," sighed Jocelyn. "I can't remember when I last had a man who was *memorable*."

"Lucky you," retorted Mathilde. "You haven't got Hank snoring beside you every night."

"You know, ladies," said Helen, "we do need to add some life to our entertainments. I just happen to be in charge of next week's reception, and not even Major Radcliff can ignore an official invitation from the Commander to our Hathian guest."

They all laughed.

"Does Hamon need to be told?" queried Marthe, all innocent trepidation. "Surely the Commander has supreme authority over prisoners. As long as you ladies keep Jaca occupied, and well away from us for the night, I will manage Hamon."

"With pleasure," they chorused, laughing low and soft.

"Our invitations have arrived for the Comptroller's reception," announced Hamon at breakfast later that week.

"How nice of the establishment to notice my existence."

"The Commander's dinner still rankles?"

"Of course it does. Do you know what I did that evening?"

"Went to bed early with a reader?"

"Yes, if you must know."

"I did," he confirmed wryly. "A private dinner, my dear, is not a place for potential spies, whereas I doubt even your ingenuity could succeed in a crowded reception among the babble of nonsense that will be spouted. Plus your lady friends were quite insistent you should come. Jocelyn, in particular, was most persuasive."

He grinned smugly at the memory and her eyes flew to his in surprise.

For a split second Hamon was rewarded with a hint of pain, then to his disappointment the barriers clashed down again.

"The lady and the tramp. What a surprising mixture of bedfellows you indulge in."

"An excess of civility may pale, even on me," he explained carelessly, as if unaware of the hurtful effect of his words. Under his lowered lids, he watched for her reactions. "What had you planned for today?"

Following his lead, she talked of the new fashion catalogue Helen Ravensbot had promised to share with her, a light frippery that should have bored him silly, but he was studying her closely. He saw her shock, saw the stunned hurt she tried to hide.

"Are you sure you want to go? You look somewhat pale."

"I haven't been quite myself for the last few days," she replied uneasily. "Your Terran rations may not agree with me."

"I'll see what I can do to make them more acceptable. But now, I must be off." He rose to leave.

Lost in thought, she missed his backward glance. She hadn't been herself, now she mentioned it, and the possible causes interested him greatly.

They spent that afternoon together, and he wreathed her in such tenderness that she almost dismissed his words of the morning—till late that night, when they came haunting back. Could he truly be tiring of her? Did it matter?

She pushed the question angrily aside and began thinking instead of a design for a gown for the reception. It didn't suit her purpose to be abandoned just yet. Her mission was too crucial. If there were other matters at the heart of her anxiety, she refused to name them. Not out loud. Not yet. Not till she had to.

In one aspect at least, he wasn't tiring. A secret smile tickled her lips as she reviewed her own, private journey since her capture.

Enemies they may be, the barriers separating them ever present, but she had thought that in this one thing there was truth between them. Granted his lovemaking was more experienced than her own, but he had taught her so much; and might not the instinctive well of sensuality she'd discovered within her have taught him also. Surely such loving as theirs had to be unique, could not be merely another night or woman to him? And now there was another worry growing in her.

She twisted yet again, hunching her shoulders down. So she was only one among all his women. Yet a principal one at least, she would have said. No others shared his waking as well as his resting moments.

Cold comfort. She punched the headrest and threw herself down.

"If you've finished conquering your personal nemesis, do you think that both of us might get some sleep?" came an amused voice from beside her.

"God, are you even spying on me at night."

Hamon lifted his head suddenly at that and she felt his surprise. "Come here," he said gently, turning her so that his eyes looked straight into the deep shadows hiding her face. "It's personal, isn't it? My urbane mistress doesn't snap like a freighter's second mate. "

She'd blown it. But her voice rolled inexorably on. "Jocelyn Hart. Are you really sleeping with her?" The pinprick of tears roughened her voice.

"What's it to you if I am?" he teased gently, hopefully.

"I'm pregnant, that's what it is to me," she said, bursting away from him as his shocked arms released her.

"What!"

"I'm going to have a baby, mine and yours. A baby whose father is already looking elsewhere for his pleasure."

"I take it this news is less than welcome? You would have preferred another father for your child?"

She turned back then, to stare in consternation. "Oh, Jaca," she murmured as the light slowly dawned. "What the hell, you aren't interested anyway," she spat, suddenly feeling savage and with no pride. "The truth is, I want this baby more than I can say. It's mine and will know all the love I can give it—unlike its father." She burst into a fit of sobbing, cradled unseeingly in the arms she wanted more than anything else.

"What do you mean, exactly?"

"I mean that you're Terran and don't trust me; that I'm Hathian and your people destroyed mine. I mean my brother died fighting against you and now my people are out there somewhere instead of here at home. I mean, I'm having the enemy's baby and loving him," the sobs tore at her now, "only to find he's turned to another woman. I've sold my soul, to no end."

"I see," was the slow reply.

"You see!"

"Yes, I see. I see at last the real Marthe I knew existed, not the lovely shell I've had these past weeks. I see you human and hurting and, I'm sorry love, but that makes me so happy. It tells me you love me as much as I love you. In this one place we will have truth between us. I have never shared any other woman's bed since I found you that day in my rooms, and will never, as long as we are bound. I am so proud that it is you who will be my First Union partner and mother of my firstborn."

The voice was so infused with love that she couldn't ignore it. Silently and slowly, she turned, to be embraced in wordless joy as his body told hers the truth of his words.

Seemingly hours later, she lifted up her face from the warmth of his shoulder. "Hamon Radcliff, you fraud. That tough front of yours is only a cover."

"In some things, yes," he agreed, turning to nuzzle the dark waves of her hair, "but don't tell anyone, especially my superiors. Speaking of which, I'd better arrange to have our liaison recorded tomorrow. Which will cause quite some surprise."

"The ogre with two heads has finally caught you?"

"Something like that. Ferdo will be livid and will probably start plans for the dissolution feast, rather than the union one." The puzzlement on her face was plain. "We celebrate both ends of a relationship," he explained then smiled at her disbelief.

"Ending a marriage … that's strange enough, but to celebrate it. Ugh!"

"We no longer have marriage on Earth, so you can ease your conscience. Now, go to sleep, my little, mother-to-be. You need all the rest you can get."

"I'm only just over a month gone," she protested.

"A month. You mean..."

"Yes, I fell pregnant our first time together. I had other things on my mind at the time," she added in a piece of blatant diplomacy, "and forgot to turn on my contraceptive program. It wasn't until the next day that I thought to check my cycle and it was too late then. But what's done is done, as they say," and she snuggled farther down the welcoming line of his body.

Soon, a smile sweetly curving her lips, sleep claimed her. He could hear her soft breathing, even and untroubled, as he lay very still beside her, gazing into the blackness. A rarely known peace was on him as thoughts chased through him. For once, they had absolutely nothing to do with duty.

CHAPTER TWELVE

"Married," gasped the outraged face, the little eyes dwindling to crackled specks among the ballooning facial creases. "Married … to a Terran!"

"I do believe that was what I said," replied Sylvan an Castre. "My daughter has asked that I place her request for marriage before the appropriate body. I'm not sure if you quite fit that role, Trundain, but," regarding the puffed-up mass before him, "failing an alternative, I am left with the computer comptroller: you."

"Don't give me that fluff, Sylvan. This is much more than an ordinary marriage request and you know it. I'm calling a full Council meeting immediately. If your girl endangers the entire affair…"

A slight twinge of a cheek muscle was Sylvan's only response to the insult. Everything else he kept under tight control. "I rather think it unlikely," answered the statesman within the father. "If you will summon the Council, we can proceed to the chambers." Sylvan waited as Trundain spoke into a nearby communicator then passed with him in strained silence down the corridors and through the security blocks to the Council chambers deep under the surface of the moon Mathe, the heart of the government in exile of Hathe. In short time, they were joined by the eighteen other councilors, all confusedly questioning one another in barely muted tones. They saw the two of them already there and immediately demanded to know what was so urgent.

"Excuse the hasty summons," began Sylvan. "Trundain here has some concerns over my daughter's pending nuptials and has seen fit to foist them on you."

"Your daughter's wedding?" was the surprised comment from the closest councilor. "Congratulations … but what has it to do with us?"

"Isn't she on active duty?" came another puzzled voice.

"It would not be the first wedding via relay," Sylvan reminded them.

"Yes, but you and Trundain can manage that between you. Why drag us down here?"

"Just who might the lucky man be?" threw in one, particularly astute member. Sylvan glanced at the speaker, a dignified lady of middle years, her clear brow above the intelligent brown eyes containing a hint of a frown. The lady, an old acquaintance, caught his quickly suppressed frustration and smiled slightly.

"The gentleman in question is Major Hamon Radcliff of the Terran forces."

Abruptly, there was silence and, in the air, an undeniable wash of fear.

"Radcliff," breathed a voice uneasily. "I've heard of him. A particularly dangerous customer, they say." It was the head of the Terran information bureau speaking, his words deepening the dread he could see settling on the Council members. "Is he not her captor? Nor, I understand, has he been particularly considerate in his treatment of her? Why the change of heart?"

"The couple is to have a child. My daughter naturally wishes it to grow up with every security possible." The flat chill in his voice should have silenced any challengers, but not this time.

It was the astute Gilda again. "The people would honor the mother of such a child and ensure both are cared for always. There is no need for this kind of sacrifice."

Sylvan didn't miss the touch of irony in his old friend's voice. Gilda had always been too perceptive by half. "Both parents are desirous that the child should be born into a family unit. Its own family unit."

"You mean that the man's feelings have softened towards his captive?" said Gilda, yet again cutting to the core of the business.

"So I understand."

"And your daughter's feelings?" the harsh voice of Aaron deln James asked, another rather too awake to the undercurrents.

"She is desirous of the connection."

Trundain an Delsin glowered beside Sylvan, obviously deciding he had gone unnoticed quite long enough. "Desirous! The girl's madly in love with a Terran, from what I can tell, and God alone knows what she's whispered to him at night."

Not even that could break Sylvan's rigidly held self-control, though it came close. "She is open to full surveillance at all times and still retains a top-level security clearance. Her immediate superior is fully confident that Marthe is alive to the cost of any indiscretion."

"Are you telling us that a highly trained intelligence officer can be so easily gulled by a beautiful woman? Radcliff is known to have caused us a great deal of trouble in the past."

"No, he is not telling you that," said a cultured voice behind an Castre. Sylvan whirled in surprise.

"Gof! Gof deln Crantz. How good to see you."

"Yes, I can see that," said the little man, his beautiful voice clashing as always with his squat body and coarsely jovial face. "Ladies and gentlemen, you're worried about the security risk presented by Agent asn Castre's latest actions. Perfectly understandably, I assure you, and I share your worry, given that Major Radcliff is still suspicious of her background. But you must see that we can't pull her out now. It would only serve to confirm the man's suspicions and set off a planet-wide search for her—which we can ill afford at this crucial stage of our plans," he reminded them all. "However, I will confirm that Agent asn Castre has formed an emotional attachment to this man and does have some sympathy for the Terran plight."

A triumphant exclamation was silenced by an icy glare from the little man. "If I may be allowed to continue," he said, the look he cast about the table silencing any comment, even from this august body. "On the positive side, there are a number of advantages to be gained from the association. She is collecting valuable information on the social and military organization of the Terran headquarters, of a kind we had never hoped to be able to acquire. Further, by reinforcing the myth of the Haut Liege, Marthe has done much to lull suspicions among the ordinary Terrans.

Sylvan watched in amusement as Gof paced up and down the room, mesmerizing his august audience.

"Regarding Radcliff, I grant that he has not been so readily duped," he now said, in that entirely reasonable tone of his, "but his interest in Marthe has distracted him, enough that he has let his surveillance in other areas slip. Nevertheless, he's still wary of her, and of the whole Hathian situation. His people provide him with a comprehensive overview of the Terran position of a kind unmatched in the occupying forces, and he's only too aware of the Terrans vulnerability to attack by a resistance movement such as ours. Our hope is that marrying Agent asn Castre will lessen his anxiety. He knows that it will bind her to him and seems to even have hopes that he can change her loyalties."

"Which he would be right to, wouldn't he? How do we know she won't come to feel that her duty lies with the Terran cause?"

"You forget that her twin brother was killed in our cause," protested Sylvan, unable to keep silent. He felt Gilda's eye on him and dreaded to think what she saw in his face.

Gof deln Crantz saved him again, once more taking firm charge. "From discussions with Agent asn Castre, and from our own observations, it is clear that she has already thought through all the arguments you raise. She is also aware of the heavy losses we would suffer if she changed sides. She will not let that happen to her own people. It's unthinkable, to her as much as to any of us. Apart from which, her studies of the Terrans has led her to conclude that Earth is the architect of its own problems and only a shock such as we will give them can force them to face reality. The Terran cause has become, in effect, our cause," he finished with a wry smile.

Sylvan heard Gilda's sigh beside him. She knew Gof as well as he, and the last thing needed right now was one of his philosophical rambles.

"Time to end this?" she murmured to Sylvan. "Then you favor the marriage," she said in a firm voice to Gof.

"Exactly, yes." The small man nodded his head enthusiastically. Then one of his wickedly dangerous grins appeared. "After all, logic aside, do none of you remember when you were young, just married and your beautiful wife was expecting your first child? A very convenient absorption for our most dangerous enemy.

Sylvan would have liked to remind his so-called friend that this was his daughter they were talking about. Unfortunately, that wasn't possible. "So, can we vote on whether the computer comptroller should proceed with arranging for a transmission wedding?" he said and was thoroughly relieved to hear the muted agreement of his fellow councilors.

The vote was unanimous, if somewhat reluctant. Marthe had her permission to wed.

"It's all very well," said Trundain petulantly as the count was announced, "But how are you going to hold a wedding with the bridegroom knowing nothing of it?"

"Major Radcliff is familiar with our customs and is aware that the exchange of vows before two or more witnesses is a binding marriage, at least upon Marthe," replied Sylvan in the same, cool tone he had striven to maintain throughout. "He knows it would make her happy and has agreed to such a ceremony. He just won't be told quite all of the technical details."

Gilda rose abruptly and offered her arm to Sylvan. He took it gladly. She was one of the few people outside his family he truly trusted.

"That's all right then," she said to the throng. "Now if you'll all excuse me, I have a deal of business to attend to." She steered Sylvan out of the room, ignoring the rising chorus of disbelieving chatter behind them.

Once past the closed door and around the corner, she slowed and turned to him, looking at him anxiously. "How about a friendly ear for those troubles." Her free hand came down to pat his arm. "You can't tell me you support this marriage as much as you claim."

"We're off record?"

"Naturally."

"Then, no, of course I'm not happy. Would you be if your baby daughter were to marry such a man? He is ruthless, charming, and all too ready to use those charms to confirm his far too accurate guesses about the true nature of our society. His is the only department that regards the Haut Liege myth as a fabrication. Why? Because he and his people alone have taken the trouble to talk to our people." He made no effort to hide the strain he felt. "They've fooled some of our most trustworthy agents into letting slip enough details to hint at the existence of a resistance group. None of it definitive, but quite enough for a man like him. He's more than capable of putting it all together and making guesses far too accurate for our liking.

Gilda's hand tightened on his, a reassuring squeeze of fingers. Sylvan sighed, then continued. "So far, he doesn't seem to have any idea of the level of technology available to us, but what he has discovered has already made many projects significantly more difficult. Is it so strange, then, that I'm not happy for my daughter to bind herself to him?"

"No, not strange."

His own free hand came around to grasp hers roughly. He avoided her eyes and took a breath. "Yet some of what I've heard of the man … it's … there is much in him I could like, though I hate to admit it. He's never, as far as we know, indulged in torture, with the exception of his manhandling of Jacquel, but that was personal. More a case of boys fighting in the sandpit."

"Jealousy?"

"Without doubt," Sylvan said dryly, then swallowed, not sure if he could ever forgive the Terran for this next bit. "Then there's what he did to Marthe. The session he inflicted on her."

"Which resulted in *his* having some kind of breakdown," Gilda reminded him.

Sylvan nodded and thrust the memory back. He took another deep gulp of life-giving air, then plunged on. "We do know that he acts out of a genuine commitment to the survival of his own people, though much in him is revolted by the Terran role here. Despite his earlier actions, I have come to believe he truly cares for Marthe. I think that's real enough," he forced himself to say. He paced agitatedly up and back a step. "What a tangled mess it all is!"

"So, the two are in love? The matter seems to have been tiptoed around."

"Oh yes. Marthe assures me that she loves the man, and he loves her, despite everything that separates them. And you know, if circumstances had been different I do believe I would be pleased with the match. They are so damned alike!"

Marthe turned up a face kissed with happiness and Hamon knew a rare joy. He returned her smile—not as freely, not as openly. That was not in him yet, but he knew she saw his love and understood. It was the night of the Comptroller's reception, and he'd managed to pull her out of the crowd and into a small alcove, needing her to himself for a precious time. They were still visible to a few others, but right now he was too happy to be concerned about anyone who might be watching them. He pulled her close in to his body and held her contentedly, letting his gaze idly pass over the crowded main assembly room of the Citadel. It looked as though every single Terran who could be spared from duty was here tonight, all competing, all aiming to appear the most elegant, the most beautiful, the most stunning. They needn't have bothered. Right here in his arms was a woman who effortlessly beat them all and, for this moment in time, she was his alone.

He had taken particular care with his own dress tonight, needing to honor her beauty with a suitable escort. He usually avoided reminding the rest of the Terrans of his position and wealth back home, but tonight, to protect this woman, he deliberately wore the expensively tailored, dress uniform his father had insisted he bring with him instead of the standard issue one the rest of the men wore.

Suddenly, his idle survey of the rooms was shattered. A flash of astonished rage engulfed him as his gaze lit upon the only other man in the room dressed to rival him.

Des Trurain.

Young and exquisite—his civilian outfit a masterful example of discretion yet with a dash of recklessness—the man was holding forth to a captivated gaggle of ladies. No longer staid, duty-bound Terran personnel, but giggling and simpering in delight as they basked in the flattering wit of their new toy. On catching sight of Hamon and Marthe, the newcomer gallantly rid himself of all but the most intrepid of the ladies and hurried forward, a welcoming smile of pure mischief upon his finely wrought face.

"My dear Marthe," he exclaimed, bestowing a flamboyant embrace upon each of her welcoming hands, before standing back a pace in admiration. "Oh, yes," he breathed, "very charming. Quite one of your best efforts. That touch of gold: just the thing," he added, indicating the artless string of gold chain and pearls slipping in and out of her shining curls.

A sadness suddenly colored his voice. "That drop necklace. If only you had it still."

"Jaca, how dare you remind me of our present poverty," she chided, laughing. "What a pretty greeting, I must say. You've not even said hello to Hamon."

Hamon was still gripped by an icy fury but managed some kind of smile. Only Marthe appeared to notice any coldness.

"Major Radcliff. To be sure, my apologies." Jacquel extended the barest fingertip in greeting. "How are you this evening?"

"Fine, thank you. To what do we owe the pleasure of your company among us?"

"It is, isn't it?" agreed the other. "It seems your commander doesn't share your suspicions and has been moved to treat me as what I am, a poor wretch of a refugee. Thanks, that is, to the kind petitions of these ladies." He took a moment to embrace each of the three still surrounding him.

Hamon looked at the women and recognized defeat. He said something, anything, whatever it took to get him away from that place and remove Marthe to the safety of his own circle of friends. Once there, he was forced to act as if nothing was wrong—but only for a short time. As soon as a diplomatic interval had passed, he hustled Marthe into a quiet, very private corner where no one could see them. He backed her into the wall, his two arms a rigid prison and glared at her furiously.

"What in hell is he doing here?"

"How should I know?" she said, in a voice that sounded far too innocent to be real. "Though it is nice to see Jaca back in the kind of world where he belongs and out of that dreadful prison of yours."

"Nice? He was there for a reason. Who did you flash those sweet eyes at to get him released?"

"Me? A mere Hathian order affairs among Terrans?"

"That's another matter," he snapped grimly. "Just answer me, who did you get to do your work?"

"Why, no one. At least—"

"What?"

"I did happen to mention some of his exploits in passing to Jocelyn Hart and Helen Ravensbot."

"Stars, the two most lascivious women in the compound. You have been studying us well. Who else are you manipulating? Apart from me," he added bitterly.

She hadn't expected that. He saw it in the sudden darkening of her eyes.

"Do I compromise your position that much?"

So many questions hid behind her words, questions that mustn't be asked. Not while they played this game of deceit. Yet still the questions lurked, still he heard them, and cold sanity returned. Anger was the last thing needed right now. Not with the bond between them so fragile in its newness and fraught with pitfalls.

Then there was his duty. She had deliberately loosed des Trurain on Terran society. Why, he could not say but he must find out. Which he couldn't do unless both Hathians stayed under his surveillance.

He took a moment, breathing slowly, aware she watched him. Then he lowered his arms to release her and stepped back. The subject was closed and she nodded her understanding before he led her back to his friends, soon becoming as seemingly ensconced as they in their game of sticks, the bets voiced quietly, with one eye always on the Commander.

Des Trurain was a huge success, particularly with the ladies. His outrageous compliments brought a blush to the cheeks of the most duty bound professional, while his stories held the men enthralled. Try as he might, Hamon couldn't avoid hearing the buzz of gossip that followed him. His men dutifully reported everything he couldn't hear himself.

The Terrans listened with envy to the elaborately embellished tales of des Trurain's travels and of life on Hathe before the fall: the beautiful women, the luxury and ease the man still took largely for granted, the wealth there had been. He considered the stunning Marthe to be almost reduced to sackcloth and ashes. Lacking any decent baubles, he declared, when the woman was parading a load of jewelry worth at least thirty thousand credits. Wealthy as the Major was, even his pockets would have been strained by their purchase, in the Terran view.

Ah, to have been one of those fortunate few. Who cared if the peasants spat *Lieger* contemptuously? The scum could not even comprehend Terran society. The dazzle of that lost world of the Haut Liege must have swept in a blazing mystery far above them.

And fun! The sheer sense of the ridiculous as he teased and cavorted with this one and that. Drinking races with the Commander even. To the Terrans, locked into the tensions of the conqueror and bound long before that to the harsh necessities of survival on Earth, the Hathian breathed freedom itself. The Lady asn Castre also. No wonder Radcliff had spread that conspiracy rumor to keep her to himself. Any man there would have done the same.

With each report, Hamon's mood worsened.

Jacquel saw it happening but didn't let it stop him. By the end of the evening, just drunk enough to view his fellows through a forgiving haze but betrayed only by the increasingly outrageous nature of his remarks, he judged it time to make his peace with Marthe's glowering fiancé. She had terrible taste, but there was a baby to be considered … and anticipation of the delights yet to come that evening with the lusciously compliant Terran ladies quelled the green devils.

He made his way over to the pair. Slowly, it must be admitted. The lovely Jocelyn waylaid him to confirm their rendezvous and a number of the younger men stopped to remind him of promised adventures, but finally he did reach the objects of his voyaging.

"Des Trurain. Having a pleasant evening, I trust." The words were polite, but that was all Radcliff managed. There was nothing welcoming in his face and he clutched Marthe to his side as if terrified of misplacing her. Jacquel let his grin widen.

"Very much, thank you," he said. "I have now come to offer my congratulations on your forthcoming marriage. See, Marthe, I got it all out. Not quite cut."

"Not far off," she chuckled, "and we both thank you very much. Would you consent to be my chief witness?"

He caught the edge of seriousness in her voice and gave her a quiet nod before letting his jovial mask drop back. "Would I consent not to be?" And he planted a less than brotherly kiss upon her mouth, whispering as he did, "Thank you. I am honored."

"Marriage? What's the boy talking about?" harrumphed an elderly gentleman. "I thought you recorded the union a week ago?"

"An archaic notion we cling to on Hathe," explained Marthe sweetly. "The declaration of vows before six witnesses is considered a legal and binding marriage contract under our laws, even if it can't be entered into the computer. I just cannot be reconciled to your temporary unions. Not when a child is involved."

"Here, what does he mean *union recorded?*" demanded Jacquel, half joking, half sternly. "Is it that half person, half marriage thing again? Never heard anything so ridiculous," he harrumphed back at the older Terran. He made no attempt to lower his voice and a crowd began to gather. "Do you seriously think that a well brought up lady like Madame asn Castre would contemplate bearing a child without due sanction of marriage vows," Jacquel declaimed with all the pompous arrogance he could muster, before adding in a cheerful aside, "or at least, nearly well brought up. Do you remember that time you wandered into the Council chambers in nothing but your night shift?"

"Yes, at the age of five," she retorted. "Must you tell the whole world about it? And show some tolerance to these people. Most have never heard of marriage." This public exposition of her private affairs was a bit much and the look she gave him made that very clear.

'Get used to it,' said the careless shrug of his shoulders.

"Ooh, a wedding. Just like in the old fairy stories," exclaimed one particularly silly girl.

Standing beside Marthe, Hamon could feel the growing anger in her. He knew just how she felt, but then he'd had the benefit of an entire evening spent controlling his rage.

"Quite," he said, throwing an icy glance in the direction of the latest and stupidest sally. He turned to the Commander, requesting permission for the ceremony and a public reception to follow.

"It was to have been a small, private occasion, but des Trurain appears to have decided otherwise. I would also be honored, sir, if you would consent to act as one of my witnesses."

The Colonel nodded. Hamon raised his voice to announce the plans to all present then turned to Marthe with a suggestion that it was time to leave.

Marthe took one look at the harsh green of his eyes and hastily agreed. A tense silence blanketed them for all of two corridors. Then they reached a stretch of passage free of monitors. He grabbed her arm, lurching her to an ungainly halt. Then exploded.

"I hope the new wedding plans are more pleasing to you," he snapped, "but in future, talk to me directly, not through your lap dog."

She breathed in deeply, not daring to reply while anger shone so brightly in those eyes. Green, brilliant green and cold as emeralds. Her gaze dropped lest he read too plainly her own eyes.

But that he wouldn't tolerate. Wrenching her chin, he jerked her face upwards. "You did plan that farce together." he said, his face suddenly bitter and weary in defeat.

Letting go her arm, he turned to leave. His back kept the defiance of its straight rigidity, but he couldn't hide the faint slump of shoulders nor chase the grayness from the air. Even his hair, that great shock of wayward black, was as still as death, not a strand astray.

Desperately she clutched his arm, pulling at him to stop. "You're wrong, you know. Wrong."

"Am I?" The retreat continued.

"Yes. Don't go like this."

He wouldn't answer her this time. Racing after him, she swung on his arm again, dragging him to a standstill. "Hamon Radcliff, you will listen to me," she cried, driven by desperation. "I did not ask Jacquel to arrange a large wedding. I swear that on the spirit of my brother and mother."

"Rather a momentous oath," was all he said. Those eyes of his stared flatly at her, flawed and cloudy with betrayal.

"It's the truth. I knew that he thought a large wedding more suitable, but I didn't ask for anything this public. I swear it."

"And it never occurred to either of you that for the duration of this fairy tale extravaganza of yours, you will succeed in removing most of the staff of Earth's central headquarters from their posts?"

"That's ridiculous. What harm would it do anyway?"

"For one, your *beloved* peasants will be completely unguarded."

"Then throw them a party as well. They'll be too drunk to think of causing trouble. How do you think we managed the problem in the past? Threw them all in jail till we were finished?" she sneered back. Convincingly, she hoped, but hating the need to act. Did he even know that those few things she promised him were true, were real? She must lie about so much, but not when she gave her oath on it. It didn't change what she must do now, and her stomach crawled with self-disgust.

"So now the whole complex is crippled. Your military genius astounds me, Madame." There was no disembodied detachment now, his chin turning down in a stabbing thrust at her.

"You do still have soldiers, or had you planned to have them parading about the reception too? Stomp, stomp, stomp."

"Stop it," he suddenly cried out, driven to his limits. "This is our wedding we're talking about. Just once, can't you be honest. Or at least keep your lies away from our private life." Jerking out of her hold, he turned to leave yet again, but she was there, barring his way in an instant.

"Not yet," she said, goaded partly by guilt and partly by anger at his refusal to recognize where duty ended and Marthe began. "I had meant to spare you this, but you leave me no choice. Jaca's main reasons for tonight are known to me, but they are not shameful, as he thought your actions to be."

That stopped him, gave her the space she needed to continue.

"He was angry that a Terran should be so ignorant of the honor he gains by union with a Hathian lady that he failed to offer marriage. Then you do, but demand a hidden affair with the fewer Terrans who find out the better. Instead of which, Jacquel claims, all Earth should bow down and give thanks that a Hathian deigns to be joined with one from such a primitive, uneducated race. Yours! And I begin to think he may be right."

"You arrogant witch!"

"You, of all people, know I have every right to be. You were here before the invasion, you tell me, and saw Hathe at its brightest. You heard its poets, saw its monuments, stayed at the hub of its politics. Can you truly compare your Terran cesspool with that?"

"Yes, I can." he hissed. "I can compare an abundance of food with a chronic scarcity. A planet teeming with resources and practically empty of people, with one teeming with starving mouths. A few hundred years of minor challenges and stability to many thousands of years of tragedy, strife and effort. Your people act like brash youth faced with an elderly parent." He flung his arms wide in frustration, then shoved them back against the wall again, trapping her. "And how do you treat us, how do you treat the first home of humanity? You desert us. You leave us to fight for our very survival while you thoughtlessly carry on, reaping all the benefits of our early care."

"By the Pillars, not that great well of self-pity again. The time honored Terran scapegoat: we gave you life, you must help now! As if we didn't try. All the knowledge in the Alliance was going begging, if you had cared to look. The technology exists for Earth to manage its problems, but no, you had to do it on your own. The colonies weren't going to tell you how to run your affairs. And now look: your medicine is twenty years behind, energy forty years and communications fifty, and your social structure relies on absolute tyranny."

"You are too kind."

"Do you know the final irony. We never realized. Not one single Alliance planet ever guessed. The only thing you were good at was keeping a secret, and the result? Your planet is dying, mine is dead, and I am to be married in a quiet ceremony, just like our old funerals."

She had said too much, yet again; but it no longer mattered. Her voice as she finished was as flat as his had been earlier and she wouldn't meet his eyes. So this was defeat. She could feel him watching her but couldn't pretend any longer.

"Very well," he said, anger still in his voice. "The wedding shall be as grand as any of old Hathe."

"The wedding won't happen. How can it, after this?"

"It will," he said firmly, "for without it, you win." His hand caught her chin and steadily lifted her head to face him. Lines gouged the sides of his mouth and his eyes were as serious as she has seen them. "My child will know and respect its father, this I vow. Which means I can't let you go. The wedding will proceed. What's more, it will be celebrated with all the fanfare you could wish for. And afterwards, you'll be bound to me for life, as I will be bound to you.

"It doesn't bind you," she said dully.

His head went up at that, but his eyes never left hers, snapping with a brilliant fire. "Your sheer incomprehension astounds me sometimes. Of course it binds me. You're not getting a one-sided bargain." One hand dragged through the thatch of his hair as he stepped back, pacing brusquely as his hand pulled through the heavy strands in frustration. Then the hand dropped, and she saw acceptance and tired defeat in the grim lines of his mouth. When he spoke, it was in the formal language she knew too well as a politician's daughter. The language of distance and enmity.

"It would be best if we leave this for now and retire for the evening," he said. "May I have your pledge that you will go straight to our quarters?" He paused painfully. "I find that I would prefer to be elsewhere this night."

She could only nod, and walk away, conscious of a pair of eyes watching her all along that endless corridor. The corner released her. She took to her heels then, fleeing wordlessly to the sanctuary of his quarters, to their great big sleeper. And her tears.

CHAPTER THIRTEEN

It was to be a long and sleepless night, not helped at all by the demons of jealousy that asked, even now, just where he was sleeping. Please let it be on his own, she prayed. Why did the Council have to extract this payment? Was it so wrong to marry the enemy that even her wedding must serve as yet one more diversion for the gathering of information? Surely there was sufficient data on the Citadel already? In the end, she was forced to admit that, no, there was not. She finally drifted into sleep—light, unrewarding, and beset by grief-ridden images of an empty future.

In the morning, she was still left wanting. Hamon sent word that she should call a guard if she wished to go anywhere. He would be unable to leave his work until evening. Her face closed and blank, she asked only to be taken to Jacquel's quarters at midday.

It was a long morning, picking up and then discarding one task after another, her mind unable to concentrate on any but the one problem. Or person, rather. Where was he? Did the cold anger and disgust of his farewell still hold him in thrall? Had he relented? Or had it hardened into something else altogether, something that would kill all they had?

Even now, a shred of something held her back: honor, loyalty, she couldn't say. Whatever it was, it kept her from rushing to do as her instincts commanded: to lay all before him and once again be enfolded in his arms, all barriers down.

Then again, perhaps it was only that she knew, deep within, that to give way to treason would finally kill all they had. Without that strong and abiding love of the culture that gave him birth, his fierce drive to somehow save his world from the threatening holocaust, would she love him as deeply? She sensed not. Just as surely, she knew that it was the Marthe who cared for her people enough to sacrifice her own happiness that he loved, not the beautiful but shallow Lieger she strove so hard to appear.

It was with a heavy heart that she followed the guard later that day to see Jaca. The years of deception had taught her well, though, enough to ensure that not a sign of her inner turmoil broke through the elegant mask of her face as she greeted his two guests.

"Jocelyn, Helen, how delightful to see you both. I see my step-cousin has not taken long to avail himself of both surroundings and companions more suited to his graces." She gazed around at the familiar Hathian touches: subtle splashes of color, an exquisite statuette, softly glowing panels of a changing luminescence lightening the standard issue tint of the walls.

"Quite an improvement on my old quarters," grinned Jacquel, watching her take it in. "Dearest Jocelyn prevailed upon the Commander and my sweet Helen managed to procure these few odds and ends." Somehow, he managed to keep both women purring contentedly at him, she noticed as she took the seat opposite the trio. "But my dear," he added, turning back to her, "you look a trifle miffed. Radcliff still out of sorts with you?"

"You rather forced him into a corner."

"Did the man really think he could get away with depriving us of a party? What cruelty. Don't you agree, my pets?"

"Oh, completely," said Jocelyn, curling closer into his shoulder. "It sounds such fun, and it's far too long since we had any of that around here."

"Is the man ashamed to be marrying you?" demanded Jacquel.

"I think he was hoping it would be more intimate celebration," she replied, half apologetically. "I must admit I'd prefer a lovely, big party. A real wedding, like we used to have. Nevertheless, his reasons are honorable; and he was worried about the peasants if they're left unguarded. Terrans have so little experience in such matters."

Helen suddenly sat up. "I hadn't thought of that."

"It's no problem," said Jacquel, pulling her firmly back. "You throw a party for the whole town and they all get blind drunk. Works a treat every time."

"And if you're at all worried about trouble, you drug the food," added Marthe. "You forget, we've had to deal with them longer than you. The only consistent emotion they feel is hatred of the Haut Liege. So, we always put in place safeguards. You Terrans are too easy on them."

"Enough of the peasants," cried Jacquel with a dismissive wave. "Surely Radcliff isn't still insisting on a small affair?"

"No, but he does claim that you and I engineered last night between us. To think all I wanted was a proper Hathian wedding, just like Maman and Father's. Do you remember when Laren got married, Jaca? My sister," she explained to the two women. "You should have seen her. She was so beautiful. Everyone came, almost five hundred at the ceremony and a thousand afterwards. There was dancing and music, poetry and games for three days after. It took us weeks to recover. And Hamon gets in a huff over a mere few hundred and one night of revelry!"

She sat down next to the Terran ladies, a picture of complete misery. Jaca's dancing eyes applauded her performance. Fortunately, both Terran women were too busy comforting her to notice her fellow conspirator's barely stifled laughter.

"You leave Radcliff to me," said Helen firmly. "I'll have a word with him."

"Oh, would you?" She let her most brilliant smile bloom on her face.

"Don't you worry any longer. I know just how you feel; men can be so heartless sometimes."

In a remarkably short time Hamon was made to feel the result of Marthe's interventions, accosted by both of her new Terran allies with stern speeches of reproach. They made worse an already pounding head, the price of a sleepless night of soul searching. He was cruel and uncompromising, the women told him. If he continued in this vein, he would soon be the laughing stock of the Terran forces. He listened carefully to all they had to say, the hammering in his head mercifully preventing him taking in more than a quarter of their tirade. Promising faithfully to make all well with his grievously wronged fiancée, he at last escaped to the sanctuary of a dark, dark room.

But that was no good. All he could do there was think. Think of the duplicity, and the sheer talent for manipulation he was pitted against. And comprehending at last the threat, could feel only admiration, more than any other emotion—more, even, than he feared it.

Cursing himself, he stalked out of the room, bent on losing himself in work—work so absorbing that it excluded all else. He took the side door to his office, unable at present to cope with the idle greetings of his staff. The pristine black slab of his desk welcomed him to its safe harbor, and it was with an eager hand that he activated his screen. The very ordinariness of the shimmering surface materializing, then settling into cream and black report mode, settled some of his inner turmoil and he sat back to study the incoming data.

He had neglected his desk these last weeks, and the number of reports waiting him had clocked up steadily. *What have I been thinking?* he berated himself grimly. Then, as he read, a growing sense of disquiet overtook him.

There were too many paradoxes, too many unexplained happenings. Most disturbing of all to his cynically analytical mind, too much was going well. The output of the mines had imperceptibly increased over the months, to a level that almost matched requirements. Food shortages were infrequent, resulting in fewer riots and military rampages through the streets by frustrated soldiers, and the number of peasants reporting sick had declined in the work camps but not, he noticed, in the village clusters next to military posts such as this.

Some kind of climax was pending, he would lay money on it. But what, and when?

He had always suspected that the peasantry was involved. Now in the data scrolling down his screen he saw it confirmed. What were they planning, and why? Did they plan to take over the planet for themselves? Or maybe they were still helping their old masters, the mysteriously vanished off-world Liegers? Or was it as he first thought? Was the whole set-up here a complete fake?

His fingers tapped a drumbeat on the desktop. The first possibility wasn't a serious worry. The peasants were too poorly equipped to be anything but a minor nuisance. The second, that they were helping hidden Liegers, was more serious but still not a major worry. The Hathians had fought bravely enough trying to keep the Terrans off planet during the invasion, but ultimately their lack of experience had beaten them. Nor would he expect the peasants to be eager to come to the aid of a class they claimed to hate so much.

As for the third option … now that was a different matter altogether.

"The problem is," he said, talking it over with Ferdo later, "if the social system here wasn't the strict, class driven one we've been led to believe existed, then what was it? Are all those peasants a complete fabrication and this whole place carrying out one colossal masquerade?"

"Impossible," declared his friend. "A whole planet of the best actors in the Alliance? That's what they'd have to be. We'd have discovered such a cover up years ago. After all, we've been here nearly five years. No resistance group waits that long to fight back."

"All true." Hamon was forced to agree. It was so reasonable. He sat forward in his chair and drummed his fingers on Ferdo's desk, on edge and unable to banish his suspicions. "Something's boiling. I just know it. And the peasants are involved."

"So it could be your first theory. In which case, why worry? It's obvious that our two Lieger friends aren't involved anyway."

"Is it?"

"Of course. That Jacquel fellow wouldn't have a serious thought in his head beyond wine, women and song. By the stars, does he know how to enjoy himself. He's got half the women in his pocket already."

"Exactly."

Ferdo stared at him. "Where's the harm in that. Even if he tried to pump anyone, no one would tell him anything."

"Maybe, but des Trurain's no playboy. I've checked the old files on prominent Hathians. His academic record is particularly interesting. He's a highly qualified historian, well able to assess the sociological set up here, along with the general state of morale and who really pulls the strings among the Terran hierarchy. Very useful knowledge to any opponent."

Ferdo was silent a moment, digesting this. He shifted uneasily, as if searching for a counter argument. "What can he do with anything he learns? A resistance large enough to be a threat would need a massive organization. You can't hide anything that big from us, not for this long."

"It depends. We've no idea what scale of technology we're dealing with."

"Nothing could be that advanced. There's never been a resistance movement yet that wasn't known to the opposition, and you haven't got one concrete fact to back up your theories."

"Maybe, but Marthe was telling me of the deficiencies of Terran technology last night. She said that in communications we're fifty years behind. A well-endowed scientific community can learn a lot in fifty years. And even if ignorance of the field leads her to exaggerate, it still suggests they are well ahead of us.

Ferdo suddenly sat up, a tight frown creasing his face.

"Ignorant? Not the daughter of Sylvan an Castre. Even on Earth, we heard rumors of the work he was doing. Unfortunately, no one in authority thought it worthwhile finding out more. But if only half the stories of his work are true and he talked to his daughter about it, then she'd know exactly how far ahead of us they are." Ferdo paced once, then turned back to stare at him.

"Fifty years, you say?" He looked at the ceiling and Hamon could almost see him turning over ideas. Then he turned back in disgust. "If that's true, why haven't they made any attempt to interfere with our transmissions? If they're that far ahead, they should be able to bring us to a standstill, but we've never detected the slightest hiccup in the network."

"Not even a twitch?"

"Not a thing."

Radcliff slumped back. He was grabbing at phantoms, but something was happening. He knew it.

"One more flaw in your argument," said Ferdo then. "The beautiful Marthe, your First Union partner. You obviously don't suspect her, not with this marriage thing you're planning. I understand it's fairly binding?"

"For life."

"So, you trust her."

"Quite the contrary," said Hamon bitterly. "I'm more and more convinced that she was planted deliberately in the Citadel. Her intuitive understanding of our real lines of influence is amazing; and she knows how to use them. On two occasions already, she's been able to manipulate our affairs enough to threaten the security of the Citadel, while at the same time increasing sympathy among her supporters." He gripped the arms of the chair as the pounding in his head suddenly exploded.

"You exaggerate, surely." Ferdo was too innocent still, too unaware that even the most trustworthy of people would stab you in the back when it suited. He was glaring at Hamon as if he'd said something unforgivable. "If you mean her introduction of des Trurain, it's only natural she'd wish to help a friend. As for the wedding, I've never seen a woman yet who didn't want an affair of which she was to be the center of attention to be as large and grand as possible."

"So everyone tells me," said Hamon, keeping his voice as low as possible. Too much exertion, he found, sent the pain level in his head soaring into the nightmare zone.

"You can't doubt it," cried Ferdo, in a voice far too loud. "You're her only prop. Without you, she'd have none of this influence you claim. You support her, then turn around and say she's betraying us. By the stars, Hamon, make up your mind. Do you trust her or not?"

"No, I do not, but I am going to keep her beside me. For two reasons. One, so that I can keep a close eye on her machinations."

"And two?" said Ferdo, his voice softening in sympathy.

"She's carrying my baby."

The torn face of the man in front of Ferdo was the only hint of what lay within, but he knew Radcliff well. A friend since childhood, he'd watched him many times bury other hurts. Long ago, he'd learnt the futility of prying deeper. There was only one way he could help, and he resolved to send an urgent, private message on the next Terran link.

After a long interval, Hamon sighed and eased his head up.

Ferdo regarded him with concern. "Why not go home and make your peace," he told his friend. "You may not have it all, but you still have more than is granted most men or women. And take something for that head you've been suffering so heroically."

There was the faintest trace of a smile in answer.

Ferdo watched Hamon leave, pondering the man's earlier words. After a time, he turned to a compartment behind him, pulling out from where he had discarded it the strange patch of material seized from Marthe at her capture. Fifty years ahead!

Hamon made his way to his quarters as ordered. Reason told him he must, if he hoped to crack the massive wall of silence surrounding Marthe. His emotions drew him to this woman, so, so strongly; but his deepest instincts said run, turn, keep out—said that all that waited was misery, suffering and the destruction of what little they now had. Did he want even his memories tarnished? Or wasn't it better to get out now and be thankful for what had been?

He couldn't do it and snarled at his idiocy for thinking he could. Not even his desperate concern for Earth could make him abandon Marthe asn Castre to all the dangers and the brutality that must come to her as a prisoner of the all mighty, common soldier. That he could bear least of all.

Quietly he entered his rooms to come upon her sleeping soundly in the bedroom and dressed still in her most elegant of tunics, her vibrant curls escaping rebelliously from their elaborate arrangement. He remembered his own sleepless night and day of agonizing with bitter regret. Then he saw the smudges beneath her eyes.

Gently, despite everything, his finger crept out to smooth the creased cheek and strayed upwards to push back a wayward curl. Her eyelids blinked open, and she stared wordlessly up at him, into the trouble in his heart. An eternity later, she reached out one small hand in uncertain plea. He hesitated still, then slowly his hand stretched out to touch, then close, then grasp tightly.

It was enough for a moment. Then he drew her urgently into him, enfolding her as close as he could manage, striving valiantly to sear the barriers that separated them. For a period, it worked. She joined with him in denying their peoples for a precious interval as with relief, with love, and with a great well of despair, their bodies said what could not be put into words.

Later, much later, the outer world again intruded. "Do you still want to go ahead with the wedding?" she asked, her buried fear emerging.

"I do," he replied, hiding all bitterness. "Do you want to know why?"

There was a hesitant lift of her shoulder and half a smile. "I'm not sure."

"It was something Ferdo said. We may not have it all, you and I, but we have more than is granted most men or women, he told me, and he was right." For an instant, a smile of pure joy lit her face. He should have left it there, but he had promised her honesty in this. "Also, we need to marry to keep you and the baby safe."

"Thank you, I think."

He wisely refrained from saying more, having reached a kind of acceptance of his own degree of compromise.

"What's more, you may have your party. As big and lavish as you like, though I do beg to be saved from three continuous days of celebration." He deliberately put a teasing slant in his voice and was relieved when she accepted the change of subject and followed it.

"Jocelyn and Helen got to you? I do admit to setting them on you, though I'm not sure they were as subtle as I'd hoped." Her finger traced a soothing path over his brow.

"No. They pounced on me at the worst of moments and led me to believe that I was the cruelest man in the universe." He could laugh at it now, the dreaded pounding dissolved by her warm sea of refuge.

"They did overdo it." She gave him the lightest of smiles and he basked in its warmth. "And the peasants? You will throw them a party? It's an old tradition, as well as a good safeguard."

"Very well." It was either true or, if a conspiracy, a way of letting her own people share in her joy. "We'll announce it tomorrow, though no doubt the grapevine will have heard of it already. How does it get to be so damned efficient?"

To his surprise, she replied. "Simple. A party needs supplies to be ordered, cleaning and cooking to be arranged. Peasants do all those things, and they're not deaf and dumb, only stupid. You may keep your state secrets secure, but day-to-day you're wide open."

"Not completely, surely?" he protested teasingly, petrified lest he stop this sudden stream of confidences.

"Completely," she assured him. "For instance, you know fat, old Captain Sandoff who's always talking about his strict diet?"

"Uh-huh,"

"His room is stuffed with secret caches. There are sweets behind pot plants, nuts in a box in the cleanser, about ten secret packets within arm's reach of his sleeper, for those midnight snacks, and a big, recessed drawer just by the door pad so he can lock up and grab a bite, all in one, easy motion."

"Do the peasants really gossip so much?"

"It's all they ever seem to do."

"And how, my lady fair, did you put up with them for so long?"

"Dreadful it was," she murmured back, squirming in to his side in a manner that sorely tested his desire to hear more of her past. "If only I had met you sooner," she added. "This is so much nicer than some of the jobs I've had."

"Oh? Just what have you been up to?"

"Are you asking for my recent life history?" she said, bestowing a kiss upon his welcoming mouth and emerging long moments later as content and relaxed as he could wish. If her habit of subterfuge was too deeply ingrained too allow her tongue too dangerous a license, much of what she said was still intensely fascinating to him, professionally and otherwise.

"Where do you want me to begin?" she said. "My first steps, my first words or my first job, none of which were particularly memorable?"

"Your first job."

"Ah, but that was quite recent. Four and a half years ago, to be exact. It was when the Terrans first started making us carry identification papers, after which we had to work if we wanted to eat. Not being totally stupid, I managed to insinuate myself into a road gang as a third cousin of the foreman. In those days, there were a lot of displaced persons, house servants and the like suddenly cast adrift.

This particular girl had used to be with us, so it was easy to pass myself off as her."

"Rather risky if the real girl turned up."

"No chance of that. She was dead." There was a shockingly callous lack of concern in her voice. He said nothing to break her mood but stored the memory up for later. "She'd been a table servant, which explained my complete inability to wield a shovel. I never did acquire the knack of it, and they demoted me to stone carrier." She snorted in puzzled amusement. "Isn't it strange that such a doltish people should be so much more physically dexterous than we Haut Liege?"

"Carrying stones about all day can't have been easy work."

"An understatement, if ever I heard one; but by that stage I'd been wandering about the place in a daze for weeks. I was hungry, and terrified of what would happen if either the peasants or soldiers found out who I really was. The relief of being in a secure place, with regular meals, more than outweighed the misery of the work."

"So how long did you last at that?"

"About four months. You should have seen the muscles in my arms at the end. Then our gang was caught up in the conscriptions to the mines. It was a good thing they were short of domestic staff for the workers' quarters at the time, or I doubt I'd be here today. It takes a strong person to survive the maximum period at the mines, and that was back in the early days, before they cut it back to six months. The eight to twelve monthers were dying in droves."

He shuddered, despite himself. The mines, that dreadful blot on the Terran record. Workers still died there occasionally, but more from accidents. The hundreds who had expired in the first year from sheer exhaustion was a shameful crime that Earth could never erase.

"That you should be in such a place!"

"Exactly what I thought myself. After two years, I'd had enough. I'd done just about every kind of job possible: cleaning toilets, scrubbing barracks, nursing the sick, cooking, laundry, and even burying the dead. The last one decided it." He pulled her closer to hide the memories he saw fleeting across her face. There was no doubting the truth of her words and the pain of it scoured him deeply.

Marthe fell silent as she saw again all those brave faces that she had meanly dragged to their last repose, bile gagging in her throat.

"Anyway, I escaped," she finally said, shrugging off the horror defiantly. "After that, I wandered across the plains for a few weeks, eating berries, roots, whatever I could find. It was lucky none were toxic because I wasn't at all discerning. I came to this town about a month later. There were quite a few mine escapees here at the time, and the peasants do look after their own. I managed to get taken in by a kind old lady. A lot like my nurse, she was. She arranged a place for me in a work gang, and I've been here ever since, mostly working on the surrounding roads. Then I was caught, and the rest you know."

She paused reflectively. "And never again will I go anywhere near a shovel. God, how I hate them. Almost as much as I despise the peasants. Moaning all the time, yet they do nothing to help themselves. It's not as if their lives are so much better under your rule than it was under ours, but at least they feared us, far more than they do your soldiers. You'll have trouble there, if you're not more careful."

Much to her chagrin, a light snore told of the deaf ears on which her elaborately embroidered ending had fallen. She thumped the headrest and flounced to the other side, gaining some comfort from the temporary interruption in her partner's sleeping rhythm.

Long after sleep had claimed her, Hamon lay unmoving at her side, his diplomatic snores abandoned. After finally hearing some truth, he'd been in no mood to listen to the fabrications she'd added at the end.

The natives were clearly able to move about a great deal more freely than the Terrans realized. By his reckoning, she'd travelled more than a hundred kilometers on foot, undetected by air or ground patrols. If the ease with which she'd been accepted into strange work gangs was to be believed, then others could do the same. The identification papers the Terrans made the peasants carry were obviously a complete failure in controlling them. Or, more likely, he thought ruefully, *we Terrans have become far too careless. Something that would change on the morrow.*

Also, she appeared to have been fully accepted by the natives, yet even the most subtle of his men had never managed that successfully. The peasants only ever tolerated them, his men said, and always seemed to know they were planted Terrans. Was it some nuance of the language, or had the peasants known all along who she was and still accepted her? Then there was that other, struggling thought, growing more and more plausible. That she and the peasants were one and the same people—the grand drama, so impossible, surely. He rose the next day with a new determination and left early for work. It was more than past time for his men to earn their pay.

It didn't take long for the local Hathian commander, Gof deln Crantz, to be made rudely aware of Radcliff's newfound zeal. From the Major's first quick strides as he left his quarters, the Hathian surveillance network was buzzing with ominous reports and overheard Terran gossip that had Gof very much less than happy. He retreated to the niche he had made his own at the back of the janitors' locker room and plugged into the feed from the central monitors covering the whole of the Citadel. He rubbed his old-fashioned-appearing spectacles and set them on his nose as he picked up the first of a set of metal bowls that needing polishing. It was a mindless task that left him free to concentrate on a summary of the day's vids screening across the inside of the spectacles, unseen by any Terran observer.

The vids started with Radcliff's entry into his office first thing that morning. The blasted Terran strode into the security wing's rooms with cold determination in his dark eyes. Gof saw recognition of that look on the faces of the veterans on Radcliff's staff and the excitement blooming in them. He listened intently to the buzz of gossip that followed in the man's wake. His inner frown deepened.

The Major had been letting things drift while he dallied with his little native, they said. But no longer, by the looks of him. In his periods of bright, fiery activity, they'd follow him anywhere, and did he ask some marvelous adventures of them! But these spells of delving into people's psyches, as he put it. Bah! The young ones could have that. Far better those first, heady days of the occupation when there was going to be urgonium enough for all of Earth, land for the taking, plunder and spoil for all, with rumors of the most beautiful women in the Alliance when they finally unearthed the damned Liegers.

Then, they had strode the streets like kings, free to remind the natives just who were their new masters, and all the security wing had to concern itself with was procuring workers, watching for rebellion and scouring the planet for Liegers.

As for the Major! The devil himself, he was. Here, there and everywhere, his finger in every pie going. He'd been but a captain then, said the oldest man in the room, sent here to assist the occupying forces because of his previous experiences on Hathe. In truth, there hadn't been a branch of the services that didn't end up with his mark on it. Even then, there had been the sign of the leader on him. And look at him now, second in seniority only to Colonel Johne. Second to none in real power, they joked. Not that he chose to use it often, unfortunately.

But when he did! The older ones laughed quietly, wondering whether the Commander had ever quite learned of all the measures that had been implemented.

Yes, those were the days. He had swept in like now, that dark devil in his eyes, snapping out orders that changed the whole face of the planet. It was he who had rearranged the work schedules, doubling the natives' output—and lengthening their life spans, admittedly. He who had set up their mighty intelligence network, delving into all aspects of native and Terran life. Now, here he was, those crisp, sharp orders of his snapping out again. The men all jumped to attention and shut up as their Major came back into the common office.

"Jones, get onto Security and tighten up the native checking procedures. Hawarth, your area is the local work force. Update native lists and bring me a comparison of work output in the different sectors. Markham, background all native domestics in Terran quarters. Reason for imprisonment and length of duty, then interrogate any who seem suspect. By *my* methods," he added, turning to fix a black stare upon the unfortunate man. "You're apt to discover more than by the Commander's methods.

"Hector, I want our ten top men in my office within three hours, and I don't care how difficult it is to pull them out at such short notice," he snapped in answer to the man's aborted protest. "Hanley, bring me that report on family relationships among the Hathians."

"But, sir, it isn't quite ready yet. There are a few permutations I have yet to explore."

"I want the complete report on my desk within the hour," was all the sympathy he got. "Contact me immediately if I'm needed, Hanrahan," he threw at his secretary, and the tornado swept out as bracingly as he had arrived.

That, said the looks on the faces of the old veterans, is that, smirking at the unfortunate young anthropologist who had only just discovered that he was, in fact, part of a military operation. Gof almost felt sorry for the man, then smiled inside. No, he didn't. He'd have given the young idiot as little sympathy as Radcliff had. He kept watching the vid.

"You can't scrabble together a conclusion to a paper in an hour," Hanley was protesting huffily to any who would listen.

"Maybe, lad, but I'd get the facts on the old man's desk within the time," said Jones, a wily elder statesman who Gof's records said had been head of Radcliff's security wing since the first days of the conquest. "This place may not be a paradise, but it's a sight easier than living on Earth."

"He wouldn't."

"He has done," said Jones, and looked fully satisfied with the blanched face and busily shuffling hands of the young researcher in front of him.

Gof switched to other vidfeeds. The whirlwind that was Radcliff swept on to the other departments. A few searching questions, a reminder of his influence, and there was the beginning of a new vitality and a curt wariness throughout the Citadel. "After all," as Gof heard a soldier remark, "you might be able to get the odd trick past the Commander, but the Major, now, he can look straight through you, as if to see the very secrets of your soul. Sure, the occasional dodge slips through, but only a fool believes the Major didn't know about it."

True to form, so the growing muttering among the soldiers said, it was Radcliff who noticed the false sense of security that had crept over the Terran forces this last year. By the stars, they had been here nearly five years and would be here forever. But no, reminded the Major. They were here by dint of their own alertness and would stay only by more of the same.

Within a very short time, Gof's opposite, Colonel Johne, became as interested in Hamon's actions as was the Hathian commander. He soon noticed a newly proud step in his men. It wasn't hard to guess who caused it. Johne did nothing yet, beyond increasing his personal surveillance of his junior officer in case the man planned a coup. The Colonel was in silent agreement with the need to find a purpose for his bored troops and chose to bide his time. As yet, there was no cause for concern. Radcliff was too well born to be satisfied with a back planet, far from the power plays of Earth. But for himself? Ruling over this misbegotten mud heap suited him nicely, and he meant to hang on to power for many years yet.

Within a few days, Gof deln Crantz became more than concerned. After the tenth challenge that morning to his persona of Old Raphe, the Hathian resistance commander was becoming downright annoyed. Radcliff's actions had set alight a vicious spark among the Terrans, and Gof wasn't about to let it get worse.

Silent messages whirled through the Hathian sector and soon, but not as quickly as usual, more disturbing reports flooded in. The checks on work gangs had been stepped up, and IDs were being requested more frequently. The number of Terran spies in town had doubled, infiltrating practically every street and gang. Strange questions were being asked of domestics, especially those working for Terran officers.

Damn that girl. She was supposed to direct attention away from the Hathians, not increase it. Deln Crantz sent out an urgent command to Marthe and grimly awaited her report. His grizzled face clapped in maddened lines, he strode back and forth in the safety of his cubby room. Then, a thought struck, banishing the grimness.

Minutes later, he sent a second storm of messages out over the secret Hathian channels, spreading through the town and deep into the heart of Terran headquarters. He switched on his vid screens to

Marthe's rooms, knowing his two captive agents were together there. The horrified gasp from agents des Trurain and asn Castre as they scanned his orders was every bit as satisfying as he'd hoped.

A joyful wedding to you, Major and Madame asn Castre. May it be a memorable one!

CHAPTER FOURTEEN

Marthe woke slowly, a strange quaver roiling in the pit of her stomach. It was only gradually that its cause dawned on her. Today was her wedding day.

Yet apart from the uneasy churning, she felt numb. That couldn't be right. Wasn't a bride supposed to feel something? Fear, eagerness, anxiety, excitement? Maybe as the day wore on it would come. If she made it through deln Crantz' latest scheme, would she be able to feel again?

The morning's diversion, then the evening's ceremony. Normality seemed to be sliding away from her. She tried to yank it back, deliberately flouncing out of the sleeper.

It woke Hamon. He jerked upright, and she could feel the retort rising in her to whatever he might say. Hamon must have seen it in her face, for he asked only where she was off to so early in the day. Nor did he protest when told simply, "Out." But, then, he would know he could trust in the guards who always accompanied her. As soon as she set foot out of their apartments without him, one of his men would appear at her side as if by telepathy.

Now she did begin to feel something, if only anger. With a wrathful glance at his reclining figure on the sleeper, she marched out of the room. Hamon had recently said she could use his personal flyer, and she made for it now. In short time, she'd lifted off, edged the craft through the tunnel leading to the outside and was speeding across the bleak, endless plains beyond the Citadel.

In her urge to fly faster and faster, she ignored the silent shadow of the soldier sitting behind her, all seeing but never speaking. For what seemed hours, she soared and soared, skimming just above the endless tussock, with the ghostly wail of the wind her only accompaniment. Occasionally, a small ground creature would scuttle away, or an aerion sweep majestically down from the sky and over the dips and gullies below.

More often than not, all she could see of the life of this great wilderness was the constantly moving grasses, the small, hardy shrubs and the creeping ground plants of the barren waste. All must struggle to survive the elements set against them—the scouring winds, the searing heat of summer, the even more biting cold of winter, and the fierce competition for the pitifully few resources of the rocky soil.

Right now, all that struggle answered some savage need inside her. As she flew, swift and silent over the heart of the plateau country, she felt the winds scour away the icy walls encasing her. Slowly, silently, the tears came, pouring from the blind cataracts of her soul and loosing what could never be loosed elsewhere but which, for too long, had been buried deep inside her. She let the stream flow, shoving open the canopy and throwing her head back to let the wind tear away the drops. It was a great emptying—the last she could risk, but necessary. She had to let the deep well of tears dammed inside her drain away to make room for the flood of sorrow the weeks and months ahead would bring.

A short while later, the guard made his presence felt. He took over the controls and returned with a set face to the Citadel. No longer did they hug the contours of the land, at one with the wind and the soil, but cut straight ahead, flying high enough to set a direct course for home. Though her soul begrudged it, her mind welcomed the harsh denial of the land as the man-made machine rigidly imposed its will. In its mechanical rule, she found an equal discipline in herself. She scrubbed her face with her hands, obliterating all trace of weakness. Her head rose, her shoulders came back, and her hands draped gently in the elegant posturing she had been taught as a young woman of the political elite. She stepped down at the shuttle port, with a gracious smile fixed on the haughtiest face she could manage.

Hamon welcomed her back with a sinking heart, seeing the mask set firmly once more upon that strong-willed face. For once, he was relieved that the demands of public duty denied them the chance of private words.

"My dear, you've returned," he said blandly. "I was becoming worried. We seem to have a disturbance in the town."

"The peasants?" she said with a knowing uplift of an eyebrow.

"Yes. They're demanding that we deliver you and des Trurain up to them. And while I wouldn't mind seeing the last of him, you are far too beautiful for whatever mayhem is on their minds."

"Torture and rape, most probably." She appeared totally unconcerned and in reply to his questioning look, explained: "It's the usual demand, once they become intoxicated. I take it there aren't enough guards on the square to control them?" He nodded brusquely, and she sighed. "I daresay we'll have to intervene. If you could procure a couple of weapons for Jacquel and myself, I will go and change."

"Impossible, and well you know it."

"Hamon, we only need one charge each. You may post as many guards behind us as you like, but we need weapons if we're going to get out of this alive."

"You don't seem particularly worried."

"I'm used to this sort of thing," she replied coolly. "Meet me inside the doors to the public balcony in a quarter of an hour and, in the meantime, let the rabble know we're coming. They'll behave till then."

She turned and strode off, calling to a guard to inform des Trurain of events.

When next he saw her, he scarcely recognized her, or her companion. He'd seen nothing like it since his pre-invasion visit to the planet. Both she and des Trurain appeared to be in full Hathian court dress. Though where they'd procured them at such short notice, he couldn't think.

On closer inspection, he saw the cloth was cheap and the jewels fake. But from a distance, from the crowd mobbing the square outside, she would look to be richly clothed, the stiff folds of her gown falling straight from shoulder to floor and every inch bejeweled and embroidered. Formal and regal, not cheap and bizarre. The close-set sleeves molded to the exquisite slimness of arm, and her hair was carefully coiled about the long strand of pearls she favored with what appeared to be ambrosite and diamonds winking here and there among the rich bronze.

Des Trurain, in a white, close-fitting coat and soft, bagged trousers caught into boots of whitest synleather, appeared less bejeweled but just as magnificent. Not for the first time, Radcliff recognized the body of a natural athlete, set off today by a sash of deep, shimmering black, studded with false diamonds, jaridite and even what, at a distance, would appear to be a huge, yellow lignosite, rarest stone in the Alliance.

Low-slung about the hip of each was a girdle, equally jeweled and embroidered, carrying a holster. Their presence on the magnificent figures could only be regarded as sinister by any viewer, Terran or Hathian.

"Where did you get those?" was his stunned reaction.

"We've been expecting such a disturbance since the wedding was announced with so few precautions," replied des Trurain. "The outfits may be fabrications, but at a distance they'll serve our purpose."

"You have the weapons?" Marthe's cold voice was unlike anything he'd heard from her. Even his soldiers were falling back in awe. Silently, he signaled for the two hand blasters to be passed over. Both took them in a completely familiar grasp, sighting with professional assurance.

"You've used Terran blasters before?"

"For hunting. You made the best in the Alliance," answered des Trurain, making the compliment an insult.

"Remember, one false move and the guards have orders to destroy you both."

Neither Hathian gave any sign of hearing him.

"If you go first with a few men to announce us, we'll follow behind," said Marthe.

Hamon passed through the doors, to be greeted by a sea of angry, chanting faces, many with hoods thrown back for the first time in public to reveal the greasy, native hair. For once, their heads were up, their voices raised in angry challenge. Violence hung over the crowd. Shouts of 'Kill the Liegers', 'Down with the tyrants', 'Death's too good for them', reverberated across the packed square.

As he held up his hand, the shouts died to a low, fierce rumble. For now, they would hear what he had to say.

He spoke the words exactly as Marthe had dictated them.

"We have brought the Haut Liege as you requested. You may lay your grievances before them. However, know that we regard this to be a purely Hathian matter, and the outcome is your own affair. I give you Jacquel des Trurain and Marthe asn Castre."

As he pronounced their names, the rumble grew to a loud, angry swell. Then, all noise ceased abruptly, and a strange silence quivered in the air. Turning involuntarily, he saw the cause.

Two grim-faced, aristocratic figures strode arrogantly forward. Giving way unconsciously, the Terran soldiers allowed the pair to proceed to the balcony edge, to stand revealed in all their glory to the silent menace beneath. At first, they merely gazed sternly down at the crowd. Then it happened. A stone flung through the air, followed by a vicious dart. The stone grazed Marthe's forehead and the dart embedded itself in des Trurain's left arm. In a flash, two blasters drew, fired and two white clouds were all that remained of two protesters.

Chillingly, des Trurain's voice cut across the stunned silence. "As you heard, this is a purely native matter. Remember, therefore, who you are and who we are and disperse to your homes without further nuisance. The next malingerers will not be so fortunate in the speed of their punishment."

Hamon saw the effect of that chilling voice on his soldiers and cursed silently. Below, the natives subsided, their heads fearfully downcast.

"There is to be a feast for you today, in honor of the Lady asn Castre's marriage," continued des Trurain, bowing haughtily to Marthe, who now spoke for the first time.

"There will be food and drink dispensed to all, as there used to be. Ensure that the standard of behavior is also as it used to be. Any deviations will be dealt with according to the ancient customs of this planet."

Hamon watched her eye the rabble. Her performance, if it was that, was as effective as des Trurain's. A disconcertingly wan cheer rose on all sides. There were half-hearted calls of 'Blessings to the Lady' and 'Many thanks' as quietly the crowd broke up and left. In a few moments, all that remained was an empty square, bare of all but the dark stains left from two piles of ash, the sole residue of two human peasants who had dared to stand against their past overlords.

The threatening figures of that deadly retribution turned and walked back inside. Not till they were safely behind the shielded doors did Hamon see any sign of relaxation in either Hathian.

"Now that's taken care of, let's get on with the preparations," he heard Marthe say to Jacquel as they passed their weapons back to him.

Hamon looked at the settings. Destruct. They had been on the lowest setting when he'd issued them. In the deft swiftness of that deadly instant, he'd missed the quick finger flick of both on the controls.

Beside him, Marthe was easing the dart from des Trurain's shoulder, causing a slow flood of darkest red to trickle down his arm. "You'd better come along to my quarters and let me bind that for you," she said in an unconcerned voice.

"And you had better clean up that graze," returned des Trurain. "I hope you've some covering screen for tonight. You're going to have a bruise."

"Mmm," she replied, gingerly putting her hand to her head and suddenly swaying in pain. Hamon jumped in to take her arm before the Hathian could touch her again. He was surprised, and secretly relieved, to feel the slightest of tremors.

"Those rabble," he ground out.

"I thought we came off pretty lightly," said des Trurain. "Nice to see you haven't lost your touch, Marthe. Good shooting."

"The same to you. But I will have you know that stone was thrown quite hard."

"You were expecting trouble like that?" Hamon demanded.

"After your leniency? Of course. A second uncle of Jaca's was killed by such a crowd only ten years ago."

"It was his own fault," Jaca added. "Reckoned he was going to reason with them. Hah! Not even armed, the idiot."

Hamon hauled her round to face him. "You went out there, knowing you could be killed?"

She looked surprised. "What do you think I've been telling you for days now?"

He didn't have to say it. That he'd believed her then as little as he believed most of what she said about her life as a Lieger; but those few moments on the balcony had shaken his convictions, just as the relief and fear he felt deep in her was shaking him still. All he could do to calm it was to urge her to get her head checked by a doctor.

For once, he and des Trurain were on the same side as the Hathian added his urging. Her long and wrangling reply that she would do no such thing till she was rid of this ridiculous get-up didn't help in the slightest, and it was in fraught bickering that they made their way to the medical section.

There, Marthe's temper was flayed further by the 'primitive hack hands', as she put it, of the hospital staff. To which the Terran doctor finally growled that she would have to be at death's door before he would come near her again and slammed out, leaving her in command of the treatment room. Hamon tried to reason with her, and had his head snapped off too. It was only des Trurain she would allow to remain. Hating it, but still terrified for her, Hamon was forced to concede and leave them to it. Worse, he couldn't mistake the locking of the door behind him. If anything happened to her, she was now beyond his help. He rammed his hand hard against the wall and began pacing, refusing to go any farther from her. That was asking too much.

Marthe had seen the anguish on his face, hidden to all but her. There was nothing she could do about it, but it didn't make her feel any better about hurting him again. She hugged her arms as she watched Jaca sweep the room for bugging devices. He shook his head and grinned in reassurance.

"By the Pillars, thank God that's over," she breathed, her rigid control breaking as she sank against him. He gave her a quick hug while at the same time urgently contacting base to learn what she'd been too scared to find out.

"You can relax, Mimi. We hit the dummies."

She let out a whoop of joy and burst into tears at the same time. "I was so sure I'd missed."

"You're not the only one. It's so long since either of us has fired a shot. But we did it!" He leaped up with a shout, then was caught by the pain in his arm, and suddenly sat down again. "Damn them. Did they have to be so realistic? Our people may not like your marriage, but they could've expressed it in less painful ways."

"Mmm," she agreed, nodding her head vigorously then stopping abruptly as a sharp pain shot across her brow. That stone had been decidedly bigger than needed. "Come on. I can't keep Hamon out of here for long, and I need to find their cerebral scanner. My head's not made of concrete, no matter what that idiot thought when he decided to chuck a boulder at me." She sorted through the room, opening cupboards and recesses before coming upon the control panel for the cerebral scanner. She slid it out disbelievingly. "This can't be it. It's not even three-dimensional. Don't these people know anything?"

"It will show you something, though?"

"Yes, in a time consuming and inaccurate fashion. I'll have to take a whole series of oblique shots to get any kind of usable image. Here, press on this control pad when I tell you to." Thoroughly exasperated, she fed in the brain scan program, then sat still while Jaca took a series of cross-sectional shots, and was partially satisfied to see no visible abnormality. But worse was to come. "They call this a neurometer?" she scoffed, glaring at the array of figures and tracings.

"It seems to put out a great deal of information," he said soothingly.

"Yes, and a lot of use it all is to me. There's no analytical or correlative function. It'll take me at least an hour to sort out this rubbish, and it leaves out the two most important variables. That does it. My head will just have to be all right. Give me your arm. I should be able to fix that at least. They must have basic medical supplies."

If her head didn't hurt so much, she would've been amused at the relief on his face. He never had liked being on the receiving end of her fouler moods. Fortunately, in tending to his wound, she managed to work off the better part of her pent-up terror.

"Feeling better now?" he asked shortly afterwards.

"Yes. Sorry."

"No worry. I saw your face when that stone hit. Didn't you know how much our people dislike your marriage?"

"I do now. That man really meant it. Did you see who it was?" She'd seen but needed his confirmation.

"Your cousin Griffith, who else? He said he was best fitted to do it, apparently. He did promise not to make it too damaging—only enough to be realistic."

She grimaced. "Trust him. Griffith's always disapproved of anything I do and can't resist letting me know it. His throwing is as accurate as ever, though. That bruise will take days to come out properly."

"You do know he's not the only one who disapproves of your marriage? Don't go into town unguarded for now. This new program of civil violence our superiors have decided on may succeed in distracting the Terrans, but it's also loosened a few too many restraints among our own people. The word's gone round among the hotheads that you're free game."

Jaca may have expected another outburst, but this was something she knew already. Volatile she may be, blind never. "Hopefully some of my lesser known deeds will be published later or I may find myself in an awkward spot in the new regime," she said dryly. "But enough of that. Is everything in place for this evening's ceremony and the link-ups ready?"

"Yes. The channels are booked for sunset. You're going to have one of the largest weddings in memory, as long as you remember your vows."

"I've been practicing nightly."

"And afterwards, for the sake of our superiors' questionable tempers, you will make sure you keep Radcliff out of the way for a while? You are having a honeymoon?"

"Well," She paused guiltily, "he hasn't actually mentioned one."

"Then you'd better," was her friend's caustic reply. "That man has caused enough of a stir already. He has to be stopped. Instead of which, you seem set on spurring him to even more dangerous activities."

Her angry reply was stopped only by the arrival of the subject of their discussion.

Hamon had finally lost patience and forced Citadel control to override the lock on the door. He still entered cautiously.

"Is it safe to come in or am I liable to have that bandage thrown at me."

Marthe bit back her temper. "Sorry. Being hit by that rock rather annoyed me. Overly brave rabble," she practically spat.

"At least they've been reminded of reality," soothed Jacquel, "and our Terran friends will hopefully exercise more care in future."

Hamon was shocked to see the underlying seriousness in the searching look the hated Hathian gave him. Just this once, they had a common bond, rankling though it was to both.

"Just what would happen if you were let loose in the streets?" Hamon asked.

"We'd be lucky to last ten minutes," was the man's matter-of-fact reply.

"You seemed to have exercised a remarkable degree of control over the mob today."

"Armed, on a balcony and backed by soldiers," Marthe reminded him.

"You didn't appear to need us. Your own powers of persuasion were most effective in quelling the rabble."

"That would give us the ten minutes mentioned," said Jacquel sardonically. "In a pair, we might survive quarter of an hour, but alone, now that the mob have seen our faces? No, the chances are small. You have us under tight security, but there's no real need. We've both spent five years hiding from the peasants, knowing they would kill us on sight if they realized we were Haut Liege. Right now, we're safer than we've been any time since our people left.

"My own men are not particular either, if it comes to that. Don't count on Terran protection forever."

"We survive here by dint of the claim Marthe's child has on you, and the rather tenuous fascination I hold for your female staff. We will not forget it," said des Trurain coldly.

"There is more between Marthe and me than the child," snapped back Hamon.

"You'd do well to remember it then," said the Hathian, before taking his leave.

Hamon glared at the departing back, hating the implication that he had other priorities that came before this woman's safety. Yet it was only the truth. He still took the Hathian's words to heart, hearing the underlying thread of deadly purpose in the man's voice. He continued to stare after the closed door for quite some time and it was only the gentle stealing into his arm of a trusting hand that drew him back to his surroundings. His name was spoken softly. He turned, caught the tentative smile spreading across her finely rounded features. The glinting sparkle and flushed cheeks were gone, chased away by a questioning light in her warm eyes.

He drew her within the circle of his arms, tilting her small chin up to let him gaze deep into her face. With delight, he saw the ever-ready mischievousness rising in her, the sweet smile dissolving to a laughing grin.

"Will there ever be a day when I see you and Jaca meet in friendship?" she exclaimed, half exasperated, half teasing.

"Never," he replied, forced in turn to laugh at himself, letting his face relax as he could only with her. "Does it bother you much?"

"Of course it does, you rogue. Just as it would bother you if Ferdo and I were unable to come within shouting distance without a danger of coming to blows."

"You can't tell me that what des Trurain feels for you is a platonic friendship."

"Did I say that?" she retorted. "But if you expect me to fall into a decline because a handsome young man is attracted to me, then you've spent too much time in deep space."

"Finds you attractive? The man imagines himself to be madly in love with you."

"1 know," she gloated, her dimple twinkling larger. "It would be a tragedy, if this fierce emotion hadn't arisen just about the time I fell madly, passionately in love with you. Jaca has been as a brother to me as long as I can remember. It's a bit late now to suddenly discover a fatal attraction," and she reached up and pulled his head down to hers. The hunger in her soothed him as nothing else could.

Ages later, he pulled back and, still holding her close, teased gently, "Don't evade the issue, little minx. Didn't you once say that you were expected to marry the man?"

"Yes I did, and a very good match it would have been, too," retorted the practical side of her he'd noted more than once. "We would both have been perfectly contented, after a fashion," she added with a gurgle. "Now come along, we have an important matter to discuss."

"Oh, and what might that be? The state of the world? Your intrusions into my security? Your safety?"

"No, far more important. Our honeymoon."

The pronouncement left him in no doubt of the seriousness of the matter. "Our what?"

"Honeymoon. Or do you count our marriage of so little consequence that you don't plan to bother with one?"

"What, by all the stars, is a honeymoon?"

She stopped dead in her tracks, pulled him round, held him at arm's length and fixed him with a gaze of utmost astonishment. "You're joking, surely!" He no doubt looked as blank as he felt, but he really had no idea what she was talking about.

"Earth has certainly lost much," she said with a sigh.

"You'd better explain it to me, then." He pulled her back into his shoulder as they wandered along to his quarters.

Marthe hadn't anticipated this. She hesitated, unsure how to begin. "It's a sort of holiday. After the wedding, the newly married couple goes off on their own, to … get to know each other, I suppose."

"Rather like our time together after I had tortured you so abominably."

She heard the pain of memory in the harshness of his voice and couldn't stop the inward shiver as she remembered her panic that day. Yet she also knew what doing it had cost him.

"Something like that. Only now, there is… She stopped again, laughing ruefully. "Oh, it's just too hard to explain. Really, a honeymoon is primarily an excuse to escape from the horde of relatives one is plagued with at a Hathian wedding!"

Then his face relaxed, a dawning grin tugging at the corners of his mouth. "In other words, I drag you off to a secret hideaway to perform a variety of hideous ravishments upon your delectable body?"

"Yes, please."

"Wench." His fingers reached up to softly stir the dark clouds falling about her shoulders, already escaping from the formal style. "How can I leave this precinct with so much unrest?"

She didn't have to fake her disappointment. "You can leave orders for your men. I could spare you for possibly half an hour a day to keep track of things."

He looked long at her face, studying her till she wondered what he saw there. Then he smiled, giving her hope. "Is it important to you?"

"Yes, Hamon, it is."

"Then it will be done. For now, though, you've had a busy morning and no breakfast. Would you join me for lunch, Madame?" and he bowed her on with a flourish to his quarters.

Her world sparkled into life again. "Thank you, kind sir; but afterwards I must get on to Jacquel's rooms. I cannot leave for my wedding from my husband's quarters, or the shades of a myriad great-aunts will come to haunt me."

It was a more relaxed lunch than any they'd had for weeks. For a time, she thought she'd managed to drive away his cares and suspicions, and even some of her own. The memory of it stayed with her through all the afternoon's lunacy of preparation. Agnethe had come, checking that all was as it should be and doing what Marthe's own mother would have done if she'd been alive. There was so much to be yet to do. In a growing flutter of nerves, Marthe reread the vows again and again, doubting more and more as the time drew near that she would be able to remember anything at all.

Jacquel was there too, to make sure that all should proceed as planned and according to the strict time schedule he'd been given by the resistance, so critical to a number of other engagements set for that evening. Little side affairs, as he termed them, which would have seriously vexed the Terrans if they'd known of them. It was ironic, signaled Jacquel through her patch, using the secret Hathian codes, that her great blunder and apparent treachery should turn out to be so useful to the cause. The resistance had never had such an opportunity to pry into the Terran section of the Citadel. Even her so proper cousin Griffith was grudgingly satisfied, he reported.

As for the public unrest among the peasants, better to allow the release of dangerously hot air now than on the final, crucial day, had declared the Council, conscious as they were of the need for a peaceful return to power by the Hathians if they hoped to retain the backing of the other Alliance worlds.

Unfortunately for her good standing in the eyes of her people, Marthe was unable to regard these political machinations as other than minor diversions, decidedly secondary to her own affair, the wedding. 'Dried up old men's ditherings' she laughingly labeled the steady stream of incoming orders.

"Do you have to go into hysterics every time we get an order from Central?" signaled Jaca."

"That last one wasn't totally ridiculous?" she signaled back, feeling no sympathy at all for him. He looked like he'd swallowed a can of swamp worms anyway, as he struggled to hold in his own laughter.

"So what? You know we can't stop the surveillance in these quarters. Too suspicious. And what am I going to tell the Terrans if they ask what's causing those giggling fits of yours?"

Marthe just gave him a 'what do I care' look and switched back to watching Agnethe fix her hair. The older woman was far more sensible. She bustled on regardless, secure in her own priorities.

However, even Jacquel's determined air of authority was shattered by one request, and he was barely able to repeat the message. *"They want an exact time for the 'concelebration of the couple's personal junction', at which time they 'feel that a visual survey of the Major's quarters will go unobserved'".*

"They can't possibly mean… They intend to spy on us when we… No!" Marthe was so shocked that hilarity seemed the only safe emotion. "And to perform to a set time? Ask him how long he estimates such 'concelebration' to take," she silently screeched via her patch. Her tapping in this case was so shaky as to be almost inaudible, but her meaning was blatantly clear to Jacquel, lying prostrate on the floor and vainly clutching his stomach to control his jolting chuckles.

Hamon chose that moment to go into the Terran surveillance rooms to check on the vid monitors watching over the Hathian quarters. He wondered why everyone seemed to be glued to one monitor and strode over to join the group clustered around it and muttering in puzzlement. He shoved through the crowd and stared at the screen.

The technician in control of the station looked up at him. "Some secret Hathian ritual?" the man said. "These Liegers are crazy!"

Hamon couldn't figure out what was going on either but knew Marthe well enough to realize that something was making her very angry. As well as decidedly merry. A sneaking suspicion entered his head.

"Has any liquor been taken into that room?"

"Only the occasional bottle, sir."

"Yes, but what was in them?" he wondered out loud, surprised at seeing his bride apparently inebriated. Not that he should have expected any less in the company of that reprobate, des Trurain. He just hoped she wouldn't be too far gone by the evening.

Leaving the chamber, he spent an unprofitable hour trying to analyze exactly what it was he was getting in to. It didn't help much. The only conclusion he came to was that he was a lunatic. What else would you call a man about to become joined by an anachronistic ritual to a woman who didn't conform to any pattern of expected behavior in the known universe? Doing away with marriage was Earth's only true gift to human civilization!

CHAPTER FIFTEEN

The thought refused to be banished by the chaos of the afternoon and still buzzed in his head later that day when Hamon found himself standing in the main assembly hall, the centerpiece of an alien and entirely ridiculous ceremony. In a semicircle behind him stood the three witnesses required to stand up for him by Hathian protocol, with Ferdo in the middle as chief. Around again in an expanding ripple of gawping circles he could swear stood every single Terran who wasn't absolutely needed elsewhere. He'd reviewed the security rosters himself, to make sure some staff were still on duty. If not, he suspected that the Citadel would have been left completely unguarded.

The only break in the surrounding ranks of watchers lay in front of him—a path, three people wide, down which his bride would walk. Ranged on the outer and as yet apart from the rest waited the native Hathians—servants supposedly setting up the feast to follow the ceremony. To Hamon, eyeing them warily, there appeared far too many for comfort, given the events of the morning. He tried to still his fidgeting hands, wishing he could reach for a weapon.

Then a hush spread over the crowd. Hamon didn't need to look. He could hear the collective holding of breath as the bride and her witnesses moved slowly around the perimeter. When she came within view at the other end of that empty row, all thought fled.

Her dress was that of the Hathian peasants and yet light years distant. The heavy shroud was transformed. A cloud of glimmering starshine, pale as snow and glinting with the hidden sparkle of a thousand gemstones. So sheer was it that the burnished waves of her hair were barely disguised, flowing freely about her shoulders and restrained only by a circlet of Hathe's tiny, white, astelia flowers. A promise maybe? Or a warning? Delicate and ephemeral in appearance, they could survive the fiercest of gales and frosts on the plains.

Beneath the shroud, her gown fell simply, fitted to the swells of her breast and still small waist, then billowing to fall in swirls of flowering lace about her feet. His entranced gaze had traced down the lines of her body and now saw with delight her jeweled toes peeking from under the folds.

She walked gracefully, confidently to meet him, wiping away all doubt. The circles were complete—the inner by Marthe, the second by her three witnesses, and the outer by the natives, fearfully moving in to fill the vacant pathway.

So that was why they were here. Even now, under the spell of her beauty, he glanced protectively at the surveillance vids and his men, armed and watchful on the perimeter.

She faced him now, then reached out and took his hands so that they turned as one to encompass the chief witnesses, Jacquel and Ferdo, solemnly eying each other across the couple's joined arms. Seeing her up close, Hamon was stunned by the cool dignity of her face … almost as much as by her beauty.

It was a dearly won mask of dignity. Marthe had to work hard to ensure not even he could guess her calm pose was a front, that inside she was a bundle of nerves, utterly convinced she would forget the entire ritual. She was so relieved to hear the rallying signal from Mathe

Central come through on her patch. At least if she stumbled, someone was there to remind her.

She knew that Jaca and the other natives heard the call also, but none gave a sign of it to the Terrans. Jacquel raised his head, letting her know he too felt the readiness of their people.

She glanced back, reassuring herself with the sight of her other two witnesses. To Jacquel's left and just behind Marthe, her cousin Griffith stood with her as her nearest available relative. All the way down the aisle, she'd felt his disapproving eyes boring into her back, yet it was more than comforting to have him there, conferring a seal of legitimacy by his presence. His wife Adele wouldn't be pleased at him taking such a risk, but Marthe was grateful for the courage that had brought him here today. She didn't doubt there would be repercussions. Hamon's men wouldn't let him escape without questioning him. They wouldn't learn anything, not from Griffith an Castre, but he would have an uncomfortable time of it.

Beside Griffith was the third of her witnesses. Her hood slipping back to reveal a smiling face, Agnethe stood as a solid bulwark of normality behind her.

A slight pressure on her hand brought her back to reality. Guiltily, she drew herself straighter and looked forward … then caught the barely perceptible wink of her mate. She grinned back. Cousin Griffith couldn't see her face anyway.

She turned to Jacquel, ignoring his look of disapproval, and nodded her readiness. His beautiful voice began to intone the solemn, opening words of the rite familiar to her since childhood. He spoke in both Standard and Harmish, calling on all to witness and support this pair, about to be joined before them and before God.

Hamon watched her intently, as if aware another world also held her attention. It did, but not one she could let him enter. Not yet. Not when he could not hear what she did—the registering of the unseen

Hathian congregation. Thousands of separate bands hitting the airways from all over Hathe and from the moon base on Mathe. Strongest of all, the call signs of her own family: her father, troubled and fearful, yet full of reassurance; her sister Laren, a slight quaver of warmth or tears; the affection and support of Jorven, her brother-in-law. Even the young twins, barely able to speak, tried to send their code, managing only a slight dash, followed immediately by their mother's more expert version.

Then came the official confirmation from Central that the marital record channel was open, and permission had been duly passed for entry to be made. She could relax somewhat, or she could have if she weren't strung up so tightly inside. Jacquel spoke again, a long, wordy injunction upon the duties of man to woman, father to son, and so on down all the degrees of family so dear to the Hathian heart.

Marthe clearly detected her cousin Griffith's influence and Hamon looked completely stunned at hearing such moralistic outpourings from Jacquel des Trurain.

Too soon, they came to that part most solemn. She had not forgotten the words as she'd feared. Speaking in a low, clear voice, she declared to her listening people her vows and intentions.

"I, Marthe asn Castre, present myself before the people and the Spirit. You know me. Know now Hamon asn Radcliff, the husband I have chosen. To him do I vow to cleave, his children will be mine and mine will be his. His family will be mine, my family will be his. His cares, woes, joys and triumphs will be mine. To him am I bound for my remaining days. This do I declare before duly registered witnesses here about me now, to all of the People wherever they may be and to the one Spirit who binds us all. Is it accepted?"

"It is accepted," declared the six witnesses.

"It is accepted," declared the myriad of voices in her ears.

"It is accepted and duly recorded, Marthe an Castre," came the voice of the chief computer supervisor.

It was now her Terran mate's turn. He paused, thanking her with his eyes, then spoke loudly and clearly for all to hear. Words which she would afterwards feel would mean more than any yet to come in her life.

"I, Hamon asn Radcliff, present myself before the people of Hathe and of Earth, and before the Spirit. You know me. Know now Marthe asn Castre, the wife I have chosen. To her do I vow to cleave. Her children will be mine and mine will be hers. Her cares, woes, joys and triumphs will be mine. To her am I bound for my remaining days. This do I declare before duly registered witnesses here about me now, to all the people of Hathe and Earth wherever they may be and to the one binding Spirit of Hathe. Is it accepted?"

"It is accepted," declared the witnesses.

"It is accepted," declared the myriad of secret voices, more sincerely than Marthe had expected, an answer to the true pride and love plain in his voice.

"It is accepted and recorded, Hamon an Radcliff," declared the disembodied voice of the chief computer supervisor, audible only to the Hathians.

The depth of commitment in Hamon's voice surprised Marthe. She hadn't expected it and felt overwhelmed with love and gratitude. One rebellious tear pricked her eye, and she leaned forward, her arms reaching out for him. He stopped her, holding her back and signaling to Ferdo, who carefully passed him a small box. He opened it, to reveal two, plain bands of gleaming yellow, one delicate and small, one larger and solid.

"On ancient Earth, it was the custom to symbolize such a union by the wearing of a gold ring, as you on Hathe do by the dropping of the *s*. Shall we wear these rings as a Terran sign of love and devotion?"

His tone was for her but set to carry throughout the audience. She could see nods of approval from the older ranks of the Terrans, reminded by his words that marriage was enmeshed in the deepest antiquity of Earth's history.

Tenderly, he slipped the delicate band of gold over the third finger of her left hand, then held out his own for her to do the same. "Welcome, wife," he said in the lowest of voices, audible to her alone, before enfolding her in his arms. "The ring is to remind us both of this day in the time to come. I hope it's enough."

She barely caught the last words, a whisper of despair and anguish. She held him even tighter, sensing with him the barriers to come and fingering anxiously the strange band. Would it be enough?

"Now," exclaimed Jacquel merrily, "we dance and feast. Let there be music," and the sound system suddenly woke. "Let there be food," he gestured towards the magnificent array laid out at one end of the vast hall, "and let there be love," he ended with a seductive gurgle, linking arms with a startled matron, who giggled in youthful zest as he planted a loud kiss on the worn mouth. Marthe could only laugh.

His high spirits were infectious, and in short time the hall became a mass of laughing faces, cheeks bulging with food and eyes unnaturally bright from liberal doses of the abundant liquid enticements.

Hamon was not surprised at the extravagance of the feast, having long ago discovered that old Agnethe had a soft spot for his bride. His eyes were far too full of the sight of Marthe to be worried too much about the amount of spirits available or the frequent comings and goings of the Hathian servants. They couldn't do anything. His men were here, and he trusted fully in their vigilance. For tonight, Hamon was free and duty be hanged.

Jacquel may look like he thought the same. His mask was complete, and he let not a trace show of the multiple responsibilities he juggled tonight. His first priority was to keep Marthe unaware and relaxed by keeping her constantly plied with the sweet wine of Etelia, especially imported for the occasion and guaranteed to keep a rosy hue on any bride's cheek. The sense of wellbeing evident in her as she floated through the evening was one of his many successes as he continuously worked to ensure that nothing drew attention to the staff's movements. He was so busy, and couldn't resist the thrill of it all, as he simultaneously kept an eye on the myriad strands of the gathering while still keeping amused and happy a constant stream of beautiful ladies.

A heady waft of danger gripped him and, more than once, his merry laugh rang out as he managed to intercept a relay signal from one of the Hathians right under the noses of the Terrans. Two different languages flowed constantly through the hall. Loud, gay and relaxed, the Terran Standard tongue was for once given over to ribald banter and seduction. Floating between with the bearers of trays of drinks and food, the more subtle language of the Hathian underground was a ripple of small hand and face gestures, delicate changes in the arrangement of gowns and folds, a gentle scratching and tapping on the transmitters concealed variously about the moving bodies.

Jacquel, continuously talking on the two levels, was in high flush, his mind a razor's edge of activity. All was going well, and the occasional crisis only added to the adventure. The Commander wished for something from his quarters? Hathian teams were just then planting recorders there. What to do?

Suddenly, the Commander found his way blocked by his Hathian captive. "You shall not leave, Colonel. My valiant co-saboteurs are busy delving among your boxes and bags while we speak. You shall not interrupt them."

Confronted by the apparently inebriated Jacquel, the Commander relaxed enough to join in the supposed game. "And what, may I ask, are your fellow saboteurs doing among my boxes and bags?"

"It's secret," was the confidential whisper, as Jacquel proceeded to prop his shoulder against the Commander's.

"Oh? Whose secret?" Fortunately, the Commander had imbibed quite as deeply as Jacquel appeared to have. "Could it be Radcliff's underground, monitoring my private moments?"

Jacquel laughed. "Aha, you have it! Radcliff's rats have come out of the sewer. How could we have a wedding without Radcliff's rats?" He stopped, and lowered his voice to a conspiratorial, stage whisper. "I have a plan, Commander. Radcliff's my step-cousin-in-law now, and you can't have a relation named a liar."

"No," agreed the Colonel amiably, having obviously forgotten what it was he had wanted from his room.

"So..." Jacquel paused momentously, "I am going to start an underground. Can't have people saying my step-cousin is lying about rebels, so got to have some rebels, see. Here, Jocelyn," he hailed loudly. "Want to join my gang of rebels?" He caught the woman about her waist and buried his mouth in her neck. "Shall we go and make some rebel plans?" he leered at her.

She laughed back, an expectant look crossing her face.

"Got to go now, Commander. We have seditious plans to make. Tell you what, though, you'll be the first to know when we decide to overthrow you. How about it, Jocy? Feel like overthrowing the Commander?" He let a wicked gleam enter his eyes. "On second thoughts, I'll throw you first," and with another, fuddled laugh, he stumbled off in the arms of his new companion, followed by the appreciative rumbles of the Terran chief.

"Now there's a boy who has his priorities right."

Fortunately for Griffith an Castre's peace of mind, Jacquel's brash attempts at obstruction were just then eclipsed. An awed silence suddenly blanketed the hall. Looking from beneath his hood towards the source of the abrupt change, Griffith saw a strange squad of soldiers entering through the far door and Jacquel des Trurain's antics immediately fell to the bottom of his list of worries. The superiority of these troops over the usual Terran soldier was striking, their heads held high and their uniforms of an immaculate cut. Obviously an elite corps. Why hadn't they been seen on Hathe before now?

Then he noticed the woman in their midst, elderly in appearance, slow-moving and weary, but the fear slashed upon the Terran faces left him in no doubt of her power. The riddle was solved when Radcliff came eagerly towards the lady, bringing his new bride. Griffith smiled coldly. So this was Administrator MacDiarmid, the mother of our troublesome major. How very interesting.

CHAPTER SIXTEEN

Even as Griffith watched, Marthe came face to face with the frail woman, dragged along by Hamon right into the middle of the nerve-searing squad of giants. He'd been stunned by the soldiers' arrival and had stood for a full minute, she swore, staring in disbelief. Never before had she seen the signs of emotion marked so clearly on his face. Without a word of explanation, he propelled her towards the terrifying men about the carefully guarded lady. She needed only one look at the stranger's face and the loving look on her husband's to tell her the visitor's identity. The woman's smile of welcome for Hamon was unmistakable.

Marthe warmly hugged her new mother-in-law and discovered her first impressions to be false. Frail and aged the lady may appear, but it came of a burden carried too long. The Administrator, she quickly realized, was younger than her own mother would have been, and Marthe's heart was filled with pity.

"Madame, how wonderful that you could be with us. I can see that it means a great deal to Hamon," she said.

"Thank you, my dear."

She'd been right. The voice was golden, clear, mature but not yet elderly.

Madame MacDiarmid now turned her warm smile on Marthe. "Ferdo sent me a message I'd almost given up hope of ever receiving, and I just had to meet the young woman who had finally tamed this rogue of a son of mine."

"Thank you for the kind words, Mother," her ungrateful son laughed back, "but how did you find the time to come? I was under the impression that Earth would be reduced to starvation level if you ever dared leave that desk of yours."

"It will if I stay. A few weeks' break can't possibly make matters worse. Who knows, I may even find that some of my staff are halfway to being competent." Her son's gruff snort at what was obviously an old complaint brought a quiet smile to his mother's face.

"So the food rationing is still as critical as ever?" Hamon said.

"Worse. We're down to seventy-five percent of maintenance requirements. You have to really earn your keep on Earth these days."

Bewildered, Marthe looked to Hamon in query. The words had been so harsh and his mother's callous chuckle jangled Marthe with its wrongness. It didn't match the lady in front of her. Stern she may be, but Marthe sensed fairness and compassion there.

Hamon proceeded to explain and, for the first time, Marthe learnt of the harsh reality that ruled the lives of Earth's residents. That all registered Terrans must carry a license stating the percentage of survival rations to which they were entitled, depending on work type, health and general usefulness to society, and that his mother was responsible for setting the rules governing that entitlement. She stared in horror. This woman standing before her literally decided who lived or died on Earth.

His mother's calm voice only confirmed it, as she wryly commented on her son's words. "Which is why, my dear, I am the prime target for any would-be briber. You have no idea how wealthy I could be. It's a pity they don't realize that all the wealth in the world will not buy me what I really need—a food supply greater than one hundred percent of requirements. It's the old story: for that we need more energy. Thank the stars for your planet, my dear."

Despite the horrors of the situation on Earth revealed by the woman's words, Marthe couldn't hide a flush of anger at the reminder of Hathe's oppression and she straightened grimly.

Fortunately, Hamon knew her well enough now to catch the danger signs before she did anything stupid. Even as she began to open her mouth, he was moving his mother away from Marthe and towards the converging horde of officials. She supposed she should be grateful.

"Watch them grovel," was his quiet aside to Marthe, and she had to smile at the devilish gleam in his clear hazel eyes, not in the slightest quelled by his mother's glare of reproof.

Leading the group coming towards them was the Commander, his face so fearful that Marthe was dumbstruck. Nor was he alone. All the officials were equally terrified, including the head of the Guards, a man well known among the Hathians for his cruel excesses.

Then Hamon's mother spoke to him, and Marthe was no longer surprised. She was the Administrator and the level of contempt in her voice froze out any attempt at familiarity. She and her bodyguard held themselves aloof from the reception party, as if to infer that the very air was contaminated. Hamon had told her that the conquering troops were gleaned from the veriest riffraff of Earth, picked solely for their lack of scruples. Now she saw it confirmed. Yet were those who sent them here any better? Or were they simply, as was her husband, men and women of principle forced by the harsh reality of Terran society to brutally discard aspirations to justice.

Marthe shook herself. Earth's problems were not her concern. Only those of her own oppressed people. Her new mother-in-law chose that moment to voice her opinion of the Hathian servants.

"Take him away. He reeks," said the Administrator, frowning with disgust at the too close approach of a cup bearer.

The wine Marthe had drunk so carelessly took sudden and disastrous hold. How dare the woman! To speak so of Marthe's valiant comrades, bravely risking discovery to attend her wedding.

"Their bodies maybe, but not their souls," she shot back. "Unlike others here present."

A deathly wave of silence filled the room and crashed with all the savagery of reality on her head. The insult was unmistakable to everyone.

Administrator MacDiarmid stared. Hamon looked stunned, then shocked, then retreated behind that hateful bland mask of his. The husband became again the Terran officer as he moved away from her and towards his mother as his expression dared her to continue. The elite bodyguard looked questioningly at their mistress for instructions concerning this impudent baggage; and inside her head, she heard the growing chorus of Hathian outcries.

Alone among the horde of visible and invisible participants, it was the disapproving and cool Griffith who kept his head. He sent her an urgent warning to stay still, then slipped quietly from the room, a simple peasant bound on his duties. Once outside and safe, she heard his signal to the absent Jacquel. *"Only the drunken brashness of that young idiot can help us now,"* was what Griffin messaged to her, and the sharpness of his tapping said only too clearly that she was included in the *young idiot* category.

Jacquel had long learnt to ignore such jibes from Griffith an Castre. The man was a pompous prig, but he'd trusted him with his life more times than he cared to remember. Jacquel listened to Griffith's precise description of what had happened, hastily disentangled himself from a warm embrace and raced to the servant's entrance. Donning the peasant robe Griffith threw at him, he entered the hall unseen, hoping to have been thought present all along. Quickly he summed up the scene. The initial, shocked silence had been short-lived. A loud babble of voices rose higher and higher, with the Colonel's uppermost, demanding that Marthe explain herself, though the stars knew her remark had been plain enough.

Only Radcliff remained uninvolved. The bastard was just standing there, cynically watching the chaos unfold. The only point in his favor was he still stood between Marthe and the threatening crowd. But that was all.

Luckily, Marthe had done as ordered and remained silent. Or was she merely stunned by her stupidity? Worst of all, on the underground channels Jacquel could hear two hotheads applauding her words and urging action if the guards should make a move towards her. By the Pillars! Only this morning, they were all too ready to kill her in the street, now they wanted to throw everything away by charging in to defend her. Dramatics are not what is needed now, you morons, just good, old-fashioned tomfoolery.

He smiled mischievously, then had a quiet word to a nearby peasant girl and proceeded to grab her lecherously about the waist, one fumbling hand groping for her breast. About him hung the rumpled vestiges of the peasant's outer robe, partially looped over his head and falling in a drunken knot round his shoulders.

Amidst a growing chorus of guffaws, he lurched with her towards the center of the storm, the girl's face a barely glimpsed slash of terror under her hood.

Marthe, desperately striving to know what to do next, had never seen a more welcome sight. As he neared, she could hear Jacquel's carelessly muffled stage whispers, urging the girl to come and meet his cousin.

"Itsh her wedding, you know. Anyone can talk to a lady on her wedding. Hey, Rickard, like my latest? Don't smell too sweet, but who cares," he called to a nearby Terran, then sprawled headlong as his foot caught in the robe, landing just in front of Marthe.

She rushed forward, uncertain whether he was drunk or sober. Then recognized the grin of pure impishness on his face from old and her heart sank. Relinquishing the peasant girl, he grabbed her instead as she helped him to sit up.

"Ho, ho," he exclaimed. "This is more the thing. Next best thing to a Hathian lady is a Hathian peasant. But the real thing! John, Rickard, ever been with a real Hathian lady?" With a strength that convinced Marthe he was all too sober, he suddenly grasped her about the waist, one hand clutching embarrassingly at her breast as he slobbered about her throat. She did not even have time to shriek before she felt familiar hands dragging her away. Hamon was finally galvanized to action, the green flames of jealousy sparking in his eyes. It was too much. She suddenly burst into tears and couldn't stop. Both men were so shocked they momentarily refrained from their threatening brawl to stare in consternation.

For a few seconds only, she clung to her husband. Then the memory of his desertion returned and she drew back, turning aside and moaning softly.

Hamon couldn't hear what she said, only that it was the same word, over and over. Across from him, des Trurain listened hard, then Hamon saw comprehension on the man's face. The drunken stance and girl were abruptly discarded.

"For God's sake, Radcliff, get her out of here before she breaks down completely. Whatever you suspect, she deserves better than that. And here's me thinking she'd finally learned to live without him."

"Who?" demanded Hamon, jealousy tearing at him.

"Bendin, of course. Haven't you realized yet that you've only one true rival—her five-years-dead twin brother? Right now, I'm guessing she wishes like hell he was standing beside her. After all, it's not as if there was anyone else offering to protect her. If Marthe means anything to you, Radcliff, get your mother to apologize. Those peasants, reek though they might, are the nearest thing she has to family tonight."

Hamon stood, torn between giving this rogue the hiding he deserved, finding out what really lay behind this drama, or seeing to the woman he loved, still standing so terribly rigid beside him. Her face was frozen, but whether from sheer self-control or an overburdened loss of all feeling, he couldn't say.

With an oath, he drew her in, hoping the frozenness would hold a few seconds longer, as he led his wife and mother away from the curious mob. For the first time in his life, he was grateful for his mother's deathly efficient guard as they kept at bay the staring crowd.

Jacquel let them go first, as he signaled in code to the young Hathians standing tensely on the verge of the crowd to stay out of a purely family affair. A command he hoped they obeyed. Then he followed Hamon and Marthe.

Once through the hall doors, he saw that matters had improved little. Marthe was still withdrawn, standing isolated on one side. He recognized her stance immediately; whenever the hot tongue of either Bendin or Marthe had landed them in yet more trouble, they had always stood so; Bendin tall in the back and Marthe in front but turned towards him, shielded from wrath.

Radcliff was speaking urgently to his affronted mother, but in vain. Though her reported words of greeting to Marthe labeled her an inherently compassionate woman, he guessed she was too used to the awe her position commanded to accept the impudence she'd faced here tonight. From what Hamon was saying, it seemed she'd seen vids of the peasants on her son's dispatches home, and whatever Marthe might claim to the contrary, Hamon's mother clearly had no reason to believe her new daughter-in-law was anything but one of the primitive natives of those images.

Wrong approach, decided Jacquel, watching Radcliff. The only way to soothe that stiff-necked bureaucrat was a direct apology from the offending party, and Marthe was in no state for that. I guess it's up to me, then. He moved toward Marthe.

"Bendin would have been proud of you," he drawled in Harmish.

She gasped, staring at him in shock.

"Just how do you propose to make amends for your appalling conduct, Marthe an Castre. Or do you *want* these Terrans to see us as no more than barbarians?" She shook her head slowly, as if trying to clear away the last vestiges of wine and emotion.

"Well, niece of my father's wife, will you apologize to she who is mother of your husband?"

The harshly formal words worked. He could see her thrust away the fug of misery.

"Friend of my brother, I will," was her barely audible reply. "From you, also, I beg forgiveness, for allowing the wine and the occasion to make me so forget the codes of our people."

"It is granted, sister of my friend."

He smiled encouragement and took her arm in support as he led her up to the Administrator. But the guards leapt in front of their mistress and the lady stared haughtily at the Hathian pair. Then Jacquel saw her glance at her son. Despite the cold mask of the soldier he'd assumed, Radcliff's face told the truth of his feelings too clearly to miss: He was besotted, utterly and completely.

Jacquel had known it from the start, now he saw the realization hit the man's mother. No matter how affronted she might be, it would change not one whit the look on her son's face. I know how you feel, Madame, thought Jacquel in grim humor. And you can do as little about it as I.

Even as he thought it, Madame MacDiarmid admitted it by her actions. Sighing, she called the guard to stand back.

As for Marthe, she knew she must rescue the night somehow, but try as she might, she couldn't bring herself to lift her eyes to look at her mother-in-law. At a silent prod from Jacquel and ever conscious of Hamon's intense stare, she coughed nervously and began to speak.

"Madame, mother of my husband, I apologize for my total lack of proper conduct and hope you will forgive my outburst. I fear the wine and the natural emotion of the evening overcame the somewhat tenuous control I usually strive to keep over my regrettable temper." She gulped and now managed to glance at the older woman's face. It was unrelenting, though she did receive a nod of acknowledgement.

Desperate now, Marthe was reduced to begging. "Mother of my husband, please, for the sake of the deep affection we both hold for your son, I beg you to overlook this unfortunate incident." She stared beseechingly, still hating the woman's words, but knowing that the safety of her whole planet hung on the Administrator's reaction. Not to mention her own happiness.

Then words of acceptance came, and a hand was extended. But it was cold and rigid in Marthe's thankful grasp.

Hamon had stood silent throughout, still partly caught by the curiosity that demanded he see what would happen. But the self-absorbed shield of professionalism could not stand against Marthe's humiliation. With an angry cry, he strode to stand beside his wife, grabbing her hand away from his mother's.

"There's no need for that, Marthe. My mother should have thought before acting so obnoxiously the conqueror in front of you. Not that I ever thought to hear you defend the peasants so forcibly." He smiled quizzically, relieved beyond words to see he could bring a charmed flush to her face, even here. He swung round to his mother. "Perhaps, Mother, you could apologize as graciously as my wife has done. I should take you on a tour of one of their old cities as I daresay my vids home have all been censored. You need to see the other side of this world, to balance the propaganda that has been fed back to Earth." His mother looked up sharply. "You did know that we had conquered a superior civilization."

"Superior?" He sensed she was about to add a scathing rejoinder. His arm tightened around Marthe in warning. His mother's eyes traced his hand and her lips clamped shut.

"Surely my father told you that, or have you been too buried in your own problems to look outwards to Alliance affairs. Do you not know that among the other planets, including the previous Hathian regime, we're considered something of a backward ghetto?"

"What do you mean, backward?" He saw the pain on her face at the cynicism in his voice. He'd always been her favorite child and had never before spoken to her in anger. She reached out a tentative hand.

It never reached his cuff. There was a flurry of cloth and a young man Hamon hoped had gone appeared before her, his bedraggled hair and open-mouthed grin testament to a mellow befuddlement. Before his mother could do anything about it, her hand was taken and a flowery kiss bestowed upon it.

"Most gracious and beauteous lady, pray listen no more to your son lest he further confirm everything he says. A backward ghetto indeed! When may I ask, Major, did you hear any of Hathe to be so ill mannered as to describe you thus within your hearing. Madame, look at me. Can you imagine such vulgar sentiments emanating from these lips? That the husband of my step-mother's niece should so demean your race!" He paused, sighing dramatically as he gazed sorrowfully at Hamon in regret.

Hamon glowered back. "What did you think of Terrans then, before we arrived?"

"Think of Terrans?" Des Trurain spared all of a moment to consider it, then shook his head. "Don't remember ever doing so. Marthe, do you recall thinking of Terrans?" There was a pensive frown on the man's lips, but Hamon recognized the slight touch of a dimple at the corner of her mouth as she shook her head and knew a sudden and profound relief.

"Mind, Madame, if we knew that you possessed such elegant ladies, we certainly would have cast you a thought," des Trurain said, flourishing low over her still entrapped hand. This time, she managed to wriggle it out of his grasp, just as Hamon growled at him to let go of his mother, naming him a lecherous reprobate. Which words, of course, thoroughly engaged his mother's interest. Hamon could only curse at his stupidity.

"And just who might you be, young man?" she demanded.

"Me, Madame? Nobody at all. A mere wretch marooned here by my thankless kin. Bereft of all am I," the annoying Hathian said with another dramatic sigh.

Hamon was about to seriously damage the young Hathian, but fortunately Marthe recognized his fraying temper and judged it time to intervene. Whether to protect her friend or her husband, Hamon thought it best not to know if he hoped to salvage anything from this night.

"May I present Jacquel des Trurain, the son of my aunt's husband and an old friend of my twin brother," she said. "Like myself, he was left behind when our people fled Hathe."

"And your brother? Did he too remain?"

"No, Madame. He was killed fighting to keep your people off planet long enough to allow the rest of the Haut Liege to escape." Her voice sounded flat and emotionless, too tightly controlled by her will. Hamon could only guess at the pain it hid.

"I did not realize," came his mother's equally cool reply. "I understand now your reaction to my words. Please accept my apology."

"With deep pleasure, Madame." This time, at least, her hand was accepted with a semblance of warmth. One hurdle overcome.

"Now that I've got this mess sorted out, I trust I can count on you to manage the rest," crowed Jacquel *sotto voce*.

For once, Hamon couldn't be angry. An unwelcome crisis had been averted. Marthe's choice of words still puzzled him. The stars knew she voiced her loathing of the peasants often enough, to suddenly now turn around and defend them. He filed it away for later. Right now, calling her on it would gain him nothing. He didn't need more lies between them, or barriers hindering his study of the Hathian pair, a study as essential as ever.

And at a deeper level, he did not wish this night marred.

Some while later, they returned to the reception area, Madame MacDiarmid arm in arm with her new daughter-in-law, and if any might wonder whether the Administrator's smile was a little forced, he knew he could count on her power to ensure that none dared voice the thought.

For Marthe, the evening had been scarred, but not ruined. A friendly woman was now alienated, but she pushed it aside philosophically. There were so many obstacles between her and Hamon; what was one more? Their love was doomed anyway. Why waste what time was left brooding over which of the opposing forces would finally bring the whole facade crashing down. She shrugged and turned to Hamon, leaning close in joyful promise.

He understood, his fingers clenching hers in equal pledge. He looked down and saw a curiously detached look on her face. After chatting briefly with Madame MacDiarmid, she moved off to mingle with her guests, stopping to talk with first this one, then that. Marthe was welcomed eagerly by them all. Hamon recognized the practiced art of a diplomat's daughter. Others felt only the ease she engendered, the ready dissipation of tension and the scattering of rumor.

Des Trurain was her equal, noted Hamon wryly, watching as the two worked to restore the glamour and romance of the evening. He had to admire their skill. A part of him wondered bitterly how many would later remember anything of significance in the disturbance. Then it ceased to matter, as a figure of glimmering moonshine danced over to him, the rosiness of her cheeks and the sparkle of her eyes only enhancing her beauty. He smiled at her bubbling joy and took her outstretched hand, holding firm to the quiet contact of finger to finger as both turned back to address the others about them.

Barely noticed at first, then just there, the musical notes stole into Hamon's mood. He stood relaxed, watching the people in the room. It was late, yet none had retired. Hidden niches enclosed gentle rendezvous and matters weighty and philosophical flowed freely in discussion. Ponderous affairs of the world and soul, solved ingeniously now by protagonists utterly safe from acting upon their thoughts.

The music entered as a delicate counterpoint to the hum of human words. So quiet was the refrain, at the barest threshold of audibility— reedy, feather light, delving into relaxed and cogent minds— acceptance and surrender were unconscious. His gaze took in the native onlookers standing apparently aimlessly about the perimeter of the room in barely defined pairs. Briefly glimpsed under the cloaking hoods, he caught faces smiling in precious recognition.

Slowly, as if on a time scale outside human experience, the strange tune became louder. So gradual that, once acknowledged consciously by the crowd, none questioned its existence. Melodies and harmonies tumbled in, building a music both haunting in its simplicity and beguiling in its complexity. He had always loved music, but this was something new.

He was holding Marthe lightly within one arm and could feel her response. He looked down and noted the upward curve of her lips and the touch of a faraway gaze. The strains were as familiar to her as to the other Hathians. Idly he stayed listening, noting hints of primitive Terran music forms. Was that a touch of a Celtic lament? Or there, a strain of a Renaissance court dance overlaid with the exotic complexities of the Indian sitar. But they were superficial similarities. The cadences now permeating every corner of the room originated not in any soul of Earth origin.

The sound began to swell. Slow and stately, yet with an underlying call that tugged deeply at the core. The chattering groups grew silent. Entwined couples were still. A space had cleared in the center of the room, and the guests clustered about, waiting. It was as if a cloud of tranquility had descended.

Two Hathians approached from the outer part of the circle and proceeded towards them. He and Marthe now stood isolated in an island of space, he realized. As the Hathians came nearer, Hamon saw they were holding a large goblet of intricate and antique design. He appeared to be expected to drink of the odorous brew within.

Even in his torpid state, his suspicions hovered and, with a reserved air, he held back. Marthe must lead here. A quiet air of excitement and, yes, nervousness surrounded her, lessening not one jot his caution. She stood still as a rock as the natives held the goblet out for her. A Hathian ceremony then, known and expected by her. Yet she hadn't spoken of it in all the tiresome briefings to prepare for this day.

One of the natives, the taller, spoke in a strange language, unlike any he had heard before. To his surprise, Marthe answered in the same tongue, before turning to him.

"This man, who stands in place of my closest relative, wishes us peace and fertility." Her voice was like a soft caress, the tone lessening his rigidity despite himself. "Will you drink the Cup of Harmony with me and join in the Dance?"

Powerless beneath her gaze, he joined her in holding the cup, clasping her hand as she raised the goblet and drank deeply. There was a touch of hesitation, then, as if from some detached void, he watched himself bring that weird chalice to his lips and drink deeply. He'd meant to take a ceremonial sip only.

A fiery liquor cascaded down his throat, melting, he felt sure, every bone in his body. Surprise was on Marthe's face too. He could see the effort at control on her face, obvious for the first time in their relationship. His hand was still on hers as, coolly, she handed back the goblet and spoke more words in the strange tongue. He was dimly aware of the natives retreating, but it was secondary. His world had shrunk. Only two existed. Her hand took his and the music, never quite forgotten, seemed suddenly to be as closely linked to his melting limbs as the fierce liquid he had just drunk.

Slowly, they began to dance. To one side, he was dimly aware of Jacquel explaining the rite of the Marriage Dance to the watching Terrans. He doubted it was necessary. Their rising sensuality must have been obvious as, in slow suspension, they twined about each other, moving imperceptibly, always in circles, only their backs ever visible to others.

Marthe was in territory strange and foreign to her, and yet excitingly familiar. How often before had she seen this dance, felt the subtle timbre in the air? It was an intricate and delicate blending, this Hathian dance. Untaught, unlearned but by observation, danced only on this, their wedding night. Yet by the skills of an unknown science, the strange music and drink became one with them, investing their limbs with a unique power to love and court the other in as close a bonding as that which was to come unaided later in the night.

A tingling fire ran through her. The burnished, hazel eyes of this man became the center of her universe. His eyes, and those shoulders, that sharp-edged profile, the lazy, sweeping regard of burning depths moving over her breasts, bringing them tautly alive; her now undulating abdomen; her hips bending in subtle invitation; and her long, shapely legs, pointing delicately and arching as she moved. Smiling inwardly, she slowly twirled, feeling the long waves of hair lift about her and cascade down again.

Not once did they touch more than hands, fingertips, a brushing of gown and suit. Yet it was as if they touched all along the length of their bodies. A sinking glow encompassed her, pulsing and throbbing. She was not alone. Her husband was with her in this. It was in every movement of his body.

The music swirled in. No louder, no more strident, yet growing, climbing to such a peak, carrying them both along in a welter of emotion and sensation, across the room and out to the corridor. The dance faded to a walk, then, as if impatient, he drew her up into his arms, holding her close. They came at last to their own suite. No music was needed now. Their own bodies, and minds, and hearts brought them to that point where, at last, they came together in a long, sighing release.

It seemed much, much later. Still she held him, all her skin cells joined one to one with the warmth and firm wonder of him. His head turned, that strong hand gently bringing her face to meet his slow smile before he softly touched her lips in sweet caress and folded her once more onto his chest. For an age they lay still, lulled in the peace of love. Then sleep quietly took them.

CHAPTER SEVENTEEN

She was later to remember the days that followed with a kind of disbelieving wonder. Relaxed, lapped in waves of happiness, she had time to explain the history of all that was strange to him on their wedding night.

The most obvious was the alien music and drink, discovered early in the colonization of the planet in an underground dwelling of unknown design. The presence of carboniferous beings on the planet long ages before man's arrival was nothing of note to her, brought up from childhood with tales of the Old Ones and their relics that were found on Hathe and a few other colonial planets. To him, though, it was all astonishingly new. Did Earth never read anything from the colonies, she had to wonder? Her happiness had been too new to blurt the thought out loud.

More exciting to Marthe was the deepening communion between them, banishing forever, she'd thought, the barriers of race, loyalty and culture that strove so hard to divide them.

What a fool she'd been. They'd had their idyllic spell, yes. Achingly brief days spent far from the Citadel in an old lodge far out on the plateau, but all too soon they had to come back to reality. His mother must be farewelled after her brief trip, and his other duties could wait no longer. Her Hamon must give way to Major Radcliff again.

That was many weeks ago and, since their return, he'd increased her guards and his surveillance—whether to protect her or to report on her movements she couldn't say. It was almost as if he sensed the growing demands on her from her own people.

She was working nonstop now, reporting Terran troop movements, warning rebel groups of the enemy's presence, delving into all aspects of the Citadel's operations. Gof deln Crantz often relayed how pleased he was with her and Jacquel. Between them, they'd managed to supply the kind of information on the Terran headquarters that the resourceful Hathian resistance had given up hope of acquiring.

So her superiors were pleased with her. There was something to be thankful in that, she supposed. Come F-day, the day on which the resistance would at last strike back and reclaim their home, the chances of success had been increased by a whole percentage point through what she and Jacquel had learned. The odds were already in the high eighties, but every extra percentage point meant less risk to the native population, thus less chance of her people dying, she reminded herself, weary after yet another night spent in the maze of corridors of the administration section combing the records of the central data bank.

Tonight had been a success. She'd discovered a code that let her pull the plans for the entire planetary communication system. Most of the network had been worked out already by extrapolation from peripheral parts, but this new data meant that the rebels could link into the fortress' system for a test run before the actual assault. It was a good night.

Unfortunately, such nights were rare. More often she would steal back in the early hours, check that the sedative she'd given Hamon had kept him under while she was gone so he knew nothing of her activities, and then fall into a dead sleep for a few, short hours. Rising heavy-headed and worn out, she'd have gained nothing to compensate for the growing suspicion of her husband as he eyed the dark eyes and gaunt face she daily confronted in her mirror.

Central's demands had grown lately, and most nights found her prowling the Citadel's corridors. Jacquel was just as busy, but he showed little sign of it and could easily pass off tired eyes with a mischievously lecherous grin. She could not, not to Hamon. She was so worn out. It was the baby, she supposed, eying the growing bulge. *I hope you'll be grateful one day, little one.* She rubbed her hand over her stomach, the driving force that kept her going. Her child would grow up safe in the freedom she'd known in her youth. It was the only dream she dared cling to.

Hamon walked in just then and saw her hand and the protective curl of it. She hadn't heard him enter and he made no attempt to catch her attention. Instead, he stopped by the door, studying her far away face and biting down hard on the fear inside him. He'd reviewed all the night vids and knew how often she tossed and turned while he appeared to sleep soundlessly. It wasn't enough to explain the deadly weariness etched into her bones. She no doubt knew how much the natives hated her, but was that what drove her? Did she imagine, as he did, all the ways she could be hurt, all the ways he could lose her forever? He was so afraid for her, fear such as never he'd felt before.

Already, he'd once detected poison in her food. Now, all her meals were personally prepared by Agnethe, alone among the Hathians in her continuing affection for Marthe. He trusted the big-hearted cook in this; he had to, but he made sure Marthe knew nothing of the incident.

She did, of course, but had hoped Hamon was in ignorance until Agnethe enlightened her to the contrary. It was one of the many thoughts in the storm-tossed maelstrom that held her in thrall as she sat in the chair, oblivious to her surrounds. One more burden to add to her looming pyre. There were so many of them. On her last visit to the rebel headquarters, she'd been recognized, and the guards had to intervene to stop the angry crowd from seriously hurting her. As it was, she'd collected a few nasty bruises. Merely a fall, she'd said to Hamon in the morning.

The surreptitious spits and angry murmurs in the street were now so commonplace that she could almost overlook them. Still, she avoided leaving the fortress unnecessarily. Apart from the poison, there had been two other attempts on her life. Both had been reported to the rebel command, who promised to rein in the hotter-headed among the younger natives. Command wouldn't stop the sneers, though. The show of hatred from the populace was too necessary to the roles she and Jacquel played. If only she didn't have to know that, while the jeers for Jaca were forced, for her they were all too real.

Then there was the continuing nausea of her pregnancy, lodging a cloud of depression over her spirits. Hamon had suggested she return to Earth with his mother, just for a short break. She'd refused him so violently he'd never mentioned it again, but she'd seen the hurt in his eyes at her loathing of his home world. It was one more wedge driven between them, one added to so many others that it was rare now that the barriers could be fully set aside, allowing them a respite of peace. She slumped farther into the seat.

Hamon saw it, angrily helpless. He growled, unable to silence his grief, and she whirled round to stare anxiously at him. He could see in her eyes the shutters crashing up against him, and in the full glare of sunlight her face was more worn than ever. He asked her yet again what the matter was. She was fine, she said, as always, but today, he couldn't take it. He swung round and flung himself out the door before he gave in to the violence that demanded he shake the truth from her before she killed herself. He couldn't. He was caught too hard by the knowledge of what would happen if he gave in to the need to keep her safe above all else. So many lives were at stake, so many innocents who would suffer if he lost the constant battle between what duty demanded he must do and what he wanted to do.

Something was building, he knew it, and Marthe was involved. It was the only explanation for her tension. The doctor had checked her out, assuring him that Madame was merely suffering a difficult pregnancy; but the doctor didn't see the reports flooding his desk, didn't know of the number upon number of incidents. Trivial enough in themselves, maybe, combined they told of a well-organized and strong resistance movement, readying itself for action.

The reports alone were useless, though. Much as he hated to admit it, Hamon didn't have the authority to act on them, couldn't order the all out mobilization of troops that would halt any uprising. Only the Commander could do that, and without hard evidence, the Colonel would do nothing. In the next weeks, Hamon set his staff to try everything to break through the native facade. To no avail. He introduced agents to Marthe and Jacquel, having them pose as personal servants. After a few days, Marthe informed him that she saw no need of the girl. From which he gathered that she didn't care to be spied on so blatantly. As neither agent had learnt a thing, he agreed to get rid of them. For once he was honest, asking her outright how she'd known the girl was Terran. All he got back was a shocked tirade on the bonds of loyalty and trust in marriage. Glaring angrily at her hypocrisy, he slammed out of the room. He seemed to be making a habit of that lately.

Marthe watched him go, unable to stop a rush of tears. Hormones, she told herself, and knew it for a lie. Her hands brushed uselessly at her wet cheeks.

Now, the end was almost here. Marthe woke one morning, counting dates—a few days only until the Zenith of the Pillars of Mathe. Everything was ready, and she knew of nothing that could stop it. The tide of misery inside her surged to full strength. F-day, the day when all this will explode about her and after which she might never see her husband again. A long, slow tear slid down her cheek. One tear only, escaping the huge dam within.

Hamon was awake beside her. He saw the treacherous drop and reached out to gather her in his arms, one stray finger brushing at her damp cheek. It broke her as nothing else he'd tried, finally shattering the wall of nerves inside her.

Triumph was the one thing he didn't feel as he watched the dam of sorrow in her burst, engulfing her in a paroxysm of weeping such as he'd never seen. Holding her tightly, he rocked her quietly till at long last the storm passed and only a soft hiccup came. Her tear-swollen face moved him only to tenderness; too absorbed was he in the release from wretchedness written there.

"Hush, little love. Nothing can be so bad. You're just run down. Why not have a day in bed?"

Whether it was his voice or his words that soothed her, he couldn't say. The tears stopped, but that was all. He could see the desperation staring from those dark eyes as she whispered: "Promise me Hamon. Please promise, if you leave you will never forget me."

The sheer hell in her voice tore into him, but he held hard to what little control he still possessed, denying the urge to plead, shake her, whatever it took to wring the truth from her.

"Don't be silly. I'll never leave you." He kept his tone deliberately light. "Why would I?"

"Yes, yes, you're right." She was on guard again. "But if you do, you won't forget, will you? And you will see our child?"

"My first-born? Of course I will. And I can never, never forget you, my little Hathian witch." This time he made sure she heard the truth of his words. It must have worked for she subsided into the haven of his shoulders, soon falling asleep again, leaving him thoughtful above her.

So, whatever was to happen, it would be before the birth of the child. Less than three months away. So little time left to crack the rigid surface of these people. He pulled her closer still, anxious to hold on to every remaining minute.

Duty battled his need to stay and finally won. Reluctantly, he let her go, easing gently from the sleeper so as not to wake her.

It was not the gentle lover that strode into his offices a short time later. Today, he couldn't hide his desperation from his men and saw the shock of it in their eyes. Hastily, he pulled up his shutters again, forcing his face into its work mode to reassure his officers. Then he gave them their orders.

"Hawarth. Cancel all passes till further notice, except where the man is known to have native associations. All personnel to be armed at all times. Jones, any breakthrough yet?"

"No, sir. Plenty of vague suspicions, but nothing definite."

"Then put this in the definite category. Source confidential. We can expect the climax within three months, probably sooner."

He might just as well have said her name. They all knew who he meant anyway, but none of them had dared to blatantly voice it since the one foolhardy attempt. The tongue-lashing he'd given the fool had ensured no one else had repeated the question. His private life was exactly that, and he wasn't about to let any man of his become a party to it. Johne and his troops were bad enough.

"No idea of the nature of the event yet, sir?" Jones said neutrally.

"No, but I suspect even more strongly that every Hathian is involved. What about the rest of you?"

"As to the nature, sir, no," said Markham, "but discipline within the native gangs has stepped up recently, particularly from the elders. It's as if they are reining in the younger ones."

"Surely they're not openly ordering them about in front of us?"

"No, nothing so obvious."

They all smiled with him, aware as no other Terrans of the almost continuous web of native communication surrounding them, so subtle in kind that even these keen watchers had yet scratched no more than the surface. "Little things. One of the younger workers in the mines will start to bring up his head in response to an overseer's orders, then will stop and out of the corner of your eye you catch sight of a passing elder. And the younger ones no longer work in peer groups. There's always a senior with them."

"Do they ever speak much?" Jones put in, to be interrupted by a contemptuous snort from Markham.

"Quite," said Hamon coldly. "Whatever the mode of communication, I'd have thought you would have realized by now, Jones, that speech is but a minor aspect."

Jones subsided judiciously. Hamon couldn't afford stupidity in his men, and they knew it.

"Have any of you noticed that the natives seem to be becoming less tolerant of our agents?" dropped Hector into the silence.

This was news to Hamon. "In what way?"

"All my agents are reporting it. In the past, even though we knew they hadn't succeeded in passing themselves off as Hathians, the natives did at least put up with them."

"What's changed?" asked Jones.

"Nothing too obvious, but the natives arrange it so that our agents are given the poorest food and cop the toughest jobs. We're having to pull them in after only a few weeks for recuperation."

"When did this start?"

"About three or four months ago," said Hector.

"About the time of the riot?" Those angry scenes on his wedding day, aborted so assuredly by the two Hathians; a subject his men knew not to mention to him. Whether that was a good thing in his staff, he refused to consider. He would not talk directly to his men about his wife. Not now, not ever.

"That would be correct, sir." replied Hector carefully.

"The same time as the younger peasants started these petty civil disturbances," said Hamon. "These annoying incidents that have managed to keep the Commander's guards fully occupied in patrolling the streets. Though at least they've forced him to bring in manned night patrols. Relying on surveillance vids alone is asking for trouble in the present climate." His fingers drummed pensively on the desk as he stared into the distance. Then he suddenly turned back, his decision made. "Jones, I want you to keep our own troops free, no matter what orders you get from above."

"And what will I tell the Commander, sir?"

"Leave that to me," Hamon said with a grim smile, "and always ensure you have one cohort on full alert. To respond to my signal only. Any other thoughts on what we face and when? I want your gut feeling, not a carefully analyzed assessment."

"No idea of what, sir, but it'll be soon. A matter of weeks at most. My agents tell me you can almost smell the tension in the natives," said the astute Hector.

"Still no cracks in their armor?"

"Not a thing. The stars know what these people are made of, but I admit I'm coming to favor your idea of a huge hoax, incredible as it may seem."

"And you others?"

"It's impossible, surely," denied Jones.

"I'm not so sure," countered a worried Markham.

"I know what you mean. There are too many coincidences. And this peasant population is too subtle for so-called ignorant yokels," said Hawarth.

"My point exactly," said Hamon. "Now, does anyone know how I can put all this to the Commander? And make him believe me?"

Their black smiles were all the answer he needed.

He carried the memory with him as, yet again, he sought an interview with Colonel Johne. Maybe this time he could persuade the man that the risk was real, not part of some grandiose plan of his own to supplant him, as Johne had claimed the last time they'd argued. The stars above knew he already had almost as much power around this place as any one man needed!

Though not quite, he conceded ruefully after a few, short minutes in the Commander's office. That dim-witted, self-seeking specimen alone could provide the official sanction Hamon needed to make the complacent Terrans face up to the reality of the threat facing them.

The Colonel merely looked down his thick, red nose at his junior officer—rejoicing yet again, Hamon knew, in his petty superiority over a member of a family as powerful as Hamon's rather than listening to his arguments. Johne had fallen into the patronizing tone he reserved for their private talks.

"You claim, Major, that these backward illiterates are mounting a full-scale, secret resistance force to overthrow us, yet you have not one verifiable piece of evidence that they possess the scale of technology needed for such an attack."

"Only my wife's words regarding the degree of advancement of her people over ours."

"So your partner likes to think herself your equal. After a few years with a woman, you'll learn to disregard such quirks. They will have their little games!"

"Sir, our own communications unit confirms that her father was a leading scientist of the Alliance. Surely that would make her well placed to know what she's talking about." Despite the plea in his words, Hamon couldn't bring himself to allow any hint of supplication in his voice. He was far too angry.

"Dr an Castre. Yes, I've heard of him. A thoroughly slippery customer, our envoys tell me, and likely the daughter is as bad. I know she bears your first child with all that entails, but a healthy degree of reserve never goes amiss in a relationship."

The Colonel eyed him with what Hamon supposed was a kindly warning. He could feel his anger rising but dared not give way to it; too important was the outcome of this meeting. His silence was misread.

"Glad to see you agree. She's a pretty little thing, I grant you, but best not to let her intrude beyond the bedroom door. I sometimes think your previous arrangements were preferable; at least they gave you a more rounded view of things."

"Perhaps, sir, but not in as much depth. My *wife* is fully as discreet as her compatriots, but she does slip up occasionally. Some of what she says gives me cause for serious concern."

"Hah. There we do agree. Your words give me cause for serious concern, Major. Concern for your fitness to do your duty. Has it occurred to you that the lady may be acting on her own, single-handedly using you to disrupt our entire organization? I am not totally unaware of your meddling." The Colonel's voice was now as cold as Hamon's.

Radcliff stiffened and glared back. "Not single-handed, surely. You forget des Trurain."

"By the stars, Radcliff, you must be suffering battle fatigue. That lightweight gigolo hasn't a serious thought in his head; and his antics do help to raise staff morale, unlike your gloomy whisperings."

"What about the reports, sir? All my staff agree with me. Something's building."

"Because you've infected them with your own pessimism. Your reports are nothing but vague opinions. Bring me concrete proof of a threat, then I might consider action."

"That's your final word on the subject, sir?"

"Yes, Major, it is."

"Then, if you will excuse me, I have work to do."

"Certainly. And I warn you, Major, I do not want to hear of any more morale damaging rumors floating about the place."

Hamon could only nod. He made it through the door without further adding to Johne's triumph, but only just. He held on to his self-control by the merest thread, but once safely back with his own officers, he couldn't keep his failure from them. All they had to do was look at his face. He slammed his fist against the desk.

"Proof! Concrete proof, he says."

"The reports?"

"'Vague opinions', were his exact words. What does the man want, a full-scale revolution?"

"Perhaps. In the meantime, would an example of advanced Hathian technology help?"

Hamon whirled round to see Ferdo grinning at him from the doorway. "What exactly do you mean?"

"I've got it. Proof. Remember those patches of unknown material we found on Marthe and the others? The so-called wound dressings?"

"Yes.

"We've managed to pick up a type of transmission from Marthe's one. Nothing we can make sense of yet, and only on a couple of occasions."

Hope, sudden and badly needed. "You think you've hit on something?"

"You bet." Ferdo's head was almost swelling with excitement as he stood there as cocky as all hell. "We've found their communicator. Those innocuous scraps of material are a sight more than they appear. Hopefully, in a few days we'll figure out how to make them work."

"Can you keep on it full time?" was all Hamon wanted to know.

"Not quite. The Colonel won't let us drop our other stuff."

"Leave that to me. You've got a horde of technicians to take over routine jobs. You just concentrate on that gadget."

"With pleasure. Mind you, if they are as sophisticated as I suspect, they could still stump us."

"Not a bit of it. We all have the greatest faith in you. Don't we, gentlemen?" There was a hearty chorus of assent.

Hamon sat, grinning, for almost a full minute. Beaming at one and all and not caring how uneasy he made his men with his display of benevolence.

"Back to work, everybody," he finally said. "As for me, I think I'll join my wife's step-cousin for the evening. This news deserves a celebration, and the kind of indulgences he favors should fit the bill nicely. And don't tell me it's too early to party, Ferdo, because for once I don't care."

All Marthe knew of his doings that night was that he was late home and that he was happier than she'd seen him for some time. And drunker. He was still enough of both when he woke up to make for a more enjoyable morning than they'd had in some time. Not long after he left for work, she found out why.

"What's that husband of yours up to?" Jaca burst out with as soon as he barged into her room.

She frowned a curt warning at him, hurriedly signaling Central to block the surveillance on her quarters. As soon as it was safe, she blasted Jaca.

"What are you thinking of, coming in here like that and forgetting the most basic of precautions? For all you knew, Hamon might still be here."

Jacquel halted, his face blanching.

"As it happens, he left five minutes ago. Your luck held this time. What's he done that's so dreadful it makes you behave like a complete novice? Apart from setting the place stirring like a madhouse and earning me a severe reprimand from Central."

"He was pleasant to me!"

Marthe stared, then collapsed in a pile of strained hysterics onto the nearest cube. Long moments later, despite the occasional hiccup of glee, she managed to ask him what was so bad about that.

"That man … pleasant … to me? A man he regards as only one step removed from the devil incarnate. In fact, he was jovial, as if celebrating. Just what has he discovered?"

"You're serious!"

"Yes, I am," said an emphatic Jacquel, "so stop giggling like a silly teenager and help me figure it out. Have you noticed any change in Radcliff this morning?"

She smiled quietly, then seeing its effect on Jacquel quickly wiped it away. "What exactly happened last night?" she asked instead.

"It started out fairly normally. A convivial evening with a few friends..."

"A bawdy, licentious evening with a group of tearaways?"

He grinned shamelessly. "Something like that. I'd just managed to get my new best mates into a state where they no longer noticed I wasn't matching their drinks. They'd relaxed nicely—"

"The ladies were becoming conformable?"

"Stop interrupting. These sessions are very useful, as you well know. As it happened, it was a drinking party, no ladies present. If I may continue?" She nodded, smiling again. "They had begun to discuss some very interesting subjects, including your Major. I hadn't realized how far his influence extends. There's not a sector on the planet in which he doesn't have a say. I was nicely milking a junior member of his own staff—and they are notoriously difficult to get close to. This one had recently been on the receiving end of the Major's tongue and was only too happy to pour out his troubles. Then who should walk in but Radcliff himself. First my confidant scuttles away, then your precious husband decides we're best of buddies and starts shouting me drinks. Stars, can he drink," he added, groaning and putting a hand to his head.

"You did keep a discreet tongue in your head?"

"Oh, yes. At least, as far as I know. I would swear that wasn't his purpose anyway. In fact, I had the distinct impression he knows something. Something we would rather he didn't, and he was only too well aware of it."

"Oh? What? You did find out?"

"I was more worried with keeping a sober head. No matter how much I poured into him, he made sure I matched him. I had to hold off in the end. Only problem was, the slower I drank, the faster your husband did. My glory boy image nearly swam away with the dregs."

"So you've convinced Hamon you're a fraud. Did you manage anything constructive?"

Jacquel glared at her for that. "That's rich. Especially since I've told you I don't know how many times that your Major's reputation was well earned. The troops claim he's known in every seedy hole in the Alliance, and from his stories I'd say they were right."

Marthe glared just as heatedly back. "What sort of stories?"

"Nothing he'd want you to know. Suffice to say, no man would be shamed to be drunk under the table by him."

This bit of male arrogance was too much for Marthe. "That was your disastrous event? A couple of silly boys trying to out-drink and out-talk one another?"

"Don't be ridiculous, Mimi." Despite the nickname, she recognized the tone. It came from the stern, sharp-witted soldier hidden so skillfully beneath Jaca's light-hearted facade and silenced her immediately. "Let me make it simple for you. One: Major Radcliff, who normally detests both my company and my morals, goes out of his way to spend an evening with me. Two: he was clearly at ease, with not a hint of his usual reticence or suspicion. Three: despite viewing me as his enemy, he rendered himself vulnerable by drinking heavily. And four: he did not once question said enemy on the subject of vital importance to us both. Namely, the true state of affairs of this planet. In other words, our most dangerous opponent has had a win, and could only truly celebrate it with the one person he felt would lose most by it."

"You were not the only one he celebrated with," she murmured, bitterness twisting the corners of her mouth as understanding struck her.

Jacquel swore softly and immediately the soldier was gone, her oldest friend back. His hand lifted, tilting her chin up and cradling her cheek. "I doubt that was all there was to it with you," he said in the same voice he'd used when he held her after Bendin's funeral as she poured her grief out. He didn't ask how she was feeling, did the baby tire her, was the strain too much. He didn't have to. The answers were carved in her face, the gaunt shadows she saw daily in her mirror. Instead, he took her in his arms, lending her his strength as he had for so many years. After a long while, Marthe smiled gratefully.

"Friend of my twin, I thank you."

"It won't be long now. I've spoken to headquarters and, as of now, you're off all duties. Except Radcliff, of course. That alone is more than enough to fully occupy you."

"Be assured that my husband will be my whole concern."

"Very praiseworthy sentiments, Madame. I am delighted to hear them."

The coolly mocking words came from the indolent figure of that very husband, lolling dubiously in the doorway and speaking in Harmish as had they. Marthe broke quickly from Jaca, one thought uppermost in her mind. How long had he stood there and how much had he heard?

"Hamon, how very silent you were. Fancy listening in to our petty concerns."

"Quite illuminating they were too," he said, a malicious smile lifting the corner of his mouth as he nodded to acknowledge des Trurain; but still it softened as he looked back to her. "How are you today, my dear? Not overdoing it, I trust?"

"A little, "she admitted, hoping he would accept it as a reason for the scene he'd interrupted. "I've been helping Claud Twyford translate some of our old texts. He's a hard taskmaster."

"You'll be glad of a rest, then." She looked up sharply, her internal alarms suddenly at maximum. "It has become necessary for you to keep to your rooms for a period."

"And Jaca?"

"Will also be confined to his own excessively luxurious quarters. It's no longer appropriate to have non-Terrans roaming freely about our central control building."

"I didn't know that I'd offended the Colonel," said Jacquel dryly.

"You haven't, but don't bother appealing to him. Two of my men will be outside your door at all times and, as I am sure you're aware, I have my own means of preventing any assistance you may be expecting."

"And our door?" said Marthe sharply. "Will it also be guarded?"

"Unfortunately, my dear, my officers don't trust you quite as much as I do," Hamon replied, coolly apologetic. "Des Trurain, your escort is waiting." He gestured to two large guards, both possessing that intangible air of professionalism she'd learnt to recognize in Hamon's men.

Solemnly, she turned to Jacquel and took him by the hand, feeling a hard squeeze in answer to her 'take care' sign. "Till we meet again, sister of my friend," he whispered. Then, in arrogant defiance and staring coldly at his Terran nemesis, he walked out between his guards. Marthe watched in silence. The door shut, and she turned to confront her husband.

"So, we're back to prisoner and warder again. May I ask why?" She regarded him warily, one hand surreptitiously feeling for her back. She'd taken to wearing a blaster concealed in a skin pocket there, so natural in feel that not even Hamon in their most intimate moments could detect the pad of matter condensing material.

"You may ask, but I'm not free to answer."

"Can you at least tell me how long this imprisonment is to last? Will I be allowed rations this time?" she asked caustically, nerves on edge.

"Certainly. You have, after all, earned them."

"In what manner?" She kept her face carefully devoid of expression and switched her patch to record.

"You haven't been as discreet as you thought. I will tell you that we're on the verge of a major breakthrough, one for which I have you to thank. It will halt, once and for all, whatever it is your fellow conspirators are planning." His eyes raked her, daring her to flinch, to throw at him the wild thoughts swirling through her.

"So, we're back to that old plot again. Your story lines lack imagination, Hamon."

She spoke with such precision and control that Hamon was compelled to applaud silently. As an agent provocateur she would be superb. Was superb, he corrected himself. But two could play that game, and his experience was the equal of hers. Or so he hoped, wondering, as so often before, exactly what she had been up to over the last five years. He let none of these thoughts show as he strolled toward her.

Marthe watched him approach. The planes of his face had sharpened, throwing the whole into a harsh cast. It was a face she'd almost forgotten, one she'd not seen since the early days of her captivity. The eyes of brilliant cut emerald challenged her from beneath hooded lids as he dropped into an adjacent cube, leaning over to flick her chin with one iron finger.

Startled, she jumped. Briefly, she knew her fear showed in her face. She hid it as quickly as she could, but too late. Hamon had seen it. She saw the knowledge of it in his suddenly darkening eyes, and the pain of self-hatred as he drew back and lapsed into an awkward silence, his hand abruptly drawn back and clenched at his side.

Then his face changed. She recognized it too easily. It was the mask of Major Radcliff, just as she wore the mask of the Haut Liege. Inside, she wept as Major Radcliff broke the silence, in a voice that said nothing of moment had happened between them. He was thinking of asking his mother to return to Hathe for a longer visit, he said, and when would be convenient to Marthe.

She studied him, all senses alert. Just as Hamon had, she forced Marthe to the background and made herself become only Agent an Castre.

Why the switch of subject? It was innocuous enough, but after the fiasco of their last meeting, he must know there was little warmth between his mother and her. Was he concerned for the baby? Or was this something else. Was he in fact asking her how safe were the Terrans on Hathe? When would the resistance act? And did he actually believe she would give him an answer?

She had to admit it would be very advantageous to have the Administrator here on F-day. Madame MacDiarmid knew all the details of Earth's food distribution system and would be a valuable hostage. Dare she attempt to arrange it? She settled for a noncommittal reply, avowing her delight at his mother's visit whenever it should suit the Administrator's busy schedule. His brows lifted in spurious disbelief.

"You're sure it won't be too much for you?" He was staring lazily out the window, his fingers playing idly through her hair.

"Not at all. Make it as soon as possible, if you like," she replied, swallowing nervously. Goosebumps jumped to life under his caressing fingers.

"Probably within days, then. She's currently on an audit of our base at Outer Georgia, as it happens, so it's only a short hop to here in this phase of the Hathian system's gates. Mother said that she didn't have enough time to get to know you on her last visit, so hopefully she can stay longer this time. Or would you rather we left it a few weeks?"

She hastily began calculating interstellar times and possibilities. It could be done, just. "Within a few days would be fine," she said, falling badly into the open pit.

The hand stopped suddenly and he turned back towards her, a cynical twist to his lips. "Thank you, my dear. That was all I needed to know. You'll be happy to know that your own imprisonment will last only a matter of days also. How long, would you say—three, five, or maybe nine?"

By all the Pillars! What had she done? She dragged back a lock of hair falling in her eyes, hastily scrabbling the alert code on her patch as she did so, then tapped out 're-run recording'.

He watched her, amused at this habit of hers of pulling on her ear lobe whenever his words hit too close.

It was the only sign she let him see of the turmoil he'd aroused. "Whatever you wish. I hadn't planned to be going anywhere for the next three months," she said, looking pointedly down at the bulge of her waistline.

"I hope it will also be possible for me to remain here that long," he tossed back at her, both a question and a challenge in his hard, green eyes.

"Why ever not?" she said in a flash, daring him to bring into the open what lay beneath their words. In the event, he only grinned as if in applause, before quixotically reverting to the playful lover she knew so well, holding her easily and planting a light kiss on her brow. As if the past moments had never been. She reached up to inactivate the alert code, pensively listening to her husband as he asked her what she wanted for dinner that evening. Almost banished was the stranger of the last few minutes.

Or was he? This easy chat tore more at her nerves than the hard-eyed, interrogating officer ever could. This man she almost knew. She said little through dinner, unable for once to copy Hamon as he hid behind a chorus of banter. What had he discovered? What had changed everything so suddenly? And how was she going to distract him from some unknown event? God, there were but four days to go. Surely all would not be lost at this last moment, just because she'd failed.

Restless, plotting and weaving still as they retired for the night, she was finally defeated by sleep.

Hamon lay beside her, watching the machinations flit across her unusually expressive face. He did nothing, could not move to comfort her. Just lie here on guard, closed off and silent, torn between triumph and dread. How many more nights would they have?

CHAPTER EIGHTEEN

Marthe devoted the next day to serious socializing. Fortunately for her cover, Hamon had put out that he was worried by the increasing threat to the two Hathian Haut Liege from the peasants' violence, telling anyone interested that Marthe and Jacquel had chosen to keep to the security of their quarters. She knew he did it only to stop other Terrans from interfering with his imprisonment of her and Jacquel, but his story meant he couldn't stop them using the vidphones, barring calls to each other. Marthe made full use of the privilege while it lasted.

Her first call was to Helen Ravensbot, the Terran woman she was most friendly with … but not close to. The hardness at the core of the Terrans always repelled Marthe, but in Helen she sensed one who, if reared under different circumstances, would have been a delight to know, full of the joy of living. As it was, she retained a delicious sense of fun which insisted on bubbling up through the careful cynicism displayed by all the Terran troops—a cynicism understandable in her case. Daily, Helen's Stores department faced a battle to keep enough of Hathe's bounty on-planet to supply the garrison, in spite of ever more avaricious calls from her crowded and desperately needy home world. Simultaneously, she had to somehow wring the equipment the

Hathe-based troops needed from an Earth reluctant to grant anything to a colony from which had leaked back unbelievable tales of wealth and luxury.

Marthe had listened in surprise when she'd first heard Helen complain. Privately, she judged the Terran quarters and rations to be merely adequate. To her, they lacked an element—call it style, finesse, whatever—but the years of scrabbling for every last necessity had stripped something from the Terrans.

It was only in Hamon's rooms that Marthe felt truly comfortable. The other rooms were furnished as expensively, enhanced with personal fripperies, but it was as if some basic essence of life was absent. Or perhaps buried, to burst forth occasionally in the elegance of Hamon's rooms, or the cheeky laughter of the pretty brunette now grinning at her from the Tri-D chamber.

Her use of the chamber was one more thing to mark Marthe as different. She persisted in using the most energy expensive mode of the vids whereas Helen used the small vidscreen only, considering the life-size, full projection of the chamber as wasteful for a mere chat.

"Helen, you can't tell me there's an energy shortage on Hathe." It was an old argument, a ritual of every vidcall, without which neither would have felt comfortable.

"Marthe, that's restricted data, as you're well aware—even if I did know the answer," remonstrated the other, completing the formula. "Tell me instead of this dreadful threat to you. I can't believe the peasants are capable of causing any real harm." She shivered theatrically, the hint of danger bringing a delighted sparkle to her eyes.

"I shouldn't think so," said Marthe soothingly. "I don't know what Hamon's so stirred up about. I suppose the threat is from the natives."

Helen stared. "Marthe! You can't think it comes from our own forces." Marthe smiled to herself. If only Hamon could hear that 'our'.

He seemed to be the only Terran who always remembered that she and Jacquel were not from Earth.

"I don't know what to think. Hamon would surely have told me all the details if the threat came from the peasants, so that I'd know how to keep safe, but he's said nothing."

"But who would do such a thing, and why?" Helen leant forward, deliciously mystified.

"Who knows? Mind you, silly jealousies often surround a woman able to wear beautiful clothes and do them justice, as you of course know. Maybe that's all this is."

Marthe was amused to see Helen's glow at the flattering inference. All her life, Marthe had been forced to listen to comments about her vaunted beauty. Only her twin Bendin, equally blessed himself, had treated such talk as it deserved, and even he had admitted she 'didn't look half bad … if you like squirty little midgets'. Today, though, Marthe needed any advantage offered, and if comparing the looks of the pretty but not uncommon Helen to Marthe's more dramatic beauty would help her, she'd swallow her embarrassment and do it.

Helen giggled, then stretched in pure, sensuous joy. "Marthe, dear, I know exactly what you mean," she replied, in a languid drawl, clearly borrowed from their other friend, the sultry Jocelyn Harp. The effect was ruined by the grin that rapidly followed. "Just imagine, fisticuffs in evening gowns. How luscious." She laughed out loud and Marthe sighed ruefully. Helen was right. It was ludicrous to think any Terran would endanger her favored position on Hathe for such a trivial emotion as envy.

"If that's not it, then what is the problem? Why the big mystery? If it's restricted data, why doesn't Hamon just say so? He always has before," she added with considerable force of feeling. "What's so different this time?"

Helen didn't answer immediately and Marthe cursed. She'd been too vehement, showed too much of the anxiety that racked her. She watched Helen study her and saw the instant that recognition hit the Terran woman: Marthe was not, in fact, from Earth.

She'd muffed it. Worse, she was suddenly forced to excuse herself, overcome by a wave of nausea.

When she returned, she saw the shock on Helen's face. Marthe had pinched her cheeks before she left the bathroom, breathed deeply and scrubbed at her cheeks. Anything to disguise the washed out face she'd seen in the mirror. It didn't work. She couldn't hide the haggard planes, the deep shadows beneath the eyes, the skin stretched taut over barely covered bones, all too starkly defined by her sudden pallor.

"Stars, Marthe, you look like a lower level, non-producer on Earth. When did you last eat?"

"It's merely the pregnancy," said Marthe, a touch too offhand. "I'm one of the unlucky ones who get stuck with nausea right through, the doctor says."

"Pregnant women don't usually look as bad as you."

"Thank you very much. It's so nice to be reminded that I'm am starting to look frumpy and bulging." She made herself laugh, one hand protectively over the gentle swelling of her belly.

"You want that baby very much, don't you?"

Helen smiled, but Marthe wasn't fooled into thinking it was sincere. Helen was too much the product of a planet where a baby was but another mouth to feed. She doubted expectant mothers on Earth openly displayed the joy Marthe felt at the thought of her baby. Yet she couldn't deny it.

"Of course I do," she said now. Then changed the subject before she might further remind Helen of the differences between them. She put on her brightest face and threw herself into the normal gossip of their chats: talk of friends in common and those not so well liked, of trivia and scandal and all the small doings of the fortress, anything to dredge up some clue to the strange happenings of yesterday.

Helen joined in, but Marthe could see much of her mind was busy elsewhere. When Helen excused herself soon afterwards, Marthe contacted Central and got them to plug her into Helen's vidlines.

She had been right to worry. Helen almost immediately put a call through to their other friend, Jocelyn. And the topic of conversation? Marthe and Hamon, of course. She listened with growing dread as she heard the two women indulge in a half hour of mutually enjoyable character shredding.

Helen couldn't wait to tell Jocelyn of her chat with Marthe and described her loss of looks all too vividly. From there, it was a very short step to the kind of speculation Marthe least needed. Was all not well between Hamon Radcliff and his beautiful Hathian? Could Radcliff be cooling?

"He's already kept her far longer than any of us expected," she heard Helen say. "It's been nearly six months now. How romantic."

"And how stupid," replied Jocelyn, as they both laughed cruelly.

From there, it didn't take long for the two women to move on to wondering about the sudden confinement of the Hathians. Could there actually be some truth to Radcliff's scare mongering? Marthe couldn't listen to any more. She left the rest for central to record and analyze. She'd heard enough.

From this tiny ripple, the damage quickly spread in ever widening circles of distrust. Increasingly, she noticed a new coolness, a tightening of the Terran ranks signaled by ever more frequent apologies and refusals to talk when she put through a vidcall. Jaca was soon on to her as well, demanding to know what was going on. He was getting the same treatment, and neither could do anything to stop the ripples gaining momentum. By the following evening, her reports told her, they lapped at Hamon's feet.

A sharp salute from a soldier was Hamon's first sign that his position was changing. It was so unusual, so different from the normal half-hearted hand jerk he got these past months that he was shaken rudely from his current worries. It was obviously time he took as much notice of the Terrans as he did the Hathians that threatened them. And once he did, the new air of alert readiness among the troops was unmistakable. Even more unsettling was their growing willingness to cooperate with his staff's orders. That was almost frightening in its novelty. Nevertheless, he used the change to his full advantage, grateful for any help.

The presence of Johne's ferrets hanging around his office signaled that the Commander was finally taking an interest in the changes. Or more probably, thought Hamon cynically, Johne was worried that if he didn't take action, he was in danger of losing all authority to his so-called 'junior'—something the man would never countenance.

So it seemed he was no longer the joke of the garrison. He smiled sourly to himself amidst the growing confidence of his men. At least, he reflected, you can take comfort in the knowledge that you have done your duty. For along with growing awareness of his own success, he couldn't miss the worsening tension in Marthe, sapping the life from her. From the surveillance vids he knew that scarce enough food passed her mouth in a day to feed the child, let alone the mother who nurtured it. Nor was the little she ate much use to her. The digester records showed that her nausea led to vomiting more than once each day. The hope emanating from Ferdo's workshop fueled a rare excitement in the professional part of him, but he kept it from her and never told her of the signals they were picking up regularly. Why trouble her further, when none had yet been decoded? She guessed too much already, and it was literally killing her.

He entered his apartment on the third night of her latest confinement beset with fear and was immediately aware of a new aura of desperation surrounding her. He stopped a moment in the doorway, watching her taut figure curled up in one of the cube chairs, her head sunk beseechingly into her cupped hands as she stared out the window. In silence, he studied the stark etching of her bones through the translucent skin, the grey smudges filling the deep hollows of her eyes, the softly swelling belly pushing on her gown sharply contrasting with the dangerous angularity of the rest of her tired body.

She was so thin, wasting away before him. The records showed that when not calling acquaintances, she spent her days sleeping. The number of calls had decreased as the coolness in her Terran confidantes grew. Des Trurain had likewise spent his time calling on hoped-for allies, but the change in atmosphere among the Terrans had given Hamon all the excuse he needed to transfer his nemesis back to a security cell, stopping any further outside contact.

Hamon made no attempt to deny the dark thrill at knowing the Hathian was once more locked away in the prison wing. He wondered if Marthe knew of it yet. Probably, he concluded sourly. From the coincidental nature of their calls these last days, he had to assume they were still in contact. Despite the complete lack of any sign of it on the surveillance records.

He realized, then, that she was not sunk in thought as he'd first assumed. Rather, she was asleep where she sat. Had sat for some time, but it was not a tranquil rest. Stark despair shivered in the grim cast of her face. Sleep had come hardily, breaking down the barriers on guard about the tired fortress of her mind. Yet her rigidly held body fought back. Sleep could only stop the pacing, the restless prowling he saw in the vids, the endless plotting scribed onto her face as she searched for ways to defeat him, to keep faith with whoever it was who held her loyalty. Right now, her overtaxed body had finally defeated her, forcing a temporary surrender.

All this came to him at the deep level below consciousness that was their only channel left to breach the distance between them. Politics denied them the language of words, but not the language of the body. That didn't lie. Yet it could not tell all. It could not tell him whether he would win this deadly battle—or what would be left to them afterwards.

Marthe was not as fully asleep as she seemed. Dozing, lost in plans, she still plotted, still drew on the core of strength she tried not to let Hamon see, still fought back as, one by one, he crashed doors shut on her. Desperation held her in a stranglehold. Desperation, but not yet its twin, despair. She refused to succumb to that, to the black pit that waited when nothing more could be attempted.

She could feel it pulling her in, even as she denied its lure. Instead, she gave in to the state of mind that filled her before every mission, multiplied so many times greater now. Power hummed through her, and she was strung up to a high pitch, capable of whatever wild and crazy action might be required. The orders from HQ had been very clear: in the event of disaster, use any means available. Far better that she and Jacquel be sacrificed—all her hopes of life, love and laughter lost—than the terrible carnage that must follow premature discovery of their plans.

They were so close to success. All she had to do was hold out till tomorrow, the long-awaited Zenith of the Pillars of Mathe—the day unique to this solar system, when sun, planet and moon would come together in a configuration of devastating effect. It occurred only once every ten years, and the Hathians had developed their technology to cope with the anomaly created in that time. The Terrans were ignorant of this foreign system. The hated conquerors would be vulnerable then, and the resistance would attack.

When even her home system conspired against the Terrans, how could she fail her people?

She moved fitfully in the cube, twitching angrily. She should be happy. She was about to achieve everything she'd fought five years for, but there was that other thought that gnawed at her constantly. The knowledge that with her state victory must come private disaster, hers and Hamon's. Here she could no longer fight. Despair won. Once she was forced to action, there was no way for her and Hamon to stay together.

Unless? Was there a hope? What if Hathe offered Earth the help it so badly needed? "We must," she vowed. "We must!" Her clenched fist lifted angrily against the cube and came down with such a blow that she frightened herself from her doze. Startled, she toppled sideways, to be caught in strong arms. Still half-asleep, her arms came up automatically, to wind hard around his shoulders, hold so tightly that never would he leave.

Gently, Hamon eased her onto his lap as he sat in the cube. It was still molded to her slighter figure, but soon flattened out to suit his larger frame.

For a while, she fought to wake, to sit up and talk. As if with a baby, he gentled her down, calming the harrowed fears haunting her face. It worked. Subsiding back into the warm shoulder with a whispered "Hamon", she drifted off again, a tired smile hovering about her mouth.

They stayed like that for most of the night, Hamon fearful of moving lest she wake from her much needed sleep—the first true sleep she'd enjoyed in many days. He sat—still, stony, but warm and comforting to his woman despite aching shoulders and a cricked neck.

Well after midnight, he finally relaxed into sleep, letting the cube mold and cosset them both as he drifted off.

Marthe woke slowly and looked out towards the big bank of windows at the end of the apartment. It was still night, the sun not yet risen to obliterate the delicate trace of moonshine lingering still.

Then it hit her, a hammer blow to her gut, what that faint glow signaled: the rarely seen, delicate wash of light that was the fading into day of Hathe's smaller moon, Mathe. So faintly it shone normally that it never seemed clear to a watcher whether it owed allegiance to Hathe or the larger moon, Dromorne.

Tonight, it had decided. At midnight, Mathe had shone brightly in the Hathian sky. On its dead slopes stood seven ghostly columns, ancient relics of an unknown people. The Pillars of Mathe. On Mathe, this night just past, the shining circle of Hathe rose high in the lunar sky, almost reaching the middle of the seven pillars. Tonight, it would stand over the central one, a shining beacon of triumph announcing the end of the ten-year cycle that brought the heavenly bodies together once more. The night of the Zenith of Hathe.

CHAPTER NINETEEN

When next she woke, it was the sun that shone in her eyes. Blinking, she peered over Hamon's comfortable bulk to the brightly lit balcony beyond. She was not the only one awake. They had left the windows open last night, and a tiny Hathian flitter, alive in a riot of gaudy livery, was perched on the overly green leaves of Hamon's Terran plant. The creature sat quite still, peering closely at the wrongness of the carbon dioxide-enhanced plant, then flicked up and jumped around, to stare at her with disdain. No bigger than a thumb and less than a meter away, it was totally unconcerned by her nearness. Almost she could believe that multi-lensed eye winked at her in conspiracy. Then it took a cautious bite of the tainted plant. Immediately, it spat out the green stuff, clawing at the foulness of its mouth in disgust. Marthe would swear it was revenge that drove the tiny claws to shred the offending leaf to nothing. Then, with a last, defiant sprint round the balcony, it flew off—no doubt to seek genuine Hathian fodder.

So much for Terrans, eh little one? She smiled to herself, delighted with the arrogance of the tiny animal. Sitting up, she stretched, feeling laughter gurgle up through her body.

The movement woke Hamon. He rolled onto his back and grinned up at her. "You've woken in a good mood this morning."

She was glad he was awake, glad he could share in the life coursing through her. Rapturously, she launched herself into his quickly opened arms.

"Oof! Assault so early in the day?"

She barely gave him a chance to catch a breath, before her mouth fastened hungrily onto his and her fingers set to rousing his avid interest. He showed no reluctance to join in her game, quickly catching her mood. They were vigorous cubs at play. Tickling here, smoothly caressing there, stirring up laughter and passion both.

The cube had spread out to become a wide couch during the night, but still they tumbled off, Hamon swinging quickly round to cushion her from harm before they cheerfully righted themselves, only to drown once more in shared wonder. She could feel the hard mass of him, the sleek lines of trained muscles that knew very well when to change from gentle caress to a hard, insistent masculinity. Eventually, laughter was defeated by passion, but even as his firm strokes drove her onwards, she felt their smiles linger, caught in the corners of gasping mouths.

Afterwards, she snuggled in to his chest, one hand straying still to comb the dark curls at the base of his neck as he slowly traced the curve of her belly, placing a soft kiss there for the baby. His eyes caught sight of the timer and he caught at her hand, bringing it tenderly to his lips before smiling ruefully.

"I ought to be going. If, that is, you have finished with my services?"

"Yes, for the moment, thank you."

She leaned back, reclining on one elbow in sensuous nonchalance then spoiled the illusion by hurling herself at him and grabbing him in a huge bear hug that tumbled them backwards in a sprawling heap, a look of panic on Hamon's face till he saw the grin on hers and she broke into giggles as they slid farther over. The door chime sounded as they hit the floor. One of Hamon's guards no doubt, wondering what had become of him.

Hamon was the first to untangle himself, still laughing. "Can't let my staff see me like this. They might think I'm human after all." He began to scrabble about for his discarded clothing, calling over the comms channel for the guards to wait a moment.

He quickly cleansed and dressed for the day while Marthe tidied the debacle of the lounge. All too soon, the only remnant of their moment of refuge was the smile still hovering inside her. She disappeared while Hamon spoke to the officer at the door and did not see who the man was. Hamon came in to the bedroom, to say only that he had to go, urgently. She knew better than to ask questions but clung to him wordlessly as a thought came to her: this may be their last time together.

"No time for more games, love," Hamon remonstrated, failing to pick up her change of mood. He gave her a quick peck on the forehead as she released him. Dimly, she heard him leave, clapping the other man on the shoulder.

"Right, we'd better see what's got Captain Braddock so excited."

At the time, the words failed to penetrate the cloud of sadness that fell on her, as quick and as real as the joyous abandon of her early rising. But there was no time for sorrow when Hathe needed her. Time to begin her preparations for the afternoon's action; she threw herself with relief in to her duties. As a distraction, it worked, until later that morning when Hamon's careless words suddenly came back to her in a rush.

Captain Braddock—his friend Ferdo—who was also a highly trained communications scientist. Ferdo had once told her that he tolerated the harsh, military regime on Hathe solely for what it gave him—the chance of a lifetime to test Terran equipment in an alien environment. Diplomacy had kept her silent but had not quelled the angry rebuttal inside. Surely someone who had heard of her Father's work would realize the more advanced Hathians had long ago solved all the problems that now excited him so much!

Still, Ferdo was one of the few Terrans with any knowledge of more recent Alliance advancements in technology. She put an urgent call through to his office.

A guardswoman appeared on the screen. "The communications room is not open to personal calls at present. May I know the nature of your business?" came the coldly impersonal voice.

"It was nothing important. I merely wished to ask Major Radcliff when he will be home tonight. I'll call him at his own office later."

"The Major will be here all day. I will tell him of your request, Madame an Castre."

The screen went blank.

Bendin's foulest expletive exploded from her. How could she have overlooked the most obvious source of danger? She hastily blocked the Terran surveillance vids in her room and contacted Central with her fears. To no avail. Everyone was busy with last minute checks. Eventually, she managed to get through to Jaca, but he, too, was fully occupied with getting ready for the final assault on the Citadel and had no time to talk. He did hear her out, sparing her a half-distracted moment.

"What can they do at this late stage?" was his harried response.

"Make the whole thing a lot bloodier than necessary, that's what!"

"Only if they manage to discover anything, which is unlikely. Earth doesn't have the expertise." There was a distinct lack of sympathy in his tone. "Radcliff's your ball game. If you suspect a problem, deal with it. The rest of us have enough to do already."

He broke off, leaving her staring into space and biting her lips. Carefully, she ticked off the contents of her concealed body pouch. Most particularly, the blaster hidden there. Her practice shots left a gaping hole in the bedroom wall, impossible to explain if Hamon should find it, but it was reassuring to find her accuracy as sharp as ever.

She toyed with lunch, scarcely tasting the nourishing fare she forced herself to swallow, and was very pleased to see Hamon enter soon afterwards, forgetting for a moment the damage to the bedroom. Luckily, he was in haste. Then she saw the grim cast of his face.

"I hope you've finished eating. Your presence is required elsewhere."

"Hamon, it's midday. Whatever would people say," she replied coquettishly, deliberately misreading his words. He didn't answer, seizing her by the arm and leading her out of the room.

"Please, you're hurting me." She tried pulling away from his harsh grip.

"Sorry." The tone was curt, but his hand relaxed a fraction—though not enough to let her escape.

She let a brush stroke of fear color her voice. "Whatever's going on?"

"Nothing will happen to you, I promise. No matter what." There was a desperate hollowness to his words; and while she felt excitement in him, she also sensed anger. At what, she couldn't guess, unless it was her pathetic delaying tactics. She forced her body to subside, appearing to acquiesce. Yet every nerve and muscle was taut, ready, as so often in the past, for whatever might be needed.

They soon arrived at their destination—the communications wing. There was no surprise in her. The guard appeared to expect them, waving them through to Ferdo's inner sanctum: the Terran central communications control room. Lights, screens and banks of equipment covered the walls in a threatening array. In the far corner sat the duty technician, constantly monitoring a myriad of channels.

The only other occupant was Ferdo, listening intently to a crackling, distorted fragment of sound coming from a nearby speaker. Beside him, an energy cone had been set up and beneath it, she saw, lay one of the old patches. That crackle of sound told her they'd found nothing dangerous yet. Despite that, her internal alarm was on high alert and there was no relaxation within her. She cleared her mind, setting aside the personal and letting the familiar, icy logic of her training take over.

Ferdo's head turned as they entered, his face glowing with anticipation. "Hamon, you're back, and with Marthe. Good."

"Nice to see you, Ferdo. Now, by all the Pillars what are you two so eager to show me?" she said.

Hamon tensed up, as surprised as Ferdo looked at Marthe's apparent willingness to cooperate. It was too abrupt a change from her earlier fear. But Marthe was not Terran, and right now that was what he must remember. The survival of all those millions on Earth must come first, whatever it cost him. The cost to her he dared not consider. Not if he was to do his duty here. She would be safe and physically unharmed; that was all he had the right to promise, and he grimly checked the room for possible escape routes. Hamon would have sworn her earlier fear had been real and, since entering, she'd never once turned her back on any of them. Not even on the harmless technician at the far side of the room.

Ferdo put down his probe and took a step forward. "Marthe, thank you for coming. If you would just take this seat and stretch your wrist out here, we can begin?"

"Begin what?"

"A little experiment," said Hamon in a tone that brooked no argument.

"It's that unusual patch you once wore," explained Ferdo enthusiastically. "I feel sure the key to it is bringing it in contact with the owner. We're going to return the patch to your wrist, then cover the whole with a cone. Hopefully we can then make some sense of these noises we're picking up. The Colonel will have to listen to us then."

"What arrant nonsense!" Marthe snatched her hand away. By the Pillars! This was more than she'd bargained for. Hamon caught hold of her wrist again and returned it firmly to the table. Coldly, he called Ferdo's duty officer over.

"Technician, as the Colonel has seen fit to limit our use of force field generators," he said, a grim cast to his face, "you will restrain this lady and prevent her from moving."

The next minute, Marthe found herself pinned tightly, her right hand firmly held behind her back. If she even tried to struggle, the man would surely break her arm. Her other hand was pulled onto the bench, palm up. She glared at Hamon, daring him wordlessly to explain. He merely stepped back, hiding whatever he felt behind the implacable barrier of his set face.

The technician who held her was too well trained and too strong. Despite all she attempted, her wrist was brought relentlessly under the cone and the patch placed against her skin. Please, God, let it not be activated.

Ferdo hunched anxiously over his toys, but for all his furious twiddling, the crackling cacophony was unchanged.

"Maybe if we enlarge the field of reception to take in the whole body," he said. The cone tilted towards her as his finger played on the controls. Still the crackling. His fingers moved viciously, then stopped, frustrated.

Hamon stared at Marthe, thinking hard. A memory jarred at the edge of consciousness, some niggling habit of hers. They had to be close. She was too unhappy with their activities, despite her innocent veneer.

"Of course, "he exclaimed suddenly. Taking over with a hold as strong as the technician's, he grabbed her other hand, bringing it inexorably forward.

"What do you think you're doing," Marthe demanded, but knew too well. Try as she might to avoid it, her hand was brought round and the fingers pressed firmly against the patch. So tight was his grip that she couldn't move her fingers, couldn't warn her people with the alarm code. The patch was fully active and the Hathians had no idea of it. Horror engulfed her.

"I think it's activated by finger contact," she now heard Hamon say to Ferdo. "I've often seen Marthe tapping her arms in the past, or more recently, tugging her ear." And despite her outraged gasp, he pushed her hair aside to pull back her earlobe. "Nothing there," she was relieved to hear him say, as his fingers brushed across her improved patch, snugly sitting in the ear crease. "Try it again, Ferdo."

Tensely, Marthe watched the Captain. Again, a babble of sound broke through, but this time, they were undeniably human sounds. Ferdo flashed a triumphant grin. Again, he adjusted his controls. The babble broke up, separating into its parts. Until only one damning voice spoke. The accent was the same as her own, the language, Harmish.

"Section nine reporting. All units set and ready to move."

"Central receiving, section nine. Confirm all go to move at third pillar. Mark Zenith start at 19.00 hours, sun at one degree below horizon."

Marthe heard the words in dread. Hamon still held her, even as he translated excitedly to Ferdo.

"That's it. Our proof!" Ferdo shouted exultantly.

Hamon grinned back in triumph. After all this time. He hurriedly reviewed the Hathian calendar and the difference between Hathian and Terran standard hours. "That's for tonight!"

Releasing Marthe, he strode across to the nearest vid. "I'll let the Commander know immediately. He has to turn the guard out now. We've won, Ferdo!"

As his hand reached for the call pad, a blinding pain slashed through his arm. Gasping, he swung back. Marthe's hand was stretched out in front of her and she stood eerily still, legs apart and braced. In her hand was a strange blaster. It was aimed directly at his heart.

One agonizing beat, and hope ended.

"I wouldn't make that call," said his beloved.

"Or?"

"A repeat of the last pain,"

"I can bear it," he warned,

"Then Ferdo's death or damage to you."

He believed her. Her stance was too real, had too much the mark of a trained professional. She had used a low blaster setting on him, but he'd seen before how swiftly she could change it. She had already moved to bring both Ferdo and the technician within range and, for the present, it seemed he must play along, waiting all the while for his own split-second chance. Must forget that it was Marthe at the end of that blaster—an agonizing blow he would deal with later. For now, he had to see only an enemy. He forced himself into battle mode.

Conceding with a shrug, he moved away from the wall and towards her. Sudden, killing heat seared a line a hair's breadth in front of his foot.

"No closer," she threatened. He saw the concrete cast of her face, the poised shoulder, the practiced finger upon the blaster.

"You should watch where you point that thing."

"I know what I'm doing."

It wasn't a boast. Not after that scene on the balcony facing the angry crowd of Hathian peasants. He moved back, ever aware of her eyes watching, then saw her free hand go up to tug at her ear. That old, not so innocent habit.

Marthe saw the recognition in his eyes as she tapped out the alarm signal, eyes which constantly raked her for any sign of weakness.

"Report," came the voice of Central in her head. Quickly, she explained the situation. The silence as she waited for a reply seemed endless.

"The room is sealed and a temporary recording in progress." It was the cultured voice of deln Crantz.

"And the technician function?"

"We will send a replacement. It's imperative that you keep the Terrans inside that room. They must not be allowed to reveal what they know until the assault has begun. Estimate one thousand casualties if you fail." Her commander signed out, no reply needed.

She looked at her husband. No, her foe. That was what she must see now. Her enemies—the Terrans she had to keep confined here—and she noted the fear in the faces of Ferdo and the technician as they watched her.

It wasn't surprising. She was still using the resistance code to communicate with Central—a mix of words and taps on her ear patch. All they would hear was the odd word spoken. Unimportant, meaningless phrases, easily woven into a covering conversation, to add to the tiny movements of her fingers on the skin behind her ear— the secret language that had surrounded the unknowing Terrans.

On Hamon's face there was no fear, only jaded comprehension.

A glacial answering image to her own posture, he'd chosen to prop himself against the far wall, legs insolently crossed in languid carelessness.

"You may try the vid," she said to him," though it will be of no use to you. This room is now sealed."

"Within five minutes, someone will miss the controlling technician and realize something is wrong."

"We have temporary control of that function until a replacement of our own arrives," she returned.

"You don't mind if I try anyway?"

Hamon didn't wait for her nod to move over to the panel, but he moved slowly enough not to spook her, ever conscious of her weapon. Even before he pressed the button, he knew there would be no response. He turned to shrug at Ferdo at the very moment the duty technician panicked and broke for the door. Quicker than he would have thought possible, that deadly weapon swung about, spat out a missile, and the technician slumped to the floor.

Ferdo stared at him, wide-eyed and slack-mouthed. "Stars, you've killed him," he spat in disgust, any lingering trace of friendship for Marthe banished from Ferdo's voice. That was something at least. Ferdo needed to understand exactly what kind of enemy they were up against here. If he didn't, the cool disregard in her voice should have told him.

"It is no more than your people have done to mine often enough," she said.

Hamon bent down to inspect the man and saw the steady breathing, the scorch mark of a low-grade charge against the back of his neck and the faint pin mark on his neck. He looked up, eyebrows raised. "Drugged?"

She nodded, the blaster rock-steady in her hands.

"For how long?"

"Twenty-four hours, unless I give him the antidote sooner."

"And will you?"

"Only if he shows signs of a serious adverse reaction. I can last as long as I have to, if that's what you're asking."

"So we're next?"

She shook her head. "I carried only one dart pin."

"If you want to stop us, you'll have to shoot Ferdo—or me."

His eyes held hers in challenge. She never flinched.

"Yes."

Would she do it? He didn't know and dared not risk it. Not yet. For now, he must give way. There was time yet. He let his lids droop down to hide his frustration as he turned and stood, moving to take a nearby chair.

Unfortunately, Ferdo wasn't so sanguine, not with one of his own staff lying unconscious on the floor.

"Hamon, stop talking and do something!"

"Do what, exactly? Marthe appears to hold the upper hand at present. Don't you, my dear?"

Marthe nodded grimly, already hating this game of taunting mockery he'd chosen.

"I don't know," cried Ferdo, "but there are two of us, against a mere woman."

"Well trained and, let me point out, with a blaster of greater capability than our own. I assume it has a destruct function?" He looked at her, as if to clarify an interesting detail, and again she nodded grimly.

"Yes, but she wouldn't use it. By the stars, under their law she's your wife."

"I assure you, my *wife* is quite capable of blowing us both to perdition."

The cold anger seeping through the mockery sent a chill through Marthe. For an instant, she glimpsed an icy fury and knew he was fighting to control it as hard as he was fighting her. So many hours to go. Could she do it? She must. The penalty was a thousand deaths if she failed.

"Thank you for your vote of confidence," she said, making her voice as cool and mocking as his.

Ferdo gasped angrily and began to stride towards her. One blast to his foot sent him reeling backward. He caught his breath then looked down. His foot was untouched, whole and safe.

"Neuroillusion. A small refinement we picked up from you," she said. "The next time, it will be for real."

Ferdo retreated angrily to the far chair. Hamon merely hooded his eyes, hiding from her the rage written in their shining brilliance. She saw enough, saw they had become brittle shards of emerald green. There was no trace left of the soft hazel glow she'd seen in them just that morning, the color that said he loved her.

CHAPTER TWENTY

Hamon waited until he judged the strain must be starting to tell on her, despite any outward sign of it. Only then did he choose to speak again, in a light tone as if continuing an academic discussion. "One thing puzzles me still. Where do the peasants fit in?"

"There are no peasants. It was a hoax."

"A very well acted one. Who were the peasants at our wedding, then?"

She ignored his reminder of intimacy. "Various relatives at hand. My cousin, Griffith an Castre, stood in for Father."

The inner door slid open just then. Hamon tensed, then saw that the newcomer was a native and that the outer door was already closed to prevent the escape of any sounds. Imperceptibly, he slumped in his chair.

Marthe didn't look away from her hostages, having already been alerted by Central of the arrival of the replacement technician. Once she was again confident that the room was secure, she turned to the newcomer. Startled, she met the clear, grey eyes of her sister.

"Laren? What are you doing here?" she signaled in astonishment.

"I was the only one available with the necessary expertise," Laren signed back. "Everyone else is too busy and this function is vital. We can no longer hold control via remote without compromising other channels. But I'll talk later. For now, we both have work to do."

Her soft smile belied any harshness and, despite her worry, Marthe was grateful for the rock-steady presence of her sister as she settled complacently in front of the console.

Hamon had watched closely as the native entered carrying a food tray, as cover he supposed. A female from her walk. He saw the few gestures of hand and cloak, so subtle one might almost think them imagined. Then the woman settled at the console, patently familiar with the instrumentation.

Marthe made no effort to speak, but he noted her continual fidgeting, her fingers tugging and tapping at her ear. Code? The newcomer confirmed his guess.

"Marthe, will you stop jabbering in my ear." Laren spoke in Harmish. "I'm trying to concentrate on these archaic controls."

That voice. He lifted his head and stared at her in shock. He'd last heard that voice more than five years ago. Laren an Castre was skilled in communications, but surely not here and now. It was too great a coincidence. Then his mouth straightened in self-derision. After the events of the last hour, was anything too great a coincidence?

"From the Major's politic silence, I'm quite certain he knows who I am. Isn't that so, Major?"

"As astute as ever, Madame asn Castre," replied Hamon also in Harmish and using every ounce of the duplicitous courtesy he'd learnt from his diplomat father, exaggerating his urbane politeness further when he saw how much it set Marthe on edge.

"An Castre," Laren corrected, untroubled by his manner and using the same polished tones in which, years ago, he'd heard her present a paper at the college. "I'm a matron with two children these days."

"And as beautiful as ever, I'm sure."

"Jorven thinks so, anyway," Laren replied, chuckling. "But I am remiss, Major. Welcome to the family. Or may I call you Hamon. It seems only right in such a case."

"Of course, and my thanks, Madame. Though I didn't expect to meet my wife's family in such circumstances."

"No? And we had always assumed you were fully alive to the real situation here. Surely you realized it would have to come to this one day?" She spoke as one mildly scolding a small boy. He refused to admit she was making him feel like one. "Never mind," she added, "it will all be over soon, and you can do your manly stomping then. You will find, Marthe, that men never can be angry silently, but, then, I am forgetting your own temper."

"Thank you, Laren," said her sister dryly.

For her part, Marthe was grateful for Laren's diversionary tactics in this game of nerves with Hamon.

Now Ferdo also came to her aid, though she doubted that was his intention. His bottled-up anger finally boiled over as he listened to the overly polite tones of the unknown exchange between Hamon and the peasant who'd had the effrontery to take over his control post. He jumped up and made for the control chair, obviously planning to drag the insolent native out of it, and probably send out an alarm as well. Marthe hit him with a burst of blaster fire. Amazingly, he ignored it, fighting against the pain and pressing on. She was forced to switch the setting. Still he came on. Two, three steps more.

It was Hamon who dragged him to a halt and held him hard to keep him still.

"Let me go, you traitor," Ferdo snarled. "No illusion is going to stop me doing my duty.

"By the stars, Ferdo, look at your damned foot. It's no illusion this time." With one, strong arm, he forced the other's head downwards, to see there the smoking remnants of what had once been toes. And still Marthe held her blaster on him.

"One step closer, Captain Braddock, and you will lose a leg, not a toe. After that, your life."

Ferdo looked into her face, and Hamon saw his shock as Ferdo recognized what Hamon had known since the moment she'd pulled her blaster. She did not bluff.

"Very wise, Captain Braddock," said Laren, switching to Alliance Standard. "Marthe is one of our best shots. Now perhaps you could numb that foot for the poor Captain, Marthe—if he will behave."

The Terran captain gazed in horror at where his toes had been. His face blanched and pinched with pain, he nodded in dazed agreement and sighed in relief as Marthe switched the setting back to the lowest possible, angling it over the nerve endings, and a welcome numbness spread over his foot.

"Lie him down on the floor and prop the foot up on a stool," ordered Marthe, partly glad to have eliminated an opponent; but there was another part of her, one that demanded to know how she could inflict such pain on a fellow human. She heard the echo of it in Hamon's voice.

"Congratulations, Madame Wife. You're whittling the numbers down very neatly. Only one to go. What are you planning for me?"

"Boiling in oil," she snapped back, not caring if her momentary loss of control afforded him the greatest satisfaction, though never did she let her hand on the blaster waver.

"Now, now, children, such tantrums," said Laren. "Hamon, you haven't introduced me to your angry young man.

"My apologies, Madame. Your sister will insist upon these minor interruptions." He gestured to Ferdo's missing toes. "Madame Laren an Castre, may I present Captain Ferdo Braddock, head of our communications section. Ferdo, my sister-in-law."

Hamon bowed as he finished, using the ironic flourish to put his hands momentarily out of sight. Almost immediately, a burning heat slashed along his left side. Just in time, he drew his hand back from the smoldering remnants of the tiny handgun he always wore. Damnit, he'd hoped she'd forgotten about it.

"Marthe, a bit radical, dear," said Laren, staring at the apparently senseless shot.

"My husband carries a small blaster in a pocket on his left side, Laren. He drew it then."

Marthe could feel herself shaking. How could it have come to this, to be forced to shoot at the man who, the stars forgive, she still loved above all else?

"Your memory does you credit," drawled Hamon in mocking congratulation.

He revolved slowly to inspect the charred hole in his suit, carefully pulling the edges together to conceal from the others the fiery welt rising on the singed skin.

That shot had shaken his confidence. While his mind had told him she would shoot, his heart still believed that he, at least, must be immune. No longer. For an instant, he nearly succumbed to the black depression hovering over him. He thrust it back, glancing at the clock. There was still time. The guards could be called out in an instant. He could still win, unlikely though it may seem to his opponents—as he must think utterly of the two Hathian women.

"Are you all right," asked Ferdo from below.

"Don't worry. Nothing more than a singed tunic. Lie still and leave everything to me."

Hamon studied his enemy. No break yet in that façade. For the present, he would have to wait, and he cursed the long sleep he'd gone to such pains to allow her last night. Yet still the shadows lingered beneath her eyes and the skin clung to her bones. Soon the strain must become too great and the debilitating spells of nausea return.

There was also the sister to consider, but instinctively he knew her experience didn't match Marthe's. She lacked the alert readiness for action that branded Marthe a trained agent. As was he, he reminded himself grimly. His enemy had five years of war service and superior weapons. He had ten years gleaned throughout the Alliance and the knowledge that no weapon is superior to a simple gadget used to best advantage. Idly, his eyes swept the room, marking potential weapons and noting possible positions of attack. As he did so, he deliberately strove to appear relaxed, settling back in his chair and checking on Ferdo from time to time. All the time, he watched Marthe, staring coldly and setting his voice to taunt her, slamming it against the hard shell she'd flung up against him.

It was his voice Marthe found the hardest to endure. That uncaring, constant battering of scorn, tearing away at her defenses. A nightmare parody of the deep tones that had bathed her in past delight.

Much later, she retreated to a stool, still poised for combat despite the pains beginning to throb in her head.

Laren watched her, a big sister frown on her face. Don't do it, thought Marthe. Don't beg. But it was a forlorn hope. Laren had seen the fatigue she could no longer hide.

"Major, since the Terran case is now hopeless, can you not accept defeat gracefully? There is really no point in continuing this ridiculous resistance," said Laren.

"But it is so amusing, Madame. And if you're so assured of victory, why waste your time here?"

"Estimate of casualty figures following premature discovery is a thousand fatalities." It was Marthe who replied, her voice flat, hiding all trace of the wearisome burden that number had become. "We will win, though. It is too late for you to change that," she added, before again relapsing into silence.

They were the first words she'd returned to his banter for a long while, and Hamon's aching, angry heart cried out in disappointment that she didn't fight back more. Did what they had mean so little to her?

Marthe didn't have enough energy left to wonder what lay behind his closed face. All she could do was endure. There was no hope of anything else, and now she must concentrate on what she could win, not on forlorn hopes. From the moment she'd been forced to draw her blaster, she knew she'd lost Hamon. For months, she'd been dreading this day. Unlike Hamon, she had never expected what they had to survive, but having failed so disastrously in her marriage, she must succeed in her duty. Her people must be safe.

Yet need he make the end so hard? His taunts were all that penetrated the growing haze in her head. They had been in this room for days, it seemed. Soon, her concentration would break. She glanced surreptitiously at the clock. Not long now. Valiantly, she roused herself for the last spell. Just a little longer, stomach. Don't forsake me yet.

Always the shielded eyes of her husband watched her. Waiting for that final moment when she could no longer anticipate his subtle maneuvers. She'd had to use her blaster once already as he tested her concentration. It wouldn't be long till he would do so again, and succeed.

Their deadly play continued. The drift of the talk changed. No longer did Hamon prod and jeer. His words were now the ordinary gossip of their evenings, achingly familiar and even harder to endure. She could only retreat, deep into the fastness inside her. When would this day finish?

Hamon watched her closely, searching for signs of collapse under the stony façade. It was usually Laren who met his sallies now, but from time to time Marthe would answer, her voice always the same. Dead and stripped of all that was personal. He asked about the crowd scene on the morning of their wedding, so obviously staged, now he looked back. He was not surprised to hear that the victims were mere dummies, only awed by the incredible skill required to hit two small targets so far away and so quickly.

At last his waiting paid out, and not a moment too soon. There was less than an hour left. Quietly, he signaled to Ferdo, also intently watching the nodding woman as her blaster hand began to wilt. He pointed Ferdo to the control panel, signing that he would take the weapon and go for the door. A few minutes longer, the relaxed pose carefully held.

"Now!" he cried. They leapt as one, Ferdo to the panel, Hamon to Marthe, grabbing the blaster as she collapsed in a heap on the floor. He ignored the wretched bundle and raced to the door, slamming it open...

To meet Jacquel des Trurain, in military dress, with a patrol of strangely uniformed men. Still he refused to give up. He brought up the blaster and pressed the button. Nothing. He threw it away, thrusting madly through the body of men in front of him, but his enemies were too many. They beat him down, though more than one was left maimed on the floor, felled by moves learnt in the streets of Earth, and all would wear his marks for some days. In the end, des Trurain grabbed his lower tunic, raised it to slam a hand against his lower back, and next second a shock wave blasted through Hamon's backbone, dropping him to the floor in helpless fury, his legs numb and unresponsive.

"The effect is temporary—usually," growled the Hathian. "I've patched you, so lie still or I'll repeat the shock till it's permanent."

From the look on the man's face, he would be only too pleased for an excuse to do just that. Not that Hamon could move anyway, as other troopers swiftly bound him hand and foot, leaving him trussed up against the wall. From there, he saw Ferdo reach the controls and Laren an Castre politely relinquish them. Ferdo frantically attempted to raise some help. It didn't need the silence to tell Hamon the result. The Hathians had already made that plain. No matter what Ferdo tried, the result was the same. Nobody answered. All that came from the console was an eerie whistle.

"It's no use," said Laren apologetically, kneeling to check on her sister. "You made your move too late, Captain."

"But the attack was scheduled for 19.00 hours," he heard Ferdo protest.

"The Zenith of the Pillars of Mathe will begin at 19.00 hours. The unique alignment of our solar system, which causes the failure of all Terran equipment, took effect at 18.00 hours. Ten minutes ago."

Hamon heard the words. Too late.

He felt his captors haul him up, felt the agony of his wound as they dragged on his arms. None of it registered. He was too late. He'd failed Earth and his people would die.

Lying on her side on the floor, Marthe woke to the hard stare of her husband's eyes from his position on the other side of the room. Eons away, she heard the words of a patrolman.

"Shall we take the Terrans away now, sir?"

"Yes, except Major Radcliff. As husband of Marthe an Castre, he merits privileged accommodation," said Jacquel.

He was interrupted by the harsh voice of his prisoner. "You are mistaken," said her husband. "I have no connection to any Hathian. The union you refer to was nothing but a military stratagem."

He would not look at her again. She lay still, watching as they dragged him up and took him away, and could do nothing. She had lost the right. It had been so short, their time. Now it was over.

Voices. That was her next memory. Voices forcing their way into her misty fastness. Anxious, fearful, nervous, the voices of love and childhood memories. Then smells, of anesthetics and disinfectants. *I am in a hospital*, came the thought, the smells familiar, the voices safe.

"Wake up, Marthe, please." Father, his voice deep, gruff, male.

"Marthe love, wake up. Open your eyes." Another voice filled with memories of childhood and love. Laren.

"Agent an Castre, wake up. Now." A military order from her commander, Gof deln Crantz.

So many voices, all demanding she return. *But none was the right voice.*

She kept her eyes shut and sought oblivion once more.

Later, it was much later. More voices, the brisk talk of nurses and medics. The reality of her years before the war, when peace and routine filled her days. No more. There was an emptiness inside her now. An emptiness that could never be filled, not after what she had done to him. She fled to the darkness and welcomed the floating mists that kept out the world.

A sharp sting, awareness spreading, unwelcome and unwanted. She had been trained in this. Someone, some doctor was forcing her to return to the world.

"No." Dry lips and a voice long unused. She heard only a cracked whisper. "No, leave me," she tried again.

"I am sorry but that is not possible, Madame." A new voice, and a new face leaning over her. The voice of an older man, vaguely familiar. Doctor, said a memory in her head. He has the manner of a doctor—like you.

She had been a doctor once, a lifetime ago. Another trace of memory returned. She was one no longer. Now she was a soldier, now she destroyed lives.

"You will wake, Madame, for your baby's sake. You cannot go, not yet."

She placed the voice now. Dr an Dothen, from her maternity care team on the moon base. She concentrated, let her senses test the gravity well. No, she was still on Hathe, still planetside.

"You should be on Mathe, not down here."

"The war is over, Madame. We are all returned to Hathe, thanks to the heroism of you and your comrades."

It was over? *Yes*, truth. A part of the memory she sought to escape.

"All over, all gone, nothing left," she murmured. "Time to go."

"Not yet," said the voice of her doctor. "There is one more life left for you to save."

"I don't save lives," she muttered. "I destroy them." Just as she had destroyed her husband's.

A shaking, nurses forcing her to sit up. She tried to struggle, but her body failed her. So weak, so useless. She opened her eyes and saw tubing and grey walls, then her doctor's face, grim and uncompromising.

"There is an old saying, Madame an Castre. While there's life, there is hope. So, equally, without life, there is no hope. Would you deny your baby all hope?"

It was the one demand she could not refuse. Not even when the pain of it tore through her. She nodded her surrender. "What do I have to do?"

This time when the grey mists claimed her, she knew she would be returning. She had made him a promise: her baby would survive, and he would see it.

PAY THE PIPER

CHAPTER TWENTY-ONE

The Hathians had trussed him like an animal and discarded him here in the corner of the room. Hamon Radcliff glared at his enemies.

It was all he could do. He'd tried to resist, fighting back with all the bottled-up rage within him. Bruised and battered, held down by enemy soldiers, still he kept punching, kicking, using every half remembered, low down street trick he'd learned growing up on Earth. But then the leader of the Hathian soldiers had slapped one of their patches on his back and used it to blast his spine with a shock wave that dropped him flat, his legs flopping uselessly and refusing to answer his furious need for action. Defeated, swiftly bound hand and foot, he was left with nothing. All he could do was watch as the Hathian troops finished rounding up the rest of the Terrans in the communications wing.

Cleaning up the leftover flotsam. That's what it felt like.

He'd nearly won. So close. After all the months of trying to pierce the enigma that lay behind the facade of this world, he thought he'd finally succeeded in keeping Hathe and its precious urgonium firmly in Terran hands. That was before he opened the control room door and met Jacquel des Trurain holding a blaster on him. Now, the

Hathian was master and Hamon the conquered; very soon, by the look of it, the rest of the Terran forces on Hathe would join him.

It was supposed to be the other way around, had been so for five years.

Ten native soldiers were in the reception area, clearing out all the rooms in this section and commanded precisely and efficiently by des Trurain—for once, observed Hamon bitterly, dispensing with the foppish mannerisms the man had assumed during his imprisonment by the Terrans. Had they been as false as everything else about the Hathians during the Terran occupation? A character the man had assumed to cover his spying for the Hathian resistance?

Few words were spoken by their captors, yet all the Hathians appeared to know what to do, working in an automated silence that frightened his fellow Terrans more than anything else their captors did. The Hathians were using those secret communication patches of theirs, he guessed, in that constant web of communication that had all unknowingly surrounded the Terrans. What words were spoken were in the native Harmish, a tongue alien to all except Hamon; and those were only single words or phrases, meaningless fragments that left him none the wiser.

Too soon, all the Terrans were tied up and forced into a line, two by two. On the other side of the control room, the cause of his downfall still lay where she'd collapsed, held by her sister and worked on by medics. He watched them work, watched the faint rise and fall that meant life. Soon, he would be taken away and this would be his last sight of her.

Her eyes opened then, to hear the Hathians speaking of their prisoners. He watched her face as they spoke his name and saw the change in her eyes as he answered their questions.

As he denied all claims between them and declared himself for Earth.

After that, he was dragged roughly from the floor and yanked into place at the back of the line of captured Terrans, the soldiers half carrying him as his legs slowly recovered their use. He stared straight ahead, refusing to look back at the inner control room and that crumpled figure. Whether from fear of what his blind anger at the sight of her would do, or from a desperately battened down streak of anxiety at his core, he refused to think. Instead, he shoved viciously at the Hathian soldier restraining him, sending the man tumbling backwards.

All he gained for his trouble was a resounding blow from the soldier on his other side, strong enough to send him crashing against the door.

"That's for my brother, dead in your mines," his assailant said, dusting his knuckles and helping up the soldier Hamon had pushed over. Both Hathian soldiers waited contemptuously while the throbbing waves in Hamon's head receded enough to allow him to stand unsupported. He thought he heard a woman cry out, but deliberately ignored it and stumbled to take his place. Maybe he couldn't fight back yet, but it felt mighty good to give these upstarts a taste of the future.

He was shoved back into line and the pull of a force field captured him, preventing any hope of escape. His legs were untied and they moved off—the once proud conquerors forced to march pitiably from their former domain.

Along the endless corridors of the Citadel they shuffled, at last reaching the vast assembly hall buried deep within the complex. En route, Hamon saw a number of other lines of his fellow Terrans, all marked by the same bewildered looks on their faces. Occasionally, there would be one, bruised and beaten as his own must be, telling of isolated rebellion but, for the most part, the Terrans appeared too dazed to fully comprehend their fate, let alone rebel.

What, by all the stars, had happened? How could the whole fortress have fallen so quickly? This was the center of Terran control on Hathe, stuffed full with soldiers, weapons and the best surveillance technology available to Earth. He refused to accept it, futilely holding on to hope of something … anything.

"Forget what you're planning." It was Ferdo, marching beside him, his best friend here and the chief communications officer in the Terran occupation forces. Captain Ferdo Braddock, who had finally given him proof of the existence of a Hathian resistance by cracking the secret of their communications system. Ferdo had been in that control room with him.

"We nearly had them, Ferdo. We nearly beat them."

"Maybe, but nearly isn't good enough. Not this time; and I don't like that look on your face—not if it means what I think it does. If des Trurain can keep it professional, then so can you."

Hamon glared angrily. He'd done much on Hathe he would never forgive himself for, or forget, but his treatment of des Trurain wasn't on his list of regrets.

"The man was obviously a spy. If he's a professional, as you say, then he knew the risks he took. Wait to see what they do to us, now they're in charge, before you start regretting what we did to them."

"Maybe, but—"

"Leave it, Ferdo. Not now."

For a minute, Hamon thought Ferdo would ignore the warning in his voice, but the Captain closed his mouth and obeyed. Thank the stars. There was so much fury boiling inside him and talk of des Trurain was just what it would take to send him over the edge. He couldn't afford that. Not yet.

One day we would have married.

She'd said that to him once, long ago in the days when he'd first held her captive. Marthe an Castre, his other Hathian Haut Liege prisoner—his wife—and the man she would have married, Jacquel des Trurain, who was now force marching Hamon to detention and who knew what else. Marthe who lay…

No. Don't think of that. Not yet. Not ever. He wiped his face clear and set his eyes forward. A black smile touched his lips at the harsh orders from a guard to stop talking. *With pleasure, and thank you for your timely intervention.* He almost said it aloud, just to see the look on the man's face. Anything to protect him from questions he couldn't face answering, though he doubted that the Hathian had meant to benefit him. Not their most hated prisoner.

They entered the assembly hall and halted. The huge room was half full already. Anxious groups dotted the hall, talking softly in scared voices. Between the doorway and the crowd, a faint luminescence announced the presence of a confining field, shining a brighter white in the narrow arch through which incoming prisoners were being processed.

Soon, their coffle was brought up to the two Hathian clerks. Even here, Hamon's anger was denied the relief of defiance. The clerks had facial analysis records of every Terran and, once in front of the screen, the instant identification brought up a full dossier on each captive. Normally, he would have admired the efficiency of the operation, but not now, not with a black haze shrouding all his thoughts. Later, he would use all he now unconsciously observed. For the present, all he could do was hate. It was less painful than thought. Even so, he could not stifle an angry growl as he saw his own record come up:

Major Hamon Radcliff, Head of Special Services.

Priority ranking – Category 1. Detain at all costs.

Connections of Importance:

Father: Alliance Ambassador Garth Radcliff

Mother: Administrator Freya MacDiarmid

Wife: Marthe an Castre, Hathian citizen

"Your last entry's wrong" he forced out. "The marriage was a sham. Part of her cover story."

The clerk looked up, then back at his record. He checked a file. "No, it's right here. Entered into the register and signed by voice recognition print. It's legal," the man said without looking up again.

Hamon was stunned, then angry again. He knew enough of Hathe's traditions to know what the man meant. A true marriage, entered into the almighty Hathian genealogical records—no sham but a promise given in full honor.

He hadn't known.

He was barely holding on, barely keeping up the shield of anger, when the Hathian clerk read the flag on his screen and urgently gestured a nearby soldier. "This the one Councilor deln Crantz wanted?"

The soldier looked at the record, then up at Hamon. "Hamon an Radcliff. Yes, that's the one. Never thought I'd want to be this close to him."

The soldier smirked at the knowing look on the clerk's face. "Doesn't look too fearsome now, does he?"

Laughing triumphantly, the man signaled over his troop and pulled Hamon out of the line. Hamon tried to shove him away but the rest of the soldiers grabbed him as well, holding him tightly and leaving no chance for escape. With his hands bound, all he could do was glare at them, hiding nothing of the fury burning him up. He was pleased to see those not holding him finger their weapons nervously. They had reason.

"Chin up," called Ferdo desperately after him. Hamon was forced to watch helplessly again as the communications officer was processed and passed through to join the dazed collection of Terrans.

Once inside the hall, the newly caught Terrans were released from their bonds, but it made no difference. They were prisoners.

Hamon was taken away from the main hall and thrust into a small side room, recognizable as once having been a stores cupboard. The soldiers were none too gentle, shoving him in as hard as they could. He hit a shelf and stifled the automatic gasp. He'd hit the burn in his side, striking the dull pain of his wound an agonizing blow. All he could manage was to keep it from showing on his face, keeping his reaction to a slight grimace. These scum must not guess how badly he was hurt. It was the only advantage he could find in his present situation.

"The Councilor is busy now. You'll have to wait here till he's free to fit you in." The leader of the soldiers grinned maliciously. "Whenever that might be."

They switched on a field over the entrance to keep him away from the door, then slammed and locked it as they left. He could hear them laughing as their footsteps disappeared. Something told him he was in for quite a wait.

He was right. The long hours of the night brought no change. He knew how much time was passing only from his timer. The lights dimmed, but never turned off completely, and he was forced to use a bottle found on a shelf to relieve himself. He refused to call out for food or water. He wasn't yet reduced to begging … not from Hathians.

His captors had forgotten him, it seemed. Could it be they'd met with difficulties? Stars, he hoped so, desperate for a ray of promise. A black haze of anger carried him through the night, riding him like a giant bear on his shoulders. At first, he gave himself over to it in relief. By morning, he'd had enough. He forced his brain to turn away from its useless treadmill of 'what if' and began to plot, to consider ways and means of countering the Hathians. First, get rid of that patch des Trurain had slapped on him, but after too many attempts and useless scrabbling, he had to admit defeat. He knew where it was, knew what it was meant to look like and feel like, but it made no difference. This patch was nothing like the one he'd taken from Marthe. He couldn't touch it, see it, do anything to get rid of it. It was there, and a continual threat to his ability to fight back.

But it was Hathian, and once he got back to the other Terrans, Ferdo would want to analyze it. He gritted his teeth and forced himself to ignore the presence of the blasted thing.

Next, he needed to find out what had happened, how widespread was the takeover. Just how could a resistance be so discreet as to be barely glimpsed until that last, fatal day?

She'd looked hurt, so badly hurt. And the child? She carried his child.

But no. That picture he wouldn't remember. Not yet. Possibly not ever.

He shook his head, viciously banishing those last moments. It had been galling enough to wake up this morning after a fitful doze on the floor to find his left thumb clenched down firmly on his wedding band. Cursing, he'd snatched it away, but couldn't bring himself to pull off the ring as he'd first intended. The incident had soured him again, and it had taken some hard self-flagellation before he regained a semblance of cool thought.

Finally, well into the next day, he heard the sound of the door opening. He tensed, pulling himself up and standing as far from the door as he could, poised for whatever might happen.

The soldiers looked every bit as wary of him as he could wish for. Their leader looked in, eyes unblinking as they locked on Hamon's position at the far end of the room. He stared silently back. The man switched off the field guarding the room and Hamon sprang forward, but the leader was ready. A tap on the control pad on his arm set off another spinal shock through that damned patch and left Hamon yet again in a helpless heap on the floor. Twice in short succession? He already had a massive back ache from the first one. Fortunately for the continued functioning of his nervous system, the effect of this blast was brief. Within seconds, he was held firmly by a personal field, the paralysis had faded, and he was hauled to his feet to face his foe.

"Des Trurain. I see our roles are reversed," he drawled slowly. "Your restraint does you credit, considering."

"We are a civilized nation. Undue retribution was never part of our plan."

The Hathian's whip-like strength, barely held in check as he stood balanced for action, belied his words. Hamon fought for sanity. Whatever his heart might want, logic said he must back down this time. He was too badly injured, too much in need of food. He nodded briefly, giving way. One day, he promised himself, there would be a reckoning with this particular Hathian, but not till he was fit again and capable of giving him the drubbing he so richly deserved.

His enemy stood a moment, his face viciously hopeful; then, seeing there would be no satisfaction today, he turned and gestured to his men to lead Hamon away. He did, though, check the strength of the restraining force, turning it up till it felt like a tight band about Hamon's chest that made each breath an effort. Coupled with the previous treatment, he was in real danger of collapsing before he got to wherever they were taking him. Des Trurain would succeed better than he hoped in rendering him amenable, Hamon mused grimly. It was this thought alone which kept his head high and his shoulders proudly straight, but he thanked the stars when he found their destination wasn't too far. He barely recognized Colonel Johne's office, now turned into the hectic and crowded headquarters of the

Hathian forces. He was hurried through a horde of people in the outer room to the large inner office.

Here, he would have laughed if the situation hadn't been so serious. Behind the huge desk of the Terran commander sat a gnome-like figure—short, balding, a ready grin coming to the hoary features. Only the man's eyes gave the lie to his appearance, alive with intelligence and coolly assessing his Terran prisoner. The guardsmen secured Hamon by a field in the center of the room, then all except des Trurain left. Hamon had hoped for a chair but allowed none of the deadly weariness dragging on him to show in his face. Especially not to des Trurain.

"Major an Radcliff. A pleasure to meet you at last."

Hamon gave the briefest of nods in recognition. "Councilor deln Crantz, I assume. You have the name wrong, though. Major Hamon Radcliff, of the Terran forces," he said, emphasizing the word Terran. As he was speaking, a figure moved into view from the edges of the room, unseen till now. For a second, Hamon hesitated, not sure that he was up to this. Then collecting himself, he bowed again. "The good Dr an Castre. Welcome." The words were fair, but his tone was infused with warning.

Unfortunately, the older man ignored it, smiling warmly. "Thank you. I have been looking forward to getting to know my latest son-in-law." The warning in Hamon's voice was equaled now by the tension in his body. He scowled at the man, but an Castre chose to plunge on regardless. "You do not ask after Marthe, Major Radcliff?"

A dark cloud swept across him as he fought for control. "I hope both your daughters are in good health."

An amused smile played about the doctor's eyes. "My youngest has had to be admitted to hospital, but I am certain she will be glad of your good wishes when she recovers. It seems she has been over-exerting herself lately. Your fault entirely I understand, Gof," he added, glancing at the councilor. "However, I am assured that both she and her son will be fine."

The words knifed into Hamon's gut. A son. Stars, couldn't they finish this!

"Shall we get on with the real business of the day, gentlemen?" Hamon spoke tersely but with restraint. "I am sure you're both far too busy to spare the time for idle family gossip."

"Not so idle, Major," returned deln Crantz. "It is your marriage to Councilor an Castre's younger daughter that concerns us."

"It need not."

"I think you misunderstand us. We are not at all displeased. Your marriage places you in a unique position—one from which you can act for the betterment of both our peoples."

"I fail to see how," said Hamon coldly.

"It's quite simple. As the husband of a member of a highly respected Hathian family, you have acquired a number of influential Hathian connections, and may thereby, if you wish, approach the Hathian forces from a position of trust and respect."

"You forget that I am also associated with the imprisonment and occasional death of your people."

Deln Crantz' eyes were too intelligent. Hamon shrugged his shoulders, legs apart, hands in pocket and let the challenge show on his face. *Yes, I've done all that, and I don't give a damn.* It didn't deter the Hathian commander.

"That may be, but our people will make allowance for the necessities of war."

Hamon raised an eyebrow. This man believed that about as much as Hamon did. The corners of Deln Crantz' mouth lifted in recognition, the barest of movements only. But the man wasn't finished. "There is also the matter of your widespread influence among the Terran forces. In the present change of circumstances, their attitude and actions will depend on whatever lead you choose to take. Either way."

"Exactly."

Hamon was surprised to find he could yet inject such precise malice into his voice. For the rest, it had been rather too long a day.

The two Hathian councilors eyed him guardedly, clearly uncertain whether to plough on regardless or gracefully concede. Eventually, the fires within Hamon won, bursting forth in angry denial.

"Why don't you spit it out, gentlemen? You want me to keep the filthy Terrans cooperative and amenable." He spoke softly, but it was the quiet of an anger so great he could taste it—the venomous, bitter fury his tongue etched into every syllable. "Sorry. I don't feel like playing your game. I will say it once and once only. I have no intention of cooperating with the Hathian regime. Not now, not ever. I am a citizen of Earth alone, the affairs of which are quite sufficient to occupy me. Find someone else to be your go-between."

"And Marthe an Castre?"

"Severed her connection with me by her own actions." To say her name was more than he could bear. They persisted still.

"What about the child?"

"Is mine," he yelled from the unthinking depths of his pain. Wrenching about, he tried in vain to break free of the force field and quit this hateful room. It took too long, but finally the Hathian leaders accepted defeat. The field was deactivated, and the guards directed to return him to the Terran compound.

He barely suffered their rough grasp in his rage; but his weakness defeated him, their cruel hold alone keeping his feet on the correct path. At least they finally freed his hands and removed that cursed patch—regrettable, though, the loss of it for Ferdo's study. If only he were fit enough to fight his captors. Pain, anger, hate, all swirled within. These Hathians … were they all machines?

Again he saw her face as it had looked in that dread moment of time when he had turned. His wife, his own one. Bleak, narrow-eyed, facing him down the deadly length of that sleek weapon.

Her eyes: they were the worst. Shuttered, their color the non-reflecting black of ebony, taking in all but releasing nothing. For once he couldn't even begin to read her emotions, only that other affairs concerned her. Somewhere behind that stony facade, her brain was pitched on high, busy with hearts not his own. He had been callously struck out, no longer worthy of concern. And he remembered his anger—the rage, the frustration and the betrayal.

Furiously he fought to shut out the tormenting vision. Throughout the night, her face had returned to haunt him, but he'd managed to chase it away. Now, overtaxed and worn out, he could banish it no more. She stood forever frozen in time, those dead eyes gazing soullessly at him. The guards were all but carrying him now, his defenses assailed once too often. One night only and the mighty Terran crumbles, he heard them scoff as they flung him into the Terran compound, a sad heap in an isolated corner.

Only for an instant. Even as they turned to leave, he started to rise, the dark memory of her eyes driven away by the jolt of landing.

As soon as the Hathians had gone, a worried figure broke from a nearby group to hurry over. Ferdo looked down at him in consternation.

"Stars, what have they done to you?" breathed Ferdo.

He glanced down and saw his dusty clothes, the bruising showing already where his torn jacket gaped.

"There was a minor difference of opinion."

All he could produce was a cracked whisper, but Ferdo caught it.

"Can I get you anything? Food, water, a change of clothes?"

"Yes, yes and yes." He managed a kind of smile this time. "Water first, then food. Then, I'd better get myself cleaned up. Can I do that?"

"We have all the amenities available, as they say in the holiday ads. We'll soon have you fixed up as good as new. Hold on here a minute and I'll be right back."

Ferdo rushed off to organize his needs and Hamon sagged back into a heap. He'd managed to hold on in that dreadful office, but now that his defenses were down, he had no resources left. For now, he let the facade crumble, giving in to the pained cries of his body. When Ferdo returned, he was nearly asleep, but not so deep that Ferdo's blundering attempts at light footedness didn't rouse him. He lifted a sleepy eyelid.

"What took you so long? I could have passed away while you grew that stuff."

It was a weak attempt at humor, but the old joke worked, easing the concern on Ferdo's face. "The queues here are longer than on Earth. Makes me quite homesick," he grinned back as he passed over the bowl of broth.

Hamon eyed the container of brown sludge. Benign and unexciting odors drifted upwards. "Is it quite safe?"

"They tell us it has a high nutrient quotient, and no one has died yet." 'Though soon will, of boredom,' said the amused grimace on his face.

Feeling very courageous, Hamon threw back the mess, gratefully chasing it down with the offered water. Surprisingly, it did refresh him, restoring some of his lost vigor. Soon, he could even ignore his hurts enough to rise and walk among the various groups of Terrans, talking and probing as he went.

"I must find out what happened," he explained desperately to Ferdo.

The stories were all depressingly similar. A sudden interference with their instruments and the failure of their machinery. All exits had been locked. Then, the strange soldiers had arrived and they had been brought here, to finally learn the identity of their captors. The officials had coldly advised them that Hathians once again ruled Hathe.

"But you? You were outside in the streets." Hamon stared accusingly at one of his own men, a soldier.

"Same story, Major. We were suddenly surrounded by a group of peasants, all pointing those strange blasters at us. We ordered them back; they just stood there. So we took retaliatory action, but none of our weapons worked and they carried field generators. Within minutes we were rounded up, bound and stripped of arms, and they toted us back here like so many trussed borsch. Razzing humiliating it was. The weirdest part, though, was the silence. No jeering, no celebrating our defeat. They didn't so much as glance at us, all too busy with their own affairs."

"And the village. What about that?" said a second trooper, pausing dramatically. Hamon raised one eyebrow and the man hastily continued. "We were on duty outside the wall, so we got to see the changes in the town as they brought us through. It was incredible."

"Do you think you could be more explicit, soldier," prodded Hamon in the voice he reserved for parade-ground dressing downs. Did the man think they were on a holiday excursion?

"The whole village was a fake," the trooper quickly explained after wiping the look of asinine amazement from his face. "The sides of the houses rolled back and out came hordes of soldiers, with carriers, aerial scooters, and more. A full scale, armed invasion. There was even a spaceport. A short-hop craft came down over one of the shacks in that slum on the eastside. The roof rolled back, and it disappeared right inside."

"What do you know," exclaimed another. "All that right under our noses and we never guessed a thing."

"No, you didn't." Hamon turned the full force of his bitter contempt on the soldier, who rapidly acquired the sense to slink away.

"You were rather hard on that man, sir. You can't blame the rest for not believing you earlier. Not even we were aware of the magnitude of the resistance."

Hamon swirled around. The new speaker was one of his agents, one of the many who had so miserably failed to pierce the native facade.

"Johnson, how kind of you to join us. Did the luxury of life in the new regime pall so quickly?"

Johnson suddenly assumed the blank face of the common soldier. "They pulled me in at the same time as all the rest, sir. One minute, we were all working together; next, the leader of my gang, Griff they called him, straightens up, points one of those new blasters at me and motions to another man to tie me up. Then he says, in precise and fluent Standard, 'My compliments to the husband of my cousin, but we no longer require your services, Sergeant Johnson.' And with that, I was led back here."

Hamon hadn't thought he could feel worse. He was wrong.

His sergeant coughed cautiously. "Do you know the man Griff, sir?"

"Griffith an Castre, I know of him." That was all Hamon could bring himself to say.

For long minutes he fought against it—against what must be. He'd done enough for Earth. Given five years of his life to this wretched undertaking because he couldn't face knowing what would happen to his home planet if he didn't. It was no use. The decision had been made before he'd even started considering it. He straightened to his full rigid height and looked at his sergeant.

"Tell Jones, Markham, Hawarth and Hector that I'll see them in the far corner, in exactly twenty minutes." Johnson stood undecided a second. "Well? Or have you, too, forgotten on which planet you were born?"

The man scurried off, but even before Hamon's select officers had gathered, he knew the news was spreading through the hall. Radcliff was moving … but in what direction, the looks cast his way said. The past twenty-four hours had been shock enough for the Terrans. So far, they were relatively unmolested and had all they needed. What kind of a ruckus was he contemplating?

They grossly underestimated him, as his men could have told them. Bloodthirsty and angry he may be still, defiant even. But foolish? No. Or so he hoped.

In short order, he gathered together all that the Terrans knew of matters so far and set clear in his mind the identity of the various groupings in the hall. More importantly, he took stock of the mood of the confused mob. Then, he tersely gave his instructions. Not for all-out assault and mayhem; any junior officer knew the time for that was not yet. By noon, he had the auditorium discreetly organized, and had ensured each man and woman was once more secure in the routine of assigned duties. It was a start.

By late afternoon, he saw a change in the attitude of the previously contemptuous Hathian guards posted outside the perimeter field. They were talking almost continuously into their patches, hands roughly tapping on ears. He smiled bleakly. If he guessed right, the native troops were becoming seriously disturbed by the rapid change to orderliness among their captives. Which was just what he'd intended.

He moved from group to group, ticking off his internal list of tasks completed. No longer was food distribution a matter of individual pushing and scurrying in endless queues. His staff had put in place a roster system of collectors based on the various occupational groups, a management system familiar to the Terrans from the previous five years. The amenities had been set up to give some degree of privacy and hygiene procedures put in place. A sick bay had been set up for minor injuries and overly shocked Terrans, though he stayed well away from it. He didn't need anyone stopping him from working.

Most helpful to him were the improvements to the sleeping areas. They were now properly furnished, with screens of whatever was at hand set up to give each person a much needed space of their own, free of the constant surveillance of their captors.

Fortunately, the Hathians were as secure in the effectiveness of their interning arrangements as he'd hoped. He looked over the growing collection of personal gadgets in Ferdo's group area with grim satisfaction. Timers, recorders, vids—innocuous enough in themselves but, together, they made up of an array of very useful components. With them, there was a good chance that Ferdo could once again link into the Hathian communication network. He almost felt a trace of a smile on his face as he strode from group to group.

The Hathian councilors, watching on the vidscreens, were too far placed to catch any smile but couldn't miss the arrogant spring in his step or his defiantly erect stance.

"We've lost him," concluded deln Crantz. While the man's efficient organization of feeding, sleeping and hygiene arrangements made it easier to confine the Terrans, the speed with which he'd achieved it left deln Crantz decidedly uneasy. He turned to look at his friend, Sylvan an Castre, also watching the blazingly vibrant man.

"A pity, a pity for us all," was the Doctor's quiet reply. And deln Crantz didn't have to be told that it wasn't only of the Hathian nation he spoke.

CHAPTER TWENTY-TWO

Marthe woke to the familiar smell of starch and antiseptic. Something inside her relaxed, then tightened. Had she fallen asleep on night shift again?

She opened her eyes to an even more familiar sight. The soft cloud paintings decorating the wards of First Hospital in The City. It was a standing joke amongst all the interns that if a city had to have such a prosaic name, then the hospital ought to be the same. So had decreed the first head doctor, changing the fanciful name honoring an unknown past hero to First Hospital and every medic since had followed her tradition.

Then Marthe realized where she was. In a patient's bed in a private room, and wearing a hospital gown. Now she did sit up, then just as urgently slumped down again as waves of dizziness threatened to engulf her.

"What do you think you're doing, Madame an Castre?"

A strange woman bustled through the door, dressed in the First Hospital nursing uniform. "Trying to get up," said Marthe, quite reasonably she thought.

"You'll be doing no such thing, Madame. Not today, and not for many days yet. Your doctors have worked too hard to undo the mess you'd made of yourself for you to spoil it by being silly."

Marthe felt all of two years old … and a dawning suspicion was taking root.

"It's Doctor asn Castre," she tried.

"And when you are better, you may be called that, but right now, Madame an Castre, you are my patient and you will lie quietly here until you are in a fit state to do otherwise."

With which the woman ruthlessly pressed Marthe firmly back onto the bed, pulled up the single sheet covering her and tucked it tightly, and straightened the pillow under her head, then gave her a shot of a sedative that finished the argument for the time being.

When next she woke, Marthe remembered enough of her last time to lie still and consider before moving.

She stared at the walls, the bed, the nutrient fluids infusing her and the shut door beyond. Nothing encouraged her to move, not yet. There was a sensor on the bed and a surveillance vid on the wall. If she more than blinked, her privacy would be gone.

Memory was coming back, and something more. Her fingers felt an unfamiliar ridge on her left hand, a ring that hadn't been there when she'd worked these wards. And something more. The nurse had called her Madame an Castre, not asn.

She was married.

Then it came back. All of it, years and years of it—the long fight for freedom and the deeply personal. Her hand strayed to the mound of her stomach. She was pregnant and married. She clenched her hand protectively over the rounding of her belly and remembered hard— all the strife and uncertainties she had endured—but try as she might, none of it came back as strongly as that last day, that one cataclysmic moment.

She had shot him. Hamon Radcliff. Her husband and the father of her child. The man she loved.

Now she had lost him.

She must have moved, or the bed registered the tight clench of her left hand. There was a beep and the sliding of a door. Outside, she glimpsed soldiers in the new uniforms of Hathe. Her guardians or her guards? Probably both, she guessed, given the ordinary Hathians view of her by the end of the occupation. Then she heard footsteps coming in to her room. Not the dragon nurse. Please not.

"How are you today," said a beloved voice, and her father walked in.

She couldn't help it. She tried hard to stop them, but the tears wouldn't obey.

"I've lost him."

The strong arms and warm smell of her father enfolded her. "Yes, I fear you have," he said, and told her of the offer they had made her husband. Then her father held her for a long time.

After that, the days in her bed seemed interminably long. There was little for her to do but rest, eat and sleep. Her doctors allowed little else. "You must avoid all stress," they told her. "You are badly underweight and worn out. If you want your baby to live, then do as we tell you."

"Not knowing what's going on is more stressful than anything," she said to her father on his daily visit, fretfully tugging at the bed cover.

He was uncharacteristically silent. When she'd been a child and hated being laid up in bed, he would chide her and tease her into enduring it. She looked up sharply and caught the strained look he swiftly hid.

"Out with it." She hitched herself upwards and glared at him. "What are you hiding?"

"Nothing, nothing."

She took a guess. It wasn't too much of a leap. She'd learned how the world worked in too harsh a school. "The soldiers outside. They're there both for my protection and to keep me under control? I've become an embarrassment."

Her father shrugged, and she saw the recognition in his face. He couldn't fool her, not this time.

"Both. There's too much anger out there still bottled up. The public has no release for it. We can't mistreat or take action against the Terran prisoners—not if we want to maintain good relations with the other Alliance planets—and, right now, we badly need their good will to help us recover."

"But I'm still the wealthy, spoiled daughter of a prominent family who betrayed her world."

Her father nodded grimly. "In the gutter press, at least. Your actual history has been published, but not widely reported. It doesn't make such a sensational story."

She saw something else in his face, something he still hid. She crossed her arms and waited, waited until he sighed in defeat. "There's more," he agreed.

His hands had tightened on the chair arms and he avoided looking her in the eye. He really didn't want to tell her this part, but she wasn't about to let him use her health status against her. "If you want me to get better, then tell me the truth. All of it. I need to know what I'm fighting."

He nodded in defeat "We can't take action against the Terrans. Not even put them on trial for what they did here—not if we want to be a part of the force sent in to run Earth and ensure they don't mount a second invasion. The Alliance has made that quite clear."

"If you don't want a second invasion, then you better do something about the disaster that must be unfolding there now," she retorted.

"I'd heard you had petitioned the Council."

"Everything I said is true. I couldn't live with another occupation, but I also can't live with what I know will be happening on Earth now. They're dying, and we have to stop it, have to teach them more advanced energy technologies. There's no other way to bring peace."

"I have a feeling you are right on this one, and I promise we'll do something about it."

Something in her relaxed at that. Her father didn't give his promises lightly. She could trust him to get the Council to act, but she wouldn't let him think he was finished.

"Now you can tell me the other thing you've been avoiding."

He glared at her. Then slumped back and stared at the ceiling, before taking a deep sigh and turning to her, his face filled with such sadness.

"They can't put the Terrans on trial, but they can try you."

By the end of the first week of captivity, Hamon had been forced to hear Ferdo telling him how well the Terrans were doing once too often.

"None of it would have happened without your leadership. Look what you've achieved," Ferdo would say.

He had a point, Hamon supposed sourly, sitting in a corner of the screened-off area he'd earmarked as his personal retreat. From here, he could watch the rest of the Terrans if he wanted or pull the makeshift screen of old tunics across and grab a moment of precious privacy.

Today he watched and was forced to acknowledge the truth of what Ferdo insisted on telling him so often. Seeing the way the

Terrans moved as they went about their duties, he could see a lighter step in them as a sense of purpose once more guided them. All of them were working tirelessly to learn as much as they could of the new regime, without letting their captors know. Colonel Johne had met with the Hathian authorities on behalf of the Terran forces, with more meetings to follow, though Hamon doubted their captors were fooled about whose words Johne spoke. The man had finally learned to listen to his despised second and had let Hamon brief him fully beforehand. Thankfully, the Hathians allowed their facade. He didn't feel like talking to the Councilors himself. Not after that last meeting.

One gain Johne had made at the meeting was permission for the prisoners to watch local newscasts. Though he probably didn't have to try too hard for that one, mused Hamon grimly. All the casts showed the Hathians to be in full control of the planet and spoke of the trouble-free incarceration of the Terran forces. Ferdo's team had managed to break into the Hathians' communication network and confirmed the reports to be all too true.

Building on what little he'd learned from Marthe's wrist patch, added to secret recordings of every Hathian device that came within range of his team, his group had discovered the fundamental difference between their own equipment and that of the Hathians.

"It's quite simple to master, once you unravel the basic workings," Ferdo enthused to Hamon a bit later that day, when he'd foolishly asked how they'd managed it.

"Oh?" He supposed he should be interested, but there were too many other things on his mind. Yet what Ferdo was learning was vital to the Terran cause. He dutifully stopped a few moments longer to listen.

"It's their intramachine transmissions," explained Ferdo, a look of real passion on his face. Hamon looked at him blankly, having no idea what he was talking about. It didn't stop Ferdo, too full of the simple genius of what he'd discovered. "In our system, when you give a machine an instruction, by finger, voice control or whatever, an electromagnetic pulse is activated. The Hathians, on the other hand, use an entirely new system. Our physics can't even explain it, not fully, but it creates a very tightly banded signal with minimal energy loss. That's why we couldn't detect it. There's no leakage from their devices. We tried copying their stuff with our own equipment, but it was useless. I had to filch some components from the food dispensers and adapt them to our needs. Absolute wonders of micro-engineering they are."

"But can you use them?" That was all Hamon wanted to know.

"Yes, but—"

"Then do so," he said gruffly, before stalking off to oversee the work of yet another group.

But Ferdo wouldn't let him go. Not this time. He felt his arm grabbed and pulled back.

"What?"

"That's my question. *What* is the matter with you? We've achieved so much, and everything is going so well, all thanks to your leadership. Yet you stalk around here like the hounds of hell are on your heels … when you're not skulking away in that curtained-off area of yours, that is."

He looked at his friend's hand on his arm, thought about hitting him, then looked up and realized all the anger inside him must be written on his face. It was beyond him at the moment to hide it. Ferdo dropped his hand, but still refused to leave.

"Not now, Ferdo. Not now."

Ferdo tensed then stared back at him. Finally, he shrugged. "Your funeral," he said tightly and stalked off.

Hamon could feel only relief. He turned and gave in to Ferdo's prediction, making for the security of his sleeper. Once there, he pulled across the screen of tunics, blocking out the rest of his fellow prisoners then made sure everything in his space was pristine, lined up in tidy lines. This at least he could control.

Lying on his bed, eyes squeezed shut against the pain that throbbed always behind them, he wished he could have handled his friend better. Ferdo was right, after all. Just a few minutes, a bit of rest, and he'd go out there, keep it all going. He had to. There was no other option.

In the coming days, he kept up the pressure on the Terrans, helped by an endless stream of incoming reports that strengthened the resolve of every one of the captives. Ferdo's team was working round the clock to monitor as many Hathian transmissions as possible. They all told the same story, of a well-planned program of repair and return to normality, flawlessly executed. Already the broadcasts spoke of the resumption of diplomatic and trade links with the other Alliance planets. The entertainment groups were performing again, and the schools had reopened. As if from nowhere, all the mighty infrastructure of the planet had magically reappeared. The spaceport was open again and the cities once more bustling, though how that could be, considering the deadly radiation levels that had coated those places during the occupation, he was at a loss to know.

He also seemed to be the only one not star struck by what the Hathians were doing outside their prison.

"And of Earth, and ourselves? What do they say of us?" was all he wanted to know, cutting ruthlessly through the childlike awe of the Terrans at the great process surrounding them.

"Rarely mentioned now," admitted Ferdo sheepishly. "Just that the hostages are securely interned in conditions which satisfy Alliance prisoner-of-war codes, and that Earth has been informed of our return in due course."

"Nothing of how Earth is surviving without urgonium?"

Hamon could see the dawning on their faces. In all their wonder, they had forgotten their home world. A horrified silence crashed down. Earth held scarce any stores of the precious mineral; too badly needed was every particle sent back for day-to-day energy production. Now, no more supplies would be arriving. Hathe was the only mineable source of the mineral, Earth's primary energy source. Even if the Alliance authorities hadn't already seized any consignments in transit, no longer constrained by Earth's control of Hathe, the Hathians would assuredly stop any further exports to the Terrans' home world. Earth would soon be without urgonium and the whole planet would grind to a deadly halt.

While they stood here congratulating themselves so heartily on each small success, many of the basic amenities on Earth must already have closed down. Heating, ventilation, and most of the transport system would have gone. Only those services essential to the production and distribution of food could remain. The riots would worsen as, inexorably, more and more citizens were struck off the infamous list of useful producers. No longer eligible to queue for hours for the plain but highly nutritious fare, millions of Terrans were doomed to a slow and miserable death.

"You see how vital is our little game of resistance?" Hamon's voice was harsh, uncaring of the shocked faces about him. He'd been living with the specter of a devastated Earth since Marthe an Castre had first drawn that blaster. His spark lit, he strode away to the privacy of his cubicle, there to lie rigid while the wildfire he'd started spread through the Terrans.

After that, a grim purpose took hold of the Terrans. Hamon saw it and wished he could rejoice. Even when Colonel Johne announced that they had been given permission to visit their former quarters to retrieve personal effects, not one had a thought but to hunt for anything that may be of use. Here was a chance to leave the hall and see for themselves just how strongly entrenched the Hathians were.

That hope was short-lived, as Hamon saw, gazing about his beautiful rooms. So neat, with so many painful, hurting memories, and so meticulously stripped of those things he needed by one who had known where to look. Even the pot of healing salve he had acquired on Cantor was missing, the one he'd used to such good effect on Marthe. It was a pity, for he was beginning to be in rather desperate need of it.

The others were as unsuccessful. They had more clothes, their personal treasures about them, but that was all. The Citadel, it turned out, was almost deserted, cast off as useless by the Hathians and, looking out his balcony window, Hamon had noticed a shimmering iridescence in the sky. Presumably a second, confining field surrounding the entire fortress. It served only to strengthen his resolve. He would either destroy the Hathians or escape and wreak what havoc he could. Somehow, he had to get back to Earth while a society still existed to be saved. He was even prepared to go cap in hand to the Alliance planets, begging them to intervene before anarchy and starvation preyed too deeply. The Alliance planets with the exception of Hathe, that is. That once admired world was now only the object of a bitter and abiding hatred.

He could find it only cruelly ironic, then, that when help did come, it was from a totally unexpected and unwelcome quarter.

Gof deln Crantz had been watching the prisoners' endeavors with increasing concern. Disdainful amusement turned to a wary watchfulness when monitoring showed the first recordings of Hathian transmissions, a development as surprising as it was unnerving. Hurried messages flew from his office in the small garrison in the Citadel to the new HQ in the city. Everything was going so well. The last thing needed now was trouble among the Terrans.

"Jacquel des Trurain should know how to handle these Terrans. Especially this troublemaker, Radcliff," one of the Councilors put forward during the daily session of the new governing council.

"I don't know that it would be politic to send him," countered the troublemaker's harassed father-in-law.

"Nevertheless, there is no one else available."

Deln Crantz leaned back in satisfaction as the vote was called and carried unanimously. One problem solved—or buried. Right now, he didn't care which. He moved the Council on to other matters.

So it was that Jacquel discovered he was to be sent back to the Citadel, to deal with this one annoying Terran who refused to accept defeat. After barely two weeks of freedom, he had no desire to return to the dreary coils of the imprisoned, despite the roles being reversed. In particular, he did not want to face Major Hamon Radcliff again. After all the bitterness between them, he just didn't know whether he could deal with the man as fairly as was required. Did he even want to try?

He stared through the monitors at the Terran captives.

"Zoom in on Radcliff," he said glumly. The man was walking stiffly across to the food counters. Once there, he spoke to a woman who immediately moved off elsewhere. "Still ordering everyone in sight." Jacquel could feel the old, familiar anger at the sight of the Terran. What, by the Pillars, was the man doing here instead of among the Hathians looking after his wife as he ought to be?

He gestured to the soldier beside him.

"Major Radcliff is requested to report to the Hathian command," blared across the speakers in the hall. Nervously, the Terrans stopped and looked towards the troopers constantly in attendance just outside the field—except Radcliff himself. With barely a pause, the Major continued his course towards the cleaning area where he could be seen checking the hygiene rosters.

Jacquel allowed him ten minutes then gave the order for his men to follow him, blasters at the ready. Once in the hall, the field surged forward with them, protecting them as they moved out among the Terrans. The hostile glares on the faces surrounding them told clearly the wisdom of their precaution. At least Radcliff made no attempt to escape. Instead, he turned, leaning nonchalantly against a partition wall to await their arrival and barely demurring as the field enveloped him. There was only a stern look at a nearby man, recognized by Jacquel as Captain Ferdo Braddock.

"You play fair," noted Jacquel dryly.

"Just accept certain inevitabilities," was the even drier reply from his prisoner, gallantly refraining from flinching as the man on his left grabbed at his arms, dragging them roughly behind his back and binding his hands with tape. There were some growls among the nearby crowd, but a look from Radcliff quelled any protest.

"You wish for another friendly chat about mutual interests," he asked, irony touching that steady voice.

"If you please," said Jacquel.

But there was no real choice in the offer. Amid a hissing chorus, they quickly retreated from the hall, and soon he had Radcliff back in his old quarters. In answer to his raised eyebrow, Jacquel said merely that it seemed the most appropriate place to detain him.

"You're stirring up an annoying amount of trouble. It was decided that you should be made to cool your heels for a bit."

Even now, the Terran refused to give any ground, refraining from asking for how long. Instead, taking advantage of the release from his not so friendly guards, he carefully lowered himself into a nearby cube, nodding to Jacquel to take the one opposite as if he were still in command and still owned this apartment.

As Jacquel sat, Radcliff leaned back and arrogantly crossed his legs while somehow managing to disregard his strapped hands. Flashing a challenge, he eyed Jacquel.

"Well. Out with it. It seems unlikely that you interrupted your busy schedule merely to ensure my comfortable installation here."

"No," agreed Jacquel, damnably pleasant. He leaned back himself, gazing at his former captor and now prisoner. To his disgust, there was no sign of discontent, though he would swear that cool, outer mask was a very thin veneer. The bitter lines about the hated faced were too well marked. Or perhaps hate was too strong a word, he conceded. He had always understood what drove this man, politically and personally, and long ago realized that his own bond with Marthe was quite unlike what Radcliff felt for her, or she for him.

Which made no difference to how he felt about Marthe. She was too much a part of his life for him to easily accept the Terran as a partner for her. She and her twin brother Bendin were his oldest and closest friends, as near to family as made no difference. Bendin was dead now, one of the pilots who had flown out in the suicidal attack that kept the invading Terrans off planet long enough for the Hathians to evacuate to a secret base on the moon Mathe those not needed for the resistance. A desperate space battle at the limit of their system from which all too few had returned.

Bendin must be writhing in his grave, he reflected in bitter grief. It was only his innate sense of humor, prompting awareness of the black comedy of the situation, that kept him from beating the man opposite to a pulp. He did, though, take great delight in riding the Terran mercilessly for the next hour, using all his skills to probe the Major's stubborn resistance. They were as well matched as ever, and at the end Jacquel was forced to concede, grinning ruefully,

"I see I am going to get as much out of you as you ever wormed out of me."

"Which was precisely nothing," admitted Radcliff.

"You look tired. Not sleeping well lately?"

Radcliff refused to answer him, and suddenly Jacquel discovered a glow of victory among the ashes. "It comes of having too much on your mind. You should cut down your workload. I know how working nights used to get to me, when our positions were reversed," he said. "Or is it sleeping on your own again? I daresay it is difficult to get used to at first," and knew by the sudden clenching of jaw that he had scored a hit. As he stood up he smiled wickedly at the Terran suffering for his sins. "I'll leave you to the enjoyment of your quarters. Just one more check and we're gone."

Turning, he spoke to one of his soldiers, who pulled out a scanner and swept it across the Major. Suddenly the man stopped and hauled the Terran out of his chair.

"There's a large area of heat on his left side, sir. In fact, his body temperature is high all over."

Jacquel gave a signal and two soldiers grasped either arm, Radcliff's hands were untied, and his tunic dragged off. Even Jacquel gasped. The faded yellow of severe bruising covered the whole of the torso and there was a large bandage covering the left side. Jacquel gestured again and one of the soldiers gingerly peeled it off. Beneath, the skin was an oozing, scabby mess, with angry streaks of redness reaching up to the armpit and down to the hip. Some effort had been made to keep it clean, but the wound must have caused unimaginable agony and, now that the bandage was removed, the smell sent Jacquel gagging.

"What the hell happened to you?"

Hamon stood still for a moment as he caught his breath. His side had been banged again as they dragged him up, but experience had taught him to cope with the pain. "I thought the sight would please you," he said as soon as he could speak.

"Of course it doesn't."

"Strange. I would at one time have taken the greatest pleasure in seeing you similarly afflicted," he said, unable to keep the touch of breathlessness out of his voice.

"Sit down, man, before you fall down." Des Trurain turned to give an order to his second officer, his voice gruff with angry concern. "Get a medical team in here immediately. One of ours. Marthe tells me theirs are primitive."

Hamon tried to protest. He mustn't lose contact with his fellow Terrans. They had their orders, but would they keep their resolve without him? And he definitely did not want to be cared for by Hathians.

"The lady is no judge of medical care. It was she who singed me," he managed to retort. Then the burning in his side cantankerously flared up again, just when he least needed it.

Those hostile words were the last, coherent speech he was to make for weeks.

CHAPTER TWENTY-THREE

Marthe stared at the monitor. Inside the hospital room, a man lay on a bed. All she could see was the still shape of him and the shimmer of a med field covering his torso.

She reached out to touch the monitor, then pulled back.

"3-D," she ordered.

"Privacy and security modes on. Access denied," said the disembodied voice of the hospital control system.

"I have clearance. The patient is my husband."

"Enter ID"

She put out her thumb, touching it to the soft pad below the monitor and waited while the system checked the DNA in her skin cells.

"ID verified. Subject: Marthe an Castre, registered wife of patient Hamon an Radcliff. 3-D on."

She stepped into the sim field and entered a projection of his room Moving silently, she walked around the bed, gazing her fill at the man there. His face was as strongly marked, his hair as darkly vibrant as ever, and she reached out to touch it, but her hand passed through, insubstantial, the touch of a ghost. She was not here. Not truly, and couldn't be here if he was awake. She was barred from this sterile room. His medical staff dare not risk his reaction to that.

She pulled back and leaned over him. His eyes were shut, and she could only wonder what color they would be if open. The soft hazel of their nights, the eyes of love? Or the hard green she had last seen as he rejected her forever? He was so big, so strong, so badly injured.

He slept still in the induced coma his doctors had kept him in since he arrived. She could see the bruises, see the healing wound of the burn that stretched over his side. She reached out a hand, hovered just above the field and traced the path of the yellow, black and angry red of his healing flesh.

She had done that to him.

Her hand punched down and the simulation vanished, plunging her back to the outer room. She lifted her hand one last time and placed it on the flat monitor image of him on that bed. "I'm sorry," she whispered softly—and wondered whether he would ever let her say it to his face.

She pleaded daily with his doctors, but it wasn't till weeks later that one of them let her enter his actual room. His burns specialist, Doctor asn Marvell, was still naive enough to fall for her pleas and unfamiliar enough with the changes the occupation had wrought in her. He remembered only the laughing med student of their shared youth. She needed to see her husband in the flesh, she said, to believe in his recovery. The good doctor had spent the occupation safely on the moon base of Mathe. Any dirtsider could have told him he was being taken in, but Marthe had no sympathy for him.

She couldn't stop the trembling as she went through the hygiene procedures before passing through to Hamon's room. He was waking longer now, half aware of what was happening around him. Would he recognize her?

She clenched her fists, lifting her chin as she walked in. The doctors were finishing their daily checks, poking at the nearly healed skin and comparing readouts. She'd seen them already, had studied them hungrily in her lonely room at night. He would recover fully. Despite what she'd done to him.

She walked softly to the bed and leaned over, drinking in the faint hint of the smell of him, just present under the chemical blanket of hospital antisepsis. Something locked into place inside her again, a missing part of her that had been skewed out of alignment.

Then his eyes opened.

Cloudy grey-green at first, lost still in the haze of his dreams. Then she saw recognition, first a softening, then phasing into the brilliant green of his anger. He began to rise, a furious growl echoing the struggle of his arms to lift him. A guard snatched her back and the nurses hurried forward.

"You'd better leave now, Madame an Castre," said the senior nurse in a tone that brooked no argument. She could do nothing but nod agreement and back off. All she could do here was hurt him, and she'd done enough of that already. She left and did not return while he slept.

Time passed for Hamon in a haze of faces and disembodied words. How long, he couldn't guess but, lying heavily sedated, his body finally got the help it needed to recover. Once, struggling out of a drug-laden nightmare, he saw her bending over him and strained upwards, growling angrily. At once, she disappeared, not to be seen again. When at last he was allowed to return to consciousness, he knew only an angry despair. How long he'd been incarcerated, he didn't know, but was certain that he wouldn't have been brought back to awareness if his influence was still important to the Terrans' defense. His despair was not lessened by the face he saw bending over him.

"Mother! What are you doing here?"

"It's a long story. Suffice to say, I'm holidaying here at the expense of the Hathian government."

"A hostage!"

"You might call it that, but you're not well enough yet to be worried by it. Rest a bit longer. I'll come back later and tell you everything."

"I have been resting. For years, it seems. The damned Hathians have had me drugged up to my eyeballs," he growled, trying to rise but failing as an inexplicable tide of weakness engulfed him.

His mother cried out for a nurse. One came running, tranquilizer at the ready, but he swept a hand out with the last of his strength and smashed the vial to the ground. Then collapsed back, exhausted.

"You're feeling more yourself then, Major?" remarked the young doctor who had followed the nurse in. He had spoken in Harmish, but quickly switched to Alliance Standard as the despised language made Hamon rise up again. "Nurse, we can dispense with the sedatives. His skin is sufficiently healed to withstand a few knocks. As long as the Major is not too foolish."

Hamon had been aware of various manipulations of the damaged skin on his left side, and now strained to look at it. To his disgust, the effort was useless. His fit of temper had exhausted him and he could no longer even raise his head.

"Don't try to do too much yet, Major. You were very ill, and it will be quite some time before your body regains its normal strength. I should have known Marthe would finally choose someone like you for a husband. That scowl of yours is almost as fierce as the one she's been wearing lately."

Which was exactly the wrong thing to say. Hamon tried madly to rise again, then collapsed in defeat. "Who the hell are you? And let me out of here."

"My apologies. Doctor Claud asn Mavell. For the past eight weeks, I have become so intimately involved with you that I forgot you wouldn't know me. That burn was quite a challenge. Where did you get it?"

"You can thank my *wife*."

He saw his mother's shiver at the venom in his voice. Unfortunately, the young doctor didn't know him as well.

"Marthe? She's about the place somewhere, though busy at present. If you would like to see her, I can find out when she will be available," he offered helpfully.

"Here!"

"Y-yes. Shall I fetch her?" The doctor was at least beginning to realize his error.

"No, thank you," exploded Hamon.

Fortunately, his mother had the sense to bustle the doctor and nurse out of the room before he reopened his wounds. Then, taking one look at him, she kissed his cheek and told him to get some rest, before absenting herself as well. It wasn't until the next day that she returned, to finally answer the question that had been tearing him apart.

How was Earth faring?

He listened bleakly as she told him in a voice that gave no hint of what she'd been through. His mother had been living with the harsh reality of Earth's situation too long to show emotion, but her report was fully as bad as he'd feared. Within four, short weeks of losing control of Hathe's energy resources, cold and hunger had driven Earth to the humiliation of begging for help from the Alliance. She refused to speak of the scorn with which their pleas had been met, but he guessed much from what she didn't say.

"They didn't believe you," he surmised flatly. "So how many people have we left?"

"We lost a number, yes, but it is not quite so bad. Fortunately, they were persuaded to change their earlier opinions. By a Hathian," she added in response to his look of surprise.

He became very still. "Continue."

"There isn't much more to tell. Emergency supplies were sent in, along with an Alliance relief team charged with overseeing the rescue operation and assessing the state of Terran affairs. Following their report, an aid team is now being readied. To help us 'catch up', as they put it. I never knew we could be regarded as barbaric savages needing civilizing," she laughed, not at all bitter. In truth, Hamon realized, a great weight had been lifted from her. For a change, someone else must shoulder the horrific responsibilities that had been hers for too long. "But as barbarians, we are still not fully trusted," she continued, "which is why a number of prominent Terrans have been removed to various Alliance planets. Hence my sojourn here. In all honesty, I can't say I mind in the slightest. This place has certainly improved since my last visit, and the Hathians are being quite delightful, everything considered."

For the first time in his life, he glared at his mother in dislike. "You change your opinions very quickly."

"No, just learned many years ago when to admit I was wrong … and it was wrong, what we did to these people."

That was a mistake, too. His face told her this was a burden he had been forced to live with for a long time now, and she sighed for him. Why must life be so harsh to this one son of hers? Or perhaps, why must he be so harsh to life? "You are so like your father," she exclaimed in exasperation.

His fists clenched. She had fallen into idiocy, and made herself step back, letting fall the mask of the Administrator to cover her mother's worry and turning to fiddle with the buoyancy controls on his couch.

"Leave that," he waved in irritation, "and tell me the rest."

"That's all I know. The Hathian side you'll have to learn elsewhere."

It was intolerable, but no more would his mother say.

Slower than he would have liked, his strength did return. Each day, he enjoyed his mother's warm but stubbornly uninformative company. They talked of family matters, the new Hathians she had met, even once, angrily, of his father. He was, it seemed, busy negotiating at Alliance Central for an increase in aid for Earth … without the political controls on which the other planets insisted. Not surprisingly, it was proving a difficult battle. After the shock of Earth's invasion of Hathe, it would be many years before Earth was trusted again. The Terrans' long history of disdain for their colonial offspring—who, unknown to those on Earth, had raced past them to adulthood—was coming home to roost with a vengeance.

For the first time, too, he told her the tale of his years of self-imposed exile: all the trivia and the escapades of his travels, roaming the Alliance as whim suggested. He could see her surprise at the cosmopolitan education he'd picked up, both in the gutters and in the high academies of the worlds he'd passed through.

"Didn't you have to take political science at the Military Academy on Earth? How we ever got you to finish that, I'll never know."

"It was a good, general education, and at the time I didn't know what else to do."

"Then why a Cantor degree?"

"Their course on interplanetary politics had a slant rather different from ours."

As usual, she thought dryly, understating his point. In these few days, she'd learned much about the passionate animal this son of hers kept hidden so skillfully behind reserved words and a cold exterior, but still she refrained from discussing what, she was coming to realize, more and more occupied the greater part of his mind. Then came the day she found him up and about, restlessly pacing the hospital room like a caged tiger. It was time.

"You want to know how the Hathians routed us so easily."

"Of course I do," was the testy reply. "Are you finally going to tell me?"

"Not I, no, but I have brought someone who can."

She called to someone standing just outside the door. There was a pause, then a woman entered—a woman bulky and slow with her seven-month pregnancy.

Hamon stared, his face white, fists clenched. Marthe. Her face a little fuller, the vibrant hair coiling about her head and shoulders as beautiful as ever, the large eyes dark and questioning. The high cheekbones were not as harshly outlined as when he had last seen her, nor her posture as upright, bent with the weight of her belly.

"Get her out of here," Hamon shouted.

It was his mother who left, giving his enemy an encouraging smile. Marthe stared at him with a face that showed nothing. It took Hamon some minutes to regain sufficient control to speak.

"I wonder you dare come here. Or have you a blaster hid somewhere about your no longer so beautiful body?" he sneered, subsiding into a nearby cube and wishing with everything in him that could be the truth. It wasn't. She was as beautiful as ever.

"I am weaponless, and the surveillance is switched off," she said.

"So, you are at my mercy again. It's a good thing for you that I don't harm pregnant women ... even such as you." His hands gripped the sides of the cube, but he blocked every other sign of the fury raging within him.

"I apologize for inflicting my presence on you, but I owe you an explanation and you are going to get it. I promise you that after this I will not bother you again."

Her voice was quiet and steady, and she sat down opposite. He noticed that she held herself rigidly upright, her back propped hard against the cube. He glared at her, hating the riot of feeling clashing through his body.

"I can learn all I need from other sources. You will leave," he shouted, jumping up and crossing over to grab her arm and push her out of the room but, at the touch of her, he leapt back as if burned. Even now, he could barely control the impulse to pull her into his arms.

Marthe flinched at his touch. She had once meant everything to this man. Now she must watch him range about the room seeking escape.

"I cannot leave till you know the full story. After that, I promise, swear by anything you wish, you will not see me again."

"All right. Give me your excuses, then go!"

It was the barest of capitulations and he stood now as far from her as possible, caught in the far corner of the room. She forced herself to ignore his distance and ploughed on with the words she had rehearsed so hard all the way here.

"First, I must go back five years, to when your people initially landed."

"Just get to how you so effectively sabotaged us. This is no place for old melodramas."

"It's necessary," was her steady reply but she couldn't prevent a pause before she continued.

If she didn't look directly at him, maybe she could get through it all without being stopped. She took a deep breath and started. "No one could believe it, you see, when your ships appeared in our skies and you fired on our welcoming barge. We were at war, and it was all too obvious we would lose. Our only chance lay in subterfuge, to pretend to be less than we were until we could find some means of defeating you. So, we hid in the one place you would never think to look—right under your nose. To give us time, we sent out what few fighters we had to attack your ships—that paltry holding action you so easily defeated. Not surprising as most had never fired a shot except in practice or play. But they were there only to delay your ships while the rest of the planet did the real work, turning hunting villages and camping shelters into the crude towns you found. The township at the Citadel was once a popular outdoor education center. The scientific settlement on Mathe became our headquarters in exile. A refuge for the councilors, technologists and scientists. We abandoned the cities, evacuating to the new towns, and left behind radioactive signals to guard our homes."

"Signals?" interrupted a startled Radcliff.

"Yes. The readings you picked up were false, artificially generated. We knew your equipment would accept them as real. We'd learned early in the holding battle that, technically, we were well ahead of you in many areas."

He started to move again, raging back and forth. She fixed her gaze on a spot on the wall behind him.

"And the dead plants? The whole city stank of decay."

"An olfactory and visual illusion, borrowed from the theatres."

She waited, letting his pacing burn off the worst of his anger. At least he was listening to her. Yet still he stayed as far away as possible—out of disgust at her presence, she presumed miserably. She ploughed on. She would have one chance only to say all this. One chance to tell him everything.

"It may please you to know that we nearly didn't finish in time," she offered, steeling herself to continue. "The protection of the cities and mines did get done before you landed. It seemed they would be your first targets.

The next year was chaos. There were flaws in the rushed transformation to a race of peasants, and the construction of the Mathe colony and the underground control centers still had to be completed. It was six months before we even discovered that you were technically so far behind us—that you were solely dependent on urgonium-generated, electromagnetic energy and knew nothing of infrareactor pulses."

She ignored the question in his sudden stillness, knowing if she stopped she would never be able to start again.

"As soon as we discovered that, things became easier. We could move about much more freely. In the second year, an effective communication system was developed and a clearly defined goal established, with a time scale to guide us. We found that we could readily subvert your surveillance devices and so, at the start of the third year, could begin regular flights to and from Mathe. We hadn't dared to risk sending out ships before in case you detected them but, now, we could give those based on Hathe some badly needed respite and shift the sick back to Mathe for proper treatment. Up till then, we could only patch them up in makeshift field centers and hope for the best.

Then it was just a matter of gathering as much information as possible so we'd be ready to move on the Zenith of Hathe. This year. It would be our only chance to defeat you without bloodshed. We were cutting it fine all the same, hence the heavy workloads of the past months. I was starting to feel like a walking data bank."

Her weak attempt at levity fell flat. "Why the Zenith of Hathe?" he wanted to know.

"The magnetic fields of Hathe, Mathe and our sun overlap at that time, creating an anomaly which disrupts any electromagnetic field. None of your machinery could operate while the effect lasted, but our own was unaffected, leaving us free to take control again. Thankfully we didn't have to wait the full ten-year cycle."

"And the time difference? You made your move before the Zenith."

"The fields overlap enough to cause the disruptive effect one hour beforehand, when Hathe appears to stand over the third of the Seven Pillars on Mathe. The time we *call* the Zenith starts when Hathe first casts its shadow over the Fourth Pillar. And when Hathe is placed squarely over the Fourth Pillar at midnight, as seen from the ancient observatory on Mathe, it is the time of *full* Zenith."

She stopped, unable to dredge up any more trivia to fill the silence, and sat stiffly to await his reaction.

She saw amazement amidst the fury. Then acceptance.

Hamon had heard of the pillars found on Mathe by the first colonists, had seen the holovids of the Zenith showing the white globe of the planet Hathe standing high over the central pillar and casting long shadows over the eerie lunar landscape. Shadows that converged, to some unknown purpose, in the center of the strange, bowl-like valley that held the alien structures. Some kind of observatory, it was thought.

Yes, he had heard of the Pillars, and what she told him set him thinking furiously. Her singsong recitation had made the fantastic story seem quite unreal. Yet the more he thought about it, the more plausible it sounded. Humiliation set in, adding to the anger. "The planning, the detailed knowledge of us it required!"

"We had three years and, fortunately for us, you relied mostly on automatic surveillance not human patrols. By feeding our own vids through your receivers, we were free to move about as we liked. The only places we couldn't study were those under permanent manned guard, such as the Terran section of the Citadel. Then you captured Jacquel and me, and we were brought to live there permanently. It was the closest the resistance ever came to being discovered, but it did have a very useful side effect. For the first time, we could directly access your central data banks, confirming much that we had only been able to extrapolate from the peripheral centers. It cut down the possibility of failure significantly. It also allowed for the peaceful takeover of the Citadel, with no serious injuries to either side."

She was babbling, she knew, but forced herself to keep talking. Anything to ward off his response. But this last claim proved too much.

"No serious injury? Your little pot shot laid me up for eight weeks."

"You shouldn't have gone for that side weapon. I had to stop you."

"Just as you *had* to use our so convenient arrangement to steal all our secrets? No wonder you were so worn down, what with keeping your entry ticket satisfied and amiable, and delving into our terminals. I'm amazed you found time for it all."

He threw himself back into the cube again, his chin buried into his chest as the hawk-like eyes bore in to her. It drove all life from her voice, reducing it to a mechanical whisper.

"The data gathering had of necessity to be done at night."

"You were in my bed at night. I checked the records each morning." Then he stopped. "You mean...?"

"Yes. I substituted the vids and drugged you before I left."

"You were busy! And the rigmarole you gave me that night? How hard life had been for you since we arrived?" His chin jutted forward, as if to stab her deep to her heart.

"It was based on truth."

"Very loosely," he sneered back. "Perhaps you'd better tell me the whole. What *you* were really doing these last five years."

So she told him. It was a bald recital, leaving out much. Despite all, she hadn't yet been reduced to begging for pity.

She told him of the first year, travelling by foot to carry messages between groups before the communications network could be set up, and assisting the medical teams—both during that first holding action and later, after the conquest, in the mines. A makeshift effort that had been, patching up where they could without letting the Terrans know, burying their patients more often than not. Even as her voice brushed lightly over that time, she could still remember how pitifully relieved she'd been when she was recruited to the special training schools in the second year. She had frequently tramped in the desert before the war and showed a real aptitude for undercover work in her early assignments, so had been co-opted into the elite section.

Of the next three years of grindingly hard and dangerous work, she gave a bare sketch only—the facts but not what lay behind them. Always her assignments had been of the worst. Roaming from group to group, it had been she and others such as Jacquel who had crept right under the enemy's nose to set up the surveillance devices for monitoring Terran personnel and their routines. On occasion, they would also sabotage the supply trains to steal the equipment they needed.

"If you stole from us, how was it we never found out?" demanded a disbelieving Hamon.

"We altered the lading bills. Your clerks could never remember exactly what they'd ordered."

"You seem to have little respect for Terran clerks."

"Or Hathian ones." But the placating sop was a failure.

She hastily continued her recitation, still giving only the cold facts and leaving out what had accompanied them: the deadly fear that threatened to sap her will to go on, the hunger and cold, the beatings, and the many times she had narrowly escaped discovery or death. She finished with that last day. The day neither of them would ever forget, when she had held him at the point of a blaster in the communications room, watched and listened as he taunted her, until, finally, it was too late for him to do anything to stop the Resistance takeover and she could give in to the weakness of her body. The day she had shot him.

"I woke five days later, here in First Hospital."

"And since then?"

"Helping in the hospital and catching up on medical studies," was her only reply. Nothing would induce her to tell him of the unpleasantness she had faced since Hathe ruled its own again, that this time of freedom for which she had waited so long was proving to be the hardest of all to endure.

Most especially, she would not tell him of the coming trial. For 'undue fraternization'. Her superiors promised that it would be a mere formality, but how she dreaded such a public exposition of her private affairs.

He stared at her for some time, all the while keeping as far away as possible. For a moment, a suspicion of doubt crept across the harsh features. Then it was banished. She had lost.

Her fingers brushed across her swollen belly, nervously pleating the lower edge of her tunic. But that was not permanent either, the shimmering material falling softly back to its pristine silkiness as soon as her fingers released it. Bitterly, she sighed and looked up again, then wished she hadn't.

"Is life not as salubrious as you anticipated, then?" His eyes held hers and the sudden blankness of face she could not control confirmed it for him as much as her hasty disclaimer. "What a pity," he murmured.

To what he referred, she was unsure, breaking off that disturbing eye lock and bracing herself for the last, and hardest, part of this most difficult of interviews.

"There is one more matter we must discuss." Her lifeless voice came out a shaky quaver.

Hamon straightened instantly. Before this, though he might ask all the pertinent questions, he had kept hidden the utter concentration with which he'd listened to her words. Her hesitation was the signal for that to cease. Abandoning all pretense of disinterest, he strode forward, coming to a halt right in front of her and forcing her to look upwards if she wished to see his face. The deadly tone of his "Oh?" killed any such attempt.

"You hesitate. Is it possible you finally feel some guilt? Some hint that you acknowledge your betrayal?"

"It's not that. I've explained the reason for my actions. I didn't intend it to be seen as an apology." The words might be defiant, but her voice had sunk even lower. Again, she hesitated. Then: "It's the baby."

"What about it?"

He stepped forward, menacingly closer.

She braced herself before continuing, taking a deep breath to make her voice a fraction stronger. "Since we're unlikely to meet again, I have to know whether or not you retain a claim. If so, we must decide his future."

Suddenly and viciously, he caught her by the elbows, hauling her up till her feet barely touched the floor. The white fury etched on his face made her flinch as if struck.

"Understand me, and understand me well, Madame," he snarled. "You will not steal my child from me.

"I never said that," she exclaimed. Then blanched. "You wouldn't! You couldn't be so cruel as to take him away?"

"It's what you were planning to do to me, wasn't it?"

"No, never that. Only to work out some sharing arrangement."

She was pleading now, her arms aching where he still gripped her. Wordlessly, she stared up at him, too aware of his closeness and filled with a dreadful yearning that he would hold her closer still, but in another way entirely. Something of the same must have been in his mind for, with no warning, he let her drop, snatching his hands hastily back.

She landed on the cube in a thudding whoosh. Thankfully it gave on impact, cushioning some part of her fall, but she was badly jarred. Her attention bent urgently inward, all other worries driven out in panicked fear for the baby.

"Much more of that and we won't have a son to worry about," she snapped, forgetting everything she'd come here for as her hands cradled her belly protectively and her temper flared.

It was the worst possible moment. Hamon had almost begun to lose the black rage that had driven him so long, dismayed by the flash of panic washing her face. Then her black eyes sparked into fury, telling him she was safe. Freeing him to discard the tenderness, and once more give into his craving for revenge.

"You dare to pretend that losing my son would worry you unduly," he jeered.

"The child is also an Castre. That is sufficient to cancel out any flaws in his genetic make-up," she jeered back, every bit as arrogant now as he and bent only on causing him as much pain as she felt.

"The records will designate asn Radcliff. I doubt even your father can get the almighty Hathian genealogies tampered with."

"Perhaps. But I can spare my child from knowing the truth of his father. What you really are."

"Which is?" he asked dangerously.

"Terran rabble. A ragtag adventurer, scorned by his own father, whose only claim to fame as far as I can learn is that he is known among all the scum and dregs of the Alliance. Well, you needn't think you are going to bring my son up like that." She had shot back up again and stood, leaning forward in her fury, the bulge of her stomach stretched tauntingly towards him.

"If you value your life, you had better leave. Now."

He was a magnificent sight, and even in her anger she drank him in. But his eyes were fully green and brittle, and his skin was dark with flushed rage, a stark contrast to the white hospital gown. Deliberately he turned away, white knuckles grasping the edge of the sleeper as he stared fixedly out the window at the opal luminescence of the Hathian sky.

"I am counting. You would be wise to be gone before I reach ten."

Cold sense came crashing back. What had she done? She stood a brief moment longer, looking at the unrelenting line of his back, then turned and left, unnecessarily slamming the door panel shut behind her.

Once outside, she held tightly to her facade of control, walking out between his guards and around the first corner. Then she found a quiet side hall, and there, the trembling won. She leaned back against the cool hospital walls, her mind as whirling and smoky as their marbled blues and whites. She had fouled that up nicely. She cursed long and silently, heedless of the cascade of tears streaming down her face. Stumbling, she turned and crept slowly down the endless walls, intent only upon her flyer.

And then? Home. Home and the privacy of that sweet room where, undisturbed, she could drop her hateful front of self-control. Safe in that fortress, the tears would come, the pain break out and the howling within her be released.

But none of it would help.

CHAPTER TWENTY-FOUR

Hamon twitched angrily. Yet another damned Hathian doctor, prodding and poking at his side. He had not seen this one before and the man seemed particularly inept.

"Stars, haven't you finished?" He pulled away from the irresolute hands. "I've already been examined ad nauseam by your fellow ghouls."

He scowled angrily, causing the middle-aged physician poking so reluctantly at him to pause. His brown eyes caught Hamon's and he gave up his half-hearted examination.

"Well? Out with it," rasped Hamon. "And don't try to con me into thinking you want to discuss my skin wounds. You haven't seen a burns case in years."

The other still hesitated, worried concern written on the freckled face. Then plunged in: "You guess right. You're not my problem, as it happens."

"What is then?"

The man stepped back, taking a resolute breath. "Let me introduce myself. Dr Raph an Dothen. As you guessed, I am not a burns specialist."

"That's obvious."

"Though young asn Marvell has done a fine job here, I must say," the older man continued, ignoring the interruption. "No, I need your help with another patient of mine."

Hamon glared. How could he be of help to anyone, given his own uncertain confinement?

"I'm in O and G, you see," the doctor informed him somewhat diffidently. Hamon only stared in bemusement. "Sorry, obstetrics and gynecology," the Hathian explained then retreated in haste as Hamon suddenly towered furiously over him.

"And your patient's name, doctor?"

"Marthe an Castre, naturally. Your wife. You see…" and then halted.

Hamon couldn't stop the harsh, gasping breaths of his shock.

"Are you all right?"

"Quite, thank you," replied Hamon, hating the time it took him to recover. He had half guessed it would be her at the start of this weird interview. Stars, it had only been a few days since that last, hellish meeting. Couldn't the woman leave him alone?

"You may tell my wife that I have nothing more to discuss. I don't need to hear from yet another of her messengers," he snapped.

"Marthe doesn't know I'm here," an Dothen replied, clearly determined to ignore any kind of rejection, regardless of the force of it, "but I'm becoming seriously concerned about her. I told the Council months ago that they were expecting too much from a pregnant woman but, no, they had to have her working all hours."

Hamon broke in on the embryonic monologue. "The an Castre woman's welfare is not my affair. You may state your business, briefly, then leave."

"As I was explaining, my business is Marthe an Castre. Her poor state of physical and mental health is endangering both her own and the child's wellbeing. You're her closest relative. It's up to you to do something. You are the child's father, after all." Doctor an Dothen, Hamon was rapidly discovering, could summon a quietly persistent core of determination when needed. He finally recognized defeat and abandoned his threatening stance. He slumped into a nearby chair and gestured to the doctor to take the other, hating totally the necessity.

It was too soon for this. Too near still to that gut tearing, nightmare meeting … when her presence had forced him to acknowledge the yearning that still lay there, deep within him. She was part of him, still the most beautiful woman he had ever seen, and nothing could change what he felt for her. Long after the hurt and betrayal subsided, as he supposed it would one day, the yearning would remain. Silently, bitterly, he cursed the day he saw that treacherous lock of hair.

"Continue, doctor," he said, unable to keep the flat note of defeat from his voice. "As you say, the welfare of my child is at stake."

"Thank you. As I said, I am concerned for Marthe. It is less than two months now till the birth, and her condition is far from satisfactory."

"You're a doctor. Prescribe rest. Isn't that the usual treatment?"

"I have. I've also tried re-admitting her to hospital, but it's no use. She knows all the staff and can't resist becoming involved. She's still working at emergency pitch, hasn't yet adapted to peacetime needs. Well, none of us has, and the special operatives more than most."

"What did you expect? That after five years of war everything would return to normal in a couple of months?"

"No, you're right of course. There is a training course for ex-agents—to redirect their talents and skills to more useful pursuits, so I'm told."

"Why bother me then if the government is looking after her? Let them sort out any problems." He thrust one hand through his already abused hair.

"Marthe is in rather a peculiar position. That damned course only added to the stress. She hasn't the energy for it, though certainly the will power. I had to pull her off it."

There was an ominously familiar pounding at Hamon's temples. The kind that hit him every time he thought too long of Marthe an Castre. If only the doddery old fool would get to the point, then leave. He would do what he could to safeguard his child, but beyond that…

"What, precisely, is the point of this discussion, doctor?"

The man gave him that look doctors often gave. The one that said they had seen too many of the intimacies of their patients' lives to be fooled by whatever you might say. Hamon suspected this doctor knew exactly how he was feeling at the moment. But would it stop him? The doctor hesitated a moment longer then, to his relief, relented, launching into a stark outline of Marthe's case.

"Marthe is underweight, has been so throughout her pregnancy, yet will not eat enough to keep the smallest flitter alive. Her nerves are strung too tightly, and she will not rest and relax as ordered. I suspect she is severely depressed, but she refuses to consult a therapist. Control of emotion is second nature to her from her years as an operative. As I suppose it is to you. But in her current situation, it can only bring her harm. Her true mental condition is impossible to ascertain. All of this could have serious implications for the baby and later on, during labor. It also bodes ill for the development of a strong maternal bond after the birth. If Bendin were still alive, I would seek his help. As it is, you seem to be the only person who can break through the wall she has thrown up—the only one who can make her slow down and start taking care of herself."

"When last I saw her, she appeared to have put on weight," argued Hamon defensively.

"Not nearly enough."

"What do you expect me to do. The lady and I are finished, as well she knows."

"Exactly what I suspect is the core of the problem. That, and this stupid trial our righteous leaders insist upon."

"Trial?" queried Hamon. Anything to distract the doctor.

"Marthe is to be tried for undue fraternization, due to your relationship. Right now, it's the last thing she needs. You would think those moralizing upstarts would have some heart. That is why it is so desperately urgent that this estrangement of yours cease. She needs all the support she can muster. If I can just minimize the stresses as much as possible. As it is—"

"Razzing stupid to try her. The lady should be given a medal. For supreme dedication to duty under duress, or some such, grand-sounding epithet. Undue fraternization indeed," spat Hamon. "Stars! That two-faced hypocrite doesn't know the meaning of the words."

His head fell back and he stared at the ceiling, desperately battling the half of him he had come to hate—the half that demanded he believe this man. His tortured gaze switched back to the Hathian, a driven plea in his heart.

"You may leave, doctor. Go look after your own patient, and don't bother me again. Not with her."

He began to laugh—wildly, bitterly, so much anger and despair exposed in the eerie cry.

Still the Hathian doctor persisted. Why, Hamon couldn't begin to guess, refusing to remember his own fears before the Terrans' fall and the picture that haunted his dreams, of the listless, slumped face of a once vibrant young woman.

"Could you not put aside your personal feelings, at least until after the birth?"

"Doctor, I can't help you. That is final."

A word that had never registered in an Dothen's vocabulary. "You deny your own child? Are your hurt feelings so important that they must come before a little one's life? For that is what I fear. Don't tell me of the wonders of modern medicine," he added, interrupting before Hamon's already opening mouth could voice its angry denial. "No amount of technology can fight a mind bent on despair."

"It's no good, doctor. I cannot help you," cried Hamon, leaping to his feet and pacing hard to fight off the pounding waves in his head. "We are finished, Marthe an Castre and I. Stars, I couldn't even vouch for her safety if left alone with me. Don't you know who it was gave me this burn on my side, or what she was doing in those months we lived together? The woman is a highly trained espionage agent, quite capable of using a sexual attachment to gain access to top secret information. Even that damned marriage charade she went through… What a joke! The woman has the word 'duty' in the place most wear a heart." He stopped again, glaring hard at the older man before slumping once more into his chair. "The only emotion she feels for me that has any truth is fear," he snarled bitterly, "and well she should."

Doctor an Dothen was silent as the tirade came to an end. He looked long at Hamon, defensively thrust backwards in the far chair, before saying calmly: "Then there is no point in further discussion." He stood, nodding his head in grave farewell. "And if you believe all that, my boy, it's more than I do," he said quietly as he disappeared through the door, leaving a fuming Hamon to once more vainly seek his couch. Would nothing stop this endless pounding in his skull?

It was still there later in the day but beginning to lessen. Then the door chimes signaled another visitor. He waited tensely, but it was only the comforting figure of his mother who entered, the harsh lines of strain upon her face lessening daily in the Hathian air.

"Hamon, how are you today?"

She had her 'mother' smile on, he saw with suspicion.

"Fine, thank you. Merely a slight headache," he added in answer to her disbelieving snort.

"I hear Doctor an Dothen has been speaking to you." His closed face warned her not to continue. "Very well. I actually came to tell you that you are now well enough to leave hospital, though you're not yet ready for space travel. As soon as you're packed, I can take you out of here."

"To go where?" he said harshly. "In whose protective custody are we to be kindly placed?"

His mother, wise in the ways of the world and beginning to be wise in the ways of this strange adult who was her son, said simply that a suite had been procured for them in a secured government complex. "Up till now, I've been staying with the an Castres, but it was felt it would be diplomatic if you resided elsewhere."

"Mother, how could you? In that nest of vipers?"

"Nonsense. I've had a very pleasant time. The only cloud on the horizon has been Marthe's lifelessness, but I know I can rely on you to remedy that." His sudden fury shocked even her.

"So now they've set you onto me. Stars, they've won the war! Can't they leave me alone?" he shouted. "What game are they playing this time?"

"It's no game. Marthe really is ill. She has lost all drive and willpower. We've all tried, but no one can rouse her. Heavens, you most of all know how far beyond her limit she had been pushed by the ordeal of the takeover. And while you may blame her for that as much as you like, I never thought to see you shirk a responsibility. Has it even occurred to you to check on the fate of your men?"

A knife edge of guilt lanced through him. Of course he had thought of it; but to question any of those about him must take him back, with the inevitability of a doom, to that hateful last day.

"Why? What's happened to them?"

"Don't worry. All the Special Forces were shipped back to Earth at the earliest opportunity. You and your men seem to have aroused an extraordinary degree of ill feeling among the Hathians. Whatever did you do to them?"

"Merely our job." His shoulders straightened defensively, and his look asked how she dared condemn him.

"Sorry. I am allowed to move about so freely and have been so well received that I sometimes forget how recent was the occupation. Sylvan was speaking only the truth, then, when he said your guards are as much for your protection as for any other reason?"

"They needn't bother."

"Perhaps, but the Hathians maintain that any reprisals against former members of the occupying forces could harm Hathe's standing among the other Alliance planets. And at the moment, they are almost as much in need of Alliance help as is Earth."

He grunted in disbelief, refusing to answer that, and turned to pack his few belongings, grateful only that he would not have to cope with too many Hathian officials.

Her words came back to him as they were driven through the streets of the City. From the darkened windows of their car, he could see that it was as beautiful as when he had last seen it, that long ago, fateful day with Marthe. Now, though, throngs of brightly dressed Hathians once again filled the wide walks, and the magnificent gardens no longer echoed in eerie desertion. Once, he was recognized, despite the dimly lit windows, and immediately the rumor spread. A queer restraint checked the protests, but he was glad of the grim-faced, efficient soldiers surrounding their vehicle. The Hathians may not have been militarily minded before the occupation, but they certainly seemed to have learned fast.

His training alone gave him the pride needed to maintain his sternly uncaring front during the brief journey to the secured building but did not stop him wishing heartily that he could catch the first flight out of this cursed paradise.

But he had made a promise. One that he would keep no matter how much he may loathe the recipient.

"I told the an Castre woman that I will be here at the birth of my child and, by the stars, I will be. But don't worry, as soon as that responsibility is discharged, I will be on the first flight out."

"Very understandable in the circumstances, sir, I'm sure," said the official accompanying them. "It's up to the Council of course, but I will certainly let them know of your request. I understand from her relatives that Madame an Castre is not well. Of course you wish to stay."

At that point, Hamon sent the official a look designed to remind the man of some of the nastier stories of his activities during the occupation. The Hathian decided to leave, immediately and with all haste.

"If one more person tries that 'poor Marthe' routine, I will be forced to take drastic action," growled Hamon desperately at the disappearing back. "That includes you, Mother. I promised the woman I would see the baby, and I do want to know my firstborn. The stars know he can't help who his mother is; but I do not wish, now or ever, to be bothered by that lying witch again!"

Madame MacDiarmid opened her mouth to speak.

"No. Don't tell me again that the woman is wasting away. One thing I know about Marthe an Castre is that she's made of solid titanium. She's not capable of failing to cope … with anything!" he said, the black hurt and anger of that day still eating at him. How could she? Betrayal, from the one woman he had trusted with his life and his heart.

No. She would not lure him back with fake stories of illness, and he thrust to the deepest recesses of his mind his own fears and worries of those last weeks—before she had turned to face him as his enemy. He would not remember her sunken eyes, or the too hollow cheeks. She had looked fit enough when last he saw her. As full of fight as ever.

Sick? Ha!

When a week had gone by and he had still received no word on whether he could stay or not, he couldn't deny his growing anxiety. It was for the child. He wanted to see his child born. If he told himself that often enough, maybe he'd begin to believe it.

Whatever the cause, after another day of pacing, he demanded to see deln Crantz. If he had to beg from anyone, he'd rather it be the resistance commander. Only if that failed would he try Sylvan an Castre or Jacquel des Trurain. He wasn't that desperate, not yet.

He still had to wait another day, pacing angrily in the comfortable rooms that now imprisoned him, before he was brought by a posse of guards to an office deep in the same complex. The little man was the same as ever, his round body and cheerfully wrinkled face still sitting as oddly with the intelligent gleam in his too knowing eyes as he waited to hear his inconvenient prisoner's demands.

Hamon lost no time in telling him.

"I propose a swap. Send my mother home and keep me as a hostage instead."

Deln Crantz didn't look surprised. More resigned.

"No."

But Hamon had expected that. "Why not? You need important, well connected hostages. I qualify, on both sides of the family. As you know, my father is the Alliance ambassador, Garth Radcliff, and other family members on both sides hold prominent Terran positions."

"And your father would hold off taking action against us to protect you?"

So, the man had done his homework. Hamon was too experienced at reading people to argue. He shrugged acknowledgement. "I'm still well enough connected to ensure the good behavior of Earth."

"But not as critical to Terran wellbeing as your mother. Your world cannot afford to lose a woman who knows as much about supply and distribution as the Administrator."

"Maybe. But unlike my father, she would hold off acting against you to protect me. Let her go and keep me, and you would have the same surety as you have now."

Deln Crantz looked skeptical. "No," he simply said again.

Hamon surged from his chair in frustration, pacing angrily. Deln Crantz made no attempt to move, as if he knew Hamon would not give up that easily.

Why was he so determined to stay? Earth needed him, needed his skills very badly now.

He sat down and tried again. Taking a deep breath, he pulled out his next card.

"Let me access my financial records on your screen."

Deln Crantz showed real interest for the first time. Hamon didn't fool himself into thinking that meant the man was bribable. The amused grin on the small man's face confirmed it, even as his fingers reached out and activated his screen.

Then he sat back and waved his arm in invitation. "It's all yours. Input your access data."

Hamon leaned over, let the light beam read his skin cells then added his code to the system, making sure all the while that deln Crantz had full view of what he did.

A few more entries and then he was finished. He switched it round to let deln Crantz see the full display on the screen.

"That's my current financial position. As you can see, the connections I mentioned aren't confined to Earth alone."

Deln Crantz looked at the screen, his face a bland mask, then it changed. Hamon wished he could take some pleasure from the shock on the man's face. The Hathian leaned forward, his fingers reaching to the figures, poking at each balance and tracing down the lists.

"You own all this?"

Hamon nodded.

"You're worth… Is that figure at the bottom accurate?"

Hamon nodded again. "You can have your finance ministry run through the data. Most of the companies are owned by double and triple blinds, but my ownership is traceable if I tell you where to look."

"How did you accumulate so much? You were serving here the last five years. And kept busy at it. Our agents can attest to that."

Hamon shrugged this time. "I found I had a knack for reading economic cycles and I needed a hobby to take my mind off my work here."

"Some hobby. You do realize this makes you wealthy on an Alliance scale?"

Hamon nodded again. It was getting to be repetitious. "So, does that make me important enough to be a hostage? If anything happens to me, a number of significant Alliance companies would be badly hit."

Deln Crantz nodded this time, very slowly, then stared at the figures one last time before switching his attention back to Hamon.

"Why?"

"I want my mother home, safe."

"No harm will come to her here. You know that. Try again."

Hamon refused to answer. He'd hoped not to, not unless he had to, but it looked like he wasn't going to be so lucky.

"Does Marthe know about this?" the other asked suddenly.

"No," he replied curtly. "Nor do I want her to."

"One of our best agents doesn't know she's spent months living with a man this wealthy?"

"She knows some of it," he conceded. "That I have off-planet interests and enjoy following the markets. The extent of it? No. I tend to accumulate rather than spend my wealth. If it's news to you, she obviously doesn't know," he couldn't resist pointing out.

Deln Crantz acknowledged the hit, then placed his hands together again, still studying him like some prize specimen.

"Tell me again. Why do you want to stay? And make it the truth this time."

Hamon had never felt so trapped. He thrust back up, pacing hard, but could see no escape. He stopped, caught.

"Because I made a promise, that's why. I promised to stay here till my child is born."

Deln Crantz must have been laughing his head off inside, but outwardly he merely gave a small smile of satisfaction, as of a complex puzzle now solved.

Hamon stepped back in disgust, hating the sense of failure. "I've taken up enough of your time. Please call the guards."

"You can stay, Major. Until the child is born and properly settled. Your mother may go whenever she decides to."

He stopped short and stared. The man was serious. Deln Crantz nodded confirmation.

"Thank you," said Hamon. And wondered why he suddenly felt free.

CHAPTER TWENTY-FIVE

Madame Freya MacDiarmid sat lost in thought, faced with the all too familiar dilemma of a problem that seemed to have no solution. This time, though, it wasn't the strident needs of Earth gnawing at her. It was her son. Her son and her barely known daughter-in-law, Marthe an Castre of Hathe.

She was at an evening reception, her chair placed near the railing of the balcony to allow her to look down in pensive contemplation on the room below. She could see Marthe there, seated in the middle of a crowd. Yet she seemed utterly alone.

Fear struck the older woman anew. They'd had a bad start, this new daughter-in-law and she, and were still not close. But since the stunning end to the occupation, Madame Freya had been forced to review many of her past attitudes and not least this one. The Hathians had lifted the worst of burdens from her; she could afford to be generous in return. The sheer relief of turning Earth's problems over to the Alliance couldn't be put into words. For the first time in generations, there was food for all Terrans. To the loss of liberty to run their own affairs she gave never a thought. There was little enough before.

She'd arrived here dreading the imprisonment she expected as hostage for Earth's good behavior only to find that her status was more that of honored guest than captive. She was free now to return home if she wished and must leave soon. Earth needed her, but she hadn't expected to be so torn between worry for her son and her home.

Not that she was blind to why she'd been among those originally taken. She knew too much about how Earth worked and was too important a member of the past government. The Alliance had wanted gone from their home planet any who might be involved in founding a resistance to the new order—such as her own son, she acknowledged ruefully. The stars help the Alliance if he were to be let loose on Earth in his present frame of mind.

That brought her back full circle to her first worry. She looked down again at her daughter-in-law, heavy with child and slumped in a seat. Her face was pinched and withdrawn, so different from the rest of the lively crowd of women surrounding her. Then Freya noticed again what she had seen on other nights. There was a space around Marthe, an unconscious shrinking away from her by the other Hathians. No trial, however fair and open, was going to wipe that gap away.

Not that Marthe appeared to notice. She sat, still and quiet, making no attempt to join in any conversation, and soon, Freya saw, she rose and made her discreet farewell. Her walk as she left was slow and ponderous—not just the slowness of pregnancy but as if a great burden of grief and despair was upon her. Her son might claim that Marthe had lived with him out of duty only, but Freya seriously doubted that—though not that Marthe had used her position to spy on the Terrans; it was what her loyalty to her people had demanded of her, just as loyalty to Earth had forced her son to interrogate and extract information from this woman he adored.

Why, Freya wondered, having been forced to act so contrary to all that love and trust demanded, could he not understand the forces that drove Marthe, so exactly his mirror? Instead, he wallowed in his pain, hiding from the truth behind its buttressing shield. Without that defense, he might have to come to an evening like this, might see what his mother saw—what this cruel separation was doing to the mother of his child.

Marthe had withdrawn behind a high wall of despair. Daily, Freya listened to her family's fear as they saw the shadows beneath her eyes deepen. She ate, yes, but only enough to keep going. Not enough to nurture her and the child she carried. Her burgeoning pregnancy seemed as nothing. Yet Sylvan had told her of a Marthe once fiercely driven by the need to provide a safe home for her baby. And Freya knew fear again—fear for her yet-to-be-born grandchild, fear for its mother, but most of all fear for her son. She knew what he said, but if anything happened to his wife and child, how would he survive it?

Down below, Marthe knew of her mother-in-law's scrutiny, but gave no sign of it. Madame MacDiarmid and her own family might guess at the cause of her decline, but they couldn't know the whole— that inside, Marthe was more deeply lost than they imagined. All around lay nothingness. This new Hathe was too foreign, too bereft of any guidelines. Long forced to survive in a double-edged world of shadows, deceit and danger, the normal, peacetime world seemed instead a place beset with hidden snares.

It was a world that had rejected her. Her family may think she no longer noticed the unconscious recoil by all who met her, with the exception of the close circle who knew the truth of her history, and Marthe had no intention of spoiling their illusions. To her, it was but an inescapable part of the grayness, not worth fighting.

Looming over her too was her coming trial. To be condemned to a public display at the whipping stand was more, she thought, than she could bear. Not after all she had endured.

Overriding all was losing Hamon. She sank into the shadows, seeking oblivion as pain cut in anew.

He had known the rules they lived by, had always accepted, she assumed, that she must act against him; but that didn't mean he would one day come to understand what she had done to him that day. His pride was too strong and his commitment to his people too deep ever to forgive her triumph—not betrayal, no, despite what he thought. Merely the last chapter in that awful game they had played so long. She had always known it would end like this, but it hadn't stopped her fighting for an alternative while she was with him.

Now, there was no hope, nor ever would be, she realized bleakly, threading her way out of the garish reception. She'd felt his mother's eye upon her and knew of the Administrator's attempts at reconciliation. She could have told her not to bother; it wouldn't work. But why, please God, did she have to miss him so badly? Like a great gash in her side that bled and bled and bled.

That last interview haunted her. How angry he'd been and, damn it, how angry she had become. She laughed mirthlessly, amazed that she could ever have felt so much emotion. Now, mere weeks later, it was all she could manage to get through the daily rituals of living. Periodically, unknown to her family, she would escape the protective guard they insisted on, concerned still with the anger of the crowds in the street. To someone of her training, it was easy enough to evade her escort. Unrecognized, she would take her skimmer up and over the lush, down-country lands, across the harsh dividing range, to seek solace once more in the emptiness of the high plateau. There alone, it seemed, she could find rest. There, where a moment's neglect could lead to death. That she could understand; but this peacetime world, with its petty intrigues, its trivial concerns and twisting of facts. Here, she was lost in an ever-winding maze…and had no guide. The only one who could have helped was barred to her forever.

He was still in the City. Barely a mile away in a carefully guarded military complex, so close she could almost feel his arms reaching for her; but he might as well have been on another planet. Once his child was born, he would be gone … taking the baby with him, she didn't doubt. Not after his angry words. So her son, too, was gone. No point in dreaming of days of playing with tiny hands and feet.

Her doctor was concerned. The physician in her recognized it, as if she were looking over the case notes of a colleague's patient. He urged her to eat, to rest, to talk out her fears and worries, urged her for the sake of the baby. She tried—she had made a promise to Hamon that his son would be safe—but couldn't. Couldn't stop the restlessness. Couldn't face the food they shoved at her. Couldn't even begin to talk. That might make her begin to feel again.

Her medical training told her the truth of it. She'd been pushed too far, too often. She recognized the breaking points but only as words on a chart, unconnected with reality. Worn out with lack of sleep and overwork, by the end of the occupation she'd been in no state to cope with the devastation of Hamon's loss. On top of that, she'd been thrust into an environment even more hostile than before. Deprived of revenge against the Terrans for the horrors of the occupation years, her own people had instituted a witch hunt, and she was the target. Facts were lost in popular myths. She was guilty and must pay, said the pop banners.

The Council had no choice but to agree to her trial. Anything else would look like a cover-up. They promised her it would be a formality but coupled with the hate and fear she met every time she braved the streets, it was too much. Her overstressed mind and body reacted in the only way it could—denial. This strange new world did not exist, the baby was coming to another woman, this growing body belonged to someone else, and Marthe an Castre the person retreated to a refuge deep within the worn out, listless shell that was her body.

Her father had tried to shake her out of it; Jaca tried and failed; her mother-in-law was most persistent of all, goaded, Marthe guessed, by the need to have her own son whole again. In vain. Deeper and deeper Marthe fled, coming to dread their kind thoughts and words. Increasingly, she shunned those public engagements she wasn't forced to attend. The birth was so close now, it was easy to make her excuses. One by one, the number of her friends shrank down to a close, loyal circle, and even they didn't bother her much.

So, it was with detached surprise that she heard her door chime one day. Listlessly, she signaled the unknown guest to enter, all the while continuing to gaze blankly out the window. She had no welcome for this intruder who bearded her in her private chambers. She sighed heavily and turned slowly to meet the interloper.

A wave of nausea and fright surged up from the bowels of her stomach. She sat down abruptly on the nearest chair and stared in dismay. For once, the lethargy had fled.

"You! What are you doing here?" she managed to gasp, staring at the cold face of her husband. Goosebumps tingled all over her and she hugged her arms to her body. Stars, but the sight of him warmed her. The dark hair curled as crisply as ever at his temples. Still that harsh mouth sent a shiver to the base of her spine. Then she saw his eyes, cold jade, and the growing hope within her was abruptly quenched.

"Glad to see me, Madame? You shouldn't be. I have come to put a stop to this ridiculous charade of yours."

"Charade?" she stammered uncertainly.

"What else would you call these claims of illness my mother keeps forcing down my throat to get me here? Though how you managed to fool her is beyond me."

There was ice in his voice and he had come no farther into the room than was absolutely necessary.

"I'm not ill."

What role was required of her, she worried, dragging a lock of hair back from her face.

"Then why does my mother continually nag at me? Are you deliberately starving yourself just to spite me? I had thought even you would have some feeling for your own child's safety."

"The child? I know I owe you that. Your child, whole and well, I mean. He'll be all right, you can take him away safely," she said earnestly, trying to assure him of this, at least.

To Hamon, her voice possessed a weird, otherworldly quality, as though she were speaking from a far distance, he realized suddenly, really looking at her for the first time. Her eyes were not quite there, and dark shadows clung beneath them. Nor was her hair as glowing and full of life as once when it had clung so closely to his hands, and the bones of her face made cavernous hollows and ridges. As if on a skull.

He checked himself hard. One more maudlin thought and he might almost begin pleading with her to come back to him, on any grounds.

"What do you mean, take him away? The baby's yours. Did you really think I would relieve you of the burden of our union that easily? Deny myself the pleasure of knowing that, as our son grows in your loving care—and by all the Pillars, it had better be loving—all the while you will see me in him?"

He took a step toward her. "And when he is old enough, then I will teach him what he needs to know. Of loyalty, of trust and love, of faith in people. All that he cannot learn from you. That is, if he's ever born. Do you hate me so much, that you neglect your own unborn child?"

His strode over, grabbing her to shake a response from her, some lie to his words. And, yes, to feel if she hurt the way he did. No sooner had he touched her than he sprang back. As on that last occasion, it was more than he could bear.

She was not dropped this time, at least. Marthe stared at his chest in confusion, He couldn't mean those ugly words. No. She clung instead to the new hope. The child—her child, she remembered with shock—he said she could keep him. She could cuddle him, feed him, love him as she had not dared to dream of since that angry day of their last meeting.

As for the rest of his words? The fury-filled hate filtered through, but not the sense. How could it, when all she was aware of was the sweet smell of him filling her senses once more? Here was the only home she would ever have. Crazily, she reached out and lifted her hunger-starved mouth to those haunting lips.

It was the worst thing she could have done. Hamon couldn't stop himself. His mouth must answer her call and he drowned in her sweet magic, even as his mind raged at this attraction he couldn't deny. Disgust and shame conquered. He tore himself away from her, to stand caught by the far wall.

"Keep back," he cried out, panting harshly in desperate flight. "Surely you've done enough. What more do you want?"

She stood where he had left her, still caught in the magic. On the far side of the room, she heard him fight for control. His slow, harsh breathing filled the air, the jagged edge of it amplified by the imprisoning walls. A little only of his anguish came to Marthe, still dazed by the sudden joy, then loss. Her mind no longer able to think, formulate, say whatever were the words needed to banish this dreadful time. All she could do was stand, caught in bewilderment. And that was no help at all.

Defeated again, admitted Hamon in despair, drinking in the sight of her. It was no good. Always, it would be like this. That the woman he loved had probably never existed was irrelevant. Maybe he had dreamed her. Whatever, this shell, this body, was hers, and he could not deliver himself of it. He breathed once, praying to be capable of cool speech.

"I will stay and see my son, as promised; and always I will do what I can to teach him something of myself … but have no fear. Once the birth is over, I will trouble you as little as possible, as long as he is happy and well cared for. For that, I trust, even you have sufficient honor."

Then: "Why the hell did you ever get pregnant in the first place? Or don't tell me that was part of the plan, too?"

"No. Oh, no. Of course not. I never meant—"

"I apologize for that, then."

He could yet manage a degree of calm. It wouldn't last. Soon, he must leave this room.

"Don't! I do want our son," she cried out, reaching out one, small hand, her voice still sounding dazed. "You must believe me. More than anything, our baby is precious to me. This I do promise, Truly."

It was the end for Hamon. Another cunning trick, or truth? Either way, it was more than he could bear. With a gasped exclamation, he tore himself from the wall. One last, hunted glance, and he was gone.

For a long time, Marthe stayed where he had left her, trying to understand. He seemed to hate her still, but she would swear that there was something else there too. If she could just hold on to that.

She stood silent, remembering all he had said. For the first time in weeks, she started to think of a future. To believe that there might be one that held joy. She began to plan, but one thought only stood clear.

How much there was to do if she was to be ready for this little one. She made lists, then discarded them again. No use. She couldn't come to the decisions she needed here. Not in this bedroom which would now remind her so vividly of Hamon. No, she knew where she must go.

Quickly, she packed all those things she would need. Including, with a wry smile at her thin face in the mirror, some high value rations. Soon, after a last, practiced check of her room and gear, she slipped from the house as silent as the night. A little while later, her small craft sped off into the air.

In strident impatience, the door chime rang and rang and rang. Hamon cursed, then harshly ordered whoever disturbed his tortured rest to go away. The chiming continued. Bitterly, he released the lock and the next moment, Jacquel des Trurain shoved forward into his room.

"Where's Marthe?" the man blurted, looking hurriedly round the room.

"Hardly likely to be here," snapped back Hamon. "Now I'll thank you to leave."

"She must be. There's nowhere else."

Hamon suddenly noticed the other's face. "What do you mean?"

"She went missing yesterday. No one's seen her since before lunch."

"No, I spoke to her in the afternoon. You have asked around?"

"Of course. I tell you, no one has seen her."

Without another word, Hamon threw on his clothes and strode out. "I'll contact you at the an Castres' when I have news," he threw over his shoulder.

He made it one step outside his door before the two large guards stationed there blocked him, weapons up and ready for use. He looked them over. Both bigger than he and as well muscled, he didn't have a chance of getting through. He tried anyway.

One very unproductive instant later, he was on his back and forced to admit the pair had the equal of his own street thuggery.

They dragged him up and back into the room to face des Trurain.

"If you've finished time wasting, do you have anything useful to tell me?" said his enemy, looking as frustrated as he felt.

"Let me out of here long enough to find something, and maybe I could."

"Don't be a fool, Radcliff. Let you loose on Hathians? Not likely."

"You have plenty of guards, my face is too well known thanks to your razzing journos, and I'm sure you have a tracker planted in me. Escape is impossible, even if that's what I planned." He thrust his hands on his hips, daring the Hathian to contradict him.

He wanted to. You could see it on his face.

"Damn it, man. That's my wife, my child out there. Not yours."

Des Trurain's face lost its pale coolness, a dark flush spreading angrily over it. "And Marthe's my oldest friend left alive."

Hamon couldn't answer that, but she was his wife.

For long moments, neither of them said anything, deadlocked in fury. Hamon could feel his hand clenching. "By the stars, des Trurain, anything could have happened to her!" He could see the Hathian's hands, fists forming in parallel to his. "Can you find her?" Hamon demanded. "If you could, why come here?"

"And you think you can do better?"

"Yes."

"What can you know about her that I don't?"

Her face came to him again. There was no choice. "I know how she feels." he said. "I feel the same."

It took too long, too many precious minutes lost when he needed to be on his way. Then finally des Trurain nodded. "The guards will go with you and you're limited to this complex, her home and unsecured parts of headquarters. And yes, we have you under full surveillance."

Hamon nodded back. "Just let me in to your flight records. On a view basis only."

"Agreed, but you don't get to operate the access. Tell the technician what you need to see. I'm setting your tracker to kill mode. You make one wrong move, and I will personally hit the button to end your miserable life."

They were wasting time, and Hamon could feel the anger in him growing. He was only surprised des Trurain thought to warn him. But he could see the look on the man's face. Des Trurain meant every word he said and would love nothing more than to rid Hathe and Marthe of his presence—permanently.

"You'd have to join the queue. How long is it?"

Des Trurain sneered back. "Almost every Hathian except one is in that queue. Unfortunately, she's the one who counts." Des Trurain breathed in hard, his eyes hot with anger. Then nodded a 'Yes'. "One wrong move, and I will kill you. Do you accept?"

It was the best deal he would get. He had to agree. His child could be at risk, and he throttled down hard on any other reason.

Des Trurain gave the guards his orders and linked in to his central command, communicating in that infuriating mix of coded taps and single words that Hamon still hadn't managed to work out.

"You'd better change," said des Trurain. "You'll be recognized in an instant in those clothes. We don't need a riot."

Hamon glared but knew it to be true. His face had been splashed all over the newsvids for weeks now, despite the Hathian government's best attempts, and in his Earth gear he had no hope of hiding. He had to stand around even longer while one of the guards fetched an overwrap from his room. Hamon was too big to wear anything of des Trurain's and would have refused if offered. He tugged a hat over his dark hair, pulling it down low. Then finally he could go.

His child was at risk. That's what he told himself as he rode through the streets in a darkened security car, as he forced himself to question her family and learn exactly how deeply and how long they had worried over her, as he scoured her room in her home.

It wasn't the same room. She had moved out of the one where he'd taken her body so brutally. Where he'd forced her to abandon the seductive pose of her subterfuge and face the honesty of what lay between them. He had never forgiven himself for it, and never would, but today he made himself enter her old room and search for clues to her disappearance. It hadn't changed. Untouched, even to the traces of dust from the occupation. The only thing removed was the vid cube of her twin brother.

My child is at risk, he told himself repeatedly, and yet again as he bullied the technician in the flight control room into checking the log-ins of every single flyer that had left The City in the last day.

"Does she have a flyer code?"

The technician glared at him and turned to his guards for help.

"Check the routes to the plateau," Hamon added on a sudden thought.

"Stand back first, Major, out of the sight line," ordered the taller guard. The man was about as happy as the technician at having to help a Terran. He didn't care. It wasn't their family at risk; but he stepped back and turned away to let the man enter the search code he needed.

"I have it, Major."

Hamon swung round and studied the screen. A single flyer, lightly laden and with no destination entered. He looked at her route as far as it was entered and remembered her face as he'd last seen it—the shock and despair—remembered how small and fragile she'd looked. The missing clog inside his heart was suddenly and painfully wrenched back into place.

"Oh, stars."

CHAPTER TWENTY-SIX

Less than an hour after he'd left his room, he faced des Trurain again. "She headed off in her skimmer, coordinates set to the desert region. Your surveillance records show her course as far as the middle of the fourth sector. After that, she disappears.

"To ground. That's where she's gone," said Jacquel, his relief showing openly on his face. "She's taken to her hide. She'll come back when she's ready."

Hamon glared at the tame rejoinder. This, after the way the man had barged into his room? "The baby is due in less than two weeks. What if something has happened? If you know where she is, take me there. Right now."

"That's just it, I don't. She'll have gone to her own hide. All the special operatives had one. A secret place of refuge for when life became too interesting, or to rest between assignments. The location was known only to the owner."

"What about your much-vaunted technology? Can't that find her?"

"Only if Marthe lets us."

"Well I'm going anyway. You coming?"

Jacquel nodded, giving way to the urgency in Hamon's voice. Hamon wasn't surprised, but he was relieved. The Hathians weren't going to let him follow her without des Trurain running security, nor would they let as prominently connected a Terran as himself wander off unaided in to the hostile high plateau country.

"She can look after herself. She'll come back when she's ready," des Trurain said again, almost as if trying to convince himself. Hamon gave that the attention it deserved. Des Trurain didn't know the cause of her flight. Fear shot through him, and not for the baby alone.

Scarcely an hour later and with full emergency kit on board, their skimmer winged its way upward, over the lowland and set for the same gap in the hills through which the reports said Marthe had disappeared; but even at maximum speed, it was a long trip. Long, gut-wrenching hours were to pass before they hovered over the sector where Marthe's craft was last sighted.

Jacquel looked out at the endless vista of waving tussock grasses and grey rocks. "What now?"

"We survey the sector in strips until we get a reading. Unless you have another suggestion. You did work with Marthe. You must have some idea of the kind of spot she would have chosen."

Jacquel sat thinking a moment then said he supposed she would have looked for the same kind of terrain as he. "…with something to confuse detection devices: hills, rocky outcrops, that kind of thing, and clay or rocky soil to build into. She'd need a water source, too, though she may have been able to tap into an underground stream."

"How big a place are we looking for?" asked a dumbfounded Hamon.

"A large cave, or something similar—big enough for a kitchen, living area and sleeping compartment.

Hamon stared. "How the— No, don't bother. I had thought we were looking for a simple cave or shelter, not a razzing luxury apartment."

He laughed shortly, some of the tight knots of tension in him loosening. So she had gone to earth with all modern conveniences. What a fool he'd been to worry so much, yet he couldn't rest, some nameless warning driving him onwards.

They began the long search, backwards and forwards over the bleak desert landscape. Beneath them, the harsh scrub spread unbroken over the rolling plain to the horizon and the hills. Always the wind whipped the land. Occasionally, a promising outcrop would warrant a closer look, but for the rest, it was bone wearyingly the same. Nothing.

After what seemed hours, they finally picked up a signal.

"That's Marthe," yelled Jacquel. "I told you we couldn't find her unless she let us—not the best damned agent in all of Hathe." Suddenly, his jubilant cry ceased. The tone of the beep had changed, tapping out a new cadence.

"The distress signal. She's in trouble."

The two men looked at each other. "But she's two weeks early," was all Hamon could say.

Hastily, Jacquel locked on to the signal. "If you pray on your world, then pray she's keyed the signal to guide us."

Hamon waited the longest minute.

"Got it." Relief swept briefly across des Trurain's face as Marthe's system locked onto their machine, and Hamon felt the pull as it was hauled down into the ground. At the last moment, they were abruptly wrenched sideways and dived down and over the lip of a hidden ridge concealing beneath it a twisting, almost subterranean stream, only one thin crack revealing the sky above. The skimmer whipped along the narrow gully, twisting from side to side to squeeze through places where Hamon would have sworn it couldn't pass.

"I told you that Marthe would have hidden it well. No one would ever think to follow her along here."

"No," agreed Hamon, holding on grimly to the contents of his stomach. Just at that moment, the craft stopped dead, dropped vertically, then veered sideways into a narrow gap. They passed through an echoing blackness before again rising suddenly and coming to land in a softly lit alcove.

A desperate sense of urgency gripped Hamon. "How do we get in?"

"Over there. You can see the doorway in UV light." Sure enough, in the luminous glow Jacquel shone upon the wall, a doorway appeared and silently slid open in answer to Jacquel's 'friend in succor' signal. Quickly, the two ran in. Hamon barely glanced at the rooms as he rushed through them, never noticing how uncannily the decor resembled his own tastes.

At last he came to her bedroom and found what he had feared. Sitting cross-legged on the bed was Marthe, a grim look of concentration on her face.

It was the strained intensity he saw first. In the second instant, he saw what only he could see—deepest fear etched in to every weary line of her body, fear such as never before had she shown him.

It wiped out what little bitterness remained after the anxiety of the search, and his voice as he called to her was the calm, soft voice of the ally she so badly needed. "Marthe?"

Relief flooded her face as once more his arms enfolded her in secure comfort. Tears flooded her gaunt eyes.

"Oh, my precious one," murmured Hamon.

He held her tightly, the buttress of his shoulder a solid touchstone as the convulsive sobs overcame her, stopped only by the cramping spasm seizing her womb. His muscles carried her through it, and he would not allow himself to relax his hold until long after her sobs abated. The fear had almost gone from her face, but still lay there, ready to swoop with the next contraction. He waited, holding her close till she looked able to speak of the essentials. Then he saw her remember, and she struggled to untangle herself from his arms, her head twisting to hide her face.

"I'm sorry. They shouldn't have bothered you with this nonsense. The baby will be fine. You can go back now."

"Don't be stupid," he shot back, guilt lancing through him. "I'm here because I want to be, and I'm staying—for always."

She looked up at him, studying his face intently. Looking for truth, he guessed. He returned her gaze in full, and when he spoke, it was with the solemnity of an eternal promise.

"These last weeks have been the worst of my life. I need you. Now and forever."

"But what I did to you? I can't apologize for it. It was the life of my people against my own happiness."

His mouth creased grimly. "I know. I made the same choice, remember. Did you betray me on that day? Yes, as I did you. That feeling, it's still there; but I will not live without you again. Somehow, we will find a way to make us work. Though right now doesn't seem an ideal time to figure out how," he added with a wry smile. "Our son isn't going to wait that long. Just know that I love you." He held up his hand, one finger rubbing over the twisted band shining there. "This ring never left my finger, no matter how black the day. Nor will it."

She held up her own, touching gold band to gold band. "Nor has this." She drew his hand to her, lips gently touching his ring in promise, then the palm of his hand. He closed it on her face, encompassing it within the shield of both hands as his mouth completed the pact. Then pulled her firmly once more into the protection of his arms as his eyes traced her body and face in uneasy appraisal. She was so thin. He held her close, feeling her trust in him return. He had come so near to losing her.

"How long ago did the pains start?" he said quietly after a while.

"About four hours, I think. They're still reasonably far apart."

"Why didn't you call in?" demanded Jacquel, bringing a black look and rapid interruption from Hamon. She was still too fragile, the tension barely submerged.

"It doesn't matter. We've found you now," he said firmly.

"But it does," she gasped, the tears resurfacing. "I panicked when the first contractions started. I rushed around trying to do something, and in my hurry, I knocked the long-range transmitter off the table. It won't work now. I thought I was stranded!"

"Well, you're not," said Jacquel brusquely. "There's a transmitter in my ship—and one in yours, too, Marthe."

"Oh. I forgot. My stars, I'm going crazy. I should have thought of it." Her fingers plucked in confusion at the bedcover.

"No you're not," said Hamon, holding her close again. "Des Trurain, instead of upsetting her, why don't you make yourself useful by putting a call through to the medicos."

Des Trurain gave him one, appraising look. Hamon glared back over Marthe's gently cradled head, and in short order, des Trurain did as suggested. Hamon took a deep breath and looked long at Marthe, considering. The memory of the last contraction was still with her. Her fingers dug in to his arms and the fear was strong in her eyes.

"Hamon, help me. I can't do this."

"Of course you can," he shot straight back. "You're a trained doctor. Stop a minute and think. What do you remember?"

It brought her back, the sensible words pulling her from the edge. He could almost see steel wires pulling her upright as she sat, silently enumerating facts. Then she gave a shake.

"You're right. What is there to fear? After all, I've assisted at more than one labor before now." Just as the words left her, another contraction crashed in and Radcliff felt the tension snap back. "They get worse than this, and already I can't do it," she cried out. "Why can't I?"

"Shush. It will be all right. Des Trurain—Jacquel—" he forced himself to say, knowing the familiarity would reassure her, "is calling the City doctors. Help will be here soon. In the meantime, you must have some kind of pain relief with you."

"None that is safe to use in labor. How could I be so stupid?"

"Marthe!" His voice was harsh now. No more the soothing lover, but bracing, authoritative. "It doesn't matter. The child is not due for hours yet and help will be here long before then. Until they arrive, you have me, and Jacquel, and your own skills and specialist knowledge. Remember your lectures. There must be something you can do to help ease the pains."

"Breathe. Breathe over them," she said automatically.

"See. You do remember. And relax. During the occupation, there must have been countless times when you needed to force yourself to relax, to beat the fear. This is no different." He frowned at her sternly. Soon, he saw her almost invisible veneer of control slide back. It was only then that he realized it had been missing. For the first time since he'd met her, her face had been naked and, unconsciously, he was sealed in that instant even closer to this one woman above all else. All his adult life he'd been forced to maintain an iron front, knowing that to reveal the very human frailty within could endanger his safety if not his very life. Now he'd finally found another forced down that same, hard path. He was no longer alone.

"Forgive me for behaving so stupidly. It was being here on my own, and not expecting it to start, and everything," she finished lamely, leaving him to wonder what she'd omitted. Jacquel's return prevented him asking.

"Marthe's doctors and a full team from the hospital are on their way. They'll be here as soon as possible, bringing the entire contents of the surgery with them … so you can now relax, Madame," he said to Marthe with a twinkle.

A cynical snort was her only reply as, yet again, her face tightened in pain. Hamon held her close, feeling her subside into his shoulder as the spasm passed. A secret sigh of relief broke in him. This time, she'd been in control. Marthe, with her dry wit shielding her, made him feel a whole lot more confident than did the frightened creature who had greeted them. To think how often in those early days he had tried all he could to find a way to lay her bare. Now, he knew that he never again wanted to see her so lost.

Within half an hour, Marthe was almost back to her normal self, busily supervising the conversion of the cavern into an efficient medical ward and autocratically delivering orders from the throne of her bed. Once the changes were completed to her satisfaction, Hamon and Jacquel took the opportunity to relax for a moment, Hamon loudly moaning for her benefit at the decidedly unpalatable rations that were all she had available.

Marthe excused herself from the pleasure of joining them, infusing instead a much-needed nutrient and electrolyte solution. With it, she felt more up to facing what must come—until another contraction brought back the secret terror she couldn't shake, reminding her of the inevitable course ahead.

What if the ambulance couldn't find her, or had an accident, or couldn't get down the gully to her entranceway?

"And what if the sky fell? None of your farfetched scenarios would matter anymore." broke in Hamon's amused voice.

She jumped. "What do you mean?"

"You forget, I can read your face. Though not, I admit, as well as I once thought," he added with a wry grin. "Right now, you're imagining all the problems that could delay the relief team?"

She nodded, comforted by his percipience, and snuggled back into the shelter of his sturdy body as he joined her on the bed.

"One: nothing will happen. Two: you forget who is really delivering this baby. You and our son there. The best doctor in the world can do nothing without you."

"I know you're right. The problem is, I also know what can go wrong. That most babies are born with little help is not something that's emphasized at Med School. It implies that doctors aren't necessary," she added with a grimace and a chuckle.

"Doctors like you, remember? You've delivered babies before?" She nodded. "And neither I nor des Trurain is exactly witless. We should be able to understand a few basic instructions."

"Yes, bu—" She was forced to stop again. "No one ever told me it hurt so much," she finally finished, the fear strong again.

Hamon held her tight, kissing her with all the love in him. His instinctive response steadied her as nothing else could and she clung wordlessly to him.

Jacquel took one look and decided to leave them together. It was clear that he could safely leave the care of Marthe to Radcliff, and he remembered with cool amusement the angry man of a few short hours ago. At the same time, the cynic in him wondered how long the present ceasefire would last. Trust Marthe to pick a man with a temper as hot and durable as her own. He chuckled then turned again to the matter that refused to stop niggling at his peace. How exactly were they to get a relief team in to such a hide? The entrance gully had been barely wide enough for his own skimmer, let alone one large enough to hold a full medical team.

He knew Marthe well enough to expect her bolt hole to conceal a number of hidden tricks, but he preferred not to disturb her with questions unless his own explorations failed. Radcliff may utter soothing words, but Jacquel remembered too well the anxiety of Marthe's family and doctor. Even Radcliff must realize how dangerously thin and vulnerable she was. Jacquel had spent time in the mines in the early days of the occupation, and had seen the effect of poor food, stress and weariness on the burgeoning mothers there. That first sight of Marthe sitting on her bed had brought back the memories of those women with stark and frightening clarity.

He prowled through the rooms, hunting for anything that could be of use. It was not a large hide, he soon realized, but cunningly wrought to confuse attackers and aid its owner. Cursing, he yet again found himself turning a corner only to come back to the spot he'd just left. He'd discovered the secret arms and stores caches, but so far there was no sign of an alternative exit. There must be at least one, if not more, but he was not unduly perturbed by his failure. He'd worked with Marthe too often to underestimate the subtlety she could employ when needed.

After a further search, he began to feel somewhat aggrieved. Finally, he was forced to admit defeat and make his way back to Marthe's bedroom.

"Des Trurain, where did you slope off to?" came the harassed bark from an anxious Terran.

"Just checking out the place. My compliments, Marthe. You've done a fine job here. Even I got lost on occasion."

"Thank you. It suits me," she answered, clearly prompted by politeness alone.

Jacquel glanced at her keenly. "Very fine indeed. In fact, you've succeeded in flummoxing me. I can't seem to find your other exits. You wouldn't like to ease my curiosity?"

She smiled, fortunately not yet seeing the point of his question. "They are all personal-coded so it's not surprising. Would you like me to show you?"

"Only if it doesn't entail you moving. I don't want your husband out for more of my blood than he's after already."

"I think a truce could be called for the present duration, des Trurain, but would you kindly stop annoying Marthe with such trivia."

"Sorry. Just professional interest."

"It's all right, Hamon," interposed Marthe hastily from her bed. "I must admit to being rather proud of this place anyway. There are three more exits. Two, small bolt holes, which I'm in no shape to show you at present, and the freight entrance in the landing dock."

"Yes, we entered that way," Radcliff put in.

"No, silly, that was only for small, one or two man skimmers. I mean the freight carrier entrance, directly into the air above. How else do you imagine I brought all this stuff in?" She broke off, suddenly struck with bitter understanding. "You want it for the ambulance, don't you, Jaca?"

"It would be easier for them. That skimmer entrance calls for some tricky aerobatics, even with your guiding signal to help."

"Why are you so concerned? What do you know about this baby?"

"Nothing," denied Jacquel hurriedly. "What do I know about babies? I just know people, and doctors hate making house calls. I merely assumed they would rather work in their portable hospital than in this poky room," he explained airily.

"Des Trurain is talking nonsense. Yet again," interrupted an exasperated Radcliff, twisting round with a growl. "If all you can do is upset Marthe, then take yourself elsewhere."

"Hamon, the doctors have told him something I should know about. Is the baby all right? I have to know," she pleaded.

"Of course it is. Now calm down. Tension can't be good for you or the baby."

She frowned a moment longer, then, clearly receiving an answer to her question in her husband's eyes, acquiesced.

Hamon stayed beside her, until an almost imperceptible flick of her eyes released him.

Quietly, he crossed to the far side of the room, to where des Trurain was assembling some odd boxes. Lying beside each was one of the Hathian patches.

"What are those?" he asked warily.

"Communitabs. One set for Marthe and one for the baby. They'll enable the medics to record her reactions and will also feed back artificial nerve stimuli to moderate the pains if necessary. The boxes are to boost the signal, and the system is linked to both the hospital and the ambulance. The other two patches are for you and me, for transmissions the medics don't want Marthe to hear."

"Why?" Hamon looked across and smiled encouragingly at Marthe, then turned away from her knowing eyes. "You were rather clumsy there, but something's wrong. Out with it."

Jacquel continued to fiddle for some time, then stopped, took a breath as if coming to a decision, and looked at Hamon, all his old antipathy clear on his face.

"The doctors are worried that Marthe is not up to the rigors of labor. You haven't seen her lately."

Hamon flushed at the reminder.

"It's as if she was in another universe and didn't give a damn if she never came back. Mentally and physically she's a wreck. Classic overwork and stress syndrome, according to the doctor. By the Pillars, I know how tired I was when the Zenith finally arrived, and I wasn't pregnant. Afterwards, I was given respect, a rest and honor. All Marthe got was work, more pregnant, a marriage split and dishonor, if not outright hatred from everyone she came across. I heard her doctor saying to Sylvan a week ago that he wasn't certain if she could survive till the baby was born, let alone the rigors of labor."

Radcliff blanched. "You're joking!"

"No, and you know it. I owe you nothing, Terran, but for Marthe's sake you need to know the truth."

Hamon read the enmity in his eyes … and the honesty.

"So they're bringing a mini-hospital?"

"Yes. Full life support for both. You can speak to the doctors yourself in a minute; but they're still a good few hours away. Even with our technology, there's a limit to what can be done at a distance." He looked hard at Hamon, a bitter glint in his eye.

"What are you trying to say?"

The Hathian paused, his fists clenched. Then: "Look, I don't know what your real feelings are here, and if it wasn't for Marthe I wouldn't particularly care; but you have quite deliberately caused her enough suffering already. The war is over and this is your child and, by the Pillars, if you don't somehow get her through this, you will have me to reckon with," Jacquel finished in a killing tone.

"I'm surprised you let me anywhere near her."

"Unfortunately, you're the only one she really wants. If not for that, I would throw you out on your filthy Terran backside this instant."

"Then it's a good thing for me that you wouldn't be able to carry out such a threat."

Each stared sickly at the other, all the former antagonisms boiling up. There was a quiet cough behind them, and Hamon spun round in fright.

"It's nice to know that I still look good enough to be fought over; but your timing could be better."

He and des Trurain smiled guiltily at the wearily delivered jest.

"Our apologies. Hostilities will be suspended for the duration," Hamon promised, noting anew the blanched thinness of her face and the black etched into her eye sockets. Remembering Jacquel's words, fear knifed through him. He quickly hid it from her beseeching eyes and moved over to the bed, folding her in his arms.

"Is it bad again?" He could feel the tension in her body—and the weariness. It was still early in her ordeal.

Soon afterwards, he settled her down on the bed. Squeezing the patch onto her wrist and the second to her abdomen, as directed by Jacquel, he hugged her gently.

"You must rest if you can. The doctors need you to lie still while they examine you." He checked the position of the patches one more time, staring in amusement at the small circle. "I still find it hard to believe you could have worn something like this for so long without my knowledge. It was not as though I didn't search you thoroughly— purely in the line of duty, you understand," he added with an intimate chuckle. It calmed her, as he'd hoped, helping her to cope better with the next contraction

It hit her as he crossed the room to speak softly with Jacquel. He saw it out of the corner of his eye, but this time she didn't call out. He continued walking, guessing that she needed to manage this one alone, if only to reassure herself that she could. It was the hardest task he'd faced, but he gave in to her, giving no sign he knew of her pain but relaxing his discreet scrutiny only when her change of breathing told him it was over.

There were hours to go yet. Hours.

It was to seem a very long wait and, well before the relief team arrived, Marthe was forced to ask for help with the pains. The medics could apply nerve blocks, but they could do little to halt the steady depletion of her resources as each fierce spasm took its toll. His son was pushing hard to be born, as if he sensed that his mother could not endure long.

The team was still a way off, but Hamon had taken to anxiously watching the door, silently urging their arrival. It seemed to him he was watching the life force being leached from her. His imagination, he chided, and battened down his fear lest she sense it. The visible effort she put into each contraction was written clearly in the lines of her face, her iron will never so evident as now, when it must force onwards her worn out body.

For Marthe, the world had shrunk to a vague, shadowy place of effort, pain and Hamon. It was to his arms and voice she clung as her muscles bunched and squeezed. She could sense his fear, but it was beyond her to calm it. She could barely hold back her own. With each, coiling spasm, she held tight to him, willing all the tension to ooze out along those comforting arms, breathing away this stupid dread.

Soon, even the contractions seemed less real, a constant surging of muscles like the waves in the sea. Always there, a constant backdrop of tension and release. There was no pain; the doctors had stopped that through the patches, but they couldn't stop the relentless draining away of the strength she needed. Terror rose in her—not the simple fear of the contractions, not fear of pain, but gut wrenching, crippling terror for her baby. She must not fail him. Not now, not so close to the end. The contractions were coming in frantic succession, each new one squeezing tight as the previous had barely released her. Soon, she must work harder still, pushing and pushing her precious little one out to the life-saving air.

Hysteria grabbed hold of her. "I can't do it, Hamon. I can't do it."

"Yes, you can. I'm here. We will do it together." But not even the calm voice of her beloved could help. She could feel the desperation in him as he gathered her into his arms, cradling her exhausted body in the strong bulwark of his.

"No, you don't understand." It was a struggle to keep her thoughts clear, to tell him what he must hear. "I can't do it. I need proper help."

"Don't worry. They're nearly here. In the meantime, they're doing all they can."

"Not … no." But then she must turn again to the inward struggle. Wave after wave swept over her.

Hamon saw her weakness and his eyes caught des Trurain's, full of the same frightening thought that filled him.

"They're almost here," affirmed des Trurain.

"And if they don't make it in time?" Then he saw Marthe slip into a faint. Tenderness forgotten, Hamon shook her with all the strength in him. "Marthe. Wake up. You have to be able to tell us what to do."

His only answer was a dull grunt, but he saw her eyelids flicker and she strove to sit.

Suddenly: "They've landed," came the triumphant shout from Jacquel. There was the blessed sound of running feet. Hamon drew back, standing aside from the business-like ministrations of the medical team as they swamped the bed. An urgent cry from Marthe brought him hastily back.

"Quick, into the ship with her," said one of the doctors. Hamon clung tightly to her hand, all he could reach through the smothering crowd of attendants. Marthe was placed on a stretcher and whisked out to the cavernous bay etched out of the rock, filled now by the large ship that had descended through a newly opened hole in the roof. The seemingly natural rock face had slid back into the surrounding hill. At another time, Hamon might have been amazed at the sight, but for now he was more concerned with the woman being passed quickly into the ship.

Never had he been so pleased to see a hospital ward or to smell the reassuring odor of disinfectant. Through her hand, he could feel the relaxation in Marthe as she took in all the familiar paraphernalia— the pristine walls, gleaming metal and functional grandeur of the bed, enthroned in the center of the portable theater.

Marthe knew, oh how she knew, that she needed help with this baby. The small part of her mind still capable of rational thought recognized the dangerous weakness of her body, too long robbed of its strength by that ridiculous weltering of self-pity. With one ear only, she listened and made some kind of response to her doctors' questions. With the other, inner ear, she became aware of a first, faint surge.

"I'm starting to bear down," she informed her helpers between harried breaths, and the level of activity around her suddenly increased.

The doctors closed in, and Hamon started to back out.

"You—the father, aren't you? Where do you think you're going?" Hamon looked up in confusion. "Get back beside your wife. We need all the help we can get with this one."

The gruff voice had an underlying kindness to it, and within seconds Hamon was back where he most wished to be, using the lifeline of his body to support and encourage Marthe's efforts.

Life in the room became very busy

"You can push whenever you're ready," said the nurse to Marthe, who sensibly ignored her, aware of the fact already, and instead clung tightly to Hamon.

Half an hour later, it was an exhausted woman who clung to him still, pushing valiantly with what little energy she had left.

"We're losing uterine strength. Stimulate contractions," came the order. The technician monitoring the screens urgently activated the emergency program, compelling the tired muscles to keep bearing down.

"The baby?"

"Signs still normal, but a slight weakening in heart rate."

"Come on, Marthe, we haven't much time."

Tears on her face, exhaustion coating her face, she pushed again.

"Nearly there. We have the head. Come on, Marthe, you can do it," urged the doctor, simultaneously gesturing frantically to a colleague to infuse a stimulant. Hamon held her close with one arm, ignoring the painful squeezing of her hand on his as she bore down.

"Right, hold it a minute."

"Head's out. One more push, that's it. Down." There was a moment of silence. "Got it! Congratulations, you have a beautiful baby boy," said the doctor as he placed a wet, squirming bundle on Marthe's waiting stomach.

Marthe glanced down then sent a stunned smile to her husband, also gazing at the ugly little bundle.

"He has your mouth," was all she could say, before turning back to feast her eyes on the miracle.

The peace lasted but a second.

"Blood pressure's falling!"

Now Hamon did find himself thrust aside. The baby was hastily removed, and urgent hands moved in to work on the tired woman. She was sealed inside a large bubble, surrounded by instrumentation, with a tube protruding from her mouth and transmitting patches, like diseased splotches, covering her body. His precious baby, too, was the center of medical activity. Gently but firmly, Hamon was forced out of the ship and left to sit anxiously in the lounge area, his only companion a nervously pacing Jacquel.

It seemed an interminable time but was really only a few minutes before a young nurse came out, her smile and brown eyes friendly and efficient.

"The baby is fine. He's fit and healthy, a bit tired, but no ill effects at all. He's a little small, but an Castre offspring tend to be small at birth. Would you like to come and say, 'Hello'?"

"And my wife?" Hamon interrupted, fear clawing at his gut.

"Will be fine, too. At present she's quite ill, but her doctors are very confident of a good outcome, and she has the best medical help available on Hathe in there. Now, come along. Your son is waiting."

There was, unbelievably, a hint of nervousness in Hamon's stride as he entered the ship for a second time. At first, his gaze could not be drawn from the still, quiet figure of Marthe within her hi-tech cocoon. Then, finally responding to the persistent young woman at his elbow, he looked down, his arms tentatively reaching out for the tiny bundle she was thrusting at him.

"Mind the head," she said, helping him to settle the awkward scrap into his inexpert grip. He stared bemusedly at the strange creature: the little face screwed up and squashed-looking, with damp, wispy tendrils clinging to the seemingly too big head, the tiny hands and feet clenching and unclenching, blindly grasping at his tunic. The little eyes blearily opened, peering out at the great world, shut, then opened again. Suddenly, he wriggled around and then flung out his arms as he frightened himself, the little mouth opening in an angry squawk.

"Shush, shush," Hamon found himself crooning, gently cradling this so precious bundle closely to his big, clumsy body. He put out a questing finger to stroke the tiny palm and found it clenched in a vise-like grip. He chuckled and made a silent promise then and there to this small part of himself.

Trust me, little one. Somehow, somewhere, we will make it work.

Too soon, the nurse intruded. "He has to go back in his cabinet now. The doctors want Madame an Castre back at First Hospital as soon as possible."

Reluctantly, he placed the baby in his clear cocoon, watching closely to see that she strapped him in carefully. The baby gurgled happily as the swaddling band caught him. Only then did his father relax.

He turned and moved to a nearby seat, strapping himself in. Jacquel entered and was seated immediately, having once more sealed Marthe's hidden refuge to intruders and set the skimmers for automatic return. There was a general scurrying as the rest of the team took their seats, then the craft lifted slowly and was soon winging back to civilization. The great doors slid to and in no time the wild desert was bereft of human life once more, undisturbed and silent, untouched by the near tragedy played out in its midst.

As soon as he could, Hamon shrugged off his restraints and strode across to Marthe. A doctor was bending over her cabinet. "What's wrong? Why doesn't she wake up?" Hamon demanded.

"We're keeping her asleep until her vital signs stabilize. Don't worry. With proper rest and care, she'll be fine."

"Then why are you in such a hurry to get back to First Hospital?"

It was old Doctor an Dothen, who had tried so hard to tell him the truth weeks ago. He stared thoughtfully at Hamon, as if in judgment. Then he seemed to come to a decision. "Sit down, Major."

"When a doctor tells me to sit down, I feel nervous," half-joked Hamon, feeling behind for a seat.

An Dothen didn't reassure him.

"I don't know if you realize it," he said, "but if we hadn't made it here in time, there's a good chance that one or both of them would have died. Marthe came in to labor debilitated, lacking in sleep and emotionally depressed." It was a repeat of what des Trurain had already told him, but Hamon had no thought of interrupting the man. "Labor, as you may have observed, is a stressful process, and in the immediate, postnatal period, there are massive changes in the mother's body. With appropriate care, we can carry her over the vulnerable period, but I want the reassurance of as much backup as possible, as soon as possible. She will also need the support of as many of her family and friends as will give it. She needs them to come visit, congratulate her, tell her how like Cousin Joachim her baby is. All the minor trivia of a new baby's life. Pride and love of her baby will bring a new mother through the worst of dangers.

"But she has me," protested Hamon.

"Has she?"

Hamon met the Doctor's eye fully. "Yes, she has."

"Then, young man, I'll be damned if we can't do it," said an Dothen. "Now, since you can do nothing for Marthe at present, why don't you go and look after that young tyke of yours." The doctor grinned, pushing Hamon away as he bent once more to his readouts, glancing frequently at his still sleeping patient.

Hamon paused reluctantly then, drawn by a loud cry, crossed quickly to the infant cabinet, already unconsciously spellbound by this tiny new son of his.

CHAPTER TWENTY-SEVEN

For a week, Marthe swung in and out of consciousness, her over tired body at war with her newly discovered need for her baby. Time and again, Hamon would come into her room to find her dissolved in tears, one hand desperately clutching her son's tiny, outstretched fist. He could see how it overwhelmed her, this knowledge of her absolute importance and, worse, her total inadequacy. How could she be the mother this precious scrap needed, she would ask dismally.

There were other moments, ones he locked deep inside to treasure always: their son's first feed, a fumbling failure to start with, then elation as mother and baby both discovered what was required; the pride in Marthe as she watched her son suckle busily, and then slowly drift off into contented and full sleep; his first, tentative attempts to peer at her face, as if trying to fix a pattern to the voice he already preferred above all others; the look on her face as she felt the soft fuzz on his solid little head nestling into the groove seemingly designer-built at the base of her neck.

On these rare occasions, when Hamon would glance through the doors to see a magical glow on her face, he softly stole away, puzzled at the wonder of this new, little person in their lives. But he never went far, was always there when the black walls came crashing back.

After another week, when he could see the desperation within her growing, he decided it was time to take a hand. Cornering her doctor in his office, he first paced in front of the desk then turned, his mouth set in grim determination.

"This can't go on. She's getting no better."

Doctor an Dothen sat back, gazing at his desk in thought, then looked up. "I agree. Physically, yes, she's improving, but the nurses tell me Marthe isn't sleeping at all well."

"It's being in hospital. She hates being a patient. The tension literally radiates from her. I want to take her home, to her own surroundings. Surely you could arrange some kind of nursing supervision?"

The doctor nodded. "I think you're right. There are two kinds of mothers, in my experience. One revels in the postnatal hospital stay, the other loathes it. Marthe's of the latter and while, from a medical viewpoint, she's still weak and needs help with the baby, these things can be easily arranged in her own home. I presume you refer to the an Castres' house. Quite large enough to hold an entire hospital corps, if need be. That is, if one were available. We're rather short of medical staff after the war, and of those we do have, most are tied up with treating those civilians who suffered the harsher treatments of the Terrans, curse their souls. If you will excuse me," he added, belatedly remembering to whom he was talking but not sounding particularly apologetic.

"Nevertheless," an Dothen continued, "I do know of one person who would suit admirably. One of our older midwives, all but retired now, but who would be very pleased to be working again. Oh, not too old. Don't worry." He'd caught Hamon's new fatherly doubt. "More importantly, she has the clinical experience which will be invaluable in a case such as this. With debilitated, depressed mothers, the trick is to know when a good, stiff push is needed, as much as when to offer a shoulder to cry on, and that's not the kind of judgment you acquire overnight. No, I think Ruth an Cracknell is just the woman you need. I assume you will be there also?"

Hamon nodded. "Already arranged. The authorities and the an Castres have agreed to my internment there. The security forces have checked it out and said they can make it work."

The doctor barely raised an eyebrow. Hamon wasn't surprised. His patient's wellbeing came first with this man. It was the reason he trusted him so completely.

So Marthe returned to the home of her childhood. Cradled within the security of its familiar walls, her husband anxiously guarding her and with the cool, common sense of 'Ruthie', as she soon came to be known, easing her newly discovered maternal fears, Marthe slowly began to blossom. As she grew in strength and happiness, the baby lost his newborn frailty and turned into a chubby, smiling bundle.

"We're soon going to have to call him something other than Baby," mused Hamon carelessly one day, a finger gently tracing his son's dimpled hands. "What do you say to Riardan Bendin? In grateful memory of a certain peasant girl I once knew, by name of Riarda," he explained with a teasing grin on his face.

"And Bendin for my twin." Her eyes glowed in gratitude as he leaned to kiss her. "I know you didn't like him when you met, but it means a lot to me to have something of him live on in this little one. Though hopefully Riardan won't be quite as naughty as Bendin. He was a fair devil, my mother always said."

Hamon gathered her and the baby closely in to him, pleased to finally hear her laugh. She was almost whole again … though not completely. Nor would she ever be, he sometimes felt. Could she ever forget all that stood against them? It was quite a list: the memory of what they had both been forced to do to the other during the occupation; her people's hostility towards both of them; his own feelings of dislike and more for this planet. And then there was the knowledge that soon he would have to leave, never to return. Hathe would not tolerate forever the presence of a leader of the Terran occupation force.

If not for Marthe, it would have been a day he longed for. He was Terran to his core, impatient to return home and help to rebuild the shattered world of his childhood. But just as he loved his world, so, he knew, did she love Hathe. They couldn't live here together, though and, after the trial, it was possible she would be banished with him. The cruelty of that he was still learning to live with, even if he understood it politically.

The anger of the populace couldn't be held at bay forever. The news vids had made sure the public were constantly reminded of his presence and of their marriage. She refused to discuss it, and the peace between them was still too fragile for him to bring it up. He wasn't even sure how he felt. Guilty? No … but he knew he ought to. Anger at the Hathians who would put her through this? Yes. Understanding of why they did it? Yes to that too. When he returned to Earth, many of his own people would want to do the same to him.

For Marthe, the trial loomed larger and larger. 'A formality', said her superiors in reassuring pomposity. Her record of service to the resistance was too well respected for it to be otherwise, but Marthe wasn't naive. The harsh school of experience she'd endured in acquiring that record of service would not allow her to ignore the undercurrents penetrating even to the fastness of their cocooned world. The government would have to take action against her. Just what that might be kept a small, worried frown from ever quite leaving her.

Hamon saw it and knew he could no longer avoid the subject. "Should I testify?" he asked her one day.

"Do you have any choice?"

"I'm not that out of practice that I couldn't evade the Hathian authorities if I had to and hightail it out of here … if you think it would help." He drew her slowly into the cradle of his arm as they both turned to greet the newly arrived visitor. It was Marthe's lawyer.

After Hamon put the same question to him, the man frowned, taking a long moment before answering. "Two possibilities exist. On the one hand, most of the population have such a fixed opinion of your despicable character that nothing you might say would help," he said at last. "On the other hand, running away," and he ignored Hamon's angry disclaimer, "could well reinforce the impression that Marthe acted in collusion with you to aid the Terran cause, particularly since she was so instrumental in organizing help for Earth after the occupation."

"She was?" broke in Hamon, surprised.

Marthe waved a hand in dismissal. "I merely dropped a few hints in the appropriate place. Even I couldn't face the thought of Terrans dying en masse."

She might dismiss it as of no consequence, but to Hamon it meant everything. "Thank you," he said softly, dropping a gentle kiss on her forehead and pulling her in closer. The lawyer coughed.

"Nevertheless, the prosecution will bring it up. They have already subpoenaed you, Major, as a witness for the prosecution."

"What!" exclaimed an outraged Hamon. "Never."

"Didn't think you would like it."

Hamon had researched the lawyer's record. Although just older than Hamon, Yurin an Begum was a seasoned campaigner of the Hathian courts. He eyed Hamon now as if summing up his available tools of strategy, then continued. "Since it's highly debatable whether your evidence will help or hinder Marthe, I don't think it really matters which side calls you."

"Then I disappear."

"Too risky, as I've said already. My advice is to stay and front up to the court. You're just a name to most of these people, and a decidedly black one at that. Appearing in person may help to dispel some of the myths. At least let them see that you haven't got two heads," he added with a ghost of a smile.

"No, just a damned stubborn temper," teased Marthe as she rose, hearing the voice of her son stridently announcing his hunger.

The men stood as she left, then settled down again, the barrister sitting opposite and quietly studying Hamon. He tolerated it at first, then refused, suddenly driven to confront at least one of these cursed Hathians.

"You don't like me, do you?" he said.

"No," said an Begum, with no hint of apology.

"Then why all the effort on our behalf?"

He hadn't really expected an answer, but this was a day of surprises.

"Marthe," said the lawyer in a dispassionate voice quite at odds with his words, "is one of the true heroines of the war. I owe her too much to stand aside and let her present treatment continue. You, however, I would be very happy to see in the dock."

"Which won't happen. Sorry to disappoint you."

The lawyer shrugged, but there was a tense set to his mouth. "Did you know that I also lost a brother in the holding action? He was in the same squad as Bendin asn Castre. My father died in the mines. I nearly lost my wife there, too. In childbirth. Marthe saved her and the baby and smuggled us all out to a safer location. No, Terran, I would be only too happy to see you pay for your crimes; but I would lay down my life for Marthe."

The evenness of the man's tone didn't fool Hamon. The man meant every word he said and was hating having to talk to him, but tonight Hamon needed answers. "If you still feel like that after having met me, then why do you think my appearance at the trial will help Marthe? I would have thought you'd rather have me tossed off this planet and out of her life."

"Don't tempt me. Unfortunately, I remember too well how she suffered during your recent estrangement. No, you will attend her trial, and testify. If for nothing else, so that you can learn just what kind of woman you married—and how much it has cost her," Yurin an Begum added bitterly. He left soon after. Before departing, he handed a disc to Hamon.

"Watch this later … all of it." He spoke quietly so that Marthe couldn't hear. "Technically, we'll win this case, but that's all she'll win. It won't make any real difference."

Puzzled, Hamon watched him leave then activated his screen and settled back to view the disc. He nearly snapped it off as he realized what it was—a newscast of the *Heroes of the Resistance* being granted the highest honor on Hathe, the Medal of Valor. He was even more disgusted to see des Trurain amongst the small coterie. It had obviously been an important public ceremony, judging by the number of uniformed VIPs and the large crowd applauding at the end. He was about to switch the nauseating thing off, when he noticed there was more. It was an amateur recording, set in a small, private room containing what looked to be the senior members of the Hathian Council and a few military leaders. Including, he saw, the resistance field commander, Gof deln Crantz and, yet again, the accursed des Trurain. Then he noticed Marthe.

This, too, was an award ceremony, but what a contrast to the previous occasion. Although the personnel attending were as high ranking, this one was private, almost secretive—no crowd, no public acclamation. It was, he soon saw, to honor Marthe. She, too, was the recipient of the Medal of Valor, with bar—the only resistance fighter to be so honored, said the proclamation. He watched as she came forward. It was during the last weeks of her pregnancy, her face drawn and her steps slow. The respect and esteem of these, her erstwhile colleagues, were obvious. He listened to the citation:

'For continuous and unremitting service, in the face of danger, persecution and extreme hardship, to the people and culture of this planet'

and, at the end, a barely audible apology from the chairman that she could not have been publicly honored alongside her fellow recipients, due to the 'delicate legal position' she at present occupied, and the regretfully expressed hope that one day her people would accord her the position in history owed to her. The tone of the speaker was not optimistic, and Hamon recognized the bitterly amused cynicism on his love's face.

The recording finished then, but he stayed seated a long time, staring at the screen. He was still there when Marthe returned. To her query, he switched on the disc. At the end, he said in a bitter, sad voice, "Congratulations. You never told me."

"You always knew what our love cost me," she replied to his unspoken thought. "As I always knew what it cost you."

"We're so alike, you and I. It's ironic that we ended up on opposing sides."

"Don't you dare say 'if only'," she warned. "Just love me."

"Always." His arms reached out for her, his mouth blindly seeking the harbor of her lips then slowly exploring her warm body, as gently, then increasingly urgently, they renewed the binding promise between them.

The following days fled by. Frighteningly soon, Marthe found herself seated in a courtroom, vainly attempting to ignore the hostile crowd packed into every available seat. These were only those who'd passed the strict security checks needed to get a seat. All over the planet, millions more were watching proceedings via the vid channels—an unusual concession from the pathologically private Hathian justice system in response to the high level of public interest. The dictates of diplomacy may have denied the people their revenge, but here at least their anger could be vented against one who had broken that oldest of tribal edicts: thou shalt not fall in love with the enemy.

She sat rigid through the first day—inside a secure box and surrounded by the paraphernalia required for her safety—as the prosecution began its damning indictment. She couldn't even rely on the comfort of Hamon's presence. It would have been too inflammatory, a security nightmare. Instead, she drew on every last nanogram of the training she'd so hardily acquired over the previous five years, striving endlessly for the freedom of those who now vilified her. Would she have changed anything, even knowing it would end like this? No, her heart said. Hathian culture was too precious, had too much to offer. This time was but a painful hiatus; her wonderful world would be reborn.

The prosecution built its case slowly. The first witnesses barely knew her—operatives who'd worked in various, menial positions in and out of the fortress and who gave evidence of seeing Hamon and herself together, happy and affectionate in appearance, as well as of her seeming arrogance towards the peasants. Such tales were easily dismissed by Yurin as the expected behavior of an agent playing a part, but the suspicions planted could not be wholly eradicated— particularly as the affection was known to be all too real.

Witness followed witness. Gradually, the noose tightened, now pulling in ever closer friends and colleagues. There had been so many near misses and unavoidable slips over the years, all now recalled in damning isolation. Many gave her a half-embarrassed smile before entering the witness stand. Her cousin Griffith, she was touched to hear, protested that requiring a close relative of the accused to give evidence was highly irregular and demanded that he be recorded as a hostile witness. Never had she thought to find herself grateful for his pompous sense of integrity.

He wasn't alone but, despite the obvious reluctance of many of her supporters to give evidence, the case against her strengthened inexorably. She knew she had let slip the odd comment during her captivity, harmless enough in themselves but informative gems to a suspicious Hamon. It had always been a tradeoff between what the Terrans must learn from her and what she learned from them. Her superiors knew that, and understood it, but whether they could convey this to the jury was increasingly doubtful.

Now it was the turn of Gof deln Crantz. Truly the professional, as always, his smooth, erudite tones never hinted that this was other than a routine analysis of an operative's performance.

"Initially you lost contact with Agent an Castre for how long?" asked Prosecutor an Koth.

"Day one to day four of her incarceration."

"During which time the Terrans seized a number of our agents and took away their communitabs?"

"Yes."

"An inconvenience, surely?"

"Not really. We had anticipated something similar happening if ever an agent should be discovered. The appropriate plan was put into action and only a few, specified agents were seized."

"But you did lose the services of some of our people. They were, in fact, imprisoned and interrogated?"

"Only those we expected to lose. If none had been found, it would have appeared too suspicious."

The minute analysis continued.

"You had worked closely with the accused throughout the period of the occupation?"

"No. Only on this mission, and as an indirect liaison on other missions."

"Yet you were, at the time, the area commander of the desert sector," the prosecutor pointed out.

"Yes, but Madame an Castre had, until then, acted independently of the regional commanders, being one of an elite group of agents answerable directly to the Council. She and des Trurain were called in specifically for this mission. None of the local agents could match the breadth of their experience, and we needed agents able to recognize the subtle changes that would indicate the Terrans were beginning to suspect us."

An annoyed twitch marred the straight line of the prosecutor's mouth and he quickly turned the talk away from this inconvenient hint of praise for the accused.

"She was under your control at the time in question, though?"

"Only to a limited extent," replied an unruffled deln Crantz. "Agents of the caliber of an Castre and des Trurain generally worked free of specific direction, as they needed to be able to change their approach depending on circumstances, and often with little time available to make a decision. All they had from me was the required end point, not how to get there. I had quite enough to do already without wasting time drawing up detailed battle plans for agents who knew how to do their own jobs rather better than I."

"How could you know of the accused's expertise, if you had never worked with her before?" shot back the unfortunately rather persistent prosecutor.

"Not directly, as I said. However, on numerous occasions my officers had benefited from the results of Madame an Castre's expertise, and I was a member of the selection panel involved in her initial recruitment. Also, like all the other regional commanders, I kept an eye on the career of the independents. It helped to know when an outsider could do the job better than one of your own, and which one to use. In this case, we needed an ability to analyze both technical and social data, plus we wanted an in-depth assessment of certain key Terran personnel who were causing us concern. The combination of des Trurain, with a background in history, and an Castre, with the human experience of a physician, seemed ideal."

"So, you requested their postings personally?"

"You might say that," replied deln Crantz dryly.

"How would you put it then?"

"I merely suggested that they would be the most appropriate people for the job. I was, however, aware that there were a number of other requests for their services. Fortunately, the Council was also seriously concerned with the activities of some of the Terran officers. In particular, the persistent attempts of their security agents to penetrate our so-called peasant society. At the time, success was still far from certain. If the Terrans had once gained proof of our existence, they could have destroyed everything."

"Which would make any discovery of Hathian agents spying on the Terrans very dangerous, surely?" exclaimed the prosecutor, unable to resist a triumphant smirk.

"Every mission included that risk and our agents had been trained accordingly. They knew that in such a situation they would have to take action based on their own reading of the circumstances. The mission in question held a particularly high risk of this. It was why Agent an Castre was pulled off maid's duties when Major Radcliff's attentions became personal."

"Unsuccessfully, as it happened. Due, I understand, to the accused's own carelessness with her disguise?"

"Her hair, you mean?" said deln Crantz, having assumed the wearied impatience of one lecturing a troublesome junior. "Agent an Castre had not dulled and braided her hair for most of her service period. She was quite good enough to allow the odd quirk, and it had certainly never been a problem before."

"Except that this time it led to her discovery and worse, recognition, with all the complications that ensued."

"Unfortunately, our data base on Terran personnel was incomplete." Deln Crantz' voice made it clear what he thought of that failure. "No one in Planning knew that the Major had once, briefly, met the family of Councilor an Castre, let alone that he had cause to remember them. Our ignorance of such detail was one of the main reasons we chose to send in operatives of the caliber of des Trurain and an Castre. However, there is always the risk of an unfortunate coincidence in this line of work, and in this case, it happened," finished deln Crantz, eyeing the prosecutor sternly.

"An unfortunate coincidence?" scoffed an Koth.

"Yes," was the final, composed reply.

Marthe smiled to herself, grateful for the unsought loyalty of the small but charismatic figure in the witness box. Admittedly, much of what he said could be used against her, but she hoped that the jury would still remember his cool, non-partisan approval of her actions. In this post-occupation world, he was one of the new heroes, proclaimed as a man of wisdom and courage. Surely they would listen to him, she hoped, suddenly weary and decidedly thankful to see the clerk, bringing her a message. It was from Ruthie to say that, trial or no trial, Riardan would like a feed—*now*, thank you very much. With a feeling of escape, she slipped out quietly to the small, side room set aside for her to suckle her voracious offspring.

Here she could, if she wished, continue to follow the trial by vidscreen. More and more, though, she found herself switching it off, a welcome respite from the endless barrage of the rights and wrongs of her actions. Stars above, even she was beginning to question her guilt. War was such a crazy time and her contribution so chaotical that the line between good luck and good management had always been decidedly fuzzy. And never more than now, she sighed, drifting off instead to thoughts of arriving home and feeling Hamon's arms around her again.

Forgetting the trial all too readily, she consciously brought his face to mind: his hair, curling strongly into the nape of his neck and springing to life under her fingers; the straight mouth and the special smile that would suddenly lift it; clearest of all images, his eyes, with their ever shifting, green and brown patterns of true hazel. From the cold hardness of emerald to the gentle brown of shared love.

Anger still lurked—at circumstance, at the choices they must yet face—but under the anger was the love they had discovered in that most unlikely of times. Love that could not be denied and without which neither could be whole. He had come home.

For an instant, she felt truly blessed, gazing upon the now contented face of little Riardan. Then the voice of Ruthie broke into her solitude. She gave a quiet sigh, before rising to place the sleeping baby back in his crib and return to the bitter ashes of the courtroom.

Two more interminable days were taken up by the prosecution vilifying and questioning all her actions until her head rang. Hamon was to be the last of the prosecution's witnesses—left, in a special departure allowed by the judge, until the end of the trial. 'For security reasons', they were told, but Marthe could just see the triumphant grin of an Koth at managing to pull off such a spectacular finale.

Each night, she would return to the an Castre villa weary and dispirited, to fall into Hamon's arms. Here alone she could let down the proud shield she showed the world.

Tonight was different. Tomorrow, the defense would start to put her case and, Mathe help her, she was so looking forward to seeing the unctuous smile wiped off the face of Prosecutor an Koth.

"Let him be the one having to wriggle out of a sticky corner," she crowed to Hamon and Yurin, who had joined her in a mid-trial celebration.

"You're not supposed to be quite so pleased at the prospect, young lady," adjured the mock-stern voice of her legal counsel. "This trial is meant to be a considered legal analysis of the appropriateness of your actions during the recent conflict, not a personal feud between *them* and us."

"'Considered legal analysis', my eye," was her quick retort. "He's a weaselly little clodpole who was safely ensconced in some bureaucratic bolt hole throughout the occupation, and now thinks to cover himself in belated glory by bringing down someone who took real risks. Isn't that so?"

"Yes, but don't go around saying it outside this room," Yurin grinned back, unabashed by her volatile temper.

Hamon laughed and gave her an affectionate squeeze. "What a spitfire."

"Well, I knew Yurin would agree with me. He, at least, was actively involved in the resistance, not skulking away somewhere."

"Someone had to 'skulk away', if you wonder-type heroes were to have any backup," Yurin reminded her, jabbing a finger playfully in her direction.

"All very well, but there's a difference between serving in support staff because that's what you were best suited to or had family commitments and making flaming sure to be assigned there, well out of the way of any danger."

"Particularly if you're then to have the gall to point the finger at those who were in danger," growled Hamon, sharing Marthe's view of the prosecutor wholeheartedly.

"Since you aren't that fond of Hathians anyway, your opinion doesn't count," proclaimed Marthe, grinning and snuggling into his side.

"Don't know about that. There is the odd one I could bear." He shot her a quick, intimate smile and his fingers began to tell a secret, slow dance of seduction in the palm of her hand.

But they were not alone. The suddenly serious voice of Yurin broke upon them. "Now that is one thing I don't understand, Radcliff." he said. "To put it bluntly, you hate both Hathe and Hathians. Why?"

They were ensconced around a low table in the library of the an Castre villa, Marthe and Hamon relaxing together on the couch, Marthe's feet tucked under her as she lay contentedly in her husband's arms. Yurin was sprawled at ease in a nearby chair, his long legs stretching out to the table as he lay back, slowly sipping his wine, then paused to throw a considering glance at Radcliff.

Hamon had heard his question and seen the look, but chose not to answer, gazing instead into the depths of his glass, a half-bitter grimace touching his lips.

"You really don't want to know," he said dourly.

"I know you don't want to discuss it, but I do need to know," Yurin returned. Hamon felt his searching gaze and, beside him, could feel the sudden tension in Marthe. An Begum had picked it up too. He saw his quick glance to the side and the almost imperceptible tightening of his hand on his glass.

"Why?" demanded Marthe, leaning forward. "You're not the type to delve into people's lives for the sake of gossip. Of what interest can this be to you?"

"You forget. The prosecution may have bagged Hamon as their witness, but I will be the one to question him last. If we're to impress the judges, it has to be good. To do that, I need to know what makes your husband tick." Then he looked directly at Hamon, giving him no room to hide. "This is the one thing I can't fathom: why you should hate us. What have we done to you, especially compared to what you directly and the Terran forces in general, have wreaked on our home world? Guilt, yes, but why hate?"

"You mean, what right do I have to feel anything against you?" said Hamon to the lawyer, who nodded. "It's a fair question. There's no logic to it, I agree." He may have been looking at the lawyer, but it was the tension in Marthe he answered. "I can't forgive Hathe for what I did here. Most particularly for what I did to you," he said softly in despair, his gaze turning to lock hers. "There is no sense in that, I know, but there it is, and I don't think I can ever change it."

"You mean, you regret what you did?" Yurin asked.

"No."

"He cannot regret it when he knows that, given what he knew then, he would do exactly the same again," said Marthe, answering in his stead and staring at him, grief-stricken. "As would I,'" she finished softly.

For a few seconds, Yurin could almost see the silent message pass between them. An uneasy frisson shivered up his back and he suddenly found himself at a loss. For the first time in the trial, he understood his task in all its glaring cruelty. Grief lodged in his gullet. Then both turned to him as one, exposed and raw.

"You have no love for Terrans either?" he said to Marthe. She shook her head, barely looking at him. "But if your husband loves his home so…?"

"He is counting the days till he returns," confirmed Marthe, staring blindly ahead now.

"They need me," Hamon told her, a desperate apology in his voice.

"Why?" demanded Yurin. "What in Mathe can you do, a marked man, closely watched by the Alliance, as you will be?"

"I'm a born leader," replied Hamon, leaning back, as the lines of bitterness on his face deepened, "and I have seen how people act when repressed. You know what it did to Hathians. Terrans are no different. In a short while, Earth will be a hotbed of rebellion. They need people like me to control the mess."

"You're a marked man."

"Maybe, but I'm also connected to, or friendly with, a number of influential Terrans. In plain Harmish, I'm a spymaster and very good at it."

"So, you'll help the new, Alliance-backed, Terran government?"

"I don't know. It depends on what I find there," he replied defiantly.

"And Marthe? Will you stay here in the meantime?"

She shook her head. "It's not safe, even if the Council would let me." Yurin raised a querying eyebrow. "I've already been told that, whatever the outcome of the trial, the Council will have me exiled— for reasons of political stability," she explained, with a short, caustic laugh.

"For a few months, yes, but you will return."

"No. It will be for a long, long time. And Hamon can never return."

"But this planet; it's your heart," gasped Yurin in disbelief. Radcliff's hand clenched down on Marthe's, his head swinging back to her.

"As Earth is yours," she murmured sadly to him.

"So, you will stay together?"

"There's no other possibility," said Radcliff, pulling Marthe close.

"Then, Marthe, you will be able to make a life on Earth? After fighting against them for five years, and despite what they did here?" Images of Marthe during the occupation filled his mind.

"I … don't know," she replied, for once, he noticed, avoiding Radcliff's searching gaze.

"Then where is there for you together?"

They were silent for a long time. "Now that is a very interesting question," was the bitter reply of the Terran, finally catching and holding his wife's gaze for a very long time.

CHAPTER TWENTY-EIGHT

"Once more into the fray," chanted Marthe jubilantly, her feet beating time with the refrain as she marched with her guards to the courtroom. "Ready to slay 'em in the aisles, Master Barrister?" She turned to grin at Yurin, a shameless twinkle in her eyes.

Yurin grinned back at her. "I'll certainly do my utmost. You won't recognize yourself in the saintly figure our character witnesses will produce."

"Not too saintly, I hope. I rather fancy being seen as a loveable rogue-type of heroine."

"Hard luck. Saintly heroines win court cases. Now, behave yourself, or you'll have this lot believing our dear friend over the way," he scolded, discreetly gesturing towards the prosecution bench.

Marthe did subside, but the excitement of finally starting the attack remained with her. She sat then gave her customary direct glance to the vid receptors. Each day, this was her first act after taking her seat in court—whether to show her face and reassure Hamon at home or to remind herself of his presence there, not even she could say.

The morning proceeded as Yurin had predicted. Marthe was stunned to find that Yurin had called in old friends and colleagues from every corner of the planet, many met but briefly on assignment, yet impelled, nevertheless, to give witness to the service she'd given.

Here, a lady from the earliest days, that dark time in the mines. A face poorly remembered, last seen straining and then triumphant in childbirth. The baby had lived, managed to survive the occupation, and was now thriving, she was glad to hear.

Next, a man she couldn't remember, and only vaguely the assignment. A village cut off and short of supplies. She had diverted a Terran supply train to come to their aid. The man spoke of the injuries she'd carried—cuts and bruising mostly, from the Terran soldiers. She'd been working as a domestic drudge, a handy cover to use as she altered the soldiers' orders to make them change route. She couldn't now call to mind her hurts; it wasn't an uncommon occurrence and, short of those injuries needing hospitalization, she'd usually treated herself on the spot and carried on regardless. Still, judging by the witness's words, she must have looked quite a sight when she hit their village.

Now, a well-remembered face from a particularly trying case. It had taken her team weeks, slowly working their way into a Terran command depot. She had posed as a laundry maid this time. It was one mission she wouldn't forget. She had nearly been caught one night, halfway through downloading Terran communications data. A trio of soldiers decided to use the very room she was in for an illegal game of Fivers, staying for hours and oblivious to a very nervous Hathian crouching behind a nearby cabinet. And with excruciatingly painful cramps in her leg, she recalled with a grimace.

So it continued. The litanies of people she had either helped or worked with, all attesting to her courage, endurance and deep commitment to her home world. Also, to the cost she'd paid, again and again, in drudgery, humiliation, exhaustion and pain. It might have caused her something of a swollen head, if she didn't remember too well what those speaking had also endured.

That night, returning home, she met Hamon at the entry. Then looked away at what she saw in his eyes.

He cried aloud in negation, pulling her back to face him and staring hard into her eyes. He shook his head when she went to speak, leading her into the privacy of their sitting room first then faced her again.

"You were hurt in the occupation?"

"Sometimes. We all were."

"How badly?" he demanded.

"Nothing too serious. The odd broken leg, a few blows leading to concussion, that's all. It came with the territory."

"How often in that five years did you live normally? Proper food, a bed, clean clothes?"

"Plenty," she shot back in angry embarrassment. "I had regular breaks on Mathe, and you've seen my hideout. The ordinary citizens who put up the smokescreen had it far worse; they hardly ever got a break; and it was worst of all for the families. Watching children grow up like young animals and never, ever getting a break for fear the little ones would blurt out something to a Terran on their return."

"Oh, stars!" He drew a hand raggedly through his hair. "I do know. I was one of those enforcing it, remember. No wonder I couldn't break you. My treatment was nothing compared to what you'd already endured. You could have been killed!"

"If it's any consolation, those months with you may have been wonderful, but they were also the nearest I ever came to losing it. Physical stress ain't got nothing on psychological pressure," she threw in with a choked off laugh.

He hugged her, then was silent a moment.

"How badly do you hate Earth for what happened here? "

She stared into space while she gathered herself, then turned to lock her eyes with his. "If you're asking, don't I really, in some part of me, hate you for it, then no, I don't. 1 can't. I love you, Hamon Radcliff, body, heart and soul, and nothing you can do will change that." She gasped in relief as his lips claimed hers, drowning in the warmth of him.

Afterwards, she continued as if uninterrupted, driven by the memories of the day to bring into the open all that was unsaid between them. "Do I hate Earth? I suppose, yes. I do know I'm incredibly angry at what you did here. I still can't believe how ... ignorant you were! How could a whole planet be so selfishly, arrogantly isolated?"

He drew a hand through his already ravaged hair.

"Do you want an apology?"

"No, damn you, I want an explanation. You were educated on Cantor. You must have noticed the differences! Did it never occur to you how backward Earth was?"

"I'm not a scientist," he replied lamely.

"Don't give me that. You're pretty damned astute about everything else. You travelled, so what about your scientists? Where was Ferdo's dratted curiosity then?"

"They weren't allowed to leave Earth. We needed their talents too badly at home."

"And no one ever thought to look at the rest of the Alliance planets, to see if maybe we had solved the problems you couldn't?"

"Why should we? Earth's population still exceeds that of all the newer Alliance planets combined. We had minds enough of our own to come up with solutions that would work for Earth."

"Yes, but not minds that had been challenged as they were on the other worlds. Don't you know how the original colonies were settled?" she demanded. "Set up on an *ad hoc* basis. Earth's only interest lay in how many people they could be rid of and what could be milked from the new worlds. But we didn't sink as we should have. We swam, finding the answers to questions you of Earth never even dreamed existed. And now you expect us to understand you? To rescue you, even?"

"Is that so unreasonable?" Hamon threw back defensively. "Do you have no sense of duty, of heritage? Earth is the home of humanity!"

"I have a nostalgic sense of interest, yes, but this is my home. I was born on Hathe, as were my parents, my grandparents, and generations before. This world—it's who I am! Against that, all you offer is the sop of your own ignorance?"

Hamon released her, hiding from her now behind the shattered clay mask of his face. He stared down at his clenched hands, then slowly unknotted them and turned to face her.

"It's the only excuse I have to offer," he said. His head came up, rigid with decision. "You ask about my time on Cantor," he continued. "First, it was a political degree, not a scientific one. I do have a basic grounding in science and technology, but if it works, I'm not particularly interested in how. And yes, of course I noticed that Cantor and Hathe had a higher standard of living than us but, like other Terrans, I put it down to the benefit of a smaller population and, presumably, a higher allocation of urgonium."

Marthe leapt up at that, furious exasperation flooding her.

"But they didn't. Earth was our single largest customer, the heaviest user of urgonium in the Alliance. When you asked for more, we thought it was a business scam. Buy from us and on-sell to the small, economically vulnerable planets, or stockpile it and push up the market price. That's why you were treated so coolly. We thought it a cheeky shot. No one took you seriously!"

"And all we could do was let our precious pride be ruffled and withdraw in a sulk," Hamon said in bitter acceptance. "Our people were dying, and no one seemed to care. We saw no choice but to take action."

"If only Earth had approached the Alliance. God, do you think we wanted the last five years?"

"Do you think I wanted it for you?" hit back Hamon. "Don't you know I would give almost anything for us to be together without all—this—between us? If we must wallow in 'if only' country, then *if only* your brother hadn't interfered, we might have met and fallen in love five years ago. Maybe even have prevented this whole mess! Is that what you want me to say?"

He grabbed her roughly, but she pulled away, an irate flush heating her cheeks. "So, it's Bendin's fault now?"

He dropped his hands suddenly, a deathly tiredness washing his face. "Forgive me. I should never have said that. No, I don't blame your twin. Blame it on history, I guess."

He sat back, staring into space, saying nothing when, moments later, she rose to go to bed, shutting the door firmly after her.

The next morning, Hamon wasn't around when she left for the court. She hugged her small son convulsively. It had become too dangerous to take him across town with her and, fearfully, she returned the dozing bundle to Ruthie's kindly arms. Unsure whether or not to be glad at Hamon's absence, she left the house in a strangely equivocal state. It persisted through the remaining days of increasingly poignant testimony.

Not once in those days did she so much as glance at the vid receptors.

Then the defense came to the end of its case. All the evidence had been presented: the word of friends and those possibly not so friendly, the surveillance transcripts, medical and duty records, her service records, all the screeds of documentation needed to bludgeon the court into finding her innocent.

All that remained was for the prosecution to present its one last, controversial witness. Then, the charade could be done with.

The morning of Hamon's testimony arrived. He looked at her, a cool, assessing look, and she looked back. Marthe gave him her hand and he accepted it in the formal clasp that was all she seemed able to give him today. Too many uncertainties lay between them.

The security this morning was even more extraordinary than usual. Jacquel was in charge of the arrangements, his legal responsibilities over. He and Hamon met with their usual, cold hostility.

This time, though, she noticed something else. A kind of indefinable trust could be seen in the, for once, not arrogant look in Hamon's eyes as he met the gaze of her oldest friend.

"Des Trurain, a favor if you would."

Jacquel paused, then nodded shortly despite no hint of supplication in Hamon's voice.

"Riardan. Can you have him and Ruthie taken to Moon One transit base as soon as possible after we leave? Inconspicuously? If anything happens, find him sanctuary. Not here, and not on Earth," he added bitterly.

Marthe kept her face closed and distant. She hadn't known he would ask this but wasn't surprised. Nor, it seemed was Jacquel.

"Don't worry," was all he said. "I'll do as you say. He'll be safe, whatever."

A hint of strain left Hamon's face and she could feel the same inside herself. They turned together to enter the heavily armed, plain car. Hamon was in full Terran dress uniform, a fact Marthe was unable to comment on, confining herself to one raised eyebrow. The look he gave in reply told her he was in a 'be damned to 'em' mood.

Quickly and without further talk, their group left, one only amongst a number of similar cars to leave the an Castre house in an attempt to elude the watching and sullen crowd. The windows were darkened to shield Hamon from view. All Hathe knew that today was the day the hated Terran was to appear. As a precaution, the rest of the Terran hostages had been shipped out to other Alliance planets a few days prior. That had been fuel enough for the hotheads, now more determined than ever not to be deprived of revenge on this one Terran at least—among the worst perpetrators of the Terrans' repressions, from all accounts. And that girl had actually married him?

Just once, she wished she could be strong minded enough to avoid checking the newsvids.

Much to their guards' relief, the trip to court passed without incident. Here, they must part: Marthe to her usual seat, Hamon to a specially secured unit—for safety, they were told, until he was called. Marthe was about to move off after a brief farewell, but turned back, hesitantly. Suddenly, she went to Hamon, ignoring their minders and leaned up for his kiss.

Gently, he took her face in his hands, his mouth warmly caressing hers. Pulling back, he looked at her with all the promise of his passion.

"I love you and will do so till the end of my days. Remember that, whatever happens." He pulled her closer into the harbor of his arms for a final, brief moment before he was marched off, a grimly withdrawn figure in the center of his guards.

Marthe next saw him as he entered the courtroom, a sullen, hostile silence falling as he marched in, head erect and looking for all the world as if nothing had changed. As if, in fact, Earth still ruled this planet and it was he who sat in judgment here today. There was an audible gasp as those present recognized the Terran uniform, too hatefully familiar to so many of them.

"It's a good thing he's not on trial," muttered Yurin. "What's he trying to do? Get himself killed?"

"He's just not in a particularly apologetic mood," murmured back Marthe, in blatant understatement.

The questioning began, innocuous enough at first. Name, rank, position in Earth's administration. Almost as if the prosecutor had been thrown off stride by the reality of a Terran Major's presence. The uniform brought its memories of fear for him too, it seemed. And this was the defendant's husband?

His recovery didn't take long, and the questions increased in both subtlety and danger.

"You appear to have had little to do with the Terran military after your time at the academy."

"One automatically remained on reserve. Only a small percentage of graduates were needed for full-time duties," was Hamon's dry reply.

"Then why, if you were contentedly pursuing your studies elsewhere and had little active experience, were you called into the occupying force?"

"I happened to be in the vicinity, and I was one of the few Terrans ever to have visited Hathe."

"That would have been shortly prior to the attack, when you were attached to the staff of your father, Ambassador Garth Radcliff?"

"Yes."

"And during that visit, did you at any time meet Marthe asn Castre?"

"Not personally. I was most desirous of so doing but, as many of you may remember, young men desirous of closer acquaintance with the asn Castre sisters were a fairly common commodity in those days," Hamon returned with a slight quirk to his mouth.

"But you did become acquainted with members of the an Castre family?"

"Councilor an Castre, in an official capacity only. On a personal basis, I spoke only to Bendin asn Castre. Not at all amicably, I might add." She saw his lips tighten even now at the remembered humiliation.

She wished he hadn't as the prosecutor sensed a wrinkle of hope. "Oh?"

"We had a disagreement over a young lady. He lost, and took it rather badly. A few days later, there was an official reception at the an Castre residence. He caught me watching his sisters, 'ogling them' he termed it, and had me thrown out." There was a snap in Hamon's voice, the lingering resentment obvious still. She wanted to throw something at him.

"So, you did have some personal connection to the an Castre family, then?" said his opponent.

"A mutual dislike of the son and an admiration for the beauty of the daughters. That was all. There were never any discussions of a treasonable nature, if that is what you're trying to induce me to say. I will admit that I never forgot the ladies, particularly the younger sister, but that, I do assure you, had nothing whatever to do with politics— as you would realize if you had one, healthy red blood cell in you."

A red flare of anger drenched the prosecutor's cheeks and he swiftly changed the subject to the details of Hamon's service during the occupation years.

"Your position in the Terran forces?"

"Chief of Staff, Special Services. The intelligence branch of the occupation force."

"Your superior?"

"I answered directly to Colonel Johne."

"And he had your full loyalty?"

"I also held a watching brief for the Terran Council."

"In what way? What areas concerned them?"

"I have not been authorized by my government to reveal any further details."

"Oh? How convenient. Can you tell us anything at all of your duties?" enquired the prosecutor scathingly.

"Only those matters pertaining to this case, and which are not prejudicial to the security of Earth and its interests," Hamon replied coolly.

"You were rather more involved in the administration than suggested by your official position, though, were you not?"

"I had other responsibilities, yes. Mainly to do with the use of Hathian personnel."

Marthe knew that look. It was the public face Hamon had worn in the early days of her captivity—that of the aloof Terran Major, letting nothing out and, conversely, protecting him from the ugliness of what he must do.

"In the use of Hathian personnel?" sneered the prosecutor. "Are you referring to the illegal use of Hathian prisoners as forced labor in the mines? In the course of which many thousands of Hathians lost their lives?"

"That was an area I was in involved in latterly," agreed her husband coolly.

"Why were these responsibilities given to you?"

It was an accusation, one that he ignored. "It tied in well with the intelligence role and was useful in our attempts to infiltrate Terran agents into the Hathian population. Also, with keeping track of the various factions present in Hathian society."

"You spied on us is what you mean when you discard the official niceties. Did you request this duty?" demanded an Koth in theatrical disbelief.

"No, but I did not refuse it either. I appear to have a knack for that sort of thing, and it seemed the most efficient way for me to serve the occupation." Still Hamon's mask held, despite the scorn from the prosecutor and the rising air of animosity permeating the courtroom.

"So you were desirous of furthering the Terran occupation of Hathe. Were deeply committed to it, in fact?"

"Of course. At the time, it appeared to be our only hope of survival."

"And the effect on the population of Hathe was irrelevant?"

Hamon paused, still expressionless, but his gaze slid momentarily to catch hers before turning to look squarely at the prosecutor.

"It was not something I could afford to consider," he said.

And despite imprecations and expostulations, he refused to add anything more. A tense air of silence hung over the courtroom. Marthe had noticed Hamon marking the exits and guards when he'd first entered. He was in full, battle-ready mode—as was she. The room had that deafening throb of danger, felt too many times in the past to be ignored now. At one stage of the questioning, she received an almost imperceptible glance from Hamon, to which she replied with a brief, reassuring nod. She'd already picked out several of her fellow agents, scattered inconspicuously through the watching crowd, with Jacquel prominently on guard at the front of the room.

He stood a few paces only from Hamon. As the tension mounted, Marthe was relieved to see him move discreetly closer to the witness stand. All around the room, the agents sharpened their deployment, a couple handy to her and the rest strategically placed to quell any riot.

Marthe surreptitiously caught Jacquel's attention, using an abbreviated hand signal that only he would understand. Jacquel saw it and replied cryptically. Too many of those in the room knew body codes and could make a fair guess at a message, but Marthe knew him well enough to catch his meaning. Be prepared. We're armed and in contact with shielded patches.

It was a reassurance, but not sufficient to allow her to relax her guard. Neither, she noted, did her husband.

The prosecutor was becoming more particular to her own case, having failed dismally to wrench a general confession of wrongdoing from his victim.

"It was you who instituted the search for the Hathian servant girl, Riarda, who was in truth the defendant, Marthe an Castre was it not, Major? A search which resulted in Madame an Castre's exposure?"

"That is correct."

"Would you care to explain to the court your reasons for this search? After all, Hathian servant girls were not uncommon in Terran quarters. Why the strong interest in this particular one? Could you not have merely ordered another?"

"She had such beautiful hair."

The prosecutor stared. "You suspected a girl merely because of her hair?"

"Partially," affirmed Hamon. "Most Hathian women at the time favored a dank, lusterless style. But Madame an Castre's hair was … memorable." Hamon allowed a small smile of fond reminiscence to light his face, which she strongly suspected would bring to the women in the room a sudden, vivid understanding of her choice. "But also, there was a too timely coincidence. Just after I removed her head cover and before I actually managed to see her face, I was interrupted by a Hathian male with a bogus message requesting me to see Colonel Johne immediately. When I returned, the maid was gone, and was replaced the next day with a new girl. I have a particularly suspicious nature, and coincidence rarely fits my scheme of affairs. Hence the desire to discover just who this mysterious woman might be."

"So it was Madame an Castre's failure to adequately disguise herself which led to her exposure?"

"Yes, but if you imagine that beautiful women such as she can happily spend a lifetime dressed in sackcloth and ashes, then you live in a fool's paradise. I had seduced a number of Hathian women previously, many of whom possessed some hidden gem of nature. My reputation was well known, and I presume her superiors knew the risks entailed when they first assigned her to this mission. In fact, if I was their target, then I would suggest that they quite deliberately chose an agent with such a quirk."

Marthe saw the grimness behind the smile and all at once was reminded disastrously of his first taking of her. Startled, she recalled his words of the other night, the anger against Hathe that he still held. Had held since that day, it now seemed. He had said that he couldn't forgive Hathe for what he'd done here. Equally, it seemed, he couldn't forgive Hathe for what loyalty to her people had forced her to make happen that day. When, unable to stand the lie a moment longer, he had brought into the open the full ugliness of what they were doing by stripping away the sham of sensuality and turning a cynical seduction into a brutal taking. No, he had not forgiven Hathe for that. Had he forgiven her?

While she was turning the thought over, the prosecutor had risen in outraged protest. "That is a foul slur, sir. It is merely the pricking of your own conscience speaking," he gasped angrily.

"You think so?" was Hamon's dry reply. "Whatever, she certainly caught my attention and would, in the normal course of such affairs, have secured an intimate position from which to observe Terran affairs. Unfortunately for her superiors' plan, no one seems to have researched my background sufficiently to realize there was a high probability of my recognizing the lady. As indeed I did when she was brought in for questioning."

Hamon lolled, apparently at ease and daring the prosecutor to doubt his words. But Marthe saw the alert wariness behind the pose.

"So you identified the defendant. She was then imprisoned and held for further questioning."

"That is correct."

"Where was she held?" an Koth put in softly.

"In my quarters."

"A most unusual place of internment, surely?"

"Perhaps," allowed Radcliff. "We'd never succeeded in learning anything of value through the usual prison regime, so I thought I'd try a new approach."

"It was not rather that you wanted to rekindle an affair with an old acquaintance, whom you hoped to enlist for the Terran cause?"

Hamon paused to eye the prosecutor, as if in doubt of the man's sanity. He continued, however, in the same, even tones as before. "Of course, I wanted to start an affair. I have already admitted to being attracted to the lady. But to say that I hoped to enlist her to the Terran cause is rather extreme. I prefer to deal in reality, not dreams. Certainly, I hoped to confuse and disarm her enough to get her to let slip some information of interest to us. But to expect that a Hathian would assist the Terran cause of her own free will, was really rather beyond the realms of probability."

"And did she?"

"Did she what, exactly?"

"Let slip any information."

There was a collective intake of breath throughout the courtroom.

"Well, of course."

She felt the shock hit the watching crowd as her husband stared unconcerned at the prosecutor. "I'm not totally inept. If I couldn't discover something of a woman's background after living with her for months, then I really wasn't quite the threat your people supposed."

"Could you tell us what kind of information Madame an Castre gave you?" demanded the prosecutor hungrily.

"I wouldn't say that she gave it to me. More that I deduced it from various comments and activities."

"And you learned what?" the prosecutor urged in frustration.

"Mostly generalities. First and foremost, her behavior and that of des Trurain confirmed in my mind the existence of an organized resistance, communicating by means we were unable to ascertain. It did become clear that your scale of technology was more advanced than we had supposed. I also gained an impression of an impending event and some idea of the time scale involved."

"And what effect did your knowledge have?"

"Not as much as I hoped," admitted Hamon, to an Koth's disappointment.

"You did not ignore it, surely? A committed Terran officer, such as yourself?"

"No, of course not." There was a slight twitch of his lips. A hint of dry amusement at the prosecutor's naivety. "My own surveillance teams were immediately strengthened and put on alert, and the general security measures my staff employed were increased. Unfortunately, I couldn't proceed further without furnishing concrete proof of my suspicions to Colonel Johne. That I was unable to do to the Colonel's satisfaction until the last day of the occupation."

The prosecutor ignored most of what he said, latching firmly on to his closing words. "Something happened then, on that final day?"

"Yes, but that's already well known. As you are perfectly aware, I was held at blaster point and shot by my own wife," was Hamon's grimly exasperated reply. He refused even to glance at her now, she saw as she watched him intently.

"Yes, yes, but prior to that. What precipitated this, as you say, well known incident?" insisted the prosecutor equally exasperated.

"After many trials, our communications expert had finally managed to activate one of the Hathian patches we had confiscated and had picked up a clear signal from the resistance network. It was the proof we needed to force the Colonel to call out the troops."

"And I understand you obtained this proof thanks to the help of the defendant?"

"Not exactly. She was physically restrained by a technician and myself, then we forced her hand to touch the patch to activate it, against her will."

"But we have heard from her colleagues that Madame an Castre was a highly trained agent. Surely she could have evaded such restraint?"

"It's unlikely," was the blithely arrogant response. "I had previously had to similarly restrain des Trurain, during the early period of his incarceration. If he wasn't successful, with the same training and free to fight back, I assume that Marthe realized it would be useless to try to escape. Not that I was about to give her a chance to anyway. It was too important to us that she be forced to help. Apart from which," he added, "any attempt to use the kind of tactics needed would have blown her cover at once."

"Which she did, shortly afterwards," the prosecutor pointed out triumphantly.

"She had no choice then. I was about to set off a full mobilization of all Terran troops. Any agent worth her salt could recognize it as a point of no return."

"For one who professes not to have been fully in her confidence, you seem very familiar with Madame an Castre's thought processes?"

"We are similarly trained, that's all." Hamon replied defiantly.

Try as he might to keep control, Hamon was becoming seriously annoyed with this prying sprat, and it was only continual reminders of the consequences to Marthe that kept him from giving the man the full blast of his tongue. The tension in the room was rising fast enough already.

A smug smile crept across an Koth's countenance. "How did you learn that the patch was a surveillance device, if Madame an Castre didn't tell you?" he dropped in to the fraught silence.

"We'd always been suspicious of the unusual patches and had previously analyzed those found on the other Hathians detained with Marthe. At the time, we were stumped, and they were put by for further study at a later date." He'd again taken to lolling back to appear fully at ease. His eyes, though, kept discreetly scanning the room. He was careful to avoid looking at her directly, but he could see Marthe doing the same, aware of the knife edge they walked. The wrong word, wrong attitude from him, could send the crowd plunging into an angry mob. How could he protect Marthe from such danger yet at the same time give answers that preserved her innocence and honor while keeping some faith with the duty he owed to his own integrity? It was a question beginning to seriously exercise him. And still the prosecutor persisted.

"Your researchers just happened to have some spare time? Or was there another reason why they suddenly decided the patches were a communicator?"

"As I've already said, I had realized from some comments of Marthe's that Earth was running out of time. Hence the sudden urgency. Also, I mentioned to Captain Braddock one day the degree of advancement of Hathian science over Earth's, and he took it from there."

Hamon let his impatience show, as he wondered how often he must answer the same question couched in ever more guises. He caught a 'behave yourself' glare from Marthe and was relieved to feel an involuntary grin twitch his lips.

Marthe was not as amused. The man seemed to have a death wish! She glared once more then leaned over to catch her counselor's words.

"Is he safe here?" Yurin was asking, with a slight jerk of his head to the crowd behind. Marthe nodded, glancing swiftly at Jacquel and his cohorts.

"Deln Crantz' people," he murmured in satisfaction. "Excuse me a minute, will you," he said, then rose and left the room. Startled, Marthe looked to him, but he was already gone.

Once outside, Yurin spoke quietly to the door guard then walked over to knock on an inconspicuous door across the hallway. Inside, he was greeted by the diminutive figure seated before one of the ranked stalls of controls and surrounded by a posse of technicians.

"The Council has called in the big guns!" commented an amused Yurin. "Marshall deln Crantz, a pleasure to see you again."

"And what might you be up to, young an Begum? Shouldn't you be across the way listening to your learned opponent?" returned the little man's incongruously elegant tones.

"No, no. Got it all on recording. It's getting a bit heavy going for me," Yurin said blithely, an unashamed grin splitting his face.

"Then what do you want? As you can see, we're rather busy."

"You are, aren't you? Whose safety is the Council so concerned with? Marthe's or the Terran's?"

"Both, of course," and the shaggy eyebrows rose sharply.

"And can you protect them?"

"Marthe certainly. The only danger spot there, since you were wise enough to keep her away from the stand, will come when the not guilty verdict is delivered. We'll get her away smartly then,"

"Not guilty? You do have a lot of faith in my powers of persuasion,"

"We better be able to," came the firm reply.

Yurin ignored this, having always known of the strength of loyalty among Marthe's former colleagues, "What about the Major?"

"It depends … on his temper and your questions. For the former, there's not too much worry. He may hate every second up there, but he's good. Very good. He'll do."

"He certainly seems to feel that he had the measure of the resistance's objectives," It was a question, and Gof deln Crantz raised one eyebrow at the impudence.

"Was he accurate, do you mean?" he said. Yurin nodded reluctantly. "Of course he was. Oh, not that Marthe was set on to him deliberately. She had a number of possible targets, depending on how things fell out; but, no, Radcliff had it right. We weren't concerned about her refusal to dull her hair and her beauty was a factor in her selection. Which she never realized, though young des Trurain, damn him, began to guess at it. Nearly ruined the whole thing with his gallant rescues."

It was Yurin's turn for grim looks, unsure that he welcomed such frankness.

"You needn't look like that either, you young pup," barked deln Crantz, "Hamon Radcliff was every bit as dangerous to us as he infers. He's very astute and deeply committed to the welfare of Earth, which you would do well to remember. Marthe may have let slip a bit much to him, but equally, there's every chance that if she hadn't distracted him so effectively, he could well have wrecked our entire campaign. Don't go forgetting that!"

"I thought you admired him, sir," said a surprised Yurin.

"Oh, I do. I have the greatest respect for him—as an opponent. I will also do my utmost to ensure his safe exit from this planet. Neither of which should be taken to mean that I don't wish that he could pay, even in some small measure, for the considerable damage he helped to wreak on our home."

"Good," said Yurin. "Because I mean to make him. I only came across here to find out how well you can secure him. I may not be able to bring him to trial, but I can ensure that he is the one who wears the role of villain in this case. Just let me know when to stop. That crowd won't stand much more."

With a gruff, "Agreed," deln Crantz stood to shake his hand briskly, both in dismissal and approval, before returning to his screen.

CHAPTER TWENTY-NINE

Back in the courtroom, Jacquel edged closer to Radcliff. The prosecutor was coming to the closing stages of his interrogation. He still dwelt on Marthe's actions on that last, fatal day and was still failing dismally to trick Radcliff into implicating her in any voluntary collusion.

To hear him talk, you would think that Radcliff was utterly blameless, thought Jacquel in disgust. He noticed Yurin an Begum slip back into the room. Simultaneously, he signaled to two of his staff to move up and complete the cordon around Marthe, securing the path to the side door in the event of trouble. He could probably get Radcliff out too, he supposed. Then, glancing at Marthe, he reluctantly signaled for support for the other side door.

On the stand, Hamon was relieved when an Koth came to his disgruntled end. Yet the man could fairly claim a degree of satisfaction, and he'd managed to create a level of doubt about the question of Marthe's cooperation. Passing by his opposing colleague, the prosecutor rewarded himself with a smug bow, as he gestured an Begum onwards to the trial's denouement.

There was an amused smile in return, then Yurin moved towards his prime objective. Hamon felt a warning frisson crackle across his shoulder blades. The defense lawyer was looking almost happy.

"Major an Radcliff. Or no, you prefer the Terran form, I understand."

Hamon nodded warily.

Behind her security screen, Marthe groaned. She had played with Yurin as a child. *He's going to be nasty*, and she glared at Jaca as she caught his gleeful recognition.

"Major Radcliff. You have cohabited, to use the Terran term, with the defendant for just over a year?"

"On and off, yes," agreed Hamon.

"On and off. Does that description apply to the time of the Terran occupation?"

"No.

"So we can take it that Marthe lived with you continuously then, for a period of about six months?"

"Yes.

"Was this always by her own choice?"

"Not at first, no. Later, I cannot say. You would have to ask Marthe," said Hamon defensively.

"This would be after the mutual attraction between you had surfaced? You had, in fact, fallen in love. And she stayed with you by choice after that? You would have made no attempt to detain her, if she should have chosen to leave?"

"Not exactly."

"No? What would you have done if Marthe had disappeared?"

Hamon glared at his tormentor, then forced himself to relax and managed a slight grin. "I would have turned the planet upside down."

"Very romantic, I'm sure," was the dry reply. "In fact, that is exactly what you would have done, isn't it Major? And not only because Madame an Castre is a very beautiful woman with whom you were in love. Why would you have 'turned the planet upside down'?"

Hamon locked the muscles in his face into place and buried all feeling beneath his role of Terran officer. "Madame an Castre was a potential source of valuable information. I would have acted the same had Jacquel des Trurain decided to vanish."

"You did not, then, believe that she was the innocent refugee that she claimed?" said an incredulous Yurin.

"No. As she well knew. I was convinced that both Marthe and des Trurain were Hathian spies. Rightly, as it turned out."

Yurin paused in his pacing, casually leaning a hip on the edge of his table and turning partly to one side, thus including the audience in his amiable discourse. "Let us clarify matters, shall we? During the Terran occupation of Hathe, Marthe an Castre and Jacquel des Trurain were, in fact, your prisoners. A fairly relaxed imprisonment, surely?"

"Both were under full surveillance at all times and were always accompanied by Terran soldiers on the odd occasion either left the Citadel."

"What a trusting husband you were. I hope Marthe," he turned to her apologetically, "is not too shocked by these revelations."

"She was fully aware of the degree of surveillance I maintained over her, and the reasons for it."

"Was she also aware of what would happen if she left?"

"I can't say for certain, but it's highly probable."

"So then," proclaimed Yurin, resuming his pacing, "rather than being the adored and pampered companion that she seemed, Marthe an Castre was actually a tightly guarded, high security prisoner whose disappearance would have led to the kind of search the Hathian resistance could least afford?"

"Yes," confirmed Radcliff, warily on edge. He was beginning to sense the trend of an Begum's defense plan.

"Yet you still claim you loved the defendant. An unusual paradox, surely. You would imprison and put at risk the life of, as it turned out, your wife?"

"I believed that to do otherwise would be to put at risk the lives of millions of my own people," replied Hamon stiffly. "Marthe understood my reasons, if not agreeing with them. After all, she was in a similar position herself. No more would she have deliberately betrayed the resistance than I would have Earth," he finished in quiet desperation, not sure if he could bear the intrusion into his private hell he felt coming. Marthe, he saw, had grown rigid, rising at one point as if to leave and then, recalling her situation, subsiding into her chair again.

"Let us further examine aspects of this kindly imprisonment." Yurin was declaiming again to his audience, a slight sneer in the theatrical voice. "Immediately following her capture, Madame an Castre was confined to your quarters for interrogation. In the hope that the pleasure of her surroundings might trick her into letting down her guard, you said?"

Hamon nodded.

"Was this the only means that you used?"

"No."

"Please explain," requested Yurin politely.

"She was denied food or sleep for the first three days."

"And did that succeed?"

"No."

"So you decided you were mistaken, discarding further attempts at coercion and taking her for your companion instead? Or did you use further means to break her?"

Hamon paused, then continued reluctantly. His voice he kept rigidly unchanged. "She was exposed to a session of electroneural stimulation."

"And the sensory illusion used?"

"Of being slowly threatened then engulfed by flames," replied Hamon tightly.

"An unpleasant experience. Madame an Castre must have given you much useful information."

"It failed. She told us nothing and became unconscious after a period." Hamon held on grimly, withdrawing deep within the armor of his professionalism. Not once did he dare glance at Marthe or the onlookers, yet he couldn't miss the growing tide of horror. Few on Hathe had suspected that this type of treatment had been meted out!

"And des Trurain? He made no objection to Marthe's treatment?"

"They had no contact. I had told Marthe he'd been executed, due to her failure to talk. He was, at the time, confined in a prison cell where I interrogated him most days."

"And did you employ similar tactics of persuasion with him?"

"No. Physical methods were used in his case," said Hamon icily, challenging Yurin, or anyone else, to object.

Yurin allowed a pause to develop. His walk slowed, and he lifted one hand to his face, cupping his chin within its prop as he appeared to contemplate the witness's words. When he judged his audience to have adequately digested the morsel, he moved back to the attack.

He dwelt but briefly on Hamon's indisposition after the traumatic session, content to let it be passed over as a consequence of overwork. Then he moved on, to the peaceful calm of the following month before battle was again joined. Fortunately, some things even an Begum didn't know.

"So, over the following weeks and despite your previous treatment of her, a relationship developed between you and the defendant. You became, in fact, lovers and the defendant fell pregnant. Was this a voluntary relationship on Madame an Castre's part, or did you think she was but playing a role?"

"Both," replied Hamon stiffly, very unwilling to talk about this but knowing he must. "Her public behavior was that of a sophisticated woman enjoying a casual liaison with a member of the current power bloc—a delightful and amusing companion."

"And you did not accept that? It sounds very pleasant for you."

"It was a front," asserted Hamon harshly. "I had no proof, but I knew it to be so. The woman I loved was far superior; but to reveal that person would have been to reveal too much of the truth. We were both aware of this at all times."

"If you knew it to be a front, weren't you taking outrageous advantage of your position by indulging in a sexual relationship?"

"That is private to us, and none of your business!" snapped Hamon, leaning forward to glare his defiance. This he would not discuss.

Yurin returned the look fully. Then, seeming to pick up his message, he shrugged and changed tack. For some time, he dwelled on the various episodes of their shared life during the occupation: the wedding, Marthe's falling out with his mother, his release of Jacquel into the Terran community, Hamon's belief in the collusion between the two Hathians, and his increased mobilization of the special service troops, coupled with his frustration at his inability to take effective action. Always, Hamon could feel the growing anger in the crowded courtroom.

He would grant Radcliff courage, mused Yurin, to reply as he did knowing the effect it was having on his listeners. It didn't stop the lawyer, pacing up and down as he demanded answers of his Terran victim.

"We come now to the final day of the occupation."

Hamon straightened fractionally, relieved at the ordeal's near conclusion, yet conscious of an uneasy dread.

"By this time," said Yurin an Begum, "you were fully convinced that the defendant was a member of some kind of resistance organization, and that she and Jacquel des Trurain had been deliberately planted. That they were, in fact, working in collusion to manipulate the Terran forces for their own purposes."

Hamon nodded.

"You loved yet mistrusted, your wife and were concerned at the probability of some imminent, anti-Terran event?"

Hamon again agreed.

"And Marthe? In what state was she?"

"She was worn out by the pregnancy and, as I later discovered, from working long hours for the Hathian forces. She was quite ill and causing me a great deal of worry."

"Not sufficient it seems, to keep your distrust from her. Instead, you confined her to quarters and denied her the support of her only compatriot, des Trurain."

"It was necessary. Their continued freedom would have posed too great a security risk."

"And it was at this point that your technical officer made the breakthrough in his study of the Hathian patches, and requested your and Marthe's assistance? When, despite her ill health, you forced her to help you further the Terran cause, though you have acknowledged that you knew her loyalties to be opposed to Earth?"

"It was necessary," repeated Hamon. For the first time, a hint of desperation and the implacable hatred he felt for Hathe entered his voice. He couldn't keep it out, and knew it wasn't lost on the hostile crowd.

"So you chose to place your duty to your home planet before the wellbeing of your wife?"

"Yes."

"And this didn't bother you? You felt no guilt?" asked Yurin in amazement.

"Of course it did. It bothered the hell out of me!"

"In a disgruntled mood, then, you brought Marthe to join Captain Braddock for this experiment—a success, as it turned out, despite your having to forcibly restrain the defendant during the procedure. What happened immediately after you picked up the Hathian broadcast?"

"I went to sound the alarm."

"Did you succeed?"

"No."

"Why not?" persisted an Begum.

For a minute, it seemed as if he had finally lost his courage. Then he clutched at his pride and forced his mouth open.

"My sick wife suddenly produced a blaster and fired at me."

"And then?"

"She held us all at blaster-point until the Hathian resistance had completed its takeover of the planet."

He had to check on her now. Marthe had turned a deathly white, gripping the side of her chair as if to silence the stream of questions pouring from an Begum's mouth. He wished he could go to her but had to content himself with a swift sideways look of reassurance.

"Did you make no attempt to disarm her?" continued the lawyer, regardless.

"I did at one stage attempt to reach the weapon I kept concealed on the inside of my tunic but was prevented." Yurin looked questioningly. "Marthe knew of it. She shot it away before I could touch it."

Yurin again halted, the silence heavy in the room.

"If you could have got to that blaster," he asked carefully, "what would you have done?"

"At that point…" parlayed Hamon desperately, knowing his face was almost as white as Marthe's. He turned, looking directly at her for the first time.

"No…" she cried, trying vainly to rise against the bodies restraining her. It was only the fraught plea in the hard stare he sent her that made her sit down.

Hamon turned back to Yurin, lifting his chin in defiance.

"At that particular point in time, I would have shot the defendant."

"To stun?"

"No, I had no time to adjust the weapon. No. I would have shot to kill."

The words echoed through the room. A stunned silence fell. Not a single person disturbed the absolute stillness.

It lasted just long enough for des Trurain to scramble his forces then a violent babble of activity struck. A forward surging mass overwhelmed the barrier in front of Hamon before a defensive shield could be snapped into place, and frantically the security troops hustled Marthe and him out separate doors.

"Stop! Marthe… Let me get to her," he pleaded, trying desperately to pull back from his surrounding guards.

"She's safe. Our people have her away already," hissed back Jacquel, "but she will stay safe only if you keep dead away from her. In case you hadn't noticed, it's your blood they're after."

He grabbed Hamon's arm harder and hustled them towards the secured exit and the waiting vehicle outside. Hamon had time for only one, silent look back.

A surging volume of noise rolled over them as they raced down the hall. Voices yelled, and he could feel the upraised fists just behind, as the contained anger of five, misery-filled years finally found its embodiment in the person of one despised Terran. Though only a matter of minutes, it felt like forever before they burst through to clear air and hurried into the waiting door of the Hathian carrier. Almost before the last foot was within the threshold, the craft began to lift, racing for free space before the crowd behind could alert sympathizers to their flight.

"Marthe? Where have you taken her?" begged Hamon yet again.

No one answered; then des Trurain looked up from the console he'd been studying intently. "It's all right. They got her away, with no followers. Everyone was far too interested in stopping you to notice her. She's in a place of safety and will rejoin Riardan in a few hours. When things have died down somewhat."

Hamon caught the 'but' in his voice.

"And me?" he asked bitterly.

"You are en route to Earth. The Council has decreed that your presence is no longer acceptable on Hathe. You are to be conveyed home in all haste."

"I see."

He turned to stare out the window at the rapidly receding planet— a sight he'd longed for. Now, it only filled him with gall.

Hamon spoke no more on that trip, except briefly when they stopped at Riardan's refuge, a closely guarded military satellite. In secretly joyous relief, he was able to hold his son again. Quietly, he soaked in every feature of the tiny face, seeing the hints of both himself and Marthe just beginning to appear. For a precious time, he was left alone. Then des Trurain joined him.

The Hathian stopped awkwardly, seeing the two of them together, then coughed discreetly. "Your ship must leave now if you're to make the Earth connection. I'll take Riardan back to Ruthie if you like, and Marthe will be with him in a few hours."

Radcliff continued to stare at his son, not ready yet to lose him. Then he turned and looked up.

"And what then? Where is Marthe to go?"

"I don't know. She's to be expelled from Hathe for the time being, but will be fully supported and cared for financially, whatever she chooses."

"Which will not be with me, you hope."

"Can you doubt it?" said Jacquel, but, unexpectedly, there was sympathy there amid the residue of hate.

"You're probably right," said Hamon. "Just as, I suppose, to you I deserve what happened down there today."

He turned away in mute contemplation of the view, hugging his son to his body. A soft shuffle and a half cough was Jacquel's reminder of his presence and the waiting ship, Hamon turned back and slowly passed the baby over.

"She never had a chance to choose, did she?" he said inconsequentially. "And yes, technically, you're right. She would be better off without me. She could return home?"

Jacquel nodded. Hamon then passed over a crumpled sliver of tape.

"I was going to attach this to Riardan's clothes, but perhaps you'd better have it. It's my contact code on Earth. She can always find me or get a message to me through that. Keep it safe, and give her time to choose. Only promise to abide by her choice, no matter your feelings."

Jacquel nodded again, took the sliver, and left. Hamon swung violently from the sight, turning to stare blindly at the view of planet Hathe below. Soon to recede from his sight completely, a final and complete farewell.

CHAPTER THIRTY

The room was strewn with people—too many people. Jacquel hated it but knew he couldn't leave. They sat, stood or paced in brittle silence. There was a sound outside and someone jumped to standing then sat again. They were waiting, had been so for some time, and the strain of it hung in the air.

In the main chair sat Councilor an Castre and, beside him, his elder daughter and son-in-law with their twins, sleeping the innocent sleep of the very young—the only relaxed ones in the room. Laren was fitfully pleating her gown, echoing her sister's quirk in a time of trouble. Standing behind her, Jorven stared disconsolately into space, turning from time to time to speak to his wife, or to take her hand comfortingly in his.

On Dr an Castres' other side sat the gentle, reassuring presence of another Council stalwart, Gilda an Rathman. A widow herself, she'd been a close friend of Sylvan's wife and was now a welcome support in this hour of need. Yurin an Begum was also there, outwardly collected and chatting lightly with Jorven. Ranging around the perimeter of the group strode Jacquel, haggard with impatience. He'd tried sitting with the others. He couldn't. Where was she?

Then the door slid open. A woman entered, baby clutched to her breast. She halted anxiously, hovering half in and half out as the door attempted to close behind her.

"Marthe!"

"Where have you been?"

"We've been worried sick!"

"Why didn't you at least let us know you were safe?"

For an instant, the hunted look on her face said that the issue was in doubt: stay or leave. Then her chin rose with the courage he had seen her call on so often before, and she walked into the room.

"Sit down. Here." It was her father, the command in his voice undeniable, despite the quivering of relief. He held out his arms for his grandson but desisted when he saw how tightly she clutched the baby. Instead he reached for, and was quickly passed, a warm drink. Only when Marthe had begun to sip slowly from the mug did he resume his questions.

"Can you tell us where you've been?"

"Traveling," she said quietly, staring down into her drink.

"Where? On Hathe? Impossible," broke in Jacquel, ignoring her father's glare. "I sent out every kind of tracer imaginable and nothing could pick you up.

"I've spent five years avoiding such things. Why should you think they could trap me now?" She was still quiet, but he heard the hint of fiery despair. "I just wanted to say goodbye to it all," she explained, turning to her father. "This is my home, remember."

"I know, love," said her sister. "We were just worried. You didn't even stay for the verdict."

"I couldn't. Could not stand there and be forced to watch their faces."

"But you were found innocent, fully exonerated," her father expostulated.

"Yes, it was on all the broadcast channels. All I can say is that it's lucky I wasn't recognized that day. The public were not happy."

She lapsed into bitter silence but was brought back to an awareness of their presence by a careful clearing of a throat. "Did you hear the full findings?" asked Yurin.

"You mean, do I know I have four hours to leave the planet, or be forcibly expelled without any means of support," she shot back, abandoning her listless wariness. "That's why I'm here. To say goodbye." She looked up, swiftly encompassing them in her searing gaze, all the sorrow and bitter defiance in her soul there to see. "Riardan had a right to see it, just this once, even if he can never remember it. Hathe is so beautiful."

For a few brief moments longer, she let them see it, the angry pain shining through her, then her mask was back. "One day, I will talk to him about the planet of his birth. Now, I can at least say he's been there and tell him of this journey."

"You're going to abide by the Council's decree then?"

It was a simple enough question, but Jacquel saw by her look of comprehension that she understood the layers hiding beneath as well as he did. "Of course. What other choice have I?" She put the mug down and folded her hands in her lap with determination. "I did not give five years of my life to have all we achieved put at risk—especially by me. The plain truth is, Hathe can't cope with me at the moment. There is too much rebuilding to be done."

A living strength was back in her voice. All in the room had known her since babyhood and Jacquel could see them straightening, alert. She had come to the real purpose of the visit, the reason she had called them here today.

"Have any of you talked to the children of the occupation? The ones who can remember no other world than one ruled by Terrans?

Have you seen the shock in their eyes? That's what Hathe should be focusing on now, not this tawdry scandal of mine!"

"You were never that," protested Laren.

"No? No matter. Madame Gilda, you can help them. I have to leave but promise me you will organize something. I've seen them, seen their bewilderment. "She took a breath, took each of them in to her memories as her gaze swept the room. "That's what I've been doing these last weeks. Wandering across the planet, one more dirtsider trying to find a place to belong. They are everywhere, people who spent five years posing as members of a menial, poorly educated sub-class and are now trapped in the role. No one seems to be doing anything to rehabilitate them or restore them to their old positions. They have been grabbed already by those who were based off-planet. The moonsiders have modern skills, you see, and can slip into the jobs easily. Some of them even seem to think that the dirtsiders really are the lowly peasants they once pretended to be and treat them as badly as ever the Terrans did."

"I know. I've seen it too," said Gilda in a quiet voice. "We never expected it, so stupid of us; and there were no contingency plans ready. But programs are being developed now."

Marthe grunted in disgust. "There were plans for everything else. Why not this? They were so brave, so steadfast. I don't think you can have had any idea, up there on Mathe. It was such a long time down here. For the children, a lifetime. You must promise me to fix it."

Her eyes caught the older woman's with a painful intensity. Gilda returned the look in full. She nodded.

"I promise," she said.

Marthe seemed to relax, slumping back in her chair and cradling Riardan closer. "Thank you. It helps. Makes it all feel a bit less worthless. I looked everywhere, you see, and could find so few traces of our old Hathe. We worked so hard to bring it back, and you can't, can you?"

No one protested her words. There was nothing that could gainsay the bitter finality in them.

She did not add to it. Finally, her father could put the question they had all been waiting to ask since she walked into the room. "When you leave, do you know where you're going?"

Marthe's head shot up, surprise and a defensive anger in her gaze. "To Earth, of course. I have a husband waiting for me, and Riardan a father." A hard-edged glint appeared in her eye. Jacquel recognized it and knew too well the determination it boded.

"But you don't even know how to find the man," her father exclaimed.

"No, but I will. Jacquel, you have something for me?"

She turned full on to him. Jacquel reluctantly put his hand into his inner pouch, withdrawing a thin sliver of tape and passing it to her.

"He said you deserved the chance to make your own choice but made me promise to abide by your decision. His directions are there."

Marthe took the outstretched sliver, clutching it convulsively.

"Thank you," was all she could say. Suddenly, she clung briefly to each one gathered there, then flung herself out the door. Those left could only stare as it closed behind her.

She was gone.

CHAPTER THIRTY-ONE

Word of her coming had gone before her: to the waystations en route, to the crews of the transit ships, to the Alliance staff based on Earth. She was repeatedly faced with it throughout the three weeks of her journey.

There were four waystations in all, and the feeling on the most distant was the same as on the first. Beneath the official discretion and smooth oiling of her passage, came always that hint of recoil from the staff who must deal with her. No matter how they tried to hide it, she could see it in that first, unguarded instant, before the lines on the faces slid back into a smooth bureaucracy. Even at the last station, closest to Earth and heavily dependent on that planet for its transit business, she felt the stigma of the outcast. Traitoress. The word might as well have been branded on her forehead.

"This way," waved the official. A Terran, yet like all the rest he stayed just that bit farther from her than was normal. He pointed to the passage leading to the Earth shuttle bay, and it was with relief that she saw a Hathian courier materialize from a side room.

It was also a signal. One last and final duty owed before she embraced this new life of exile. Slowly, she came to a halt and turned towards Ruthie, faithfully by her side and carrying the sleeping Riardan. Marthe held out her hands for the baby.

"This is as far as you go, Ruthie. I cannot and will not ask you to go farther."

The Hathian woman stopped, her face falling into a fathomless dilemma. There was both unexpected grief and a sense of reprieve caught there. The usually self-contained face stared down at the sleeping child.

"I know you suffered under the occupation, Ruthie, and I have been more grateful than you can know for your tolerance of our unusual family; but can you maintain it on Earth? It's more than anyone should ask of you. Nor do I know how safe you would be."

The older woman nodded slowly, gently cradling the baby deep into her shoulder. The look she sent him was a very private one. Slowly, reluctantly, she passed the child over to Marthe.

"Take care," Ruthie whispered, one last finger lingering over the soft cheek. She lifted her eyes to Marthe. "For all your sorrows, you are aye a lucky woman." It was a blessing and a farewell. As a bright blush suddenly heated Marthe's cheeks, Ruthie turned and was comfortingly received by the station official. Marthe stared after the solid back, feeling as if her last bulwark had disappeared yet curiously buoyed by the woman's words.

She too turned, but in the opposite direction. Suddenly granted hope, she followed the Hathian official onto the Terran shuttle. She had forgotten what Earth held. Not exile, but the promise of life with her family. Life with Hamon.

She held grimly to that thought through all the buffeting and chaos of arrival. She had sent no word to Hamon and had forbidden any warning of her coming to precede her. So now she must face the harsh reality of his world without him. Never had she seen so many people, all hectically pursuing their own lives. She had lived in cities on and off all her life, but none like this.

It wasn't just the sheer mass of people, though that was overwhelming in itself. More than once, she clutched tightly to Riardan and hunched against her Hathian courier, wary of being forced into the stream or losing her baby. But no, more than that was the dirt, the soulless decay. Rubbish sprawled along walkways, carelessly fluttering about unconcerned legs. Railways and buildings wore the chips and rubbings of innumerable hands brushing past, with little sign of any regular maintenance. Or maybe, she conceded, they couldn't afford to waste resources on such trivialities.

The hostel to which she was assigned was more familiar. It had the utilitarian feel of the Terran quarters on Hathe—stark and with all the essentials but lacking that spark of life she had taken for granted all her days.

As she waited interminably for the bureaucrats to process and approve her residential application, despite its having been lodged long before her arrival, she wondered how Hamon could have sprung from such an environment. Was there a parallel world of the privileged, as like this one as night to day? Or was it something in the man himself? Whatever, he didn't belong in this place she must now inhabit and could never have done.

Four days passed and still she lay in her hostel room. Ten paces by eight. She had measured it often enough. Riardan was asleep in the hastily converted box they had brought her. She hadn't dared to ask what it had been used for previously, but with a durafoam pad, some blankets she had brought with her, and the gay decorations that had adorned his cot in his first days, she hoped he wasn't as aware as she of the gloomy strangeness of their surroundings.

The walls were nauseously bland, their mustard green obviously a mixture of all the colors left at the end of a run and used up on the cheap. After all, it's only for foreigners, she could hear the contractor say. The hostel was government accommodation, set aside for officials and visitors such as herself—those the administration was not troubled with impressing. She'd enquired about a private hotel and, yes, such were found on Earth, but security concerns ruled one out for her, or so she was told.

Staring at the encircling barrenness—that is, if you ignored the cheap hologram on the wall, and she usually tried to—she became possessed by a conviction that her placement here was deliberate, a punishment for past wrongs. Someone had decided she was in need of time spent mortifying the soul. Terran or Hathian? Either seemed possible.

In actual fact, she thought crossly, her soul had already had its lifetime share of mortification, and it appeared more was to come if what she'd seen of Earth so far was any indication.

A bright spark of anger flared deep inside her. She leaned back in her seat, grunting disgustedly at its unyielding discomfort, and stretched out her legs, feet crossed at the ankles. Her fingers twined thoughtfully in her lap and her chin jutted belligerently forwards. If she had been prone to paranoia, she might almost imagine a conspiracy to force her to acknowledge the error of her ways and bring her, abjectly apologetic, back home.

Even if that were the case, did it really matter? It was not as if she couldn't end the whole charade at any time. One call was all that was needed. She had full confidence in Hamon's ability to send this bureaucratic nonsense scurrying back into its mean and stingy hole. But that was an escape she refused to consider. That was not how she would come to him, not surrounded by the political baggage train that would ensue, with all its layers of implications.

After two more days of being stuck in a room with a grizzly baby and a decided lack of news, her resolve had weakened badly. Why had she released Ruthie so nobly? She jumped up, overwhelmed by frustration. Surprising the baby, restlessly tossing in his box, she snatched him up, wrapped him securely in his walking sling and palmed the door to exit. Ignoring the frantic "Hey" from the corridor porter, she swung round the nearest corner and slipped out the side entrance before her 'hosts' could realize she'd stirred. She pulled her overcloak forward about her body to conceal the lump of the child and strode quickly down the street. A mischievous grin lit her face. Thank the stars for the automatic habits of training that made her always find the alternate exits to any place she was in. She ducked down another street, swerving and weaving about the blocks to lose any possible pursuit. Just for once, she would face this world unfettered by the intentions of her minders. It must have some redeeming features, she thought, forcing her way against the masses blocking the walkways. She soon realized there was no point trying that and turned to let the flow of humanity take her where it would.

Riardan began to whimper, bringing startled, even disbelieving looks from those around her.

Good Heavens, do they have no children here? She shushed him gently, holding him close and letting the rhythm of her steps slowly rock him to sleep. Her frenetic restlessness had powered her forward, but now, she relaxed into the pace of the city—never a dawdle nor yet a race either, as though the populace paced itself to survive the place.

She began to look about her, leaving her direction to the whim of the crowd. For the first time since landing on Earth, she felt some of her inner tension seep away. She was free, and as safe here as anywhere. No Terran attacker could break the Hathian codes protecting her valuables or the weaponry she carried as a matter of course, while her body sensors would quickly warn her of trouble. Anyone trying to disrupt the protective field about Riardan would be in for a nasty shock. Her grin stretched wider, and then was internalized as she observed its unsettling effect on the few in the crowd who bothered to notice their fellow citizens.

She did, though, observe the labyrinth of life surrounding her. Deaf to their language, she would still have known them for Terrans. There was that same look in the eyes she had seen among the troops on Hathe, especially when they talked of home. Both listless despair and hopeless pride. Most unnerving of all was an almost total lack of curiosity: about her, their neighbors, even the weather in the sky above, every one of them set on their own path and oblivious of the others who shared the space with them. Was it fear or the only way to survive this oldest of human habitations?

Eons of human history had left their trace—a myriad of architectural styles patched together in a crazy quilt of different eras, stitched haphazardly one on top of another. Here, a fragment of intricate swirls, cut off mid-design by the cubist addition budding from the side of a large box that stretched to tower over its parent. The top had been lopped off, a coil of antennae and wires sprouting forth from an edifice built long before the technology which now inhabited it and to which it must adapt.

Over it all sprouted the most bizarre element of the crazy match-ups. Greenery, richly vibrant with life and sprawling in every available nook and cranny—window boxes, roof gardens, planters in the street. In any spot begging for dirt to settle, the natural world had invaded. In this world of people who seemed to have forgotten that blood flowed in their veins, plant life burst forth in vigorous abandon. Some of it even seemed to have been cultivated, placed deliberately in all its riotous profusion. That was another jarring element. All the plantings, even the smallest, sang with variety and color, a beguiling multiplicity such as she had never imagined.

It did not fit.

The buildings were unloved, rarely showing any harmony in their patchwork mixes, while sprawling over them, the plants came together in a living symphony. She rounded a corner and found an exquisite park—wide open spaces exactly designed for strolling and studded with the huge plants they called trees, their solid trunks reaching into the papery floss of the canopy above. Why, in this world of insufficiency and strife, such a beautiful place had survived, she was unable to say. But survive it had, and thank God. Something flashed in her head then, a wistful line she had once heard Hamon mutter.

"There is so much to love," he had said, angry and defensive. Yet he had also told her, frequently, of Earth's killing lack of resources, its inability to feed its population. Here she saw it confirmed in the pinched hunger of Earth's ordinary classes, carved into the faces of people wandering uncaring through nature's opulence. All at once, a fathomless gulf of incomprehensibility yawned in front of her. So much richness in the depths of such need. Never would Hathe have tolerated it. Nor, maybe, could she. She stood outside the park, staring.

Abruptly, her foot swung round of its own accord and she strode blindly back the way she'd come. Wrongness breathed from everything around her. Urgently she fled, unaware of her direction and badly needing the stark monotony of her room, the barren Earth of her expectations. Confused and clutching the stirring baby in his sling, she for once failed to notice her surroundings. Riardan grizzled and she automatically rocked him.

Her frantic pace was carrying her into a new area. The greenery was still with her, but wilder. Here and there lay marks of violence upon leaves and trunks. The buildings were more decayed than ever, the litter denser and the faces of the people wore the desperate bravado of failing hope.

These things she noted only subconsciously. She strode on, fitfully hurrying, every now and then slowing, as she gazed upwards seeking some hidden signpost. Jolted awake by the urgent haste, Riardan began to grizzle. His sturdy little body wriggled about and forced her to pay attention, his head now able to lift and seek the threat he sensed in the tension of his mother's body. Finally, fully awake, his grizzle became a full cry. All around, heads turned at the sound, many in stunned disgust. Also, here and there, was a quickly shuttered look of wistfulness on a woman's face.

She slowed, bringing him up to let him see her face and gently rubbing his back in soothing comfort. "Shush, shush, little bumpkin." Silly words, repeated over and over. He subsided but didn't fully relax. The tone of the words couldn't give the lie to the signals coming from her body as, brought to full awareness of her surroundings, Marthe's well-honed senses shrieked a warning.

The crowd was sparser here. It was clearly not a major thoroughfare. Though she was dressed in Terran clothing, her difference from these people was starkly obvious. More and more faces turned towards her, slowly gathering into a small mob. There was hostility here, both to her affluence and, terrifyingly, to Riardan, clutched protectively to her chest. Then it came to her, what she should have noticed earlier. Children! There were none. Certainly not playing in these streets—a few only back at the park and closely guarded by their accompanying adults, said her memory, replaying the scene.

Automatically, she moved back towards a solid wall, her training taking over as the crowd surrounded her. Her one advantage: these people would know nothing of the kind of weaponry she carried. Would it give her the time she needed for help to arrive? She urgently signaled Alliance headquarters.

"Don't worry, little one," she whispered to the now unnaturally quiet child. A cold grin twitched her lips and she felt again the adrenalin surge that had been her frequent companion for five years. Soon, soon, the closer ones would be within range.

"Outa yore territory, ain't ya?" came the guttural Terran. She knew the language, but barely understood these people's version.

"Whatcha got there?" shot another angry voice.

"It's a brat, that's what it is!"

"So?" she retorted, sparking something in the eyes before her.

"One more rich brat over quota, to take the food from our bellies, eh?"

"How much did you bribe the gyneys?"

The taunting grew, and her stance fell into high readiness. Closer they came, the voices growing louder and shriller. It was Riardan who angered them, his presence alone. For the first time, a special fear entered her. She may survive, but if she failed, he certainly would not.

They were within her perimeter now. In her hand suddenly appeared a blaster, firing out a warning shot. A singeing smell assaulted her nostrils and one man began to babble in shrieking discord. The onward surge halted in stunned dismay. For moments, there was an uneasy stillness.

"Hey, who you think you is? Some crazy police person? Know how to use that thing, you reckon?"

"Come any closer and you'll find out. I know how to use this one too." A second weapon appeared in her other hand.

The hostility lessened not a jot, but the forward creep of her assailants stopped in one simultaneous jolt. Angry eyes raked her, probing to see how much was bluff and how much expertise.

"Funny little plastic toy, that whatcha got there?"

"Come a step closer and you'll find out exactly what it can do. I swear that you will feel enough pain before the end to know all about it, too."

The coldness of her voice they clearly recognized. The voice of unfeeling authority; but she so clearly jarred with their usual order that she wasn't sure they believed her.

"Jake, you ever see anything like that?"

All eyes turned to one man—tall, with a jagged scar angling from the bridge of his nose down across the pocked cheek. She could see the dry, sallowness of his childhood poverty etched into his skin. From the expectancy hanging on his searching stare, he must be what passed for a weaponry expert round here. After a while, he turned to his fellows.

"Nope," was the single, gravelly reply.

"Think it's fake, you reckon?"

An exultant voice began to inch closer. Her fire swiftly drew a thin, burning line up one leg and across the edge of the speaker's abdomen. There was a shocked howl and he crumpled, clutching the glowing flesh in agony.

"That's the lowest setting. Care to see a higher capacity," she taunted.

"You been off-world trading," the one named Jake stated rather than asked. "It'll be faulty. The grey suits would have made sure of it."

"Not this one. They can't touch it, and I service-checked it myself only this morning. Believe me, it's in full working order, and I know exactly how to use it."

For the first time, she allowed a little of her natural accent into her speech. She saw the indolent confidence of the one they called Jake slip. Then, remembering his position, he shrugged defiantly and glared at her.

"Just who is you supposed to be then? No off-worlder would come snooping round here. Terran authorities ain't stupid enough to let the wierdies nose about on their own."

"They didn't have much say," she boasted back, "and I'm not occupying forces. My partner's Terran. I'm not," she added, the threat clearly audible. "You can also tell your friends who are trying to get the drop on me from up on that building that if they don't retreat, now, I have some nasty surprises waiting." She simultaneously felled two who had crept up under cover of the sidewalls, thinking uneasily how close they had managed to get before her sensors picked them up.

"You got some pretty good toys there."

"Don't even think about trying to get them. Even if you could take them, they are personalized to me only. There's no way you can fire them. Only my own people can tell you how to do that, and I don't think the Hathian authorities are about to help any Terrans, low-life or otherwise."

A rumble rose through the crowd.

"Hathian!"

"You're one of those?"

"Lady, get out. Now!" The last, angry command was from Jake, legs splayed and hands belligerently hooked into the belt of his overalls.

"Unless I mistake the matter, that's just what I'm about to do," she grinned back, in dawning recognition of mutual respect. As the crowd began to quickly scatter, a buzz of flyers dropped in a protective perimeter around her. Jake was the last to turn and, as he was about to go, she called out to him.

"Good luck, but don't think we'll be too easy to be rid of. Having just spent five years throwing your lot out, we're pretty set on not having you back, even if it means having to watch every one of you from now to doomsday. But have a go anyway."

Jake turned back angrily, then must have seen the irony of the situation. "That's just what we intend to do, lady."

As the first of the flyers hit the ground, he melted with the rest of his fellows into the maze of surrounding streets. Soon, a buzz of officialdom surrounded her. The very efficient-looking city police fanned out to establish a safe zone as her Terran hosts, watched frowningly by a cohort of Alliance troops, hustled her into a nearby flyer. She'd returned her weapons to their concealing pouches as soon as the crowd began to disperse, and the hand signal she threw the accompanying Hathian official ensured that the Terrans' bombastic questions were quickly silenced. It was unfortunate that she'd been forced to reveal her weapons, but it wasn't as if the Terrans would be able to use them if they'd managed to take them from her.

Still, as she climbed into the flyer, she threw a not unsympathetic glance towards where the Terran mob had been. A small part of her truly wished the man well.

After all, she knew exactly how he felt.

Within a very short time, sympathy for any Terran was wiped completely. Returning to Alliance Central, she walked straight into the midst of a diplomatic row with what she could only term the thwarted bureaucracy of this hidebound world. The little man now in front of her seemed to regard her as some lesser species of noxious pest, giving her looks at once anxious and filled with loathing while he was forced to listen to the Hathian head of the Alliance forces stationed on Earth.

"Madame an Castre is highly regarded by my government. To find that Terran stalling of her perfectly legitimate request for residence has led to her life being placed in needless jeopardy is something we view very seriously. Either Earth does or does not wish to be seen as cooperative by the Alliance; or could it be that our aid is no longer necessary?"

The bureaucrat stifled a glare, reminded by his stomach of what, precisely, this offworlder threatened.

"As you seem unable to act according to accepted protocol, Madame an Castre is henceforth to be considered an official member of the Alliance presence here, with all the resources that implies. Her movements are, therefore, of no concern to Terran officials. You will render her any assistance she may require. You will also be fully answerable to the Alliance for any harm that may befall her."

There was a gritty edge of anger in the Hathian's voice, and Marthe could almost see the ruffling of Terran pride. It was amusing, and satisfying to watch, but she couldn't feel it to be particularly wise. With a curt nod, the Terran official was dismissed. As soon as he'd left, Marthe turned to her fellow Hathian.

"I'm sorry to have put you in such an embarrassing position, Representative an Truro."

"Not at all." But his words were belied by his suddenly somber tone. "It seems, though, that the time for softly, softly is fading fast. I must admit that I've been looking forward to giving that particular, little worm a shove into place since I first landed." He paused then, turning to face her squarely. "What I would really like to know is, who is pulling his strings. Your treatment so far has been too deliberately boorish and provocative to be mere bureaucratic pen pushing."

Marthe frowned. "You think they were hoping for just such an incident?"

"Uh-huh. Though I doubt they wished for such a peaceful outcome. We may have beaten them today, but I think you better keep your wits about you in future."

"It wasn't a total failure on their part," admitted Marthe. "I was forced to reveal that Alliance personnel carry weaponry unknown on Earth—stuff they would like very much to own."

"Are you carrying anything with a high security listing?"

"No, and what I do have is personal-coded. They can't touch any of it. Which doesn't mean I would be happy if Terran forces, legit or otherwise, got hold of them."

"Then you'd better be careful, hadn't you?" An Truro fell silent a minute, looking slightly uncomfortable for the first time. He leaned back in his seat and eyes her squarely. "And Radcliff? What about him?"

Marthe refused to show how the words affected her. It helped that she was still buoyed by the triumph over Terran malice. "You mean, is he for or against us, and would he like to get hold of such weapons?" An Truro nodded. "For the first, I don't know. As for the second," she grinned, "you can pretty well guarantee it."

"So why are you taking them in with you?"

"Because there is no way I am letting go of just one device that might mean the difference between saving Riardan or losing him."

She meant it and an Truro got the message, wisely refraining from further argument. "Good luck then, and the stars speed your voyage."

He smiled politely as he rose then paused halfway up. Slowly, he straightened to his full height. Almost with a hint of an apology.

"No," cut in Marthe sharply. There was a persistent look on an Truro's face. "No," cried Marthe even louder, standing up so suddenly that her chair crashed to the floor as she took a defensive step back.

"But he might be—"

"I don't care," she broke in angrily. "For all I know, Hamon could be the leader of whole armies of resistance troops. I will not spy on him!"

"And if he is, and succeeds? He could threaten Hathe again," continued an Truro doggedly. She stepped back again, desperate to avoid this.

"Haven't I done enough for Hathe? It's time for someone else." She stopped, then cried out as if the words were wrung from her. "There's not enough of me left."

It was too much. Tears starting in her eyes, she pushed past her tormentor and ran from the room, crashing her hand on the palm plate so hard it left a red, stinging tingle.

An Truro watched her go, a hard grimace on his lips.

"I'm sorry, so sorry, my lady, but there is no one else. And you will do your duty. You can't escape it, ever," he finished softly, staring long at the door, before turning to complete his perusal of the file begun before this meeting interrupted him. His lips twitched, reading the two names on the heading. An Radcliff and an Castre. She was right; so much had been asked of her. But there was more there yet.

Marthe cleared the building, remembered her changed status, turned and strode back in, all in a haze of tears and desperate anger. Brusquely, she coded for her new quarters, ordered her luggage transferred and headed for the lift, striding so fast that she woke Riardan and he let out an angry squawk. She'd been forced to take him with her to that foul interview, too fearful of his safety to leave him for even a few seconds. Torn by inner storms, she hurried down the maze of corridors to the rooms assigned her, frantically avoiding any eye contact that might stop her. After an age of need, she finally palmed a door that answered her summons and stumbled into the offered sanctuary.

It was marginally less stark than her previous quarters. The colors of this room had been chosen with an aim to please. It was irrelevant. She threw herself into a cube and hurriedly brought Riardan around, latching him onto the nourishment he sought. She so needed the comfort of his contented suckling.

"Hamon, where are you," she sighed softly. "Oh, little one. Where is your father now? Stars, but we need him."

Some time later, the baby replete and dozing in her lap with only the odd smacking of lips, she gazed thoughtfully into space. *How to do it*, was her constant thought. How to rejoin Hamon without destroying what they had with all the complications that still lay between them—all the enmity and brutality of the past. They so needed a chance to see whether what they had was true, not some figment of wistfulness or fragment of guilt left over from the war. Did she truly believe that was all it was? No, but did he? Or maybe it was only that she wanted one last time together, before either his loyalties or hers parted them forever.

Certainly there must be no others present when they met. No Terran bureaucrats, watching suspiciously to see whether he showed too much pleasure at the sight of her and, just as certainly, none of her own, marking her with the indelible stain of 'spy' from which she had just fled so precipitously.

Gently, her fingers disengaged the baby, mopping the little driblet of milk clinging to the outer corner of the pursed-up mouth and reaching up to trace the hint of eyebrows, so like the line of his father's. Then she remembered. They were like his grandmother's too. An ironic smile hovered on her lips and she put up a hand to smooth her hair. Then she turned to the vidphone.

Two hours later, her preparations were complete. Riardan was wrapped close in his cot and she was dressed once more in the manner of her homeland, a light upper tunic thrown over close-fitting trousers. It was not outlandishly different from Terran styles, but enough to clearly mark her origin. There was only so much she would concede to this woman, the love they both bore her son their only bond. So far.

The raised eyebrow of her visitor at the sight of her dress said the message was received, but Marthe chose not to comment, confining herself to a polite greeting. "Madame MacDiarmid. Thank you for coming. I am sure you have much to otherwise occupy you." Despite herself, Marthe couldn't banish her stilted reserve.

"Not as much as I used to," replied Madame MacDiarmid, her own reserve diplomatically set aside. "And certainly nothing as important as my first grandchild. I suppose, like most young men, he's asleep just when he's needed?"

Marthe smiled in return, grateful for the offered token. "Over here in his cot. He's due to wake soon, so don't worry about disturbing him."

"I wouldn't dream of doing any such thing. Not if he's like his father. That boy would never go to sleep!"

She stepped softly over, then gave a quick gasp and stared hungrily at the sleeping baby. To her amazement, Marthe caught a glimpse of a tear at the corner of the older woman's eye, and the smile the Administrator turned on her was lop-sided.

"He is … so like his father. Thank you, my dear." One of the older woman's hands reached carefully out to lightly run her fingertips over the little bundle. "Hamon used to hold his hands just like that when he was sleeping. It was the only time he was still," she added as the ghost of old memories washed over her face. Of a sudden, a slight shrug shook her frame, and she moved to seat herself with deliberation in the only other cube in the small room. She quietly crossed her hands in her lap then looked up, a hint of amusement in her eyes.

"Now, my dear, perhaps you would care to explain exactly what it is you wish me to do for you?" She ignored Marthe's assumed air of surprise. "You've been here for some days already, and now you decide to call me before you contact Hamon. Why?"

"So you knew I'd arrived?"

"I'm not totally devoid of contacts—who all warned me rather strenuously against informing Hamon of it, I might add. Still, I'm surprised that he hasn't discovered your presence himself."

"His surveillance methods are as good as ever?" Marthe broke into a real smile then was stopped by the stiffening of her guest. "That wasn't prying, in case you're wondering. This is pure family."

"You expect me to believe that you have no professional interest in what my son may or may not be doing?"

"No, of course I don't. Hamon openly admitted he was undecided as to what he intended on his return. He equally knows that I am fully committed to ensuring that never again does Hathe suffer a repeat of the last five years; but I didn't ask you here to play politics." She paused, unable to see a way forwards. "I need to see Hamon, but I don't want him to be expecting me. To do that, I need your help. I can't get past whatever security systems he has, but I think you can."

"Again, I ask why." Distrust spoke in every line of Madame MacDiarmid's body.

"I'm not planning to harm him," promised Marthe, a hint of weariness entering her voice. "This is solely for Riardan and me. I need us to be a family, and I need to find out if that's what Hamon wants too. I can't do that if he's forewarned and watched, by his side or mine. He can hide what he really feels better than anyone I know. I need to see him on his own, just the two of us. To find out if there's a chance for us, that's all I ask."

Hamon's mother stared uncompromisingly back.

"Please," begged Marthe, a desperate anxiety treading the lines of her forehead. "I do love him. I need him so very, very badly." But she saw only defeat. She stood up and turned towards the cot. Tired beyond memory, she stared down at her son's face then, hearing no reply, turned back.

"Thank you for coming," she said in a flat voice, before moving over to palm the door. The older woman stood but made no further move.

"I will help you, girl. If only so that I may have the pleasure of being able to watch a baby grow without endlessly worrying about the drain on resources," she said, speaking carefully; "but may your divinity help you if you betray me or mine."

Which was how Marthe came to be standing on a strange hillside, in the midst of a wilderness such as she'd never dreamed possible on Earth, peering down the path leading to the house. Madame MacDiarmid had brought them here in her own vehicle. The only way, she claimed, to ensure that Hamon would be unaware of her arrival. Some distance out, she'd locked into his security system, overriding the warning signal. Hamon was down there and, as yet, did not know Marthe was near.

"You'll have to walk from here," said his mother. "It's the only unguarded route in. There's a small hut up here he often visits, so this track is covered by the house security. I've blocked that and the only other way to get to this peak is by flyer. You have the advantage of surprise you asked for. Your path lies ahead of you."

The older woman had paused then, all her distrust showing on her face. She had seemed to be about to add something further, but had instead turned, her mouth suddenly snapped shut, and entered her flyer. A whoosh of air and it was gone. They were alone, Riardan and she. At last.

Indecision hit, wrapping her in a fog. She could go back, to safety and to her beloved Hathe. Then she glanced down at the baby staring quizzically back. His little eyes scanned her face, drinking in the safe haven of her presence. A grin tugged at her mouth as she stared back. No, she couldn't leave now.

She looked down the track.

It was a long, low house, melded into the slope of the hill. From this angle, it was barely visible—a dark smudge on the slope as the eye was drawn past to the world beyond. From the front, there would be a stunning panorama.

Surrounding the house, enclosing and protecting it, were trees—trees of every size, shape and shade of green. Large ones in the distance and small, friendly neighbors close in, bearing fruits or the last, lingering blossoms of spring. The music of birds rose on all sides, ceasing as she walked forward, buzzing into life again once she'd passed.

Reluctant now, she forced herself to continue. She'd made this choice so easily at first, knowing no other course was possible … but that had been on her home ground. Here, it was different. So beautiful, but so strange. The wildness she recognized—the sense of space and freedom and the oneness with the world of the house merging into its majestic surroundings—but the nature of that world was unfamiliar, the trees unknown and the songs of the wildlife strange. She had seen odd, chaotic hints of this on her journey—the parks hiding among buildings and the brazen greenery infesting the city, but nothing like the beauty that now assaulted her, increasing with each step she trod so deliberately down this roadway. Even the path was a revelation, the scrunching of the gravel an anachronism in this world of industrial overuse. She had heard rumors of places such as this—glorious remnants of what had been, what might have been—but to have to enter and become a part of one was more intimidating than she could have dreamed possible.

The house was now in front of her. She stopped, hesitant. Even this close, the house still felt closed to her. This wasn't a part used by the inhabitants. To one side, she saw a landing pad and a broad path winding down to it. It was an entrance only, then, with a sense of more beyond—a corridor to the private world at the front.

She gave herself a quick shake, her chin jutting defiantly upwards. Then she marched those last, few paces forward and rammed her finger against the old-fashioned door chime, squaring her shoulders in preparation. Riardan stared up at her in surprise, his eyes blinking and the little mouth a wide exclamation as he clutched onto the comfort of his sling.

She waited, bearing up at first, but gradually realized there would be no opening door. Anger dawned, all her fears, her anxieties, still to be unsatisfied. Impatient now, she repeatedly jabbed at the bell, rapping a sharp staccato on the door for good measure, then stepped back to await developments.

Nothing. The door remained resolutely shut. Frustrated, she began to pace. Backwards and forwards, her hand viciously shredding the leaves of a nearby shrub. A bird flew briskly off, screeching his dislike. At her feet, a small animal rushed forward, barking. 'Dog', said her memory, as it braked in front of her, then quickly scurried down a side path. Her shredding stopped and the pacing came to an abrupt halt. She considered the path, the barking, the small dog scurrying.

"What do you say?" she whispered to her staring son. He smiled in relief at the pleased mischief in his mother's voice. Her feet turned and followed the small path. Down it crept, hugging the side of the building and following every hollow, every contour of the land. She rounded a corner to be stunned into a sudden standstill.

The front did have a panoramic view. Valley upon valley, folding away into vastness. Green rolled over the dips and gullies, lightest lime to darkly menacing giants. A river plunged and gurgled far below. Here and there, the bare earth erupted forth in mighty outcroppings of rock or in the jagged splash of a slip gouging a raw path through the trees. Patches of grass, irregular-shaped splodges, marked intermittent clearings. The sun shone strongly here, but far over in the distance, clouds formed mottled shadows racing across the land.

When Freya MacDiarmid had first landed her craft, Marthe had gained an impression of great height. Now she saw it confirmed. This was a peak, the highest point to be seen as the world fell away in front of her. Slowly, in stunned awe, she dragged her eyes from the view and back to the house.

Immediately in front of her, steps rose to the deck that must run along the entire front of this secretive house. It was designed for one thing only, a place from which to gaze out at this powerful vista. She stood stock still, drinking in the view. How long she stood, she knew not but, gradually, a sense of some other one entered her consciousness. Still she stared ahead, now fully aware then, slowly, she turned to look.

It stretched long and wide, the balcony. There were chairs, and pots of shrubs and flowers. A pergola reached out its protective arms from the house. There, at the farthest end, was a figure—a figure she knew almost as well as her own and had travelled over half of settled space to find. He stood, more still even than she, waiting. He had heard her assault on his door, then.

At first, it seemed neither would move. Then she started forward, slowly at first, placing just one foot in front of the other. Then quicker. And now, fear at last was routed and she hurried forward.

He remained as still as before. She approached and slowed till only paces away. Now the arms stretched wide and the precious smile she had missed so badly cracked into being ... but not before she glimpsed the memory of the fear in her own heart echoed in his face. Then, the remaining gap was closed, and the wonderful smell and feel of him engulfed her once more. His hands closed, one fist clenching the waves of her hair, while the other encompassed the head of his son in protective tenderness. His head closed over hers and, for a time, the loneliness vanished.

CHAPTER THIRTY-TWO

An indignant squawk from her son drew Marthe's head up from the sleeper. She chuckled. That particular cry was very familiar. For a moment, she watched his angry legs digging into the soft bedding of his temporary nest, then gave in and rolled over to lift him up.

Hamon propped himself on his elbow, watching her settle the child between them on the breast. A quiet smile on his face, he drew one finger lightly across the soft mound and down to the greedily suckling mouth. The baby scowled fiercely at the intrusion, then set to feeding even more voraciously.

"A mite noisy, isn't he?" He laughed. Then a somberness coated his face. "I thought never to see this again," he said, looking up fully into her eyes. "You took such a long time to come, I assumed… It seemed that you wouldn't come at all."

"No, never that," she promised, "but I had to say goodbye."

"It can't have been easy."

"No."

He knew it was all the answer she would ever give him, and his gaze lifted over her and out to the valleys of his boyhood. He tried to picture saying goodbye to them, and soon gave up. One hand clenched tight to hers, and he continued in a lightly teasing voice that seemed safer.

"You kept your arrival quiet. I've had the watchdogs out for weeks, but you must have come from the port to here before they could let me know."

No answering smile came to her face. "I've been here some days. Your surveillance is good but can't match the fear of losing Allied help. A few chosen words in the right place kept the officials silent."

His hand abruptly left hers and he sat up, withdrawing brusquely. "And you didn't contact me till now? Come to that, how did you get past my perimeter defenses? Or are you still working?" he asked bitterly.

Marthe sat up as abruptly at that, before the enraged shriek of her son forced her to settle back down. Being forced to look up at the closed face of her husband did nothing for her confidence.

"Your mother got me in. She knew why I wanted to come unheralded and agreed to help. Or maybe you think she's switched sides too?"

His face was still closed, but he was listening.

"I couldn't come sooner nor contact you. If I had, I would have been forced to arrive surrounded by Alliance bureaucrats watching me, and Terran bureaucrats watching you. Is that what you want? The conquering Hathian strolling in here, while you hide everything you feel for fear of what your people might think?"

She ducked her head. "I need to know what we really are. Or were you just working, too, back there on Hathe?"

His angry, "Don't be a fool," did nothing to reassure her. "Do you really believe me capable of that? I may have done a lot on Hathe I can never take pride in but deceiving you in this wasn't one of them."

His fist clenched again, but he eased down beside her, staring intently at her. Could it be a test, he wondered. After a while, the tension in her seeped into him and he sought her hand again.

"I have loved you almost from the first moment I saw you, all those years ago on Hathe; and, through those crazy months of your captivity, I grew to love you more and more. You are the other half of me, the only one who has ever known me, as I know you. We are a family, we three, and we will make a life together." He kissed her, long and slow, an affirmation and a promise. He drew away, the crooked grin on his face matching the one that eased the stiffness of hers, "Just don't ask me how, not yet." Then he added, in the foreboding cadences of an oath, "We will not be parted, whatever may come; but I cannot sacrifice the things that make me the man you fell in love with. I will not betray my world. It is the lifeblood of me."

"As Hathe, present or absent, is for me. I will not let you bring such destruction on us ever again."

His nod mirrored hers as he reached to pull her close to him, where she belonged. His mouth twitched again, in a rueful grin. "All I can say is, the next few years should prove very interesting."

She could feel his gaze over her head and beyond. "One day at a time," she murmured. She felt the tension leave then as he moved to look down at her. The self-mocking grin was in place again.

"Do we have any other choice," he said, amusement lighting his eyes. "You never know, you might just get to like Earth, and don't answer that," he added hurriedly, in response to the clench of negation she couldn't prevent. "Only, let me show you *my* Earth.

She looked long at him then nodded, A little only and very slowly, yet still a pledge.

And so, over the next days and weeks, he led her into his world. Small trips at first, to the woods and forest surrounding this isolated house. The trees were familiar to her from childhood stories yet also utterly strange. She was brought up with the lifeforms of Hathe. The large plants of her home world might possess the same sense of solidness as these trees, but the rustling of leaves as the wind played symphonies over her head, their ever-changing forms in sun or heavy rain or stark and ghostly in the evening light, were a revelation. Hathian trees did show a misleading similarity, but their so-called leaves were not like these of Earth, each independent and moving, yet part of the whole. Hathian leaves were but branch extensions, each turning in response to the tree's needs, not wildly dancing with any light air that chose to stray within the canopy.

The colors, too, were a surprising delight. Green in all its myriad shades, far more than she could ever have imagined. There were hints of the blue, yellow and browns of her home world, but always caught in a green kaleidoscope. They had strong, glossy blue-greens at home, but not the silver whisper of light on this tree, nor the mottled stripes of that. They walked past trees densely shrouded in dark foliage, through glades where the sun splashed and trickled through sparse branches and leaves, and onwards to a sharp tang and the spice of conifers, their scent vibrating through the moisture dripping on the sharp needles and leaving her hair damp and coated with the life of their fragrance.

Farther still he took her. To high mountain tops where small, hardy plants clung grimly to sunbaked gravel slides only to be plunged into glacial cold by night. Down again, to wide grasslands with hints of the golden plains of Hathe but for the alien species heavy with nodding seed heads, while above, small feather-covered birds hovered and flew. Their movements lacked the wild zings of her native flitters, more akin as they were to the ancient airborne reptiles seen in

Hamon's library. Terran flying animals hovered, soared, fluttered; but they did not zip.

Hamon had been right. There were parts of his Earth that were very, very beautiful. Something deep within her even recognized a sense of homecoming … but only a small part. The rest yearned for her own land, the strangeness of this world forever clanging against the protective shell she'd erected around her. And always, wherever they went, she took Riardan with her. She'd seen the looks on those Terran faces. Always, fear for her child walked with her.

As did confusion at the paradoxes of this world. Hamon also showed her the Earth of her expectations: the desolated fields of over-polluted, farmed-out wastes; the vast, echoing chambers of underground cities, long abandoned in favor of the haphazard towers above ground. The demands of the services necessary to subterranean life—lighting, heat and ventilation—had been too much for an energy-depleted world. She saw, too, the hunger and deprivation etched into the faces of so many Terrans, felt the essential sterility in them. Yet she now lived in a home engulfed in rich and vibrant life. Early on, she tackled Hamon.

"Why?" she demanded. "All this untouched beauty, yet you let people starve?"

"The beauty is a safeguard, too," he said. "Your world is too young to have to worry, your population too small. We long ago realized we were reaching a critical loss of biomass. We know, to the last kilogram, the exact amount of flora and fauna needed to maintain the balance of the atmosphere." He caught her puzzled look. "Clean air, with sufficient oxygen content; clear, drinkable water; and a planetary temperature range within which we can survive. The absolute basics of life," he reiterated in grim irony. "So now we regulate. Our biomass is never allowed to fall below a given minimum. We keep to the limits by setting aside areas under appointed guardians. My family has had the responsibility for this bioreserve for hundreds of years. In the cities, too, we cultivate every available space.

"Hence the greenery on all the buildings, that beautiful park?"

"Yes, there so that we can have air to breathe. The penalty for destruction of such gardens is decidedly draconian, so the population treats them with care and leaves well enough alone."

"Yet they don't see the beauty." It was a statement, Marthe's voice tinged with sadness.

"No, not many," he agreed, rising from the rock on which they sat, to stand and stare across the glacier lake they were visiting this day. She saw his gaze travel over the wind-carved wavelets stirred up by the passing breeze, ignoring the heady challenge of the shining turquoise water to the storm-threatening clouds above.

She let him stand alone. He was busy with thoughts that, even yet, he couldn't share with her, maybe never would if they concerned his care of Earth. Quietly she watched him, saw the tension in the straight back, stared as the evening breeze grabbed at the stray locks curling into his nape. Lost in contemplation of broad shoulders rising to a sturdy neck and fine head, she almost didn't hear him when he turned and said lightly.

"Some old friends are calling in tomorrow night. Is that okay with you?"

His tone might be casual, but his eyes said that he knew what he was asking. Caught unawares, Marthe bent her head in retreat. She'd known the day must come when their isolation ended. Was she ready for it, he was asking. Probably not. Would she ever be ready? Probably not, jeered the monologue in her head. Her hands fisted on the rock as she looked up.

"That's fine," she said to him in quiet promise.

Swiftly, he came and crouched before her. "It may not be so bad," he said in a whisper. "And they are only friends."

"Do they know about me?"

"Only that you're Hathian. The allies controlled outside news almost completely. Nothing of your trial got through, and you've never met any of them. None were on Hathe, ever."

His voice changed, heavy with desperation. "If we're to make any kind of life here, you have to meet people sometime."

She could only nod in grim reply. He was right. He had already absented himself a number of times over the past weeks. Some occasions were social, some, she knew, to do with his own affairs; but she'd always known that this moment must come, that their private world must once more embrace the everyday one. She heartily wished it otherwise.

She swallowed. "Old friends, you say. How old?"

She'd pinned a small smile to her face. He kissed her once, tenderly, then retreated to the polite inanity she needed. "Very old, I've known them since earliest childhood." He sat down beside her and pulled her gently into his shoulder. "There'll be about ten or so—those readily available of a group who used to knock around together in my school days. Some I've known since we were dragged along to the same crèches as babies." He smiled, a teasing self-mockery. "Don't worry, if the presence of Terrans en masse becomes too much, you can always plead the boredom of listening to too many old reminiscences and slip away."

"Thank you," she said dryly, "I'll try to endure it, but that kind of thing can be rather heavy going."

She had smiled in jest at the time, but on the next evening, her smile was stretched to its diplomatic limits. The first shock of walking into a room full of her enemies was bad enough. Automatically, she checked the exits and reached for her ear patch, until she caught Hamon's eye on her and blushed in confusion. At least it gave an impression of shyness to their guests, causing them to refrain from crowding her with conversation and allowing her to sit on the sidelines most of the evening. Fortunately, they really did appear ignorant of most of what had happened on Hathe and unaware of her connections with the current Alliance governors of Earth.

And they did chatter over silly childhood memories, alien yet utterly fascinating to her. For the first time, she saw Hamon in the whole, with friends, family and a background. It was a precious revelation. She could almost have liked these friends of his. Until a careless 'Where's Ferdo tonight?' brought a bland reply from Hamon and the gates crashing down inside Marthe. Soon after, she excused herself, shamelessly plying Riardan with an unexpected late feed to cover her early retirement.

There were other such evenings, initially much like the first—friends only, who knew little of her past and who she could come to accept at her own pace, a few even with whom she could feel a sense of ease. Slowly, she grew able to walk into a room full of Terrans without automatically tensing. Increasing her surveillance of Riardan and the house helped. Hamon knew of it, was aware of the sophisticated nature of the Hathian technology she employed, but had so far refrained from commenting. It hadn't taken him long to realize the significance of her new habit of rubbing the back of her neck, but he only teased her lightly. He understood how hard was the road she walked, and she had a feeling he was grateful for the security her additions afforded them, as grateful as she for the double protection from Hamon's monitors, constantly guarding the estate and everything in it, including Riardan and herself.

His vigilance wasn't broken by his increasingly frequent absences either. He knew too many of Riardan's growing adventures to have not been recording while away. She tasked him with it, letting him know by her laugh that she knew of and accepted his care. Her own surveillance didn't follow him, though she was certain his trips were concerned with whatever direction he'd chosen to follow on his return. She'd told an Truro she wouldn't spy on Hamon, nor would she, but, equally, she could not allow him to harm Hathe again so, reluctantly, she advised the allies of his departures. After the first few times, she chose to openly signal Alliance HQ. He watched, amusement chief in his face.

"Is that a challenge, or have you really never let your people know my movements before?"

"Of course I have," she replied gruffly. "It just didn't feel right to keep it from you."

"Well, thank you for that at least." He smiled, moving over to gently hold her. "You think that I haven't taken your surveillance of my activities into account?"

"I don't follow you once you leave the estate. The Alliance can manage that for themselves, but I did tell you I wouldn't let you harm Hathe again. Anything else you choose to do is your own business— as long as you don't ask me to help you." She looked up at him, glaring and beseeching at once.

"You assume, then, that I don't favor allied control?" he asked in surprise.

"It seems unlikely … not with the way you feel about Hathe. I can't imagine you enjoy foreign control of your home."

"I don't. Particularly by some of the more ignorant members of the Alliance—the ones who think they know the answers to all our problems; but that doesn't mean I favor resistance either."

"So you haven't made up your mind?"

"No." He smiled at the relief she couldn't hide from him "Don't be too pleased. Maybe I just haven't found the right resistance movement yet." Then the smile was gone. "Whatever I decide, you two will be safe."

"And together with you?" she couldn't help asking.

He caught her closer at that, so tightly enfolded that she couldn't see his face, could only hear the word, "Together", not his silently mouthed, 'the stars willing', that followed.

His body was a blessed refuge, and she drank fully of it, taking comfort in the smell and warmth of him, and it was only as he was about to leave that the sense of his words penetrated. "What do you mean, the right resistance movement?"

"Why, my dearest enemy, only that there are as many movements as there are people opposed to Alliance control." The special smile he gave her took any sting from his words.

Soon, too, he let her see the truth of it. Bit by bit, the gatherings changed to include those who were of use to Hamon politically as well as socially. He hadn't announced it, yet the careful tenor of any conversation within her hearing made it all too obvious. Next, he began to invite her to join him on his visits.

Her first impulse was to refuse—both from a fear of leaving Riardan unguarded and from a deep-seated reluctance to embroil herself again in the world of intrigue. The social visitors she could manage, viewing them as a part of the building process her small family must go through. For that to succeed, she was ready to endure much.

Earth had given her one very special gift: a time at last for the three of them. Safe and secure in their wilderness home and free of the sense of doom that had always accompanied them on Hathe, she and Hamon could talk openly for the first time. Talk and laugh and love and slowly, little by little, a family was growing.

Now he was asking her to go back, to let in the doom again.

It was late one night that he first chose to introduce the idea to her. It had been a special evening. Riardan had crawled right across the room before pulling himself hand over hand to a shaky stand. His two little fists were clutched rigidly to a cube, but the sturdy legs were undeniably upright and supporting him for the first time. He'd looked across to his parents with such a look of triumph that Marthe had felt her whole chest swelling with delight. Beside her, Hamon chuckled.

"That young man is going to turn out as bloody-minded as both of us combined."

Then, later, flushed with this latest sign of their success as parents, not to mention having succeeded in actually getting their small tyrant to bed and asleep at a reasonable hour, Hamon had taken the chance to show her just how beautiful, desirable and precious he still found her to be.

Now, Marthe lay replete, head turned into his broad shoulder, her leg still in possession of his lower body. Hamon's arm held her to him, the fingers of one hand gently whispering his contentment on her skin. Their movement paused as he reached down to slowly place a kiss on her turned-up forehead, then the slow strokes began again. Only this time, they held a hint of tension. She looked up enquiringly.

"You do know how much I love you?" he asked softly. She nodded her reply and reached up with her lips in promise. He took them, suddenly releasing his passion again as his lips and hands possessed her in what could almost be desperation.

Drawing back moments later, he moved to prop himself on one elbow and look seriously down at her. Nonplussed, she suddenly felt the languor of their loving vanish in a rush. She, too, sat up, drawing the cover about her as if it were a shield.

"There is a dinner tomorrow at one of my brothers'. I will have to attend," he began. "I was hoping you would come with me."

"Why," she asked baldly.

"Mostly, because I want you to."

She knew that wasn't all of it and waited for the rest, hating the cynicism that welled up inside her and the recognition of it on his face.

"Oh, hell. That was actually true. Can't you trust me even yet?"

She shook her head in distress. "You did say mostly."

He looked away for a moment—shifting, uncomfortable—then sat even straighter. "There will be some people there I want to meet. All of my family are political animals, and they attract a fairly diverse range of the groups I told you about."

"That would seem a reason not to include me."

"No," he almost shouted. Then quieter, "No. I will not repeat our situation on Hathe. I want you to know if I'm planning something. Maybe not exactly what, but I will not live that double life again."

"Yet you know I will not let you harm Hathe. What if you decide to take a course opposed to me?"

"I don't know. Can't we face that when and if it occurs? By the stars, if the truth be known I couldn't hide such a thing from you anyway. Even on Hathe, we both always knew something of what the other was about, if not the details. You think that's changed? No. Only by parting could I keep such knowledge from you, and that I cannot do," he added in a whisper.

Her arm came swiftly across to his outstretched hand.

"No, never again."

He was silent for a time then began again. "I want you to meet the factions. Whatever I decide must affect you, so I need your assessment of the various parties."

"What? Help you to decide which group will most effectively rid you of the allies? No! It's too soon to even begin to ask such a thing.

Her hand was suddenly clamped, halting her urge to retract.

"So you mean to condemn Earth to an eternity of servitude?"

"How dare you say such a thing! You, who almost succeeded in doing exactly that to my home!"

He let go of her hand then, drawing his own raggedly through his hair. "I apologize. That was out of line."

"It was." She grimaced, her sudden anger cooling. "Hamon, even the thought of an Earth free of Alliance control fills me with dread. You say you don't want to repeat the situation on Hathe. Well, I cannot. I just cannot go through those five years again and I tell you, I will do almost anything to prevent it." For an instant, she let him see the full cost to her of those years. "I will not help your cause, not if it is in any way opposed to mine, and I don't understand how you can ask such a thing."

"Because I don't know any other way to make us work. Should I divide my life into segments, let you share only the acceptable pieces? Such a lie is doomed to failure. What I said first is still true. I want you to be with me … even though, I might add, it will cost me too. After all, I am literally handing you entry to the inner world of Earth's dissidents. The allies could never hope to penetrate it otherwise."

"Thank you for permission to spy on you," she snapped. "What a pity I already told an Truro I wouldn't do so."

Hamon really looked at her now, seeing the anger, and the fear hiding beneath it. He could guess the cause too well. "Oh my love," he whispered, pulling her into his arms. "Can you not come? We have to make a life here. Your world is closed to us, and I cannot give you only half of me. Just come. No promises, no demands, just see what you make of it."

"But there's Riardan," she began. "How can I keep him safe?"

"My mother will jump at the chance to babysit, and for all I care, you can flood the place with allied militia. There's nothing for them to find. Please?"

There was only one possible answer—and, if nothing else, supposed Marthe, it was a chance to meet his family. Those three half-brothers and one half-sister she and Jacquel had been so scathing about.

As Hamon had warned, she found that they were all political animals but of widely diverse views, arguing now in tangents, then glancing hesitantly at her, before forgetting themselves and setting to again. She could almost believe herself back in evenings on Hathe. The language of politics seemed universal.

Yet the brothers surprised her. In none of the three did she find the passion of the leader that marked Hamon so ruthlessly. Only in his sister did she see it, his father's second-union child. Though not similar to Hamon in appearance, she had the same ability to command attention as soon as she entered a room. Her eyes, the only feature she shared with her brother, snapped briskly with her current emotion.

Bitterness was there too, deeper even than it went in Hamon. Caitlin had aligned herself with their father. Ex-Ambassador Radcliff had so far declined to meet Marthe but, from his daughter's attitude, Marthe felt both a profound reluctance towards making his acquaintance and a professional conviction that he was a man in urgent need of examination by the Alliance authorities. There was a limit, she was finding, to how far she could distance herself from political realities. She would not harm Hamon, nor could she stay neutral and let harm come to her home again.

"You have an interesting family," she remarked to Hamon some days later. They were seated on the balcony, gazing at the breathtaking view and leisurely sipping a cooling drink.

"I suppose you could say that," he agreed, glancing in amusement at the most blatant fishing she'd ever used.

"Your sister. She seems fond of your father."

"Mm hmm. "

"Yet you never mention him."

"No. We couldn't be called close, if that's what you're asking."

Marthe chose to ignore the wide grin plastered on his face and kept her gaze fixed on the trees of a far ridge. "Yet, though your sister is very like you, she is close to him."

"He doesn't threaten her as he does me. We're too much the same, my mother says and, frankly, the thought of turning into another Garth Radcliff fills me with horror."

"Is he so much worse than the dreaded Major Radcliff then?"

Hamon laughed, accepting her point. "His reputation certainly isn't." He chuckled again and then sobered. "He has no sense of compassion, though—is constantly driven by the goal and isn't too discriminating over the means he uses to get there. I may act in a fashion similar to his, but at least I have the grace to feel guilty."

"That must be comforting to those poor unfortunates on the receiving end."

She softened the words with a peal of laughter, and Hamon's return look recognized the irony. Nor did he argue, merely contenting himself with a reminder to her that the Ambassador had sired him, and he wasn't about to betray his own father, whatever he thought of his views.

Which left Marthe precisely where she had started, still unable to decide exactly what Hamon's plans were. She continued to chat idly of his family, but with half a mind only. The other half kept returning to the only lead she had: his sister. And her plans.

Caitlin supported her father. Might she not also wish for her brother's support? In which case, maybe she would accept the help of a concerned sister- in-law. After all, having never been on Hathe, how could Caitlin know that Marthe was the last person to foster Terran independence?

She continued to mull over the problem for some days, wondering how best to approach the woman. It was with some surprise, therefore, that she found herself being hailed on the vidcom one morning by the very object of her plotting. Hamon had left earlier for a meeting he would not discuss with her, so it happened that she was alone. Nothing could be better.

"Marthe? Hello, Caitlin Radcliff here," said the remembered voice. "I happened to be in the neighborhood today and thought I would pop in. To get to know you better and welcome you to the family, so to speak. Do you think you could turn off some of this dratted security my brother surrounds himself with and let me in?"

"Certainly," Marthe replied. "It's nice of you to call," she added, switching off the perimeter defenses—at least, those that impeded entry. She failed to mention that she was even more paranoid than Hamon, and that a large number of Hathian devices still dogged Caitlin's every step as she landed and made her way along the wide path from the landing pad.

Caitlin probably guessed anyway. Marthe could see the assessing look in her eyes. They were like Hamon's, taking on the same, metallic gleam as his under stress. Marthe noted it, but chose to ignore it, restricting herself to a discreetly courteous reply to the woman's greeting.

Just as discreetly, she switched her patch to full surveillance even as she waved her visitor out to the balcony.

For an instant, there was relaxation in Caitlin's back and she breathed deeply the fragrance of the woods.

"My grandmother always loved to sit out here," she said softly, leaning over the rail then turning back to smile at Marthe. "It's ages since I was here. I'd forgotten how beautiful it is. This really is the best homestead on the reserve."

"There are others?" exclaimed Marthe in surprise.

"Yes. This was my grandparents' home, but Father has a place a hundred or so kilometers that way. That's where I grew up and, after my parents split, I still came here to visit whenever I was at Father's. As for Hamon," a slight tightening of Caitlin's mouth, one Marthe doubted the woman was aware of, "he seemed to spend half his childhood here. Father separated from his mother when he was quite young, so Hamon never really lived on the reserve as such, but he spent a lot of time with the grandparents. He's first-born of all Father's brood, you see. That counts for a lot on Earth."

There was that hint of bitterness again.

"Is that why he has the guardianship of the reserve now, instead of his father?"

"Partially. He was very close to Gramps, and Grandma too—but enough of old family history. How are you settling in?"

Marthe was very familiar with the mask that suddenly slid into place. It was eerily like her brother's, but even harder to penetrate.

"Fine," she replied noncommittally, gesturing to a nearby chair and feeling somewhat easier when the other woman was seated. There was an air of taut readiness about the Terran woman she found unnerving and, seated, she could look her in the face.

Caitlin Radcliff was tall—almost as tall as her brother; but that, his eyes, and a sudden trick of expression were all they really shared in appearance. Her hair was not Hamon's rich earthy brown, but rather a dark blonde, chased with the lights of the sun and smudged through with a hint of earth and fire. A squarely bobbed cut kept the incipient unruliness under control. It also served to highlight the strength in the angular face, the bones uncompromisingly delineating the wide brow and firm jaw; and when she moved, it was with the barely coiled grace of a natural athlete. Even now, at ease, her long legs jutted forward, and it was as if her body accepted the chair as but a convenient accessory. She had sat in one, easy movement and appeared to need no further twitches to discover the best accommodation with its foreign angularity.

They were undoubtedly quite comfortable chairs, but Marthe, used to the self-adjusting cubes of Hathe, generally had to spend a few minutes exploring the old-fashioned construction of wood and cushions to find the best fit. It was as if, by her immobility, Caitlin Radcliff was branding Marthe as foreign. It worked all too well.

Mentally, Marthe grimaced, but many years of experience kept her mood from showing on her face. Not so the other. As Marthe had noted previously, Caitlin lacked Hamon's training. Although she smiled affably and appeared pleased as she accepted a drink, Marthe detected a trace of hostility. Whatever had brought Caitlin Radcliff here today, she had certainly not just been 'in the neighborhood'.

For now, though, Marthe watched and waited, content to chat of trivialities. Yes, she was most impressed with the reserve. No, it was not as she had imagined Earth to be, and no, it was not even remotely like Hathe.

"You must be glad to have Hamon home again, after so many years away," she said, interrupting the stream of questions.

"I suppose so. Truth to tell, he's been a wanderer for most of his life. His time on Hathe didn't seem very different," replied Caitlin.

"You didn't grow up with your brother then?"

"No. As I've said, his mother split from Father when he was quite young. Hamon spent his early years with his mother in the cities."

Marthe caught the hint of distaste in her voice.

"And you?"

"See that far ridge, over to the left?" Marthe followed the hand, seeing a long, high ridge marked with one slashing vee in the center. She nodded. "Through the pass is Father's valley. His house is just on the other side of the ridge, just to the right of the pass."

"Oh," said Marthe flatly. She hadn't realized that Garth Radcliff was so near. "And you grew up there?" It was Caitlin's turn to nod. "You must be quite close to your father."

"We share a number of similar ideas," was all Caitlin would say, before abruptly changing the subject. Marthe recognized the futility of further probing and regretfully accepted that she would learn no more at present. Soon, too, the talk drifted to a subject that she was very willing to explore at length—the wonderful uniqueness of her precious son. Once launched, she was more than happy to prattle endlessly on, blithely ignoring the glazed look that spread over her visitor's face as Marthe dotingly revealed all the small triumphs of Riardan's short life. Though only eight months old, he was crawling everywhere and already pulling himself to a stand.

"Amazing," and "Really. You don't say," muttered Caitlin at appropriate intervals, sufficient encouragement to feed the conversation for quite some time.

But Marthe was not blind to the other's lack of real interest, and she was somewhat surprised to hear Caitlin ask to see the baby, avowing an eagerness to hold her first nephew.

"I'll go and see whether he's awake," she replied, unable to think of a reason not to leave the woman alone and, as soon as she was out of Caitlin's sight she switched the surveillance systems to full alert. To her surprise, though, when she returned with her son, now wide awake and very happy to be the center of attention, it was to find Caitlin still reclining at ease in the same chair.

What was the woman up to? Almost absently, she passed the baby to his aunt's waiting lap. Her security systems were certainly sufficient to have warned of any prying by her guest. Even as she solicitously helped an inexperienced Caitlin cope with a bundle of infantile energy, the greater part of her mind was occupied in pondering the woman's actions.

Riardan was unconcerned with his mother's worries, far more interested in this new person who had entered his world—purely for his entertainment, one would have supposed from the grin on his face. Even as Caitlin sat up awkwardly, trying to keep the squirming mass within the confines of her knees, he lost his initial reserve and reached up to explore her hair, pulling hard. Caitlin jumped, as Marthe quickly reached out to untangle the flyaway strands from his chubby clutch.

"I am sorry! He's got a thing for hair at the moment."

"Don't worry," said Caitlin. "Freya did mention he took after her side of the family, and the MacDiarmids have always been rather good at grabbing what they want." A smile attempted to take the sting out of the words, not altogether successfully.

"Perhaps if you walk him. He loves being jiggled," suggested Marthe in embarrassment.

Caitlin accepted her advice, rising in one easy motion. After some moments of her rhythmic, bouncing stride, Riardan began to gurgle happily. His aunt even showed signs of relaxing as she strolled up and down the balcony, chatting to her enthralled nephew.

Marthe stayed in her chair, adding the odd comment and watching the pair's enjoyment, yet she could not banish her doubts, and an eerie foreboding began to grow in her. Caitlin was becoming braver, swinging the baby gently about as she swirled round the balcony. Riardan was laughing up at her, yet Marthe suddenly felt an urgent need to have him back in her arms. Involuntarily, she started to rise. At the same instant, Caitlin's swirls carried the pair right to the edge of the balcony. Despite knowing of the force field there to prevent any accident, Marthe could not help calling out.

"Oh, please, not so close to the edge."

"Why? You surely don't think I would let him fall?" smiled the Terran girl.

Marthe halted. "No. No, of course not."

Too late, she saw the glitter in the other's eyes. "What a fool! Of course I would. And don't come any closer, not if you value your son's life."

"You can't harm him. There's a protective field there," Marthe snapped back.

"Not any longer. You forget, I know this house better than you do. I deactivated it some moments ago. But go ahead, try to take the child. Quite frankly, he's only one more mouth to feed as far as I'm concerned, and not a Terran one at that." Jeering, she held the baby away from her. Marthe froze, watching in horror and praying that Riardan would not choose now to begin wriggling. The baby had also changed, though, as if sensing the tense hostility. He lay quiet, whimpering nervously and looking piteously towards the safety of his mother.

"Shush, sit still, little one," soothed Marthe softly, despite the panic rampaging within her. Keeping her voice as calm as she was able, so as not to frighten him further, she turned to her sister-in-law. "What do you want? Or should I ask, what does your father want?"

"How perceptive of you. Quite simply, Father wants you. Or, to be precise, he wants Hamon, and you are going to give him to us."

"Oh? And how exactly does he hope to achieve that?"

"You're to be a hostage to Hamon's support of our cause."

"Why do you need Hamon? Surely Garth Radcliff has quite enough supporters already?" challenged Marthe.

"Of course he does," the Terran returned angrily. "But Hamon, curse him, is the only one who can bring in the military—something we would find very useful."

"What, get men to follow him in a cause he is forced to espouse?"

"Ah, but you're wrong there. He is as committed to Terran independence as any of us, despite what you may wish to the contrary. It's only the means to achieve it that he hasn't yet decided. There, he needs some persuasion."

"And you think holding me will do that?"

"He does seem ridiculously fond of you, and he will be only too aware that Father wouldn't give two bits if you were killed."

"You haven't taken me yet," Marthe reminded her.

"No," allowed the Terran, "but if you don't turn off all your accursed foreign defenses and let our forces in, right now, you can say goodbye to the brat. He is becoming really, very heavy and I don't mind in the slightest dropping him right over the edge."

Marthe gave her a long, considering look. There was only one possible answer and Caitlin Radcliff knew it.

"All right, but Riardan stays here, in his own room."

"Agreed."

Marthe looked at her again, then, seeing something in her eyes, nodded grimly. Holding her wrist in open view, she tapped out an intricate sequence upon the control patch there. "They can now enter."

Within minutes, four heavily armed men surrounded her. A fifth had taken the baby from Caitlin and carried him into the lounge and, even as Caitlin began to strip the concealed weaponry from her, all she could feel was an overwhelming sense of relief to have Riardan away from the terrifying drop. Once disarmed, she was bound by a tight force band to a captor on either wrist. She could not even stroke her baby as he passed her and was placed in his cot, from where his frightened cries called to her. They did let her close the door, her hand gently touching the doorframe, activating all her defenses within his room. He might be frightened, hungry and lonely, but at least he would be safe until his father arrived.

They then dragged her back to the balcony, where Caitlin was examining her weapons with keen interest.

"Quite an arsenal you carry.

"And all personal-coded. You can't use them," said Marthe coldly. "Nor should you try dismantling them for examination. The resulting explosion would not do much for your looks."

"Very impressive. What else do you have concealed? We know you Hathians are full of devious tricks, and I can still blow this whole place to pieces, including your son in his so safe room."

Marthe glared at her but saw the implacable look, so chillingly like the one she had occasionally seen on Hamon's face. She shrugged and requested that one hand be released. They did but dug the blaster at her head sharply into her temple as a reminder of the need for obedience. Very slowly and carefully, Marthe reached around to the concealed skin slither on her back, pulling into real space her remaining blaster and one, tiny knife, old fashioned but very effective if all else failed.

"That's it?" demanded Caitlin doubtingly.

"That's it," nodded Marthe. "You have my word on the blood of my ancestors."

Caitlin shrugged in disdain, but accepted the pledge nonetheless, gesturing her to move off. Within minutes, she was in a flyer, winging rapidly towards the pass in the hills; but all she could hear, all she could think of, were the frightened howls of her baby son. Please come home to him, Hamon. Now. The plea kept repeating itself over and over in her head and she stared sightlessly ahead, blind to the harsh faces of her enemies, well and truly surrounding her now.

CHAPTER THIRTY-THREE

Garth Radcliff was not as she'd imagined. She had drawn pictures of him in her head all through the flight—images colored by the echoing memory of her son's screams. She'd thought she knew what it was to hate, especially to hate Terrans, but by the time she was dragged roughly from the flyer and through the doors of the great house set firmly on a massive outcrop of rock, what she felt for Garth Radcliff could no longer be contained by such a simple word.

It was a shock, then, to be welcomed by a pleasantly urbane and courteous man whose first action was to enquire of her choice of refreshments. She could only shake her head in refusal. Her father-in-law shrugged, and waited as the guards escorted her to a seat, fastening her hands to the sides with force bands. He seemed to be both oblivious to the extraordinary nature of her visit and yet vaguely apologetic for the treatment offered her.

In the few moments it took to secure her, Marthe seized the chance to study her captor. He looked like Hamon, yes, far more so than his daughter. The same height, the same dark and vibrant hair, though liberally sprinkled with grey. The eyes, thank the Pillars, they didn't share. Caitlin may have the same, disturbing eye color as Hamon, but it was from a more distant progenitor. Garth Radcliff's were the grey of a sea caught in a spring shower. Slate, but with a shimmer of sharp blue scattered by breaking clouds.

His face had the craggy strength into which Hamon's would one day solidify, and his body possessed the same staunch uprightness. The resemblance was frighteningly close. Almost one could imagine that here was an ally and a refuge but, always, Marthe remembered Hamon's words. "The thought of turning into another Garth Radcliff fills me with horror."

Garth allowed the survey, watching her in amusement, then coughed politely. "My son is thought to resemble me somewhat."

"Some," agreed Marthe guardedly.

"I take it you think he would have acted differently than I in the present circumstance?"

"No, not that; but he would have tried to avoid it."

Her captor laughed in delight. "You think that makes a difference?"

"Hamon seems to," was all she would reply.

"What a unique code of ethics the boy espouses. From quite where he acquired such a convenient philosophy, I cannot begin to imagine, but I must ask him when he arrives."

"You're expecting him then?"

"Of course. Aren't you? Are you not sitting there waiting for him to storm in, intent on heroically saving you?"

It was Marthe's turn to assume the amused smile. "Somewhat dramatic for Hamon, I would have said. Heroism's too easy. He prefers less obvious methods. Longer and more difficult, but far more likely to get him what he wants in the end."

Garth's face didn't alter, but Marthe clearly felt the spark of anger, then saw it as quickly controlled. "You do agree that he will attempt your rescue?" he said.

"Yes," she conceded, then stuck her chin belligerently forward. "Hamon will rescue me."

Whatever weakness she had felt in her father-in-law was now buried, though, and all she received was a gruff, "Hmmph."

"Why this whole farce?" she demanded next. "Wouldn't a simple invitation have sufficed?"

The man scarcely attempted to hide his scowl. "I've already tried that."

"And he wouldn't come on board. So now you hold a threat to me over his head. Well, you may know your son better than I," she said skeptically, "but I can't understand why you want him so badly."

"He is blessed with rather special talents and has experience with armed resistance. Not something there is a plethora of on Earth."

"You forgot to add that he's also closely watched and thoroughly distrusted by the Alliance authorities. Stars, he can barely sneeze without a full-page report in triplicate landing on the Commander's screen!"

"You think that's a problem to him?" boasted Hamon's father.

"I know it is," said Marthe dryly.

Her father-in-law grunted in disgust, then turned away. "It's irrelevant," he harrumphed, waving his hand as though he could as easily rid himself of Hathian and Alliance officialdom. "My son, for all his faults, has a superb military and political mind. He also has some very useful connections. In fact, I have an old friend of his here now. One who has been fundamental to our enterprise. I understand you know him. Ferdo, come in."

Marthe swiveled her head in surprise. It was the same Ferdo Braddock. Exactly the same. The anger of their last meeting, when she had held him under siege in the control room on Hathe, was still carved on his face. She remembered clearly that she had shot this man that day, slicing off part of his foot. Unfortunately, her present mood allowed for no apology.

"Captain Braddock, we meet again. I trust the medics repaired your foot adequately?"

He merely grunted, refusing to look at her. Hamon's regrettable parent answered instead. "Captain Braddock was treated here on Earth. His disability is fortunately but a minor hindrance to him in the very important work he performs for us," he said, gesturing to the younger man to proceed. Ferdo began pulling out various pieces of unknown equipment from the bag he had carried in. Marthe ignored him for now, still caught by the elder Radcliff's words.

"What do you mean, disability? Surely he had his foot regenerated on Hathe before he left. Or is your pride so important that you ignore common sense?"

Ferdo still refused to acknowledge her, his only response to become even more rigidly self-contained.

"Enough," barked Garth Radcliff. "Sit still, young woman!"

"I cannot do otherwise," she snapped back.

Radcliff had tired of the pose of urbanity. He beckoned the young Terran officer, who was carrying what appeared to be some kind of probe. Ferdo's next action, sweeping the small box over her body, confirmed her guess, though she was as yet unworried. Terran expertise was certainly not equal to Hathian guile.

Seconds later she was proved frighteningly wrong. Braddock paused, the probe hovering over her neck.

"Increase her immobility," he snapped. Marthe now could not move at all, her voluntary muscles locked rigidly in position. Ferdo lifted the hair from her neck, rolling down the collar to reveal a barely discernible patch of faintly darker skin. The color difference was insignificant, far too slight to be readily noticeable, but Ferdo's readings clearly marked it. Triumphantly, he peeled off the patch and threw it into a box. Marthe didn't need his brusquely thrown words to know that her only contact with her people was now utterly and completely destroyed. For the first time, she began to be seriously worried.

She caught sight of the smirk on Braddock's face—a vicious sneer of triumph. The next instant, his arm shot out, catching her in a ringing swipe across the side of her head. Unable to duck, the full force of his hate hit her. All around her was a mobile blur, the force field alone holding her upright. She tried to tense, expecting more of the same, but through the groggy haze, she dimly heard Radcliff admonishing Braddock.

"I said you could mark her a bit, not send her into the next world. It won't help us much with that cursed son of mine if she's dead."

She did receive a sullen blow to her arm and a kick to the leg that would make walking uncomfortable for some days. Braddock must have conceded after that, and she next heard the soft whoosh of the sliding door as he left. Radcliff slackened the field a bit then, allowing her to slump backwards. Her leg and arm hurt, but not enough to eclipse the pounding of her head, and she had to concentrate hard to make out her captor's words.

"He owed you those, and they should blunt any attempt to use your alien trickery. Also, thanks to Ferdo's endeavors, this place is free of Alliance surveillance. Your precious authorities have no idea where you are, and could do nothing to help you if they did."

"So it's solely up to me and my cursed alien trickery then?" She tried to smile as she jeered back. "It has served me rather well against Terrans in the past. Now shouldn't be too different."

"Don't be so sure. Remember, I still control the magnitude of that restraining field." And he gave her one, bone crushing demonstration. As the blood cleared slowly from her eyes, her returning vision showed him watching her threateningly, one finger still caressing the control pad. "While we're on the subject," he added, the finger casually sweeping round and round the pad, "you can disarm those interesting-looking weapons of yours. So careless of you to carry so many around with you. You must know how keen we are to analyze them."

"No can do," she jeered back.

"You are so eager for more discomfort?"

Radcliff's eyebrows had risen in a gesture sickeningly like his son's, and, for a moment, Marthe was cast adrift. She fought desperately to deny a horrifying sense of trust in the man, wrapping the armor of her professionalism about her. A mocking smile lit her lips.

"Of course not, but it's your own eagerness that denies you. Every one of those weapons is personally coded to me ... through my patch. I can still fire them, but not disarm them. I need that patch you so avidly destroyed to do that. As it is, no one, and that includes me, had better try tampering with them. Not that the loss of however many of your compatriots infest this place would worry me. I just have no desire to be part of the resulting carnage."

For a long moment, she could feel his gaze upon her, assessing her and then increasingly frustrated as he came to accept the truth of her words. Or at least decided that, if she were bluffing, it was not a bluff he dared risk testing.

At long last, his eyes narrowed, then he looked up at her face. "Hmph," was all he said at first, rising to his feet. Then, "I'll leave you to ponder your actions," he added, like some pompous school master. "Do not forget that we have you under full surveillance at all times."

Then he was gone, and she was left to enjoy the illusion of privacy. Hamon, where are you, she silently called, desperately hoping against reason that somehow he could feel her plea. Hamon, help, we need you so badly.

It was not an emptiness in his home that told Hamon of his loss. It was, rather, a raucous cacophony of noise. Even as his flyer hit the landing pad, jarring down in his hurry to answer Marthe's emergency call, a platoon of allied soldiers swarmed to surround him. None would answer his urgent pleas, merely passing a sensor over him and gesturing him towards the house. He broke into a run, up the path, reaching the house out of breath and frantic with worry. He was calling for Marthe as he burst through the door, but she didn't answer. All he met as he searched ever more urgently through the rooms were yet more troops, intent on their own tasks, and harried officialdom determinedly thrusting their faces at him.

Sanity was finally discovered in the person of his mother, quietly walking Riardan up and down in the sanctuary of his room. She looked up at him, and what he saw there stopped him in his tracks.

"Riardan? What's happened to him?"

He anxiously reached out for the baby, seeing the signs of distress still apparent in the puffy eyes and reddened cheeks. Riardan clung to his outstretched hands, then snuggled back into the comforting shoulder of his grandmother, one hand still clutching his father's finger.

"Who did this?" Hamon demanded again. "And where's Marthe?"

His mother didn't answer at first. Then, she raised her eyes to look him squarely in the face. "It's not Riardan. It's Marthe. They've taken her."

"Taken! Who?"

His mother would say no more, nodding at the soldier in the doorway in explanation. A Terran matter, with Terran interests to be protected.

Then he understood. His teeth clenched, and the white shock of knowledge blasted through him. "How long ago?"

"She managed to set the alarm off as they left. The local Alliance chief picked me up on his way here. They said you were still some time away."

"About an hour," confirmed Hamon bitterly. "I was visiting 'friends'."

"Do you know what he would want with Marthe?"

"I can guess."

The Alliance chief entered then, and they could say no more. He and his mother turned towards the Hathian, their faces kept equally blank, to an Truro's obvious exasperation.

"Major Radcliff, Madame MacDiarmid, would you please join us? We need to ask you a few questions. And Major, don't worry, we will find her."

The words may have been kind, but the tone was abrupt, and Hamon had seen that same look in the eyes of too many Hathians to mistake his words for those of a friend.

"Have you any leads yet?" he asked as they moved through to the main rooms and were made to sit before an enquiry panel.

"Only that she's lost her patch. Since we can't track her, we have to assume that she's being held in one of the six locations our sensors can't penetrate," said an Truro, ignoring the scowls of his staff at his frankness.

"She's out of contact?" If Hamon had thought he was afraid before, it was nothing to what he felt now. "What do you mean, can't penetrate six locations?"

"Certain Terran groups have developed systems to detect and negate our equipment. You were unaware of this?"

"I was," said Hamon. "Presumably I'm known to be too closely watched to be allowed access to such information."

His tone was carefully neutral, but he felt his mother tense as she recognized what the admission cost him. He turned to her, and they exchanged a long, intent look, ended by a brief nod from his mother.

Hamon turned back to the panel in crisp determination. "Show me these locations." The world map lit up. One marker was only a short distance away. Hamon stabbed his finger down. "There. That's where he'll have her."

"So close? Surely even he wouldn't dare?"

"Why not? Are you willing to face the repercussions if the allies should be foolish enough to mount an assault on Ambassador Radcliff's home? So far, the opposition to your rule is fragmented enough to allow a peaceful occupation, but how long do you think that will last if you attack a revered elder statesman on what many will consider a whim?"

An Truro nodded. "What do you suggest then?"

"I know what he wants. Me. Let me make contact and we can go from there."

"And why does he want you?" was the pointed question from a senior officer.

"To help him raise an armed rebellion, I'd guess."

"Could you?" another voice snapped.

Hamon gazed back, all his antipathy rising, and he leveled a long steady look at the glaring face of the Alliance leader. "If I chose to, yes I could."

"After such an admission, why should we trust you?" an Truro broke in coldly.

"Because I can get her out with the minimum of fuss—something you need."

"And how are you going to manage that?"

"I won't know until after I've contacted my father. Most likely though, I'll have to play along with him, at least to begin with, then see what happens."

An angry roar of dissent erupted. An Truro let it continue only so long, then broke in with a single, quelling, "Silence."

"What guarantee do we have that once you get in there, you won't join up with your father, leaving us with armed rebellion anyway?"

"None. But I have to get Marthe out and keep her and Riardan safe. An armed rebellion is unlikely to achieve that. Also," and he paused then, shrugging an apology to his mother before continuing in a voice strained in confession, "For all he is my father, I don't wish for the kind of independence he envisages for Earth. I've sacrificed too much to the welfare of this planet, over too many years, to let it descend into that. Oh, don't get me wrong. There is nothing I would like more than to see you get your alien backsides off my soil; but being ruled by Garth Radcliff and his ilk is too high a price even for me to pay."

An Truro leaned back, studying him. Hamon kept none of his angry pride hidden, meeting the cold eyes of the Hathian commander and not once backing off. After some time, an Truro broke off to confer with his colleagues, but it was a courtesy only and before long, he turned back.

"All right. For now, you call the shots."

"Thank you," breathed Hamon in relief. He turned to his mother, who was clutching his sleeve as if afraid to let go.

"Are you sure of this?" she asked quietly.

He nodded, slow and sad. "I think I've always known it would come to this," he said, "but, Mother, she is worth it."

His mother smiled, then squeezed his hand. "You may just be right, my son." The look she sent him was long and very private, and it was only the impatient coughing of the Alliance officers that broke it off.

"Give me five minutes to make my preparations, if you please, gentlemen," said Hamon, "then I'll be off."

He turned once before leaving, to gently stroke his son's cheek then disappeared from sight, heading for his rooms.

He left behind a particularly disgruntled group of men and his mother, her head turned down to bury itself in the warm breath of her baby grandson, hiding the fear that had clutched her as she saw her son's face when he gave that last caress to his son.

There had been an ominous finality to it.

Considerably more than five minutes had passed since Radcliff left the room, and an increasingly vocal group of officers still waited for his return. An Truro spoke urgently into his communicator, and the search began. All too soon, and with a great deal of irritation, he was brought to the realization that yet another Terran had managed to best them. Frustrated and angry, an Truro ordered a count of all vehicles in the compound.

"All present and accounted for, Sir," responded the young technician. "Except, of course, the flyer you ordered back to headquarters for back-up personnel."

"I what!" An Truro glared angrily at the unfortunate junior.

"That's what your assistant told me, sir. The one who took off in it. His ID was legit," he added in hasty exoneration, but it served only to drive the commander's anger farther into the stratosphere. Frantic search ensued. Soon an aide was discovered, unconscious and tethered in a closet and with his ID missing. An Truro's face must have been bright scarlet, but he no longer cared.

"Step up security. Retina and thumbprints required at all times," he barked. "*Both* thumbprints." Then he turned to his opponent's mother. "So he wanted us to trust him? Can you explain this, Madame, or are we going to have armed rebellion after all?"

"I'm sure my son has a good reason for his actions. He does know his father rather well."

"Perhaps, but I'm sure you will understand my request that you remain here for the time being. To care for your grandson, shall we say? My men will be here to protect you at all times, and until the present situation is resolved, it would be wise if you did not attempt to leave the immediate vicinity of this house."

Madame MacDiarmid bowed, an echo of his heavy irony, but her thoughts were all with her son.

Hamon had realized almost immediately that if he were to have any hope of success, he must approach the Terran rebels alone. The disposal of the guard had been almost too easy, and the successful theft of the flyer buoyed him further. There was a part of him that could not but exult in this one small victory over the Hathians, a rich prize after the long years of frustration.

Then the image of a hurt and frightened Marthe intruded and his delight faded. It was an image that he could not banish, no matter how unlikely it might be, and with renewed determination, he bent to the controls again, steering in a long, curving sweep away from his destination.

His path thereafter was decidedly erratic, a puzzle to any would be followers as he zigzagged back and forth through the valleys, stopping at frequent intervals to land as if searching for something.

After one such stop, Hamon emerged from the dim shadow of a tree, to watch the flyer disappear over a far ridge. The controls had been unfamiliar, so he could only hope that he had fed his program into the autonavigator, not the garbage recycler. So far, his plan looked to be working, the faint hum of the flyer fading into the distance still turning and twisting. A grimace, then he stepped back through the trees to the concealed cave. He'd hidden a flyer of his own there shortly after his return to Earth, prompted by the constant surveillance of the Alliance to organize an escape route if needed. He hadn't expected that his own people would pose the threat.

He waited some time, hoping to further confuse the Alliance probes, all the while driven by an urgent need to move on. Fear for Marthe wouldn't leave him. Finally, his anxiety could stand no more, and he eased the small flyer out, hugging closely to the contour of the hills and using the forest cover as long as he could. When he judged it to be safe, he emerged and set a swift course straight for his father's house. Trickery would not gain him entry there, would more likely get his head blown off.

Soon, he picked up the challenge he was expecting … and a warning. As soon as he sent his answering code, the defense system flashed an alarm on his console. A number of very heavy-duty weapons were locked on and tracking him. Trust his father to take no chances, he grinned wryly. But no word did he receive all through that eerie flight, across ground he had known since childhood to the house he dimly remembered from his earliest years with fondness, and later and more clearly, as filled with tension and argument. He was going home, serenaded with all the paraphernalia of a force of invading aliens.

Quixotically, as he approached the house, he ignored the main landing site, heading instead for the smaller pad reserved for family members. His father may be playing politics, but Hamon was damned if he was going to give him the satisfaction of joining the game. The only variation from previous arrivals that he chose to concede was to blatantly lock and seal the flyer to all but himself, leaving it on standby mode for a rapid exit if needed.

He stood for a full minute in plain sight of the external viewers, glaring arrogantly around, then strode forward. As he did so, his foot automatically stepped on a roughly gouged out crack. It was a relic of a childhood game with Caitlin. They had been hurling stones at a target set here on the top step. All his adult life, his foot had sought out the mark as he entered, as if seeking to renew old bonds. This time, he fought off the insidious sense of relaxation it brought. There was no sanctuary in this house today, only a lurking danger. His face was a solid mask as he palmed the door and entered.

An elderly man met him inside, greeting him with a quick smile and a warm hand on his shoulder. A flinch of horror gripped Hamon.

"Good to see you again, Master Hamon."

"Joseph. It's been a long time."

Joseph had always been a special favorite on his infrequent visits as a child, ever ready to shield him from the puzzling distance that had arisen between him and his father; and his father was well aware of his affection for the old man. He made sure he showed none of his anger at that, and restricted his reply to a polite request for his father's whereabouts.

"In the study." A look of embarrassment passed over Joseph's lined face. "He has ordered that you be screened for hidden weapons before you go in, sir."

A wry smile lit Hamon's face. "You mean he hasn't a screen on the doorway?"

"Well, yes."

"It's all right, Joseph. If Father wants to indulge in ostentatious threat displays, who am I to quibble?" he said, waiting as the old man swept the beam over him.

"As if you would be stupid enough to bring in anything untoward," scoffed Joseph.

"Thanks for the vote of confidence." Then he turned towards his father's office. "Onwards?"

"Onwards, young sir."

He rewarded the old man with a mischievous quirk of his lips.

Hamon suddenly felt a burst of confidence. Father had forgotten, it seemed, that it was old Joseph who could always lighten the younger Hamon's mood, just as his well-chosen words had done now. Maybe it was not all that Garth Radcliff had miscalculated.

The study door refused to answer to his palm, throwing back instead an "Identify" order. Still with his head up, Hamon moved in front of the beam. A moment later, the door slid away and his father stood before him.

Hamon was the taller of the two, just, but in the sense of presence, he knew there was little to choose.

"You have come remarkably promptly, and free of Alliance baggage. You are to be commended." It was the parade ground patriarch of his teenage years, the gruff voice with its familiar cold praise.

"Always willing to oblige, as you know, Father. Especially when you give me such good cause." Then his voice changed abruptly, some of his anger seeping in. "Where is she?"

"Just over here." Garth Radcliff gestured then added, just as Hamon knew an inward sigh of relief that Marthe was still alive, **"I must commend you on your good taste. She is a most beautiful woman. Or, at least, was…"**

The words reached Hamon at the same instant as the full sight of Marthe struck him.

There was a nasty cut over one eye, the bruising already congealed to an ugly, swollen mass that engulfed the smooth surface of one cheek. She sat awkwardly, arms and legs clamped to the sides of the chair and her back arched in agony. Her eyes blazed momentarily in enormous relief, then she retreated again to a shielded world. All lightness deserted him, fury such as he had never known before sweeping in a huge wave over him.

"Release that field immediately." A deep breath, eyes locked on hers as he fought for control. "What were you thinking? That I would need such stupid barbarity to prove how serious you are. Why in hell do you think I'm here if I didn't believe she was in real danger?"

"A personal whim. Ferdo felt she owed him. You remember Ferdo, your erstwhile friend? The one she injured?" Garth said, waving forward the man Hamon had been too preoccupied to notice.

He swung round in disgust. "Injured! Remind me to show you Marthe's medical file one day." He grabbed the controls on his father's desk, but to no avail. "Release her," he shouted. Garth shrugged, then obliged. Hamon leapt to catch Marthe as she collapsed forward, swinging her up and carrying her over to a couch he hoped was out of the force's reach. One finger softly traced the injuries on her head. "I am so sorry, sweetheart. I never meant for you to be hurt again. Is the face all they touched, or is there more?"

"Not much. One arm and a leg are badly bruised, so don't plan on making a run for it," she managed to whisper, then leaned tiredly into his side. "Riardan?"

"He's fine. My mother got to him soon after you were taken, and there are Alliance troops swarming all over the homestead. He's completely safe." He turned back to his father, Marthe cradled protectively against him. "What now?" he demanded.

His father didn't answer at first. He moved over and seated himself at his desk, waving a hand to Ferdo to be seated and ignoring the glowering anger on the man's face. "A discussion of matters of mutual interest," he then said, leaning back in his chair.

"Just say what you want, without the embellishments. Right now, I'm not in the mood."

"Such a lack of finesse, all over a woman … and not even Terran at that."

"My first union partner, mother of my first union child. I'll thank you to remember it, Father, and use a respectful tone when you speak of my wife."

Garth linked his fingers, staring first at him then moving his predatory gaze to the woman slumped beside him.

His stare eventually drew her attention. Hamon felt her lift her head from his chest as she returned the look. He glanced at her, caught the challenge in her dark eyes. Across the room his father— her enemy—took up the gauntlet, accepting it with a sharp nod, then turned back to his son with no sign in his business-like voice of that short exchange.

"Agreed," he said to Hamon, ignoring Marthe. "What do I want? You, of course. Your full cooperation and assistance in ridding our home of these filthy invaders."

"You can't do it without me? There's more than enough opposition to the Alliance among Terrans."

"I haven't your contacts among the military. Nor damn it, have I your knack for leading men, much as I hate to admit it. I can make them do as I wish, but you … you can make them *want* to do as you wish, and you know it," Garth said brusquely. "Must be your mother in you."

"Funny, she always says I'm too much like you," Hamon allowed himself a short grin. "And if I don't agree to help you?"

"You, and more particularly your pretty wife, will never leave here otherwise. You can watch as we dispose of her. Nor will your son be spared. He may be safely surrounded by Alliance muck for now, but you can't guarantee his safety forever, not on Earth."

"He's your own grandson!" exclaimed Marthe in disbelief, struggling upwards even as Hamon's hand pulled her back.

"I can have more," replied his father. "Truly Terran grandchildren."

Marthe stared up at Hamon, "He's bluffing, surely?"

Hamon wouldn't look at her, continuing to hold his father's gaze with a taut stillness. "No, he's not bluffing. He is deadly serious." He sat, still and silent. Then he moved. His head rose sharply and his hand squeezed Marthe's, in warning. Then he turned towards his fate. He nodded once. "You leave me no choice. You have me."

"No!" squawked Marthe.

"A very wise decision," said his father simultaneously.

A wry grin touched Hamon's lips and his head bent to meet her eyes.

For an instant, Marthe was back in the days on Hathe when they had been forced to depend on face and feelings to speak. "Are you sure this is what you want? That it has to be this way?"

"It's the last thing I want, but there is no other way." His look was both a promise and an ending.

"You always said we are alike," she said with a hint of tears.

He caught her closer, and she sent him all the strength she had as he turned back to his father. "Give me the details," he said bitterly.

"Not with her listening," growled Ferdo. "She's coned, or no deal."

Hamon glared over at him, distrust evident in every line of his body, but it was Marthe who restrained him and nodded her head at the senior Radcliff.

"On one condition only, that Hamon oversees the controls," she added firmly. She wasn't about to trust herself to the word of a Terran. Not after today.

It was Hamon's hands that led her back to the center chair and who took the control console from his father, to safeguard her while the Terrans talked. It helped, but only a little, as she sat tensely watching father and son. They were facing away from her, so she couldn't tell their words by lip reading, and any sounds were blocked out completely by the cone-shaped field surrounding her. Hamon was again the professional, leaning forward earnestly. Their only hope was that neither his father nor his oldest friend could see past the front he assumed, had missed the silent communication between husband and wife. Their lives depended on his ability to sound convincing. Like her husband, Marthe had battened down the armor of her professionalism.

There was danger in the tension cramping her muscles, and carefully she stretched taut limbs, shrugging her shoulders one by one and breathing in the slow discipline she had been taught, easing away nerves that could destroy the sharp edge of her response.

The talking lasted a long time. At one point Hamon leapt up, marching backwards and forwards and throwing angry looks at his father. Garth merely ordered him to sit down, his hands motioning brusquely. Ferdo didn't seem to have much to say. Maybe he still distrusted his former friend, but Marthe thought it more than that. He was superfluous here. This was between the two Radcliffs.

Then it was finished. One, final handshake, a clasp of promise and an intent look between father and son. Marthe searched for some hint of apology in her father-in-law's face but wasn't surprised to see none. The sensory cone was released. Hamon's hand lifted her by the elbow and moved her towards the door. His grip hurt in its hardness, and she turned to admonish him, but seeing his face kept her words to herself. There was a powerful urge in her to run, and she was sure Hamon shared it. Instead, they both walked steadily to the door and bid farewell, just as at the end of any family visit. Marthe wondered if the hairs on her arm were standing on end like those on Hamon's. She couldn't look, too afraid to lose what control she yet retained.

At the door, Hamon pulled them to a sudden stop and swung back to his father. "Until I hear from you, the old contact points?" Garth merely grunted assent. "Good." Hamon turned away without any sign he may never meet his father again.

Still, they walked slowly across to the flyer, and it wasn't till they were past the outer defenses that Hamon finally gave in to the urgent forces riding them both. His finger hit the accelerator and the craft shot forward at a speed that at last gave hope. Marthe would have spoken then, but his face again stopped her. Instead, she stared rigidly forward, never moving, through all the confusing aerobatics Hamon employed to minimize any shadowing of their route. It was not until he put down in the shelter of a hidden glade of trees that he finally turned to her, and then it was not to talk.

His lips opened, frantically seeking the reassurance of hers. Marthe made no protest. She needed as much as he to feel the touch of hands, of arms, of bodies.

It was a desperate joining, washed with the stain of terror, and it was not for a long time later that either felt secure and whole once more. They lay concealed beneath the shrouding undergrowth, closely entwined and finally safe enough in the reality of the other's return to ask the inevitable.

"What now?"

He didn't answer her at first, his hand continuing its slow course, down her face, across her shoulders, his fingers trickling along her arms as his eyes became fixed on her hand lying warm in his. He made a fist, gently enclosing her fingers within his grasp.

Only then did his eyes rise to hers. "I don't know," he whispered into her cheek. "I really do not know. Where is there left for us?"

"We can't stay on Earth?" It was both question and statement.

"If you could persuade the Alliance that I'm not a threat to their security? After this little episode, there doesn't seem much chance of that."

She moved to close the infinitesimal space between them, needing both to feel the comfort of his body and to offer the comfort of her own.

"I could always go into hiding. This is my world after all," he offered.

"For how long though?"

"Oh, quite some time. But you and Riardan couldn't come with me, so that's no good either." Her eyebrows rose in affronted enquiry. "It would be too dangerous. The first time you opened your mouth, you would be exposed as an offworlder, risking both your lives."

"I'm a rather good actress. What do you think I've been doing for the last five years?"

"And no Terran could ever pass himself off as Hathian."

She nodded, her argument lost.

"Apart from which," he continued, "the minute it's seen that I have no intention of complying with my father's orders, all our lives will be forfeit. I know him too well. He doesn't make threats lightly."

She put her hand to his face, gently tracing the line of lip and brow, trying to ease the bitterness her fingers found. "I am so sorry," she whispered.

He rolled towards her, his hand sweeping down low over her stomach as his lips tendered his thanks. The hand gently massaged her abdomen. "There is only one thing in all this I truly regret," he said. "I would have liked one child to be conceived here. To have a child of Earth as we have Riardan with the soil of Hathe in his bones. A gift of my world to take with us on our travels."

She grew still, withdrawing into silent calculation. Then her eyes opened again, catching his as her fingers played a quick cadence on the implant set into the back of her neck.

"I've disengaged the cervical shield, and the timing is nearly right. There is a chance," she whispered in promise.

His hand knotted into her belly. Then his eyes warmed in the promise of desire and he rose over her. Her hips lifted to him and his fingers dug into the brown earth beneath. The rich aroma of his world awoke to surround them, blanket and bed and a memory of promise. In frantic and earthly delight, they found the wellspring of hope.

And inside her body, a new life awoke.

CHAPTER THIRTY-FOUR

The hotel room was like all the others in a long line of temporary stops, its perfect sterility a mocking counterpoint to her pacing footsteps. Tasteful. Marthe's mouth creased. She'd had her fill of tasteful rooms—six months full. Six months, three planets and how many hotel rooms since they'd been catapulted from Earth?

It had unsettled her more than she expected, the sorrow she felt at leaving a house she had begun to think of as home coming as an unwelcome surprise.

It had unsettled her, yes, but it had torn Hamon asunder. The Alliance didn't believe that he meant to leave Earth, or so they said. No father, not even Garth Radcliff, could possibly be a threat to a son long allied to his beliefs. Marthe remembered the look on an Truro's face as he'd said that—the contempt and the dislike. She had wondered at the time whether it was personal. Had Hamon wronged the man at some time? Or was it a more general desire to annihilate any push by the Terrans for independence, with the renewal it must bring of their threat to Hathe. Hamon's face had remained unchanged throughout, his professional reserve solidifying about him. She knew, though, what it cost him. He had been granted one boon only: a few moments' privacy with his mother—an illusion; they were monitored at all times, but she didn't think it mattered.

It had been mother and son alone on that perfect Earth morning, a final farewell. Marthe owed Freya that. She didn't know the words he spoke there and couldn't have guessed their significance in any case. All she had seen was Hamon pass something to his mother, and the look on the older woman's face, before the door slid to.

It had been very quiet in that small room. Madame MacDiarmid looked at her eldest son, memorizing each line of his face and watching the color deepen in his eyes.

"I always used to dread it when your eyes turned quite that shade of green. You were either furious, or something was very serious."

She ignored the capsule in her hand.

"It's serious, Mama."

She nodded still refusing to look down, even as he put his hand on the capsule, pushing it towards her.

"I'm turning the guardianship of the reserve over to you, to be held in trust until one of my children can take it up."

"But it's been in your father's family for centuries," she cried.

"And Gramps and Grandma deeded it to me, not Garth. It is my choice what happens next. You know what the reserve means to me. I can trust you to keep it safe. One day, my children may be able to return, and it must …it *must* still be here for them. I don't think I can bear all this if the only legacy I am to leave is one of fear and deceit. You will keep it safe, Mama?"

Her fingers had grasped the capsule then and she'd slid it into a pouch, her head nodding in promise. Her arms came around him, and her words then were the age old, words of wisdom mothers give to their departing sons, hoping to shield them from the dangers ahead.

Marthe had seen her face at the end and did not try to draw Hamon's attention. Her mother-in-law had given her the gift of her son, and these last moments together were but a small price in recompense. There had been some official business, and Riardan had been held close to his grandmother. Freya had searched the baby's face as she held him close, absorbing the feel of the little body into her skin. It was a memory imprinted deep within Marthe, and she vowed that, as he grew, Riardan would know of it, would learn the treasure of his dual heritage.

Their departure from Earth had been rapid. Military figures guarded every stage, imprisoning and protecting. Just before entering the shuttle that would take them to their ship, Hamon was stopped by an Truro.

"I understand that you have sufficient funds elsewhere to enable you to survive away from Earth?" the man said in a cold tone.

"I have business interests on a number of Alliance planets," Hamon had confirmed curtly.

"Then you have no need to return to Earth?"

"I have made arrangements to ensure that it's not necessary."

"For if you do," had continued an Truro as if uninterrupted, "you will be arrested and charged with the full weight of your crimes against Hathe."

"Wouldn't that be rather inadvisable, politically?"

"I don't give a damn. You will be charged, tried and executed," an Truro had snapped, then turned and ordered the guard to escort them on board. Hamon had also turned then to march onto the ship, his eyes and hands isolated as Marthe and Riardan followed.

The sliding of the door broke Marthe from her thoughts. Anxiety etched her face as she swung around.

"Was it the same man?"

"Yes. They've found us again. Father's trackers are as efficient as ever," replied Hamon.

"I'll start packing."

"No. This time we stay. I've already informed the authorities of their presence, and Cantor is one planet that knows how to handle intruders. The stars know, we can't keep running for the rest of our lives. This time I say we stop and deal with them."

"He'll only send more."

"Probably, but I've informed the Cantorese that I intend to increase the level of my investment in this planet, and they have a profound dislike of offworlders using their soil for the kind of minor war my father favors—along with the capability to stop such. For now, we're safe, and likely to stay so."

He moved up to her, one hand going over her shoulder and the other sweeping round to cradle the bulge of her stomach. "It's a good planet, this, and I'm almost as good at business as I was at counterintelligence. They also have a fine university where you can further your studies. We could make a life here." His eyes held hers, green flecks sharpening the softness of hazel as an edge of urgency cut his voice. "We are not going to find anywhere better in the next few months, and I don't want you going into labor on some space freighter with the stars know what help available. Riardan's birth was more than enough excitement for one lifetime.

She leaned back into his shoulder with a slight chuckle. "So be it. Riardan will just have to put up with an excess of supervision for a few weeks."

"And where is that young rascal?"

"Asleep, thanks be. To think I couldn't wait till he started walking!" A fond smile touched her lips as she stared out the window. It was gone when she twisted back to face Hamon. "He will be safe?" she demanded.

"On my life and honor."

Marthe relaxed, twisting back to the window and his arms. Hamon Radcliff knew well what such a pledge meant, and what it might cost. Riardan was safe.

She was glad. She liked this world. Never would it replace her lost home. The memory of Hathe lay deep within her, a constant, raw pain which was now so much a part of her that she welcomed it as a friend; but Cantor had something of the spirit of the Hathe of her childhood. The great university of its capital wove its thread throughout the life of the planet, and here her children could grow up free, delighting in the gifts that grew within them. There was justice, curiosity and hope here, strong building blocks for a good life. She might even learn to dream again.

"Done. Cantor it is." She caught his hands, drawing them about her as a grin lit up her face. "Just don't expect a child of Cantor too soon after this one."

"Agreed," he laughed, "so long as I can keep in practice for when you do want another." He swung her carelessly up, grunting only slightly as he valiantly carried her through the doors to the bedroom and deposited her on the sleeper. "Agreed, my wonderful Hathian, beloved of my life."

To her relief, she caught sight again of the wicked grin that had first called her so strongly, whispering of laughter and adventure. She had seen it so rarely of late.

The following months were a precious interlude of mundane domesticity. They searched for, and eventually found, a home—a house set in a wide landscape reminiscent of both the high plains of Hathe that Marthe had always loved best and the grandeur of Hamon's reserve. It stood on a slash of rock gouged from the mountains, high above a great sweep of land plunging down and out from the rugged peaks behind them. This was not a region favored by the Cantorese, too challenging in its rawness for that urbane and essentially cosmopolitan people, and there was a welcoming echo of emptiness in the land.

They stood together on the balcony. Hamon needed only one brief look then he turned towards her, his smile an answer and a question.

"Yes!" she breathed back, seeking his hand, and then laughing as Riardan forced himself between them. His father caught him up, tossing him high in merry abandon then turning to show him the view.

"And what do you think, young man? Will it suit you?"

"Din, din," shrieked that young man, his head nodding happily. He burrowed into his father's shoulder, excited far more by his parents' happiness than by any view.

Marthe swung round to the agent. "How soon can we move in?"

"You can have a temporary tenure immediately. It will take some months to clear the permanent lease through Immigration, but you might as well stay here while you're waiting."

"Cleared through Immigration?"

"Our government is very careful about whom it allows to live here long term. Any lease by a non-citizen requires a clearance."

"A technicality, I hope?"

"Given the financial status of Ser Radcliff, I don't envisage any problems," assured the agent, smiling unctuously.

Marthe had heard him with reservations at the time, too used to feeling destined to always follow the troubled path, but the next few months seemed to fulfill his words. The final settlement was taking time, admittedly, but they had rapidly learnt that such was the way of the Cantorese bureaucracy.

The birth of a daughter in the new year gave further hope that, just maybe, they had been granted a reprieve.

"We'll name her Freya, for your mother. She has the look of her."

"How can you tell with such a red and wrinkled, little bundle?" retorted Hamon, putting forth his finger gently to the baby's crazily questing hand.

"She is not! She's perfectly beautiful."

"She is, isn't she? "They both stared rapturously at the newest addition to their patchwork family. "She is also very red and very, very wrinkled."

"Maybe, but you'll fill out, won't you, sweetheart?"

Marthe held her tiny daughter close, till she was forced to swap her hurriedly to the other side as Riardan rushed forward and lunged onto the sleeper. His new nurse followed hastily into the room, a young woman with a warmly infectious laugh, quick to surface. Only not at the moment.

"I'm sorry. I couldn't keep him away any longer. Ever since he woke, he's known something is different. Well, the whole house does, so I suppose it's not surprising."

"Don't worry," smiled Marthe, gathering her small son into her other side. She was overcome by an enormous feeling of rightness. The nurse, bless her sensitive soul, discreetly withdrew.

The birth had been relatively easy, and both Freya and Marthe throve in the peace of their new home. For Marthe, it was as if she had entered a sanctuary, free for a time from the buffeting of their troubles. A part of her recognized the constant vigilance Hamon maintained over them all, and knew that from time to time he was forced to take action against their enemies, both Terran and Hathian. It may be unfair, but for this time she let it all fall on his shoulders. He had been as shattered by his exile from Earth as she had by hers from Hathe and was in equal need of solace, but they could not each simultaneously support the other, and for now Marthe drank greedily of his solid comfort, a small part only watchful that he shouldn't exceed his strength.

Nor was it selfish. As she grew in ease, the laughter of his wife and children surrounded Hamon, bringing a healing of the bleakness within. Hope entered their house.

Freya turned out to be more like her grandmother than expected.

"That child runs this house," exclaimed an exasperated Marthe as, yet again, she was forced to put aside her medical texts to attend to a hungry and fractious daughter. "At this rate, I'll never qualify for registration here!"

"Why don't you read while you feed her," suggested Hamon, glancing up from a screen displaying the latest business data.

"I've tried that. She's perfectly happy if I read something lightweight, but as soon as I try anything of a vaguely serious nature, she grizzles and refuses to settle. Mathe knows why! Maybe I'm just not relaxed enough for Madame if I read study notes."

She sighed, though there was little true regret on her face as she gave in to her daughter's preferred regime, switching her reading matter to a scandalous and utterly ludicrous tale and rapidly losing herself in the improbable passages. Hamon barely caught a quick, self-satisfied glance from Freya to her mother before she settled happily to feed and smiled to himself. It was the selfsame smile he had seen on his mother's face whenever she had managed to organize an official down a path she alone favored.

His screen bleeped him. Talk about thought conjuring up reality, he mused as he recognized the code on the incoming message. Scrambling a personal note seemed rather excessive, even for his mother, and his mouth lifted in a grin as he hit the decoder.

The grin vanished. "Marthe, switch to my screen."

She obeyed, reading the decoded message, then looked up in dismay. Nor did she bother asking who could do such a thing. This had Garth Radcliff written all over it. "Can he do that?"

"Technically, no, but it will cost me a large chunk of all I own to stop him if it's true."

In grim haste, Hamon brought up the files on his various companies, and there it was. Proof.

Almost every enterprise he owned was under legal bond, all trading ceased. The claim informed him that, as a recent resident of Cantor, his businesses were still considered subject to Earth's laws— one in particular, which Hamon ironically remembered helping to draft back in his student days, during his cadetship in the office of the Finance Administrator. It had been aimed at stopping an outflow of Terran companies that, although established and run by Terrans from Earth, were claiming they were not subject to Terran taxation as their head offices had been shifted off planet.

The law firm filing against him was no stranger either. It belonged to a friend of his father.

In all, it was claimed that he owed ten years back taxes on each of his companies. The total sum must have been carefully calculated. It would not bankrupt him, but what little it left him would not impress the Cantorese—certainly not enough to warrant their continued protection. It would leave him and his small family exposed to any danger his father cared to throw at them.

He twisted round, looking up at Marthe. She had not bothered with the figures, he saw. His face told her all she needed.

"You say that technically he can't do this. Why not?"

"My companies were all founded off planet, so the law doesn't apply, but to prove that, I need to track back through the history of each company. Something I'm not sure even I could do. Most of them began purely by chance, back in my travelling days, and were set up under assumed names. They were only ever meant to make me enough money to get me to whatever place was next on the map. But I found I had a knack for coming up with a new angle and exploiting it. A number did rather well, and there seemed no point in closing down good businesses. Then, during the occupation on Hathe, I formalized the best of them and transferred ownership to my own name through a chain of bogus holding companies. We Terrans were getting nowhere on Hathe, and Earth had no other way of surviving, so it seemed prudent to organize an alternative. I learnt very early in life that all governments love a rich man and that no administration is forever.

As it turned out, I was right to be prudent."

His voice was bitter, and Marthe could only guess how much he wished it hadn't been so. Nor was there any way to deny his sorrow, and instead she homed in on an aspect that puzzled her.

"I still don't see why it should be so difficult to prove that they weren't founded on Earth. The records of the transactions must still exist."

"Yes, but to trace them would cost me almost as much as the taxes they're claiming. Also, if I do that, I will be exposed as a businessman with an even more dubious background than the one about which the Cantorese already know. Cantor welcomed us only because I transferred all my wealth here. Once that looks shaky, so does our welcome."

"Either we leave, or they look the other way the next time your father's thugs turn up?"

He nodded. "The best option is to pay the taxes. My business reputation would then be kept intact and the Cantorese may decide that if I could make money once, I can do it again."

"Which is a fair assumption."

"Maybe, but I have to say it's not an attitude I would count on them adopting. Cantor is an ally of Hathe and must know your Council would be only too pleased to have me conveniently disposed of."

"Leaving me to be re-educated and repatriated, you mean?" Her bitterness equaled his.

She suddenly found herself badly in need of reassurance. She laid the sleeping Freya in her cot, then moved across and slid under Hamon's arm, molding herself tightly to his powerful body. It helped a bit. "How long do you think we have?"

"Thirty-six standard hours. It will take them at least that long to complete the formal registration of claim in the Cantorese and Terran courts."

She wriggled then, and her chin lifted defiantly. "You'd better get started then. I'll bring us something to eat." A picture of Garth Radcliff strayed into her head. No, she was not about to let *him* beat them.

Later that night, Marthe lay watching Hamon. Finally unable to continue, he had succumbed to his need for sleep. She had dozed off earlier but now couldn't relax. Tenderly, her eyes traced the lines of bone and muscle, travelling over his shoulder and down the long slope of his back, to the tautness of his buttocks, honed to a tense fitness by the hard exercise he so often used as an escape from their worries. She clenched her hands firmly to her side, fearful that their hunger to touch where eyes explored would disturb his rest.

She couldn't stay lying there. Carefully, she rose, sliding the door quietly as she passed through to their study. He'd left his screen set on ready. Numbers shone belligerently at her. Again her hands were tempted to reach out and touch and again she clenched them firmly to her side. This time, though, it was in anger not love, driving her to slam the erase code, and wipe away the hateful figures that threatened so blindly all she held most dear.

How long she stood there, staring around her at this fortress they had created, she couldn't say. Her mind roamed wildly, seeking some obscure way out. Finally, a decision. She sat at her screen, breaking the link with Hamon's. She entered a message, setting the interspace code at the end and double scrambling with her own code. Then she coded for transmission.

It was gone. To Hathe. To the one other person she most truly trusted.

The message ended with two, short sentences. 'Help. Please come.' It was signed only, Mimi.

"Fancy living on a freight liner?"

Marthe looked across at Hamon in surprise. "What are the other choices?"

"None that I can find." His voice held a disturbing note of seriousness, and Marthe bit down hard on a shocked gasp. "My father is good. His people have uncovered most of my businesses, despite the trail of blind companies that own them. By the time I pay the taxes and bribe sufficient officials to let us move our money off planet, we should have just enough left to buy a freight liner, pay for our first cargo and cover our living expenses until I can build up a paying business."

"There must be something else we can do? What about my pension from Hathe?"

"You think I'd touch that, even if they would let me?" snapped Hamon, worn out by a night and day of searching for answers.

Marthe began to bristle, then saw the strain on his face, and subsided. "If you want to start up a freight line, fine; but why not use a planetary base? We could always lease one until we're more financial."

"I've tried that. Our story, or rather my story, is too widely known. No planet will touch me. They neither wish to annoy Hathe nor attract the attention of my father's more aggressive supporters, and I can't say I blame them. No, the only place left for us to live is space."

Marthe paused then gathered herself in with a sharp thrusting back of her shoulders. "So be it. At least there's no way your father can comb all of space to track us down."

"There is one other place closed to my father."

"Oh?" said Marthe, a warning glint in her eye.

"Hathe. You and the children would be safe there. You said yourself that without me, they would be only too happy to accept you back. A Terran couldn't touch you there."

Marthe had drawn herself up rigidly as she listened to him, her face for once reflecting her thoughts all too clearly.

"At least consider it," pleaded Hamon desperately.

"Is that what you want? Are we so much of a burden that you wish that on us?"

Hamon was about to lie, then saw recognition of it in her face. "Of course it's not what I want. No responsibility as dear to me as you three could ever be a burden. To lose my family would be to lose all that makes life matter … but at least you would be alive!"

"And have my children grow up to be taught that their father was a war criminal, some kind of perverted monster? No, thank you. We can be alive on a freighter just as easily, and with a great deal more self-respect."

Hamon held her eyes a minute longer, then finally shrugged his shoulders in defeat, a soft tenderness lighting his lips. "Did I ever mention quite how much I love you?"

Marthe grinned. "You may have … but perhaps you'd better say it again. Just to make sure."

He gave a gasp of laughter, then rose and caught her up, swinging her out in a joyous circle. "I love you, Madame Ship's Surgeon, delight of my life," he shouted.

"Thank you kindly, Captain, but should you be taking such liberties with one of your officers?"

"It's allowable in exceptional circumstances.

"Such as?"

"When the officer in question is far too beautiful to be resisted." After which, Marthe was effectively silenced for quite some time.

It refreshed them but was only an interlude.

"You estimate we have twelve hours left. Will it be enough?" she asked anxiously, lying on his chest and slowly drawing the black, living mass of his hair away from his eyes. Eyes that darkened from warm hazel to harshest green at her words.

"I don't know. I've put the word out that we are urgently seeking a ship, and my Cantorese agent is touting for buyers for my companies."

"You can't sell them that quickly!"

"Not all, no, but I can amalgamate what's left under one holding company, which the Terran authorities can seize in lieu of the taxes. The three largest businesses should be sold by then, and the proceeds will go straight to the space line. My competitors have been angling to buy them for years."

"And a ship?"

"He tells me there are one or two possibilities. It will be tight, though, so we'd better be prepared in case he fails."

"To defend ourselves here, or to run for cover?"

"Both. When this hits the Cantorese authorities in twelve hours' time, they will withdraw all protection and order our immediate departure. While they might prefer that we weren't killed on their territory, I doubt whether they would do anything to prevent it."

"Surely Hathe will protest if anything happens to the children or myself?"

"I know you have powerful allies on Hathe, but how many others would be only too glad to be rid of what they regard as an embarrassment?" His hand reached up to hold her cheek in apology for his words as his eyes read her bitter acknowledgement. "Be strong, my love," he whispered, and his lips reached up in echo. After a long interval, he drew back. "Remember, too, that they have yet to defeat us—two of the most conniving and battle-hardened operatives in the business. Between our skills and the hardware we have tucked away, if we can't give them a nasty surprise then we don't deserve to live!" he declared, and his eyes flashed in wicked glee.

What could she do but grin back? She nodded, and rolled over, swatting playfully at his thigh. "Let's get on with it then, lazybones."

His eyes opened wide at the epithet, and he refused to honor it with a reply, leaning over to reach for his clothes to dress, before attacking his screen again with renewed vigor. Marthe looked in on the still sleeping children then hurried off to check their defensive deployments.

Remembering the ease with which the Hathians had tricked the Terran surveillance systems during the occupation, she also made time to take her flyer out to personally inspect the surrounding countryside. Cantor was a world with no large moon. Instead, a cluster of bodies too large to be true asteroids ranged in a wide arc over the heavens, their reflected light casting a low sheen over the rocks from all directions with few shadows anywhere. It gave the night world an eerie, two-dimensional feel, leaving Marthe wary and ill at ease. Though there were no midnight-black pools of darkness that could conceal a man, neither were there the telltale abnormalities of line and angle which spoke of a hidden enemy. In this unreal landscape, forces moving as slowly as the languid drift of a cloud shadow could stay hidden from all but the sharpest of sensors.

It was not a comforting thought, and try as she might, she couldn't shake off a feeling of incipient doom. With a heavy heart, she turned back to the house.

Then, with just four hours of safety left, Hamon let out a whoop of success. "I've got one! A D45 class freighter, registered to the Cordoban Asteroids. Her owner needs to sell urgently and she's due to dock in the capital's port today."

"When?"

"Five and a half hours from now," replied Hamon. "Her shuttle can pick us up twenty minutes later, if we can keep the air space above us free till then."

Marthe looked across at him, hearing the enormity of that 'if'. She took a deep breath. "At least it's a chance."

Shortly afterwards, they woke their few staff and explained the situation. There were yet three hours remaining for them to leave safely, they said. Neither Marthe nor Hamon was surprised to find that, as the deadline neared, they had been left alone with their children in the echoing emptiness of the great house. The young nanny had wept copiously as she turned to board the departing flyer, but Marthe couldn't find it in her to condemn the defectors. All the staff were new to them, all native Cantorese. This offworlders' tragedy was not their concern.

They found strength, though, in the emptiness. Bereft it might be of allies and companions, but neither could it hide a threat. Only the an Radcliff family were here—this strangely assorted couple, defending their two precious offspring and, as Hamon had earlier reminded her, that was not a combination to be taken lightly.

Dawn had broken. In this arid region, the sun rose quickly into the sky, banishing the concealing eeriness of the night and exposing the plain in front of their bluff to a strong, red-white light. No cover for an attacker there.

The mountains at their back were another matter. Immediately behind the house was a smooth shelf of rock which no one could safely cross, but beyond that, the rugged canyons offered enough cover for scores of troops, hiding them completely until they had come far too close to the house. Either Marthe or Hamon maintained a continuous watch over their mountain sensors.

There was also the possibility of attack by longer range weapons but, as Hamon pointed out, it was unlikely that either the Terrans or Hathians would risk upsetting the Cantorese by loosing such destruction on their soil.

"I hope you're right," said Marthe, agreeing with his logic, but unconvinced that the rule of commonsense would favor them. It never had before.

Then time had run out. They looked at each other, each seeing the tension in the other's face. Marthe glanced towards the children. Riardan was playing on the floor with some holoblocks and Freya was happily asleep. She had brought them in here earlier, unable to believe in their safety away from her protective gaze.

Shortly after that, the screens sprang to life, incoming messages chattering in a garish display.

"You were right about the Cantorese response, said Marthe tersely. "Our permits are withdrawn as of now, and we are required to leave on the first available transport."

"Send back to say we acknowledge and will do our best to comply with all haste. Which is all too true," he added ruefully. "I just hope it's possible. Sensors already show intruders in sector two."

Marthe switched to his display. Their defenses had held this time, but other sensors were already warning of a swarm of invaders.

"Your father really is a vindictive bastard!"

"They're not all Terran," countered Hamon.

Marthe followed his pointing finger to the telltale reading. A small party so far, but the weapons were unmistakably Hathian. She had known it would happen but found herself totally unprepared for the shock of coming under attack by her own people. A tight, closed shield blanketed her.

"It's me they want, not you," Hamon reminded her, "and since we left Earth, this is the first time I haven't been protected by guards. The temptation is too much for those who hate me."

"I can't kill Hathians, Hamon. Don't ask me to."

"And if they threaten the children? You know how they will operate better than I. By the stars, the Terrans out there are my own father's people. I probably played with some of them as youngsters; but that doesn't mean I'm about to let them march in here and hurt Riardan or Freya—or you!"

"So, you take the Terrans and I deal with the Hathians?"

"It's the only way."

She took a great, shuddering breath, then forced the steel of her experience to arm her. Her shoulders came back, and she turned once more to the screen. Next minute her voice spoke out, strong and devoid of all emotion. "Hathians in sectors three, five and seven. I'll take those, and you take the rest. Let me know if you need a hand."

Hamon reached across to lightly clench her shoulder then gave a crisp, "Yes," before turning back to his own screen.

At first, their automatic defenses were sufficient, but too soon that stopped. They were forced to override, using all their hard won cunning to block the intruders. The size of the force ranged against them became frighteningly obvious.

"Shipping this lot here must have cost a fortune, let alone the bribes slipped into some Cantorese worm's pocket. I know your father is wealthy, but this is ridiculous!"

"He's probably taken out a loan against the taxes I'll have to pay."

"But they are owed to the government not the courts, and the Alliance controls that."

"Even in a puppet administration, he has enough friends to ensure he'll receive a fat collection fee," grimaced Hamon. Then he grinned as he noticed something in the attack pattern. "At least your people and mine still hate each other more than they hate us. There is not one iota of cooperation out there. Wouldn't it be a turnabout if we could get them to attack each other, rather than us?"

"You are an optimist," laughed Marthe. She looked at her screen. "How long before that shuttle arrives?"

"An hour, minimum."

The laughter vanished and both stared at their screens. Their defenses were holding, but already there were too many ragged patches.

"Hamon, you've a couple broken through the second ring in sector eight. They are into that narrow crack running down the rock face. The one that comes out…"

"…right by the house!" His finger leapt forward. A sonic blast hit the ledge above and a sudden rumble told of a heavy rock fall, burying two men. It was the first of the deaths they were to cause.

Marthe looked at Hamon and took her cue from the rigid set of his face. He was already turning to another threat, releasing a shattering burst of electric static. It wiped out the control circuitry of the weapons of the group just breasting the mountaintop behind them. They were alive, but unable to do anything and, as he had hoped, they immediately withdrew to re-arm.

For as long as possible, this was their strategy: knock out enemy equipment and block invasions with landfalls, sudden hotspots, curtains of vicious laser fire across paths over the harsh rocks, forcing the Terrans and Hathians to fall back, knowing they would only return with new tools to seek out and destroy the Radcliffs' defenses.

These were not inconsiderable. They retained full coverage of the periphery, but in three sectors, the number of sensor traps still operative was becoming dangerously low.

"Flyers approaching in four and six," warned Marthe.

"How is that air corridor above us?"

"Clear so far. No sign of the shuttle, though, and more flyers approaching. They could block our escape route."

"Activating scramble pattern," returned Hamon, switching to a separate program. Immediately, a strong beam arced over the incoming flyers, knocking out their navigational systems, followed by a series of aerial explosions, too rapid and random to be avoided by manual control alone. It worked this time, forcing the attackers to turn back. Hamon swiveled to grin at Marthe.

"Never thought I would be grateful for Hathian technology, but your little surprise worked a treat.

"I only wish Terrans had come up with something similar to stop Hathian flyers. I've got six ricocheting all over the place in sector three."

"Need some help in discouraging them?"

"No. If anyone's going to hurt Hathians, it will be me."

"You would be betraying your own if you let me hurt them again, you mean?" he demanded.

She was too busy to reply, but he wasn't fooled. She had heard his words. A sudden image flashed into his head, of her brother lying cold on a pathologist's bench, followed by his own memories of the first battle for Hathe. He had been secure on the bridge of the command ship, watching with irritation the puny crafts of the Hathian defense forces hurl themselves at the huge Terran ships. Each flash of light signaling the destruction of yet another small craft had been received with a sense of satisfaction that this tiresome, delaying action would soon be over.

Now he looked at the screen and wondered which held men or women he knew. How many of those, too, would be laid on a cold slab tomorrow, all in the name of greed and hate?

"Two flyers down," reported Marthe, the careful tone of her voice telling him her thoughts were not too far distant from his own. He braced himself. Now was not the time for introspection. His gaze locked back on his screen.

"They're starting to send in the heavy guns. I've got one carrier coming in, supported by ten flyers, and the ground below is swarming with troops," Hamon called sharply, his eyes never leaving the screen.

"Similar here. And it's a mix of Terran and Hathians. They may not be cooperating, but they are certainly watching each other closely, to use whatever advantage possible."

"Closing in on all sides. Activating inner defense shield."

"Hold for a count of three. I should be able to catch a few in its net."

"Right. One … two … three. Now!"

Hamon's finger shot out and a deathly shimmer sprang up on a globe about them, open only at one, small circle directly above, to allow the signal to the shuttle to pass through undistorted.

"We caught one transporter and ten flyers," said Marthe, reading the disordered waves on her screen, which told of vessels with controls suddenly burned out by the shield, settling on the ground in untidy lumps. Their enemies were close now, only a couple of kilometers from the house.

"That should hold them for a spell."

"A few minutes maybe," retorted Marthe. "They are bound to be carrying shield neutralizers."

"With the kind of fire power out there, I would say it's a foregone conclusion; but we need only another half hour. A few minutes may make all the difference. What about the shuttle? No sign yet?"

"It's not like you to expect fate to suddenly deal us a wining hand."

"At this particular moment, a miracle wouldn't go amiss," Hamon said dryly, concentrating his defenses on the already thinning zones of the shield. If only his father didn't know him so well!

Then there was no time for idle musings. Terrans and Hathians attacked the shield on all sides. Marthe took over surveillance, while he threw all their reserve power into its defense. Gradually, the great house was shut down, diverting everything available to bolster the shimmering wall. Finally, there was nothing left.

"That's it," he announced. "Everything is dead but this room and the flyer hangar above us. Once that shield is down, they have a clear passage to this door. Are Riardan and Freya ready to go?"

"All set. The shuttle will be here in ten minutes."

"Time to abandon this room then. You three go ahead and I'll switch over to you once you're on board."

Quickly Marthe stood up, moving over to pick up Riardan. He wriggled awkwardly, sounding his annoyance at being interrupted in his game.

"Hush, baby," soothed Marthe. "How would you like to come and show Freya the flyer?" He stopped instantly. There was nothing Riardan liked better than to be taken out in a flyer, exulting when his father let loose with some of his boyhood aerobatics. Eagerly, his little fingers reached out to the baby. "No, not yet. Freya will only get bored if you wake her too early. Wait till we've taken off."

She scooped up the baby, eliciting only a grunt from the sleeping child before Freya settled in to her shoulder, and entered the lift doors. Marthe refused to look back at Hamon. It was stupid, but to do so might ill-wish him, might make something happen to prevent his joining her. Instead, she busied herself with settling the children into the flyer, placing Freya in her restraining sleeper first, then buckling an excited Riardan into his seat and giving him the food chute to choose his own snack, a special treat that set his eyes sparkling. So far, thank the Pillars, the fear she was throttling in so tightly had not reached him. The children secured, she was free to take her seat and activate the flyer's screen, intensely relieved to see Hamon's face flash up in front of her.

"All set this end. Now, get up here quickly. Please."

Hamon grinned in affirmation. ""Closing down now and switching over to you."

A screen lit up, charged with the angry nightmare of the battle. The shield was nearly gone and she refused to look at the total readout of troops arrayed against them. Especially not at the Hathian forces.

"Some day I really must get Hamon to tell me exactly what he got up to on Hathe during the occupation," she muttered, then turned at the sound of the door opening.

He was there. His broad shoulders, his dark hair shining, the harsh mouth grinning back at her as his eyes, alive with the light of battle, softened for an instant at the sight of her.

"I had forgotten," she murmured.

"What?" he asked in surprise as he settled into the seat beside her, activating his own share of the console.

"How big you are."

One hand came across to gently squeeze hers. "I have you safe. Or I will shortly. Time we got out of here. Watch out for the shuttle signal."

She waited tensely, then crowed, "Got it!"

Suddenly, she was silenced.

"Well? Where?"

She didn't answer, pointing instead to her screen. It was displaying the view immediately above them—that precariously guarded, aerial corridor leading to the point in the sky where the shuttle should have been. The one taking them to their own ship, and safety; but it was no shuttle that blocked the airways above.

Hamon looked across at her. She spoke, said words, but knew her voice was dead with failure. "It's a Hathian battle cruiser, of the latest mode. We commissioned a fleet of them from Arcanthias in case our first plan to throw you out failed. We have absolutely nothing here that can defeat it."

CHAPTER THIRTY-FIVE

"We'll have to make a run for it." There was a starkly clinical lack of emotion in Hamon's voice.

Marthe couldn't make herself equal it. "They will have infrared tracers. Our body heat will show up as soon as we leave the shielding of these rooms."

"There'll be so much confusion when they break through that field that there's a good chance they'll miss us."

"Not the children. No soldier is that small."

"We'll carry them. Hopefully, the trace will show two bodies, not four. What else do you propose? Sit here and wait for whatever that ship up there decides to dish out?"

She shook her head, mute, then looked to her babies in anguish. She rose slowly to her feet. Hamon stood too, holding her briefly to give her the strength she needed. There was no other choice; at heart she knew it as well as he. She stepped back as he released her, straightening with resolution.

"Come on, my darlings, let's take a wee hike," she said, as she went to pick up Freya and reached for Riardan. Hamon took his son from her then turned to switch off the screens as they left.

"Wait a second. Look at this!"

Marthe looked back and followed his pointing finger.

"A few minutes ago, they were almost through in near on twenty sites. Now the shield is back to full strength. For some reason, our friends out there have pulled back."

"So? If I were a Terran facing a Hathian battle cruiser, I'd pull back too."

"Look again. Here, here and here. It wasn't Terrans attacking those points."

A subspace call sign suddenly rent the tense air. Marthe jumped, then looked at Hamon.

"Answer it."

Marthe's finger reached out to accept, fear stiffening her innards. Not for herself. If Terrans were wary of a Hathian battle cruiser, then it was likely that whoever was up there would not harm the children or herself.

Hamon was a different matter. He had just given her permission to risk his life. Her eyes locked with his as she waited for an answering voice.

"Marthe. Is that you?" it said.

Marthe had twisted her face away at the first word. It was too late. She knew he'd seen the relief she couldn't hide. He must also have seen her total lack of surprise.

"Father, it is very good to hear you," she said.

"You seem to be in some bother there. What can we do to help?"

"You've already done it. Our friends are retreating."

There was a moment of silence, then Sylvan's voice returned. "Only pulled back, my dear, and we can't bluff them for long. This ship may look dangerous but the Cantorese will not allow a full-scale war on their territory. We have only time to pick you up then must leave. I'll send down a shuttle."

Hamon who broke in to answer. "No. Our own shuttle should be arriving shortly. It will take us to the ship waiting for us at the spaceport. Once we are safe in space, then we can talk."

His voice was flat and lifeless. Marthe had heard it like that before, directing his troops on Hathe. They were the last words he was to utter on all the long journey following: the nerve-racking ascent through the shielded corridor to the Cantorese shuttle, the trip through the stratosphere and then up to the space port where their own ship waited. Marthe answered any queries, gave any orders. Even once on board the comparative safety of their own ship, he refused to speak to her, merely indicating that she strap the family in while he took the pilot's seat.

Then, finally, he turned to her.

"Call your people. Tell them to follow us. I know a safe rendezvous."

She didn't argue, seeing her betrayal in his eyes. Soon, they were at his chosen site—just out of Cantorese space yet close enough that their observer satellites could act as witness in case of foul play.

"Ask your father to join us—alone," her husband commanded, and soon a small shuttle was in the docking bay. Sensors confirmed there was only one passenger.

Hamon took the intercom. "Welcome, Doctor an Castre. Please join us on the bridge." Then he sat back and looked at her.

Now was the time to explain, but she had no idea what to say. Had she betrayed him? She didn't know.

The door slid away. It was her father. For a moment, Hamon could be ignored as her father tightly enfolded her and then was shown, to his astonished joy, his two grandchildren: a Riardan grown beyond belief in the year and more since his grandfather last held him and the new delight of baby Freya. But at last the Doctor must turn to greet his son-in-law.

Marthe turned, too, to face the blank mask of her husband.

Hamon had been watching her, and before she could turn enough to see his face fully he made sure the angry pain that had engulfed him as he looked at his family was utterly erased. As he looked his last at all that was most precious to him.

"You will be wondering why I'm here," said Doctor an Castre.

"Not at all. I presume your daughter asked you to come. The question is, what do you intend to do now you're here."

Her father chose to ignore his cold politeness and helped himself to a nearby seat. "That rather depends on you, as it happens."

"You can relax. It has been brought home rather forcefully to me that my children and my wife can be safe only in a place that is without me."

"No!" came Marthe's horrified denial, but they both ignored her.

"I would like time to farewell the children, then some hours' grace for my getaway before any hotheads on your ship decide to take matters into their own hands. The children don't deserve to live with the knowledge that their grandfather had a part in the death of their father. They will have quite enough of a burden as it is. As soon as I'm able, I will re-organize my finances to ensure that they will never be in physical need."

The words were precisely articulated, as tensely constructed as the body he was holding so rigid.

Marthe could bear it no longer. "My love, no. I only asked my father for help, not to come and fetch me home."

His eyes were so deep green as to be almost black. She saw his hand grip the edge of the seat, but nothing else of his body escaped his control.

"So you say. Even if it's true, are you sure that at heart you didn't want this? To leave behind all this sordid outlawry?" he challenged softly. The quiet voice was infinitely more fearsome than if he had loosed his anger in ranting fury.

"Actually, you're mistaken, Major," interrupted her father. I haven't come to take Marthe back to Hathe, nor did she ask me to. What I have come for is to offer you a proposition—from the Alliance as it happens—which I hope will be an answer to your present dilemma."

That was so unexpected that, for an instant, even her father must see the confusion break through. "A proposition from the Alliance? That's absurd. They have all my service records and the Hathian judicial ones. They know exactly what I did there."

"Yes, right down to every single, Hathian death due to your actions, and to every life saved as a result of an order of yours," returned Sylvan.

Hamon shook his head slowly. "You've lost me."

"When you shortened the service period in the mines, the death rate declined dramatically."

"That was only to make more efficient use of our resources. You don't survive by killing off your work force."

"You rarely tortured prisoners, unlike other officers. Most importantly of all, you granted the Hathian people the dignity of our humanity. You believed us to be capable of mounting a resistance to your rule, though other Terrans thought of the natives as little more than lower animals on two legs. All because, alone among the senior officers, you never lost sight of the fact that you were on Hathe to aid Earth, not to indulge yourself in the petty power and luxury of the life of a conqueror."

"A cesspit is still a cesspit, even if you give it a shiny cover. And your words don't change the reality of my position on Hathe. I may have 'accepted the humanity of the Hathian natives', but you can't deny that I fought hard to ensure you would have no freedom to enjoy it. There is a whole raft of Alliance laws under which I could be indicted, if it weren't likely to raise political hell on Earth. What could the Alliance offer me?" he finished caustically.

"The leadership of the colonizing mission to Annan IV," said Sylvan an Castre.

Marthe gaped. Hamon laughed, and continued to laugh, falling back into his chair and clutching his temples. Doctor an Castre stared in bemusement, then shook his head and continued to speak as if there had been no interruption.

"The leadership to Major Radcliff and to you, Marthe, as Chief Medical Officer."

That stopped Hamon's laughter. He stood up, shocked to silence in mid-guffaw. "You're offering us both positions?" he demanded in rampant disbelief.

"Of course. Is there any other option?"

"Then you don't plan to conveniently ship me off to the ends of the galaxy, while you quietly repatriate Marthe and the children home to Hathe?"

Her father stared. "Why should I think that Marthe would ever agree to such a thing?"

"Then why did you send for your father?" exclaimed a now truly puzzled Hamon, turning to confront Marthe.

"For help. That's all."

"Help to return home," he charged flatly.

"No. Not without you."

"It would not be possible in any case," added her father, "with or without your husband. Since you left, the name of Radcliff has become the most hated on Hathe, encapsulating for many their feelings towards the entire Terran race. They have been denied their revenge and have turned instead to black myth, cloaking your husband in notoriety. Neither you, nor your children, are ever likely to be safe on Hathe again." His voice saddened as he watched her, unable to hide from him the grief his words brought her. "I am so sorry, my dear," he said, catching her and soothing her as he had been used to so many years before, when she was a child.

He turned to Hamon. "I understand you had planned to become free traders, your home a ship. I have to tell you, my daughter can't live like that. You know she loves Hathe, but it is not the people alone that hold her heart. It is the very soil of the planet, the wind in the sky and the animals and plants that grow there. My wife would watch her at play as a child and say to me that Marthe almost became one with the country, listening to the rhythms of the world with her whole body. She can't survive in space alone, devoid of the seasons and cycles of a planet. And you strike me, Major, as one who would understand this."

"Yes," said Hamon quietly. "It's the same for me with Earth. Parts of it are unforgettably beautiful."

"And yet you chose a life in space?"

"We had no choice. It was decreed by my father, and by the Hathians who hate us."

"Now you do have a choice. What do you say?"

Hamon was silent. Marthe drew back from her father and gave her hand to her husband. She knew what he was thinking. Annan IV. The most recently discovered of the Earth-type worlds, but unimaginably distant, situated at the farthest reaches of the galaxy.

He spoke then, his words the echo to her thoughts. "It takes ten years by military frigate to get there, let alone by the slow freighters you would be using for settlers. It is a one-way trip you offer us."

"That's true," agreed an Castre, "though it's not as bad as you think. The settlers' ships are to be fitted with a newly developed drive system, which should cut the trip down to just two years."

"I've heard no talk of such a drive," countered Hamon.

"You wouldn't have. It was a Hathian development. Marthe, do you remember the changes we had to make to the shuttles on the run from Hathe to the moon base on Mathe?"

"Yes. They needed to be silent, undetectable by Terran technology, and energy efficient."

"They also turned out to be faster than anything built previously. The new drive can bend space to a greater extent during hyperdrive than the old standard. Hence you need fewer interplanetary hops, giving a much shorter transit time. With a four-year round trip, you're not out of reach if you strike trouble. And trade becomes an option."

"Giving the new colony both increased security and economic viability," said Hamon.

"Exactly, Major. I told the committee you were ideal for the job."

Hamon laughed and shook his head ruefully. Then he looked at Marthe and she knew it was going to be all right. He gave her the smile that she knew even his mother had never seen. "What do you say, my heart? Shall we brave it?"

"Annan IV is said to be very beautiful. Maybe more so than Earth or Hathe. Yes, I think we must," she said, and knew her smile was the equally rare one saved for him alone.

It was the turning point—not the final acceptance that they should turn colonist, but a beginning none the less. Much was still to be resolved and would be argued over mercilessly during the coming months, but right from that moment, Marthe knew she would be going. She saw it in Hamon too. She would catch the spark of excitement in his voice or see it in the sudden flying up of an eyebrow as he put forward his demands for the enterprise—then proceeded to inform the committee in blistering terms exactly why it must comply with his lists and of certain failure following any deviation.

The most obvious snag surfaced early on. They were discussing the settlers, three thousand brave and foolhardy souls.

"Are any Terran or Hathian," asked Marthe during a lull in the talk. The lull became a dead wall of silence. Hamon straightened, staring hard at the chairwomen of the organizing committee.

A hardened space merchant from Samarkan. Madame ka Merle had amassed a huge fortune from her widespread fleet, entering Alliance politics only when it became obvious that her business was becoming limited by the static condition of the Alliance. This expansion into a new colony was, to her, an economic necessity, one for which she was prepared to wield a great deal of sheer bloody mindedness—which did not mean that, at this late stage in her life, she intended to suddenly develop the habit of laying all her cards on the table, as both Marthe and Hamon were well aware.

"How many of the colonists are from Earth or Hathe," Hamon demanded now, in the cold voice that demanded an answer.

"Four hundred from Earth, maybe the same or a bit more from Hathe," replied Madame ka Merle dispassionately.

"Are they aware that you propose myself as leader and Marthe as medical officer?"

"They are."

Hamon surged upwards, glaring at Sylvan an Castre. "And you call this a safe refuge!"

"That surely is up to you, young man. You were very successful in binding men to you to achieve your aims on my home world. Now you must do the same again, with people equally desperate." After a long day of discussion, her father had lost his usual calm. "At least it holds more hope of long-term security than your first choice."

"I was beginning to think you were one Hathian I could trust," sneered Hamon angrily.

An Castre's hands reached up to grip the table as he slowly rose to glare at his son-in-law. "How dare you suggest that I would send Marthe or my grandchildren into danger! You, of all people. Or do you forget what the Terran occupation cost me? The death of a son and the exile of a daughter. Only one of my three children is left to grow old on the world to which their mother bore them. You think I want the death of any more of my family? By the Pillars, this is the best I could find."

Her father stood rigid, his eyes holding Hamon's. Her husband returned the challenge for a bare minute, then stepped back, his hand half raised as if to ward off something. He dropped his gaze, shaking his head in release, then sat down again with quiet deliberation. It was not till her father retook his seat, his face grey and showing the imprint of all his years, that Hamon spoke again.

"You have questioned the Terran and Hathian colonists on this matter then?"

Marthe sensed it was as close as he could come to an apology, his voice carefully devoid of any hint of challenge. There was the slightest trace of a nod from his father-in-law, then Father turned to her to reply. The mechanical timbre of his voice alone told Marthe that he hadn't yet recovered his equilibrium.

"The Terran colonists are all from the ranks of those who would have been classified as 'uncommitted to the communal good' under the old system, and were therefore outside the food supply system— the chronic rebels and deviants. They have no love for the Earth of old and even less for the new hierarchy. On Annan IV, they see a chance to follow their dreams, unfettered by the restrictions of a worn-out society—a feeling that you will find is common to all your colonists. The Terrans have no reason to love either of you, nor will they harm you if they truly believe you can make the colony succeed.

That is what they want above all. As for the Hathians…" he paused, and for a moment Marthe thought he would be unable to continue.

He proved her wrong. "None have any reason to love your husband, my dear. Every single one of them is from the families who were permanently stationed on Hathe—the 'dirtsiders'. Their children grew up believing they were nothing, and many of their parents almost came to believe it too. We have set up re-education programs since you left, but not all can readjust. They fought too long and cannot now set aside the habits they needed to survive then. Nor could many live with the crowds flocking the new Hathe, too used to the small villages we set up. Your Hathian colonists are exiles too. Permanently barred from their home world, not by the law as you are, but by culture and self-esteem. They may hate your husband, but if he can help them create a world to which they belong, then he will have their loyalty.

"As for you and the children. I wouldn't worry. You may be reviled on Hathe by the public brayers of gossip, but the dirtsiders know the truth of the occupation. They remember how often you risked your life to come to their aid."

No more was said that day, but her father's words echoed in Marthe's head as she stood with Hamon to address their fellow colonists for the first time. Her Hathians ware immediately recognizable, still unconsciously burdened with the self-effacing demeanor that had protected them during the Terran regime. They huddled together, carefully distinct from their neighbors and at the opposite end of the vast hall from the equally recognizable Terrans.

These, too, were branded, indelibly marked by a swaggering defiance and the pinched faces of a childhood whose only constant had been an ever present and debilitating hunger.

The whole arena was divided into similar groups, like stubbornly clinging to like, though none so signally as the Terrans or Hathians; yet Marthe also saw what her father had seen. Despite the disparity and the tensions fragmenting the crowd, a harsh similarity bound them all. First, she sensed their anger, the bitter anger of defeat, but then came the second common bond: the eagerness with which they raised their heads to look intently at their new leaders. And in the absolute silence that fell as Hamon stepped forward, she felt a bone-deep, desperate hope. For every single one. Annan IV held their only hope of a life and a purpose to it, as it did for her own family.

Hamon saw it too. It was in his eyes, and he drew it into his words. Within moments, they were his. Marthe could almost feel the committee nodding in self-congratulation as they watched the vidcast. They had picked the right man. Over the following months, he reinforced it again and again, and long before the day of their final embarkation, his position was unassailable. Even the Hathians and Terrans came to him so matter of factly that it was only as they were leaving that an amused Marthe would see the faint look of surprise on their faces, as they suddenly remembered just who this man was.

They were frantic months, filled with too much work and too little time for all the goodbyes that must be said to those they would leave behind. Many came from Hathe and Earth to see them, for however brief a moment of contact. A last hug, last words of wisdom, a last chance to see family or friend.

"We will return, one day." Marthe lost count of how many times she said this.

Her farewell to Jaca was private. The expedition was leaving for Annan IV from an Alliance space station—neutral territory for all parties. He marched down the corridor to meet her surrounded by his personal troop of Hathian guards, every bit the senior government official with a demeanor to suit. She merely raised an eyebrow, saving her cheeky grin until the door had slid behind him and they were alone.

"Commander des Trurains. Should I salute or curtsey?"

"You dare, and I'll shove you into that fancy pot plant."

He'd done that to her when they were seven and she was being particularly annoying. Bendin had held her on one side, Jaca on the other. She kept up the facade for one long moment more, then burst into laughter and grabbed him, hugging him as hard as she could manage. "Where have you been, Jaca?"

"Back home, fixing up the mess you left behind," he said, hugging her back just as hard. Then he set her from him, raking his gaze down her and finishing with an approving nod. "Motherhood suits you."

"Thank you." A softer smile, then she held him by the shoulders and looked him over as carefully as he had her. "And you? All this responsibility. How are you?"

He opened his face, dropped any shielding from her. "I'm getting there, Mimi."

It was a fair summation. New lines edged his face, but there was a definite lift to the corners of his mouth.

"Hathe is recovering?"

He nodded. "We couldn't save them all—but you know that. You have those we failed among your settlers. Overall though, we are becoming one planet again, and there are protections in place for the dirtsiders. They are now treated with the honor they deserve."

She dropped her head, and he tilted it up again to catch the tears she couldn't control.

"So, it wasn't all for nothing?"

"No, Mimi. What you did, what we did..." Then it was his turn to drop his head. She stood silent, at ease with him in a way she had feared she would never have again. When he lifted his head, it was the old smile of childhood on his face. "I have something for you. To take with you to your new home."

He pulled a small travel vial from his pocket and opened the cap. "Dirt?"

"From Bendin's grave," he pulled out a sliver and placed it in her hand, "and a holo of the three of us from that night on the plateau. That last night before everything changed."

Her fist closed, clenched tight around vial and sliver. "Thank you," she breathed.

"He would have been proud of you."

She nodded. "Yes, I think he would have. After he'd read me the riot act three times over," and she gave a choke of laughter.

They were good. Not the same as before, but good. Later, she showed him her babies. Riardan went straight for the shiny medals lining his dress uniform, having decided they were old friends, while Freya gave him that long, considering look of her grandmother's, then let her head drop against his arm and shut her eyes.

"You've made the grade," said Marthe softly. "I can count on one hand the number of people she'll relax like that with."

"A wise one, then."

Marthe grinned. "She takes after her father's family," and was relieved to see a similar grin back from Jaca.

Then it was time. Hamon came in, shook hands with that cool detachment that was the still the best he and Jaca could manage, then left them alone.

"Be safe, Mimi," said her oldest friend.

"And you, be happy," she said back.

He was silent. One long study of her face, all the precious tales of the years between them suddenly alive in his eyes. A slight grimace, then his com crackled into life. "Commander, the shuttle leaves in ten minutes standard," said a female voice. Marthe caught the trace of something new on his face and smothered a quiet smile.

One last, hard hug, then he must go.

"Good luck," she whispered as the door slid open and his official guard surrounded him once more.

He had assumed his public face and gave her a formal bow. Then just as his head came back and before his men could see it, she caught a quick wink and the rogue's grin from their days in captivity.

The last few days were even more frantic, chaos in triplicate, and it was with a sense of stunned surprise that Marthe found herself one day standing on the bridge of the command ship, minutes only from departure. Their bags were all loaded, the vast trivia of documentation fully processed and, around her, the crew pragmatically counted down the routine of departure.

What was she doing here? This was madness.

Hamon caught the change in her face as he leaned over to speak to a ship's officer. He waved the man aside and strode across to where she stood, trapped in time, with their children beside her.

"Into the Forward Gallery. I've something to show you." He took up Freya, his other hand reaching out for his wife and son.

The gallery was designed for one purpose only. The wall at the far end slid back as they entered, revealing the mighty window that was the dominant feature of the room. Through it, a kaleidoscope of stars beckoned. Right at the edge, isolated from the jostling clusters of light, was a single, winking glow.

Hamon crouched down beside his son. "See that light, Riardan. See how pretty it is. That is going to be your home sun one day."

The little boy looked at his father in awe, too young to understand the words but caught by the wonder in the voice. He turned and tugged at his sister, who wriggled to be let down. Freya was no sooner freed than she crawled over to the window, trying to catch the pretty lights shimmering through the transparent plate.

Hamon pulled Marthe in close, tucking her under his chin as they watched their children. "Look above the window," he murmured. "I've activated the rear viewers."

Marthe did as he said, then gasped. Two screens were alive and on each shone a group of stars. Stars still close but soon to become heartrendingly distant. At the center of one screen was a small, yellow sun, around which she knew orbited nine planets. The third one would be part of her husband's soul till the day he died. On the second screen blazed a larger, yellow-white sun. It owned four planets. Around the second of these circled two moons, one small and insignificant and known as Mathe. It shone down on a world that epitomized all the beauty and wonder of her life.

"Earth and Hathe," she murmured, the wetness of a single tear on her cheek echoing the grief she could feel in the arms holding her. Then they released her and Hamon twisted her round to face him, stepping back a pace. His face was a closed mask.

"You could return to Hathe, despite what your father said. You have enough friends in the military to ensure the children's safety, and yours. Given time, the Hathians would come to accept you."

She looked up a moment more at her home sun, then turned back to Hamon, a very special smile lifting the corners of her mouth.

"If we did that, you could return to Earth. Your father would welcome you with open arms, and I am fully confident you would soon manage to filch his organization from him. You could use it to restore Earth according to your dreams."

"Very likely."

He grinned, pulling her into his arms in a long kiss of promise. Breaking off, he gazed down into the warm brown eyes of his wife.

"I think it's time I gave the Captain the order to be off."

It was a question. She answered it by tucking her head under his chin, finding its home in the sturdy shelter of his chest. Hamon spoke the necessary words into the com channel, then they both turned to face forwards, to where their children played excitedly with the stars.

On the screens above their heads still shone the slowly waning images of their home suns, declining into a pale farewell.

The family stayed in that room a long time. Only once, by mutual consent, did they both glance upward—a last, long look at yearned-for and vanishing glitter. Then the screens fell dark, and their eyes fastened resolutely on the forward vista.

The children played on, oblivious, and beneath their feet, a faint vibration told of a voyage begun.

Ahead, the star at the edge of the galaxy beckoned.

Thank you for joining me in the tale of Hamon and Marthe's adventures. I hope you enjoyed their story as much as I enjoyed writing it. Please consider posting a review, or letting your friends know about this book. I appreciate all honest reviews.

Sign up to my newsletter for all the latest on my new releases, events and book discounts, and I'll send you a bonus, subscriber exclusive short story. https://mbj-landing-page.subscribepage.io/

Marthe and Hamon have now set off for their new home, and new challenges. But what happened to those left behind, to Jacquel and the Hathians left torn and bleeding from the wounds of war? Look out for Jacquel's trials and adventures as he sets about restoring the world he loves in "Aftermath: Hathe Book Three.

ACKNOWLEDGEMENTS

With thanks to all those who have helped me bring my Hathe books to reality. Firstly, to my amazing, wise and ever patient editor, Laura Daniels, who pushed me harder than I've been pushed before to make these books the best they could possibly be, and for which I am hugely grateful. Any errors remaining are purely the fault of my own pigheadedness. To Victoria for coming to my rescue with the formatting stuff and saving me from computer hell. To my fellow writers at SpecFicNZ, RWNZ and RWA, particularly the Auckland specficers and RWNZers. Thank you for your generosity, your never-ending support, the laughter and the mutual moans, but most of all for helping me to believe I can do this!

Biggest thanks of all go to my family. To my mother, for raising me in a house full of books, taking us to libraries and taking it for granted that we would all get an education and be able to think for ourselves; to my husband who is always there for me, even though I'm far away in my own world more often than not; but most of all to my sons. You grew up with Hathe – these books had a longer gestation than any baby – and now they are reality. Thank you for your acceptance, for all you taught me over the years, and for the smiles on your faces when I told you I was finally going to publish Hathe.

Now it's here. Hathe really does exist.